The Dragon Manuscript

The Sage's Legacy, Volume 2

Alexa Whitewolf

Published by Alexa Whitewolf, 2017.

THE DRAGON MANUSCRIPT

Fourth Edition. September 20, 2017.

ISBN 978-1-9993839-9-2

Written by Alexa Whitewolf.

To those that leave us, but stay forever in our hearts.

"Ars longa, vita
brevis"

— Art is long, life is short, Latin proverb —

Prologue

E *ons ago...*
   Buried deep within Ancient Egypt, on an island not easily accessible, a holy place had been built for the gods. The structure stood proud and tall, majestic and threatening at once – both a warning and invitation to the mortals on the other shore.

The outer temple court was wide, with a mix of stand and battered stone making up the ground. Colonnades ran along both sides, leaving partings wide enough to offer a beautiful view of the Nile River. The pantheon was split into different areas, each with intricately painted scenes from the Book of the Dead, as well as the history of the gods.

Further within the sanctuary, past a hall with column capitals lay a vestibule to the inner sanctum. It was there the goddess Isis had stretched over an animal rug, trying to fight the contractions in her oversized belly.

The temple had become a heaven of peace for the queen of Egypt, a place of worship. It had also, upon her husband's return to the Underworld, become a refuge. She'd chosen the emplacement to give birth to their son, but had not foreseen it would be so soon.

Biting back a cry, the goddess tried to fight the pains of pregnancy, to no avail. The child would be born tonight under the full moon, a certainty not even her powers could amend.

When the contractions became too much, she groaned aloud, her screams echoing across the hollow walls. Though she was physically alone in the suffering, Osiris' spiritual presence was next to her, gently helping out. The next few hours were blurs, until a baby's first cry echoed in the temple.

Tears of relief streamed down Isis' cheeks, even as cleaned him up, then held him in her arms. "My son, Horus, welcome into the world," she whispered.

The child looked at her with dark eyes like his father's and babbled in the language of the innocents. Isis smiled tenderly towards the little miracle, her heart strings tugging, wanting nothing more than to shelter him from all that would break him.

Lightning outside dragged Isis' stare to it, and she shivered. "Osiris, where are you?" she murmured, worry in her voice.

"Delayed, I assume."

Isis jumped to her feet, breath coming in quick gasps. The response had come from far away, but it might as well have been near, the way it thundered across the distance. She grasped Horus closer, as though the gesture itself could protect him. The newborn was quiet, sensing his mother's agitation.

Unwilling to be a coward, Isis stood up straighter. With one graceful sweep of her hand, she exchanged her dirtied clothing to full queen regalia – a cotton robe woven with gold threads, the headdress crown she always wore, and kohl-rimmed eyes.

Gold pieces adorned her ears, wrists and neck, creating a halo of lights with her every movement. Only her hair was left free of jewelry, dropping straight to her waist in a thick, black mane.

With another hand movement, she created a cradle out of thin air and placed Horus in its safe confines. An incantation escaped her lips, a wishful muttering in hopes of shielding him against that which would harm him.

"I do not want to leave you, my darling son, but I must," she whispered, then kissed his cherubic cheek.

Stepping back from Horus took most of her will. The motherly connection that existed between them was as solid as chains around the deity's heart, pleading with her to stay by her child. But Isis was, first and foremost, a goddess and a leader. She was the magician of life, supreme queen of the land, wife to the lord of the Underworld.

Throwing back her shoulders, head held straight, Isis stepped into the night. The moon had been high up in the sky before, but now dark clouds hid it from prying eyes. A thick obscurity pulsed in the surroundings, with a life of its own.

The temple was surrounded by water, an island free of shackles. Always, Isis had felt secure in her sanctuary. Yet in that moment, despite the river that defended her, she shivered. Her eyes latched onto an immobile form on the opposite shore.

Set, her brother-in-law, stood watching her.

Tall, broad of shoulders and built like a rock, the god held a dangerous appeal. He and Osiris could have been twins, were it not for the lack of warmth in Set's expression. Dark eyes glinted malevolently across the distance, and his full lips stretched in the cold smile of a snake.

"I take it my nephew was born?" There was a steely edge in his tone.

Isis glared back. "What is it you have come seeking, Set?"

"I thought it was clear. To ensure my legacy continues."

His cruel laugh echoed around them, and Isis was compelled to run back inside to Horus. They had realized too late the god's ruthlessness and will to destroy. Despite their best attempts to thwart him, Set had escaped over and over, going so far as to killing Osiris.

Isis gulped past her distress, recalling the months she had spent tracking down her husband's body parts across the continent. It had taken all her power to string him back together, and return him to life. Even now, after all they had been through, peace and happiness still eluded them.

As though reading her thoughts, Set raised his palms and bolts of lightning and fire shot towards the temple. They sizzled through the dark sky, illuminating the water and Isis' pale face. She had counted on the temple's holiness for shielding, but the spiritual force was no match for a vengeful god.

When the rays of light made contact close to her feet, Isis snapped out of her stupor. She flicked her wrist, turning the air into a barrier of fire, which she then pushed outwards.

Though she was a powerful enchantress, Isis strained as Set's attacks made contact, over and over.

The man was angry, and in his wrath, his force was accentuated. Despite being able to defend herself and Horus, Isis was stuck and unable to counter with an attack.

Osiris!

The mental scream had the desired effect. A gust of wind picked up, pushing against Set. Sand lifted off the ground and surrounded him, until it seemed as though he was in the middle of a tornado. The god had no choice but to shield his eyesight, lifting his arm against the elements and dropping the assault.

To his left, the sand sank until a hole appeared. Ripples of dusty beige spread across, then Osiris rose amongst them from the Underworld where he normally presided.

Wearing only a cotton loin cloth and his gold jewelry on his chest, he had never looked as beautiful as he did to Isis in that moment. Features darkened in fury, eyes shooting flames of anger, Osiris lunged at his brother.

"How dare you attack my wife and child!?" he growled, slamming his fist into Set's face, then following it with a magical onslaught.

Hours went by and Isis watched the fight, unable to step in, but also unwilling to tear her eyes from it. It was akin to witnessing two forces of nature battling each other. Neither was winning, but neither would stop.

Osiris had the deciding punch, in the end burying Set into the sand. As the god coughed to regain his breath, Osiris' gaze met hers across the distance.

I need your help to imprison him, beloved.

Isis nodded, dropping the protection on the temple in order to contribute her magic.

A flow of golden light escaped her palms, joining with Osiris' greener energy. As one, the magic surrounded Set until, with a cry, he disappeared – forever to be bound by the darkness he belonged to.

Osiris stood staring at the spot his brother had last been in, panting heavily. It was finally over, this fight that had started the moment they had both been born. Jealous to no end, Set had always coveted what was his. When taking by force had not succeeded, he had settled for destroying everything.

Now, Osiris could drop his guard. The amount of energy they had used would ensure Set was forever imprisoned in the Underworld, under Osiris' control. With a satisfied nod, he crossed the river and hugged Isis tightly to him.

"I thought I was too late, beloved."

She shivered as his murmured words ran across her skin. In response, Osiris' arms tightened reflexively around her waist, breathing her in. The dread gripping his heart finally let go, and his pulse returned to its regular beat.

"Your timing was perfect," Isis smiled weakly back.

Supporting her weight, Osiris threw the defensive shield back onto the sanctuary, and they both headed back in. "Would you like to meet your son?" Isis whispered.

"Nothing would give me more pleasure," Osiris beamed back.

He reached the cradle and picked up the tiny bundle in his arms. A grin of pure fatherly pride tugged at his lips for the product of their love, meant to rule over Egypt through each pharaoh, for centuries to come.

"Welcome to this world, Horus, my beloved son and heir."

Chapter 1

A s Freya floated into space, enveloped by the light, she saw something move out of the corner of her eye. A shadow, slithering closer. Her eyes widened and, under her bewildered stare, a shape formed. It was the silhouette of a man, with ebony skin and glowing red eyes.

"At lassst, we meet," his deep rumble of a voice was reminiscent of an animal.

"You're the wraith," Freya stated, shivering with the truth of her words.

"Yeesss," he hissed, "It isss I. Raksssh is my name, and I have been chasssing you for too long now, sssilly girl."

Freya glared at him despite her fear. The blaze enveloping her was giving her courage. "I'm not a child!"

"Oh yesss, you are..." he laughed. "You're the sssame sssscared little girl, in the backssseat of the car, watching as your parentsss die in front of you." He paused, enjoying her stricken expression, before adding, "I ssshould know. I wasss there."

"You're lying," Freya murmured, her throat dry. "My parents..."

"Your parentsss were weak*! Giving up that power, the relic-sss, for love. For* family.*" The disdain in his tone was apparent with every syllable.*

He stepped closer, not letting her analyze his words. *"Be better than them. Sstep out of that beacon, and help me get the orb and ssscepter. You can benefit, too..."*

"Never!" Freya glared, stepping out of the cocoon of light, as his words finally penetrated. *"How dare you lie about my parents' death, to manipulate me? I'm a lost soul in need of a puppet master!"*

The demon stared at her for a beat, before laughing that low, animalistic laugh. *"Manipulate you? Dear girl, why would I bother... When I can sssimply ussse you to get the objectsss?"*

"As if I ever would."

Again, that unnerving stare, as though Raksh knew something she didn't. Then, he smiled. *"Never sssay never, Sssage."*

Even as he was going to add something, a roar echoed around them. In the distance, a shape appeared. It was coming closer, all stripes of white and black, getting larger every moment.

"Tyr!" Freya recognized the entity before it had fully reached them.

"Stay away from him!" With one last push of its powerful back muscles, the feline lunged in the air and landed between the Sage and the demon.

"And you... I should have killed you when I had the chance."

"A ssshame you did not." The fiend retorted, and with one last glimpse at Freya, full of meaning, it dematerialized.

"Freya?"

The Sage turned to Tyr slowly, as though emerging from a daze. Shivers overtook her entire body, even as her mind refused to accept what the monster had revealed.

"Freya!"

The teenager fell to her knees, hugging herself tightly. "What's happening?" she shivered, panicking. "Why am I so cold?"

It was as though something within her was trying to burst to the surface, some memory deeply hidden, and she was afraid. A sharp ache erupted in her stomach, and she screamed.

"Freya!"

Tyr disappeared, as though pushed away by something. The agony was overwhelming, and Freya couldn't stay awake. She felt like fainting, but then a murmur rose from deep inside herself.

"I will not give up."

Another voice, weaker, denied, "I can't go on."

"I will not *give up." The first one grew fiercer by the second.*

Freya snapped her eyes open, and repeated, "I will not give up. I will not give up. I will not *give up."*

It grew stronger and stronger as she repeated it, almost a chant. A fire started in the pit of her stomach, and she enjoyed the warmth it gave her.

"I .Will. Not. Give. Up*!" she shouted more forcefully.*

A silvery light enveloped Freya wholly – coming from the deepest of her heart – and she was peaceful and serene. Her eyes closed, and her body, replenishing in the Sage's healing, fell into a restful slumber.

&&&

Freya jumped wide awake, panting and gripping the sheets. She was covered in a thin sheet of sweat, and her heart hammered against her chest non-stop.

Curled in a ball next to her, Artemis opened one green eye and stared at her mistress. Freya petted her distractedly, overwhelmed by the surge of emotions swirling within her.

Since the battle with Cadmael, she'd walked in a perpetual state of confusion, with an odd sense of missing something that night. Now, it had come back with a vengeance, and she had no idea how to respond to the hidden memory.

Tyr knew all along about the demon. And what Raksh said... Freya clenched her free fist, gritting her teeth in the process.

Was she angry? Yes, she was furious that Tyr hadn't seen fit to bring up the dream, leaving her instead to go through the last few weeks in a daze. Furthermore, she was nowhere close to exacting vengeance for her parents.

A glow caught her eye, and Freya turned to the burgundy book on her nightstand – the dragon manuscript. A soft silver glow escaped the rugged leather pattern, and she touched it, not thinking twice about it. Her eyelids grew heavy and before she knew it, darkness welcomed her with opened arms.

&&&

Freya was dreaming – or so she thought.

She was no longer in Scotland, but in a cottage in the midst of a forest. An old man stood at a tiny table, writing on a piece of paper. Long, grey hair was tied back in a ponytail, and he had warm hazel eyes.

Hunched over a paper, he didn't immediately hear someone enter. But a noise made him snap to, and he turned around. His eyes widened, and a glint of fear flashed, before his face became a blank mask.

"So, you came."

"Did you doubt it?"

Freya froze at once, recognizing the voice of the demon of her nightmares. The animal rumble, devoid of the hiss she'd heard, was unmistakable. She moved around, switching her point of observation until she could see both the wraith and the old man.

There was an almost eager look on Raksh's face, as though he was coming to collect a prized possession.

"Where isss it?" he questioned, confirming Freya's suspicions.

"I do not know what you are referring to."

There was something incredibly familiar about the old man, and the almost arrogant poise he displayed. Freya tried to place him, but was again distracted by Raksh.

"Do not lie!" he shrieked, taking a controlled step forward. His broad shoulders were taut with fury, fists clenched tightly. "You have the medallion, the key to it all. I want it!"

The man smirked, and recognition dawned on Freya – he was Brennan's grandfather!

"I do not. Not anymore." There was an almost smug undertone to the words, in spite of his blank expression.

"Foolisssh old man!" Raksh growled. He lifted a palm, and a thin black mist escaped his index to travel in the Wiseman's nostrils.

Freya gasped and tried to reach out, to help, but to no avail. The demon stepped around Thomas as he choked to death, and seemed to scan the area with his senses.

Furious at not finding what he was looking for, he stormed out, leaving the poor man dying. The vision started to fade just as Brennan entered. He took in the scene, and the despair on his features was the last thing Freya saw before waking up.

&&&

In the pale morning light, the streets of the Spanish city seemed deserted. A light breeze blew softly, pushing the dirt off the ground and towards the modest houses. Whispers could be heard, followed by laughter at sparse moments. The lifeless houses were coming to life, enchanted by the energy of the persons that existed within.

The ghosts that had, until then, wandered the hollow roads were now taking one last look at what had once been their stomping ground, and what would be, in a matter of hours, a festive city. One more glance, and they started to disappear, the nostalgia of the past days leaving with them.

Close to the middle of the city, around buildings that surrounded a massive structure, one ghost remained behind. His blonde locks fell charmingly in his eyes as he glanced around nervously, trying to figure out how much time remained until the moment of his departure.

The ghost did not seem to be older than twelve years old, and one would wonder what he was doing roaming the streets alone at such an early hour. Especially considering the charms of the city had not yet awakened.

But Sam wasn't in Spain to admire the many wonders of the town. He'd come there on a short vacation to look for something. Or rather...some*one*.

A lost friend whom he hadn't seen in years, and with whom he'd more or less lost contact.

At once, Sam's gaze landed on the amazing architectural masterpiece that kept so many secrets – the Cathedral.

The impressive church shone brightly in the waning night, its gold-plated walls attracting the eye. A large dome stood against the horizon, imposing. Thick oak doors were at the entrance, and its windows were decorated with painted glass.

In spite of him, a sad smile crept upon Sam's face as a not-so-cheery recollection drifted in his thoughts. A remembrance of a fight that had taken place months earlier in the area, and that had nearly cost Freya her life.

It had been after that same fight that Sam's friend had taken his leave. Sighing, Sam floated to the houses near the Cathedral. He'd been hoping for his task to be easy, but apparently, it was not to be.

He was now questioning whether the time to retreat had come and whether it was best to return to the castle in Scotland at once, or if one last glance around was worth it.

Before he could make up his mind, he heard voices – Spanish ones. Sam's curiosity awakened, and he subtly floated to the small cottage they were coming from. Nearing it, he noticed the window was open and enabled him to better tune in to the conversation taking place inside.

Creeping under the window seat, Sam crouched as low as he could and listened. Though his Spanish was not exactly perfect, it was enough so that he could understand the gist.

"*Mierda*!" someone swore ungallantly, then the gruff tone continued, "And the others, how can we be sure they will submit?"

"Cortés will be happy, I assure you. They are afraid of him and will unite because of it," the other person inside answered. Deeper, his inflection implied he was the older of the duo.

Sam couldn't help a frown. *The ghosts of Spain have always been divided... And now they plan to join under one person? Damn, this can't be good!* Biting his lip, the younger boy leaned further in.

"How much time do they need? Cortés is very...*impaciente*. I have to keep him informed of how this goes," the more youthful voice said.

That can't be...?

Without questioning his instincts, Sam stood to peek inside, trying to catch a glimpse of whoever was there. From his observation spot, he could distinguish rather well the two beings in the house.

One was short, wearing a faded brown robe with priestly implications. His greyish hair and the deep wrinkles in his face gave away his age. The other was taller, dressed in a formal soldier's attire – navy blue vest, old-school breeches, and sharp sword on his hip. Only his black hair and onyx eyes gave away his youth.

Barely taking time to notice the glow around them that indicated they were ghosts, Sam gasped. He'd recognized the second man, and was powerless to help a whisper escape him.

"Raoul?"

Normally, it wouldn't have been heard. But in the deep silence of the morning, the one word carried and the ghosts spun as one toward the window.

Sam froze for a split second, enough to see recognition pass Raoul's gaze, then he started walking backwards. He was attempting to get away from the house, yet not managing to unglue his stunned stare from the scene.

Almost like in a dream, Sam saw Raoul turn to the priest and say, "I'll take care of this. Just make sure nothing changes. *Gracias, Padre.*"

The priest nodded and lifted a hand in mute blessing. After a brief inclination of his head, Raoul passed through the wall of the house towards Sam, intent on catching him.

With one last glance, Sam turned his back to him and dematerialized at once, unwilling to tempt fate further than he already had.

&&&

One, two, three...

"Hiyah!" Freya breathed out loud as she once again punched the target, then moved past it. Panting, she grabbed a towel from the branch of the lively tree next to her and dried her sweaty forehead. In a black t-shirt and sweatpants, she was dressed for comfort rather than style – the perfect outfit, as far as she was concerned.

The Sage took a long look around her, surveying the trees and her secret hideout, then her wooden mannequin that was supporting large fissures on the torso and head. A head taller than her, it was sturdy enough to take hits, yet not enough for her to get hurt.

After the restless night she'd spent, and the back-to-back nightmares – or memories, whatever they'd been – Freya had felt the need for an old-fashioned workout. Glancing now at the obvious cracks in the makeshift doll, she frowned.

"Not bad," she whispered out loud. Her grey eyes turned steely recalling the demon, and just how weak she'd felt while sleeping. Rolling her shoulders to work out the kinks, Freya threw the rag to the ground and stepped forward. "But I can do better."

As she used a series of back kicks and punches combinations, Freya envisioned Raksh being there, his face being the one she was pummeling. Why Tyr hadn't brought up what had happened, Freya could only guess. *More protection.*

With a rueful shake of the head, she had to admit that though she hated secrets, the tiger knew her well. There was no point holding a grudge – not against Tyr, at any rate. However, nothing required her at this point to be as forthcoming as she'd been, especially about the manuscript.

Recalling the glow, and the last few nights as she'd toyed with the object, Freya had to shake her head to focus.

"Time to try something new." Freya stepped back from the dummy, then brought her palms closer together and closed her eyes, exhaling at once.

Let the power invade you, guide you, do not try to control it, Tyr's whispered softly.

Easy enough, was Freya's telepathic reply, even as she blocked her mind against the tiger seeing what she truly hid.

Her eyes snapped open and she clapped her palms, holding them tightly together. The vibration from skin on skin rumbled, then trembled up her arm. Freya could feel the energy build in her hands and jumped up in the air. As she started her descent, she willed the light to escape her and it hit bull's-eye.

The Sage landed in a crouch, then slowly stood up and straightened her back. A small victorious smile tugged at the corners of her lips, and she tossed her ponytail back.

Nice shot, Tyr complimented her.

Freya nodded in satisfaction. The aim had been perfect, and if it had been Raksh, she would've even allowed a surge of pride. Sensing it was time for a break, the young woman turned on her heels and was about to walk away when she caught the presence.

She whirled around at the intrusion – no one was allowed in her inner sanctum! Instinctively, after the session she'd just finished, Freya's hands rose, already manipulating the elements with her spiritual energy.

Then she caught sight of a pale glow and blonde head of hair. *Sam!*

Freya breathed a sigh of relief, and was about to drop it. *On second thought...* Feeling mischievous, the Sage shot a weak burst an inch to the side of his foot, and the ghost jumped in surprise – and alarm.

"It's just me!" he squeaked.

"I know," Freya replied.

Sam glared as he floated to her, but it only served to widen Freya's grin.

The ghost opened his mouth as if to retort, then seemed to think better of it. Shaking his head, he said, "Seamus wants a chat."

Freya narrowed her eyes, more than slightly annoyed. "Now? Sam, I'm training. Can't it wait until I'm done?"

"I don't think so, Frey-Frey," Sam's face darkened in response. "I think we may have a problem."

Lightning passed furtively through Freya's eyes, and she turned her back to Sam before he could read her expression.

Three months! This isn't enough time to prepare to face that demon again.

Tyr scanned the young woman's thoughts, and soothingly whispered, *Calm down, child. You will not have to face him again, not if I have anything to say about it.*

But Tyr, I...

The tiger interrupted her, having caught on to what was holding Freya back. *You want to figure out what the link is between the two objects of power.*

It took her a few moments, but finally Freya admitted, *Yes. I planned to spend my free time doing some research, and trying to figure out what exactly it all leads to. If it's the relics he wants, then I may be able to figure out a way to use that against him.*

The Sage knew that only by finding out the full extent of the power contained in the manuscript, would she then be able to use it to defeat Raksh. She kept the thought tightly buried in her mind, though, refusing to let Tyr catch wind of it.

Freya could almost hear the tiger sigh. *There was a reason your parents only guarded the book, without trying to do anything with it. Some things are best left as they are.*

Thinking back to the last few weeks, and to the fight with the Vikings, Freya shook her head. The book wanted her stronger – the dragon runes were speaking to her. She knew that with certainty.

I don't believe that! Call it rebellion, call it teenager impulsiveness or whatever you will, but I'm tired of being in the dark.

Instead of answering the comment, Tyr muttered, *Go to Seamus. And do not worry about the mission, you will not go at it alone.*

What do you mean?

When only silence echoed in her mind, Freya scowled and bit back a curse. *Typical.* Forcing an even tone, she turned back to Sam. "Lead the way."

"What about that?" He was pointing to the target.

Shrugging, Freya faced the dummy with her palm and wished for it to be invisible, like she'd done with the dragon manuscript not long before. It took only a few seconds, then the mannequin dissolved into thin air.

The Sage caught Sam gaping at her. "How did you... How did you *do* that?"

He contemplated his own question for a few seconds, while eyeing her. There was something new about Freya, in the way she held herself and acted. Sam was forced to admit his friend was no longer a young child, like him. "You really *have* grown stronger."

Freya nodded at him, her gaze slightly nostalgic over the lost peace. Yes, she'd increased her abilities, but at what cost? The last mission had nearly cost her the existence she'd grown used to. *How much longer will I have to fight, always ignorant of the full truth?*

Sam's voice brought her back from her ruminations. "You ready?"

"Always," Freya muttered, then followed Sam's floating form back to the castle garden. They both stopped for a few minutes to admire the place that had become their home.

Against the backdrop of twilight, the ancient castle looked enormous and threatening. The stone, which had once glinted proudly, was now washed off and cracked in certain spots, with weeds peeking through like shy wallflowers. A single tower stood off to the side, ruins of an old prison.

The large oak doors were opened wide, entering into a vast hallway, which then got lost in mazes upon mazes of hallways and bedrooms. It was a large place for only two people – and a ghost – but Freya wouldn't have given it up for anything in the world, and neither would Seamus.

In the background, mountains rose like hushed giants, peaks topped off with snow lost somewhere in the fog. The morning always made their surroundings look like something out of a fairy-tale, and the two youths were awestruck by the beauty of the place.

With the vast grounds completing it, the castle was the only habitation for miles along the coast of Scotland – something they were all immensely relieved by.

Punching Sam on the shoulder, Freya yelled, "Last one there does the chores tomorrow!" She then broke up into a run towards the gates.

"Freya!" Sam yelled. "That's not fair! You know I can't do chores, not to save my life!"

The Sage's crystalline laugh echoed all around, and the twelve-year-old couldn't help a grin as he followed her inside.

&&&

"What is it, Seamus?" Freya pushed the library doors open and entered her mentor's office.

Without as much as a second glance to the rows of books on each side of her, she walked straight to the comfortable armchair in front of the desk and took a seat in it, folding her legs under her.

Frowning slightly, Freya studied O'Keeffe. Despite his fairly young age, he now looked ten years older. The wrinkles around his eyes had deepened and his grey eyes had grown slightly dull, their usual light vanished.

With a pang on guilt, Freya acknowledged she was partly the cause of this transformation, and resolved to stop giving her old teacher so much trouble. He might be keeping a lot of secrets from her, but he meant well.

Her grey eyes rose and locked gazes with Seamus' as she bid her time for an answer to her previous question.

Rather than comply, the old man smiled. "How was your practice?"

Freya raised an eyebrow at his unsubtle attempt to redirect the conversation. "As usual – tiring, but effective."

Nodding his head thoughtfully, Seamus leaned further in the chair, surveying his pupil. Though he knew Freya's capabilities grew each day, he worried for her sake. It wasn't so long ago she'd been unaware of the legacy she carried within her. Now that she'd realized its extent, he felt she was always trying to measure herself to incredible standards.

O'Keeffe was aware that Freya was ready to take on whatever was thrown her way, innocence of the youth and all. But lately, his feelings of a darker danger shadowing her path couldn't be shaken off.

She is the portrait of her parents... O'Keeffe thought nostalgically as he took in Freya's raven hair and soft features.

Sighing heavily, O'Keeffe rubbed his forehead, wishing for the memories to go away. Thinking of Mark and Evelyn, his friends, was the epitome of idiocy this close to the teenager. Sages were very perceptive, even more so with people that were close to them.

Despite the threat, Seamus was powerless against it. His dreams of them had come back, and their loss was lately even more present at the back of his mind. Before he could avert it, his eyes lost their focus as one particular memory assailed him.

Having been watching her mentor attentively, Freya was quick to notice when his stare glazed and lost its focus.

Tyr... Her call went unanswered, further adding to her concern.

Damn it! What's wrong with Seamus? Frowning, she stood up from the velvet brown armchair and walked around the desk, prudently raising her hand to touch Seamus's shoulder. Her fingers hesitantly moved closer, even as Freya bit her lip awkwardly.

She'd barely made contact with Seamus's shoulder when his pain hit her with such force she was thrown backwards into the row of books. Freya collapsed on the floor, uncon-scious, while the recollection spread through her.

&&&

"Evelyn!" A male voice shouted through the fire. "Mark!" It called again.

There was a huge explosion and flames burst everywhere. Aside from the roar of the blaze, the silence was deafening, only adding to the eerie sensation the smoke created.

Freya peered around, noticing everything as though in a vision. The familiarity of the scene was not lost on her, hav-ing lived it once before.

Through the flames, a shape appeared. It was Seamus, but a younger version with dirty clothing, barely in his mid-twenties. His blonde hair was glued to his face, and sweat dripped off his brow. He searched around frantically, his grey eyes widened with anguish and panic.

"Mark! Evelyn!" he yelled. "*Freya*!"

Shouts answered him and he paused to listen, trying to pinpoint their location. From her vantage point, Freya watched his hand twitch as he scanned the area. Having found what he needed, he purposefully strode through the fire. She had to run to keep up with him, taking in the ten-sion in him, the way his breath was coming out in ragged pants.

The smoke is getting to him... Freya observed absentmind-edly.

Seamus reached a burning car, his eyes glistening more than before. The smoke was thick and heavy, and he coughed. Despite his discomfort, he stepped closer to the people within.

He placed his palms on the burning metal of the hood, and gritted his teeth. Freya's eyes widened at the power emanating from his palms, a surge so strong it rippled across the metal, trying to leash in the fire.

"Stop!" Seamus growled, and the blaze seemed to diminish for a moment. Before he even had a chance to speak, it burst higher, and he was slammed backwards by the force behind it.

The Sage recoiled back in shock. "Impossible..." he whispered.

"Very *much* possible," a voice came from behind him.

He turned towards it, then staggered back. "You! *You* are the cause of this!"

The shapes were dark, obscured by the smog, only a faint outline visible. Freya couldn't see them any better than Seamus could, but she sensed his wrath as if it was a living thing.

Snarling, Seamus clasped his hands together, trying to grasp the air around and use it to his advantage. He struck forward, and energy escaped towards the attackers.

"You scum!" he yelled as they disappeared.

Seamus then turned back to the car, and a female voice called from within. "Seamus! Save her!"

Freya watched in a daze as pale hands streaked with cuts and smoke held a bundle wrapped in a dirty rag. Seamus rushed closer and reached out for the child handed to him – a raven-haired grey-eyed four-year-old baby. Freya gasped, seeing the woman's hands, though she couldn't see her face as well as she wished.

Seamus held the baby securely in his arms, wrapping his coat around tiny Freya's face to shield her from the fire.

"Evelyn! Where's Mark?"

A weak voice answered from within. "I'm here. Run, Seamus... Run before they come back."

"You know... You know who they were, don't you?" O'Keeffe whispered, and there was so much emotion in his tone, it seemed to strangle him.

"Yes. *He* sent them. And they'll come back for Freya. Get her out of here, please," Mark pleaded. "Leave us, just... just make sure she's safe."

"No!" Seamus' eyes were filled with tears as he choked out, "I can save you, too!"

"There is no time," Evelyn's voice was wistful, but firm. "They will return, make no mistake. Save Freya!"

"Go!" Mark croaked from within, and the sound tore at Freya's heart. "Run, Seamus. Do it for our friendship!"

Seamus shook his head, but another plea from them both was his undoing. Wordlessly, he nodded and, biting back tears, hugged the child closer.

"I'm sorry... Mark... Evelyn..." he whispered to the air.

Seamus turned and ran through the smoke, until his chest was ablaze and he dropped to his knees. He'd reached the end of the road when he turned and looked back. He witnessed the same two shapes coming out of the fire and raising their hands, blasting energy at the car simultaneously.

Sobs burst past his lips, soon followed by the anguished groan of a hurt beast. "No..."

Seamus watched, powerless, as the flames consumed Freya's parents. Movement in his arms drew his gaze to the tiny baby, and the ache in his heart eased ever-so. "Farewell, my friends. I will protect her as my own, I swear it."

Chapter 2

Tyr moved from the spot in front of the fireplace, lifting its head in confusion at the scene playing in its mind.

Isis!

The goddess was lounging on a chaise, absentmindedly twirling her hair as she stared into the flames. At the tiger's panicked voice, she stood, frowning anxiously. "Did something happen?"

Seamus is losing control of his emotions.

"It may interest you to know that what you see has nothing to do with the old Sage."

Both beings turned to Osiris, whose darkening face hinted at nothing good.

What do you mean?

"Freya has been attempting to unravel the dragon runes in the manuscript," Osiris divulged. "Even without her awkward passes, the book has been speaking to her. Since the Vikings, the runes have enhanced her power, touching her spiritual – and physical – strength. It does not help that every night before she rests, she connects to the book, reading through it – ensuring you do not see it."

Tyr could only stare back in shock, realizing the dangers associated with such actions even before the god thought fit to expand on them.

"Yes... If she continues, with every rune she absorbs, her powers will unleash more and more. Freya is not fit to control everything she is absorbing, and the power emanates from her without her knowing. She is affecting what surrounds her, including Seamus. It is not the old man's fault that his memories latched on to Freya, desperate to answer her unspoken questions."

She wants to find out everything about her past.

Tyr's tone was flat, almost devoid of emotion, but the deep emerald-golden gaze shone ferociously.

"That may be so, but we can no longer deny she is much closer to the truth than before," Isis intervened. "It may be time for you to be honest with the young one."

No. Not yet.

"Tyr, Raksh is most definitely planning something," Isis tried to argue. "What you saw last time will not be the end, it is simply not in his nature."

"My beloved is correct. We have danced with this pest for eons. Freya needs to be aware of the full truth," Osiris continued. "She has already seen the demon kill Brennan's grandfather, it is long past due!"

She what? Tyr growled and when neither deity answered, moved closer. *Tell me.*

Isis shared a look with her husband, before kneeling in front of the tiger. "Perhaps you have been blinded by your love for her, and no longer notice all that you should. Freya remembers your encounter with the demon, and has somehow witnessed the elder Wiseman's death."

Tyr was silent for a moment, then the green eyes glinted speculatively. *Somehow?*

"She cannot be a Dreamwalker," Osiris interrupted, taking the hint. "That ability was lost eons ago."

You know that is not true. Isis' words resounded in his head, but the god uncharacteristically ignored his wife, in favor of the feline in their presence.

You do not know this young one well. Freya makes the impossible, possible.

"Have you ever thought," Osiris gritted, "that perhaps it is you who does not know your precious charge?"

Tyr was not impressed by the thundering god. *I will do this my way, or not at all. Neither of you has faced Raksh as I have. Stay out of this.*

"Tyr," Isis tried, "you are much too close to the matter and not thinking straight. Be careful."

The tiger's only response was a slight nod of the head.

&&&

O'Keeffe opened his eyes, blinking against the fog. His vision was impaired by the rivers of tears streaming down his cheeks, even as his chest squeezed painfully.

He took two deep breaths to calm himself, then wiped at his face. "Freya?" he asked hoarsely. He cleared his throat, then attempted again. "Freya?"

When he received no response, the elder man hastily jumped to his feet and searched the office. Freya's unmoving body was curled up on the floor a few feet away from the armchair she'd been sitting in moments earlier. An odd dizziness assailed him, but he fought it off.

"No!" O'Keeffe yelled as he ran to her and dropped on his knees. "Freya, please wake up!"

It took her a few seconds, but then the teenager's eyelids fluttered open and her dazed expression focused on Seamus's face. Under his bemused gaze, the unfocused gleam in her eyes turned steely.

"What happened?" Seamus gently asked her, helping her stand up.

Freya shrugged out of the embrace abruptly, then walked to the window closest to her. Staring unseeingly at the beautiful castle's grounds below, she shook with barely repressed fury at what she'd seen.

Nothing – *nothing!* – could have prepared her for the sense of betrayal coursing through her. Freya had always known Seamus was holding back something about the way her parents died, but the extent of the camouflage left her flabbergasted – and more than a little pissed.

Especially when his little story doesn't even add up!

Making sure her voice was steady, Freya spoke haltingly. "You zoned out in front of me, and I was worried. I tried to shake you out of it, but as soon as my fingers touched your shoulder, I was blasted away into the books and..." She left the phrase in suspense, wanting to see just how much she could find out before Seamus retreated back into his shell.

"My memory was shared... You saw that, didn't you?" O'Keeffe whispered, then audibly gulped.

Freya turned to him hopefully. If he was admitting it, acknowledging that she'd witnessed what he desperately tried to hide, perhaps there was chance. She was prepared to forgive, if only he could be honest.

"It was my parents, wasn't it?" she pressed, taking a few steps closer.

O'Keeffe, however, was avoiding her gaze. When he finally did meet it, his features were inscrutable. Realization dawned on Freya like a frigid shower, leaving her trembling. *He still refuses to tell me anything. No matter what, he won't...*

She turned back to the window before her mentor could catch sight of her disappointment.

"Freya, I..." O'Keeffe started, then sighed. "Yes, it was your parents."

"What happened that day?" Freya questioned neutrally, though inside she was boiling with anticipation.

"We were all driving to a cabin in the woods, to celebrate your birthday. I took a different car, and lost track of your parents'. There was an explosion on the highway, so much chaos... I could not find them, and my negligence was partly responsible for their deaths. By the time I got there, it was too late."

"Don't lie!" Freya accused through gritted teeth, despite the calmness of her voice.

"I'm not, Freya!" Seamus denied, warring with emotions within. *I cannot tell her the truth... She can't know. Not yet.*

Nothing petrified him as much as the idea of Freya launching herself on a quest for vengeance she was nowhere close to achieving.

"How did they *really* die?" Freya pressed, a frost he was unused to hearing in her voice.

Seamus only stared back, before declaring, "I... can't tell you. I'm sorry, Freya, but I simply cannot."

"Can't or *won't*?"

"What do you mean?" O'Keeffe frowned.

Freya's back went rigid with anger at his continued lies. She spun to him, hair flying about her face, grey eyes blazing with rage. "You know full well what I mean, Seamus! For years now, you've lied, telling me you had to keep secrets because of a promise you made to my parents. Even months ago, you told me it was because you'd sworn to keep everything away from me until my eighteenth birthday!" She shook her head, stepping to him. "This memory speaks to just how much you've been hiding, stuff they didn't ask you to! I'm asking you one last time, Seamus. No more secrets, please."

O'Keeffe was taken aback, but unfazed. He was torn between a need to shelter Freya, and a very real want to instill some respect into her. In the end, old instincts won and he only shook his head.

The corners of her lips turned into a sneer. "Of course you can't!" Freya taunted bitterly. "Why would I even expect something different? You can hide as much as you want to, but they're *my* parents, and I have the right to know!"

"I *am* sorry." The words could not fully express the regret he felt. They were, however, the most Seamus could give this proud teenager that was unaware what she was asking for.

"So am I."

Still fuming about his lack of cooperation, Freya walked past him, body taut with unspent energy. As she reached for the knob of the door, one last threat escaped her lips. "I *am* going to find out the truth. All of it."

She then slammed the door behind her, the shock of it causing one of the large albums to fall on the floor, revealing a photo of Freya at her sixth birthday party.

Tears filled O'Keeffe's eyes when they fell upon it. "I am sorry. But I can't risk losing you, too."

&&&

"Argh!" Freya yelled as she punched her bedroom wall for the fourth time, her knuckles having grown red and nearly cracked already.

After the encounter with Seamus, she'd furiously stormed on the fifth floor. Unable and unwilling to cry out her frustration, she set about beating it out of her sore body.

Situated in the northern tower, Freya's room was just above Seamus's, with a magnificent view of the river. It was decorated quite simply, with a canopy bed and walls in beige, a huge closet and a place for Freya to store her weapons in.

I'm sorry, I'm sorry, I'm sorry, Seamus's words echoed in her head, and tears struck her eyes again. It wasn't as if what he was hiding would be a revelation. She already knew Raksh had a hand in her parents' death – or so he claimed. But it would've been nice to have the vote of confidence from her mentor, and no secrets between them.

Freya furiously blinked to keep the tears away, and made to hit the wall again. Sam's head popped through it, and she missed his head by inches. Breathing heavily, she cradled her right hand and rubbed it soothingly.

"Freya... Are you okay?" Sam fretted, his whole body passing through the wall.

The teen nodded, not trusting herself to speak. Sam threw her a distressed look, floating closer. "Did you talk to Seamus?"

Again, he was answered by a brief incline of the head. "And?"

Freya's eyes met his, and Sam could see her sadness and anger in them. "I... I experienced this memory of Seamus's... With my parents. The night they died, or were killed."

"Killed!?" Sam's gaze widened. "Freya, what do you mean?"

"I don't know!" the Sage snapped, furiously shaking her head. "Seamus, as per usual, refused to tell me anything more!"

As soon as it came, the anger disappeared. Dismayed, Freya slid to the ground, her back to the wall, and grabbed her head in her hands.

Sam's expression showed his pity for the one he considered a sister. "Freya, please calm down. Maybe... Maybe he's right not to tell you."

She raised her head, glaring at him through her tears. "Whose side are you on? You know what, don't even answer. Just leave me alone." When he seemed ready to dispute the order, she shouted, "Just *go*, Sam!"

After a slight hesitation, the spirit dematerialized, knowing it was best to leave the teen alone for the time being. Once he was truly gone, Freya got up and grabbed the nearest book to her, throwing it angrily to the other side of the room.

She then lay back in her previous position on the floor, choking out the tears. Resting her head on a bent knee, Freya finally let go of the pent up emotions, sobs wrecking her body until there were no more.

Freya...

Tyr! the Sage cried telepathically.

I know, child. I have seen what troubles you so, and I understand your need to grasp everything. You are too young at the moment, and do not yet realize what perils lie in wait.

Then tell me! Freya argued. *Who can it serve if I don't know things, and end up doing stupid stuff?*

Tyr hesitated, but the Sage wasn't about to drop it. *How about we start with the demon I met after the fight with Cadmael? And the meeting I had with him – and you.*

There was a silence, as though the tiger was trying to figure out how best to go about the situation. In the end, it regretfully admitted, *Yes, Raksh is very much real, and involved in your parents' death. No matter what, you have to know your parents were wonderful people. They loved you with all their hearts. You were their ray of sunshine, Freya. When the accident happened... They preferred death to ensure your safety. The car had crashed and they were blocked inside of it. They could not get out through the windows, because they were too small. They knew, however, that you were a priority.*

Sensing a presence in the room, Freya slowly lifted her head from her hands and met Tyr's caring gaze.

White fur as smooth as velvet, golden-green eyes sparkling with emotions, the tiger stepped up to the Sage and nuzzled Freya's cheek. *Your past holds certain challenges you are not yet ready to face. This medallion and book you and Brennan have are not making things easier.*

The tiger paused, then asked, *Why did you not confide in me? Regarding your dream of Thomas, and your recollection of Raksh.*

Freya ducked her head in shame, mumbling, "I was afraid you would take that away from me, too."

I would never do such a thing, child. It was your mind that blocked what happened with the demon, not me.

The Sage dared to peek at the tiger, reading sincerity in its expression. *What I and Seamus are trying to do is shelter you, not limit you. But I see you do not accept my words, so here is a show of faith. That book you go to bed with every night, the dragon runes, are a path. I do not know how it unlocks the map to the relics, but I do know it will a perilous journey left for another time. Already, the book is changing you and altering your powers. You must be careful!*

"Altering how?"

Your dreams, being able to tap into someone's mind like with Seamus... You are widening your horizons. And it is not the best ability to develop when you have a demon intent on harming you and stealing what you now possess.

"But the castle keeps me safe."

For now.

"Fine, I get it," Freya muttered. "I'll ease up on the runes. But what about the rest of it? I know now my parents were murdered, and that demon had something to do with it. I want revenge, Tyr."

The tiger sighed at the fire burning in the Sage. *I know you do. That is what both me and Seamus were attempting to prevent. But I know nothing I say will dissuade you from it. I*

only ask of you one promise – that you delay **until the end of**
this new mission.

Freya stared into the tiger's eyes, then inclined her head.
"All right. Agreed."

Good. Now go to Seamus, he has something to tell you
about the new case.

Freya was about to make a face, but at her guardian's se-
vere growl, let it go and slowly stood up. Before heading out
of the room, she turned back and said, "Thanks, Tyr."

The tiger gave her a warm look, then disappeared as soon
as she was gone.

&&&

"What's up?" Freya asked as she entered O'Keeffe's office
for the second time in as many hours.

The elder Sage whirled around in surprise. After she'd
stormed out the way she had, he would not have expected
to see Freya again during the day, regardless of what awaited
them.

To his utter amazement, there were no glares or gritted
jaws greeting him, only a determined stare. Observing Freya,
Seamus realized she had no intention to bring up their earlier
fight, and he felt his gut churn in response. If her red-
rimmed eyes were any indication, she had cried, and heavily
so. He hated hurting her, or being the cause of her anguish.

At the very least, this will ensure she will keep a clear head
on the new mission. Heaving a sigh, O'Keeffe masked his own
regrets, and turned to the floating ghost above his desk.

"Go ahead, Sam. Tell Freya what you told me only moments ago."

"Right," the boy nodded, then fully faced Freya. "Do you remember your history about the leaders in the ghostly world of Spain?"

It took Freya a minute to sort through the muddle in her mind, then she caught on. "The conquistadors? Vaguely, yeah. You know my own track record with those spirits wasn't very pleasant. Why do you ask?"

Sam grimaced in commiseration, recalling all too well what Freya alluded to. "Right, well, so you definitely recall then that they're, shall we say, divided. Into cliques, if you will. It's a system unique to the country, and something that hasn't been a problem. Until now, that is. One of the groups is growing too powerful, and the others are bowing down to it."

"Okay..." Freya dragged out the word, glancing between her two companions with a raised eyebrow. "And this is bad because of the large amount of people involved?"

"That," Seamus intervened, "And a mysterious new presence."

Freya held his gaze for a moment, sorting through all the statements she wanted to hurl at him. Taking a deep breath, she instead settled on, "So we're off to Spain?"

Sam nodded hesitantly, glancing back and forth between Freya and Seamus.

"Sweet!" the Sage grinned, all thoughts of her previous temper flare set aside. "When are we leaving?"

"Not quite yet," Seamus lifted a hand as though to stop her. "We still have to wait for one more person to arrive."

"Say what?" Freya frowned, not understanding.

"We will need some assistance with this one," O'Keeffe continued, avoiding her look.

"What for?" Freya protested, stepping closer to the desk. "I speak Spanish and we can handle whatever conquistador there is all alone."

"No, not this one," Seamus continued, stubborn as can be – and still not meeting her gaze.

"Do you know something I should?" Freya pushed through gritted teeth.

"Not at all. Just a bad feeling."

Freya was about to comment, but something about the statement set her instincts prickling. "Hang on a second..." She peered suspiciously at her mentor. "Who exactly did you have in mind?"

Seamus rubbed the back of his almost sheepishly, before meeting her eyes and admitting, "Brennan."

Freya was too stunned to say anything. The insufferable, arrogant prat was coming with them?

A nightmare. This has *to be a nightmare.*

"No. Bloody. *Way!*" she reacted, finally regaining control of her vocal chords.

"You are hardly in a position to decline, Freya," Seamus chuckled. "He's already on his way. In fact, if I'm not mistaken, his plane already landed. Brennan should be here any minute now."

"Seamus!" In a very child-like show of temper, Freya stomped her foot and whined. "I *can't* work with him! He's an–"

O'Keeffe lifted a hand to silence her. Ignoring her petulant expression, he continued, "Before you get started, I am pleading with you to please make an effort. For the sake of the mission."

"I'll make one if he does too," the Sage scowled.

Five minutes later, there was a polite knock on the door and Freya groaned. She flopped down onto the armchair, sinking deep in the cushions as though they could swallow her whole.

This should be interesting... Seamus mused as he watched the expression on his pupil's face.

Chapter 3

"**F**reya, *do* make an effort."

The Sage glared at Seamus, to no avail. The elder man simply rolled his eyes and walked towards the door.

Freya tensed up, muttering under breath about unwelcome surprises, and sank that much deeper in the chair. Due to its colossal size, her form was completely hidden from anyone new entering the room, especially if they were at the other end of it. Stubbornly, she focused her gaze on the carpet, unwilling to stand and greet their guest.

She remembered Brennan and his help all too well, and though she was grateful, Freya was also confused. She knew more now about his past than she cared to, and especially about his grandfather and his untimely death. An odd sense of guilt and foreboding tugged at her, causing her stomach to plummet.

Nope, I'm definitely not ready for that conversation.

A soft click snapped her out of her thoughts, and Freya cringed at the echo of footsteps entering the room.

A cocky voice then resonated. "Professor O'Keeffe, your castle is seriously the *shit*!"

"It's good to see you too, Dublin," Seamus chuckled.

"Oh, please, do call me Brennan. Works better on the ladies."

Laughter answered him, causing Freya to grimace. *This is going to be just great,* she thought sarcastically. She'd forgotten how arrogant the newcomer sounded.

"Had a good flight?" Seamus was asking.

"More than good. Though I've been kind of worried about why you called me here..."

As Freya's ears perked up, a head came from under the desk and whispered to her, "Why are you hiding?"

Freya nearly jumped out of the armchair, but restrained herself just in time. "Sam!" she hissed back furiously. "I am *not* hiding!" They were far enough from Seamus' spot that they couldn't be heard, but the Sage didn't want to take chances.

"Oh, really?" the ghost grinned mischievously.

"Yes, really. I'm just delaying until Seamus and Brennan finish their little chat."

Sam seated himself Indian-style in front of Freya, tilting his head to the side. "Why not just say *hi*?"

"Because I—" A look of realization dawned on Freya, stopping her mid-sentence. "Hang on a second! You knew!" The Sage threw Sam a suspicious glare. "You *knew* Brennan was coming and you didn't say anything!"

Sam's sheepish smile was more of an answer than his innocent, "Nope."

"Why?" Freya whined. "*Why* would you do that to me?"

"Because you never asked. Besides, Brennan's my friend too, so technically I should keep both his secrets *and* yours."

Setting her jaw firmly, Freya muttered through gritted teeth, "You little... Sam, you're lucky I can't afford to move right now, else you'd be in a huge deal of trouble."

Sam floated closer to Freya, taunting, "Luckily for me, though, you're hiding and therefore won't get up."

Freya's hands held onto the inside of the armchair so tightly her knuckles grew white, and she closed her eyes in a futile attempt to calm herself.

Am I to guess by the amount of anger I perceive that Brennan has arrived?

Freya's shut eyes snapped open. *You knew too?*

A laugh echoed in her mind, then Tyr admitted, *Of course I did, Freya. If you remember well, when you defeated your last enemy, a special bond was created between you and Brennan.*

That, I won't be forgetting, the Sage grumbled. She'd done her utmost in the last few weeks to keep that link tightly locked, and the Wiseman at bay.

Choosing to ignore the grumpy teenager, the tiger said, *Well, considering we are also telepathically linked, the bond now applies to me as well.*

Wait, what? Freya frowned, distracted from her annoyance by yet another piece of the puzzle.

Tyr hesitated for a brief moment, but a nudge from their mental bond pulled the words out unwillingly. *You remember the light that enveloped you and Brennan, coming from his necklace?*

Yes.

Though it tried to stop speaking, Tyr found it was impossible. *Once the connection was created between the two of you, it was also extended between me and Brennan.*

Freya was stunned into silence at the new piece of information.

Yes. Now, if he is in trouble, I have come to his aid, unable to fight it.

But what about the emotional side? Freya questioned. *You once said that we'll be able to feel our emotions… Does that apply to you too?*

With a sinking realization, Tyr figured out the reason behind its sudden honesty was tied in with the cursed book manuscript Freya had been dabbling in. Somehow, much as it had affected Seamus around the teenager, it was now doing the same to Tyr.

Yes, the tiger answered gravely, wishing the Sage would stop with the questions. *But I have blocked mine to ensure Brennan will not be able to feel them. I, however, will catch onto his regardless.*

Freya was silent for a few seconds as the information sank in. *So does that mean I have to tell Brennan about you?*

I believe so, Freya. And it also means that you will have to cooperate. Both *of you.*

Tyr, he's an egotistical prick! Besides that, he wasn't able to save his grandfather, what makes you think he can help me? I can do this alone, and you know it.

The tiger pressed forth in Freya's mind, as the words themselves didn't sound like her. It only took a nudge to grasp the true reason behind her panic – the dream of Brennan's grandfather. At the end of the day, Freya didn't know how to reveal to the Wiseman what she'd witnessed, let alone be by his side as he coped with the newfound knowledge.

It was that which softened Tyr's tone enough to say, *That decision is for Seamus to take, Freya.*

What!?

Your mentor has fought the ghosts for longer than you, Freya, and knows better. If he maintains this conquistador is too much for you to handle alone, then you will have to listen to him.

But, Tyr—

No buts, Freya. Wherever is this new attitude of yours from? If I did not know better, I would say you are afraid to work with Brennan for fear of something you have been trying to hide resurfacing.

Me? Afraid? Of him? Freya mentally snorted, choosing to ignore the last part of Tyr's speech. *No way. But I am, however, anxious for my safety when working with him.*

This time, the tiger didn't bother to hide its annoyance, and Freya could feel its tremors internally. *You* will *collaborate with Brennan, regardless of your opinion of him. And enough with the childish games, I know you are afraid to tell him what you saw of Thomas' death. Grow up, child. I have a feeling that O'Keeffe is right and that you will need help.*

"Freya? Hey, Frey-Frey, you okay?" Sam whispered.

Still frowning, Freya gave the ghost a reassuring smile. "Peachy, don't worry."

The twelve-year-old took one glance at the Sage's eyes and nodded, not believing a single word. Despite her best efforts, Freya was a horrible liar, and her expression always betrayed the truth hiding within. At the moment, he could tell

something else was on her mind – something that was annoying her a lot more than Brennan's presence.

Thinking back to their last mission, Sam had to bite back
a mocking comment. Freya had certainly not been fond of
the Wiseman, but they'd made a great team. Despite Brennan's exceptional talent of always pissing her off, their teamwork had defeated an army of Vikings.

Sam shook his head, beaming widely. "Then I don't suppose you'll mind me saying *hi* to our guest."

Before the Sage could answer, the ghost floated past her
and reached O'Keeffe and Brennan. Freya heard the two
salute each other, and tried to ignore it as much as possible.

*Fine, Tyr, I'll make an effort. I just can't promise to always
be cheerful around Brennan... You know how he can infuriate
me. But I'll try.*

Good. The tiger seemed satisfied enough, as it then ended the connection.

Freya sighed and was about to stand up and unwillingly
greet her partner, when his next words froze her movements.

"So what exactly did you call me here for, Professor?"
Brennan asked.

There was a slight hesitation, then O'Keeffe admitted, "I
know you proposed your help and I vowed to only call upon you if it was absolutely necessary, but I believe now is as
good a time as any."

"What happened?" Freya was surprised to hear Brennan's concerned tone, like he actually cared. *Huh. Go figure.*

"The ghosts in Spain are being bullied by a conquistador," Seamus explained. "With their rather large numbers,

and evidence this is unprecedented, it can turn ugly if we let it to."

"No problem, I'm more than happy to pitch in." Brennan looked around the room, rubbing his hands together eagerly. "So, where's Freya? I'm looking forward to this, actually. Saving damsels in distress is my job and Freya is—"

At that point, the Sage couldn't stand it anymore and shot to her feet. She faced the door, pursing her lips, and was met by Brennan's frank golden-brown gaze.

The Wiseman stood a few inches taller than her, wearing faded jeans and a dark t-shirt with some logo or another. His hair was shorter than she remembered, setting off the square jaw line. He had a backpack slung carelessly off one shoulder, and seemed more or less fashionable. His attire, however, was not the reason Freya was struck dumb for a moment.

Rather, it could be blamed on those blasted eyes and the twinkling specks of light. When they landed on her there was surprise, then pure eagerness in them, and it was enough for Freya's breath to hitch in her throat. For that instant, she forgot the anger and its source.

When Seamus cleared his throat, the spell was broken and she narrowed her eyes. "I'm *what*, Brennan?" Freya taunted coldly, her gaze piercing his own.

Brennan glanced at Sam – who was scratching the back of his head sheepishly – then at Seamus – who simply shrugged – for help. When neither of them budged to jump to his aid, he turned back to Freya and gave her his most charming smile.

"Not one at all," he ended his previous remark.

Freya's eyes grew, if possible, even darker as she stepped up to him and hissed furiously, "Listen up, Wiseman. Last I remember, I fought Cadmael by myself – and won. As I did with countless other ghosts before him. I can certainly do this all by myself, without your help or anyone else's for that matter. So why don't you do me a huge favor and go back to where you came from, hmm?"

Molten eyes turned bemused, then unreadable as the words sank in. Before Brennan could answer, Freya extended her left palm to the rows of books on the left. An old tome levitated from between two others, and floated to her expecting hands.

Even as she flipped the pages, she muttered under her breath, "I simply cannot believe you would do this to me, Seamus. I'm not a child anymore, and I can fully take care of myself!"

Without another word, she threw the opened book to him and the old Sage caught it by reflex. He glanced down at the cover and read the title – *Conquistadors: Facts and myths about them*. O'Keeffe raised a confused look to Freya's blank one.

"A bit of reading for you," she hissed. "You might be interested to know that the conquistadors aren't all that they seem, and not as powerful as you may think."

Freya then passed by Brennan, mumbling a, "Sorry you came here for nothing."

The door slammed behind her and she broke into a run, desperately wanting to put some distance between her and the Wiseman.

What happened to cooperation and trying? Tyr interrupted, but Freya ignored it and jogged even faster towards the castle grounds, and beyond.

&&&

Back in the room, Brennan turned a puzzled look to O'Keeffe. "Was it something I said?"

Seamus slapped his forehead, muttering, "This is going to take a lot of work."

"You're telling me," Sam grumbled, still floating next to O'Keeffe.

Brennan looked from the twelve-year-old ghost to Seamus, frowning. *This doesn't seem right,* he thought. *Just three months ago, there was harmony between Seamus and Freya. Now, I can smell conflict a mile ahead. And there's something else... Freya herself is acting different. Sure, she'd get angered by me before, but now it's as if I'm stepping on eggshells.*

"Seamus," Brennan started haltingly, then barreled through, "is Freya upset about something?"

"Why do you ask?" O'Keeffe countered, his expression giving nothing away.

Brennan snorted. "Were you paying attention, just now? Not only did she nearly rip my head off, but it's pretty damn obvious she doesn't want me here. I think that was made pretty clear, don't you?"

The Wiseman didn't want to admit how much Freya's reaction had hurt him. After having fought side by side, he'd been under the impression they were friends. The last few minutes in her company, however, proved the delusion of such a statement.

Since it was nothing he could change, he preferred to focus on understanding her reaction. And at the moment, Seamus was his best bet at doing that. Nothing in the old man would've revealed the truth, but Brennan was a good judge of character. It took only a tiny prompt of his senses to pick up the tension emanating from him, confirming his suspicions.

"Since you ask…" Sam started, but trailed off when Seamus cleared his throat. As Brennan turned to the spirit, Sam only said, "It's not my place to tell, anyways."

"Freya's just a bit upset because I did not inform her you will be joining us, Brennan," O'Keeffe tried to reassure. "But do not fret. She will get over it soon, and then we can concentrate on the mission."

Brennan nodded, though a bit uncertainly. The lie rang false to his ears, and that only proved the seriousness of what was hidden. He intended to find out what that was – as soon as they could converse without Freya wanting to bite his head off.

The Wiseman then stepped up to the window, pensively surveying the grounds. The grass was lively and green, and Brennan could sense every bit of life that vibrated its own energy in the cosmos.

His eyes then noticed the small shape running towards the river. He recognized the raven-black hair flying in the wind in seconds, and resolved to reach out to her. It was better than informing O'Keeffe that his pupil was currently escaping to an undisclosed location, probably to diffuse some of her anger.

Grasping the edge of the window for support, Brennan expanded his mind and removed the blocks usually in place. The link between him and Freya was almost tangible due to the lack of distance, and it came as a relief. For the last few weeks, his attempts had been unfruitful to contact her, and he'd feared it was broken.

Luckily for Brennan, it was an easy feat to snap it into place, and he wasted no time. *Why are you so mad at me?*

&&&

Freya was heading to her training place, desperate for a bit of practice, when the question rang in her head. Though she was startled by it, she'd been half-expecting it. After all, Brennan didn't know how to let go.

Without pausing, Freya shot back, *That's my business. You keep out of it.*

She could tell Brennan was puzzled by her anger, but hoping that he'd had enough, Freya didn't comment further. It was not the most mature way to deal with what she knew, but it was the quickest. With Brennan out of the way, Freya would no longer have to be concerned about his feelings, and could focus on what really mattered – the truth.

However, peace was not to be, as the Wiseman was more persistent than Freya initially gave him credit for.

Okay, fine. But you should know, I flew here because Seamus asked me to.

Of course you did, Freya scoffed. Though she refused to admit it, she appreciated Brennan having travelled across time zones to help out. Despite the show of good faith, it was not enough to drop her guard.

Listen, I... Can't we at least call a truce? Brennan pleaded, and he seemed sincere. *We'll have to work together, you know.*

The Sage set her jaw firm as she bit back. *No, we won't.*

Freya...

Sighing, Freya came to a halt. *Listen, Brennan. I thank you for helping me fight Cadmael, so don't think I'm ungrateful. But I have never needed a partner to fight ghosts. I've done this for the past two years of my life, and I'm pretty sure I can keep it up.*

She then turned to the castle and her gaze rose to Seamus' window. Though she couldn't see him, Brennan's energy was palpable there, reaching out to her.

"Good-bye, Brennan," she said softly.

She lingered for another minute, then whirled around and broke off into a run again. The river was nearby now, and a soft smile tugged at her lips.

"Finally, I'm here."

&&&

Back inside the castle, Brennan observed Freya's speed increase as she reached the stream. Not once did she glance back his way, leaving the Wiseman frowning slightly.

Apparently, the Sage was determined to complete the mission by herself. But what she ignored was that Brennan was just as stubborn as she was. And when he planned to do something, he didn't give up until he achieved it. O'Keeffe had called him on a secure telephone and asked him to come over to Scotland to help with a mission. Whether Freya liked it or not, he *would* be a part of it.

You know how I hate good-byes, Brennan thought mischievously. He took one last look at the running Sage, then addressed Seamus and Sam. "All right, that aside, I'll need more information about the mission."

Though the Wiseman preferred not to think about it, during the past months, he'd been restless. Aside from his usual dreams and nightmares, something was pushing him to move, to reach out to the Sages. In truth, he'd been standing by, waiting for a reason to come to Scotland. He could not explain it. Maybe it was the bond, or perhaps something else, but being close to Freya, partnering up with her now seemed like the right course of action.

Since when? Brennan wondered. Yet no matter how hard he looked for an answer, it eluded him. At a loss on what to do about that particular issue, he focused on Seamus and Sam, waiting for an answer.

Instead of getting one, O'Keeffe asked, "What do you know about the ghosts in Spain, Brennan?"

"Answer a question with another question... Does this run in the family?" Brennan taunted. He then plopped himself on the armchair Freya had vacated, pursing his lips thoughtfully. "Well, not a lot. If I remember correctly, my grandfather told me that they'd split into cliques. Some were causing trouble, others not. Some were gentle, others furious. The cliques depended on religion, cults, aspirations, dreams..."

"Yes," Seamus confirmed, "That is about our understanding, as well."

When he said nothing else, rather falling into a deep rumination, Brennan probed, "So this time, trouble's stirring up in Spain?"

"Yes," O'Keeffe admitted, his features darkening. "We do not know what is causing it exactly, but Sam overheard a conversation between a Spanish priest and an ancient soldier. It seems that someone is attempting to rally all ghosts together."

"And that's a bad thing...why?" Brennan enquired.

"No, it is not bad per se," O'Keeffe said, pacing. "But it also seems this sudden gathering hides something more sinister. We could very well be referring to over three thousand ghosts. Why would someone want to be leader of so many, unless they plan on doing something with them?"

"Well, when you put it that way... That great a force can pose a problem if used to no good. But the question is, who would bother?"

"Ever heard of Cortés?" Sam interrupted.

Brennan turned to him, a questioning gleam in his golden eyes. "What?"

"Cortés," Sam repeated. "It's a name I heard in the conversation. I figured it might give us a clue or something."

Brennan shook his head. "Sorry, I can't place it."

"Neither can I, Sam. But I grow old, and my memory may be failing me. I can throw a look in my books and files, do a bit of research before we head off."

"Can I help?" Sam offered, though the thought of flipping through dusty, boring manuscripts made him want to sneeze.

"No, it's quite all right. It might be best if I go and search through those right now, see what I can gather."

With that said, O'Keeffe bid both Brennan and Sam good-bye and left the room.

&&&

Having reached the river, Freya stopped her run. Her eyes took in the clear water and the fish swimming in it. *I wish everything could be this peaceful,* the Sage thought.

Shaking her head clear, Freya then brought her palms together. She concentrated on the energy filling her, and before long, her whole body radiated of a clear silvery aura. The sun's light bathed the Sage in its warmth, enveloping her in a calm cocoon.

The Sage reached out with her mind to the river, feeling its immovable energy and destructive force. "Let me in," she whispered, pleading for permission, always respectful of the element itself.

The water swirled for a moment, then stilled as the current lessened.

Freya's body became lighter every second, and the Sage could sense it. She detached herself from the ground, propelled her spirit forward, and imagined breaking her roots and flying free. Her body slowly rose into the air – one centimeter, two, three, and right above the ground.

Nothing else existed except for the water ahead and below her. She called upon the substance whose strength would keep her floating, and felt its power get in touch with hers. They contoured each other, as old friends would, Freya's essence and the water's, and then finally mingled. An invisible net was set above the river, so that its turbulent waters could not harm the Sage.

Still keeping her eyes closed, but inwardly smiling, Freya stepped up to it and headed to the other side. To an outsider, it would appear as if she was walking on water, but to Freya it was much more. As she used the water's strength to keep going, she got in touch with its primitive side. The clarity and pureness of the element filled her wholly, and all anger and frustration was left behind.

Freya had discovered the river a long time ago, when she was only six years old. She usually came to play over by it, feeling deeply attracted to the place. As she grew up and found out about her abilities, Freya had learned to use them to her own benefit, as well as the world's. Since the fight with the Vikings, she'd used some of her elevated abilities to create a little heaven of peace for herself.

No one could cross to the other side unless they could levitate or, as Sam, pass through the water. It was an efficient way to ensure the sanctuary on the other side of the river would be for her, and her alone.

Freya sighed in satisfaction and opened her eyes when she touched the ground. She stretched her limbs as though awakening from a deep slumber, then stepped forward. She thanked the water for having cooperated with her, and let its essence return back to where it belonged.

Her gaze fell on the forest ahead, and a slow smile spread on her lips, before she ran towards it impatiently. The location was where she always headed whenever she needed to train, focus, or simply when the need to be alone arose. The sanctuary of silence allowed her to leave all problems behind, and to retrieve them only when she was ready.

Beaming as she reached the edge of the clearing, Freya kept moving towards its center, onto a path she knew only too well. Ducking branches and leaves, she only stopped when the way opened onto a meadow.

Her meadow.

Chapter 4

B rennan stared into space for a while after O'Keeffe's departure, his thoughts on a certain Sage. After what Seamus had told him, he'd fallen deep in thought, worried for Freya. Fighting a few hundred ghosts was one thing.

But all of Spain's phantoms and badass leaders? Multiple Sages would be required to complete the mission – and get out unharmed. And since that wasn't possible, it left them with the option of working together.

And there was something else. With the Vikings, the spirits had been united – as much as they could be. This meant they presented a cohesive target. In Spain, they were divided in groups. And Brennan was not sure that he and Freya could spread themselves thinly, following them for recon.

Which means… Brennan mused pensively, wheels churning to find a solution. *The easiest way to go about this is to figure out the one leader most powerful and keep an eye on them. But in order to do that, we have to actually work together.*

It didn't take him long to realize the futility of his thoughts, considering Freya wouldn't even speak to him. *Let alone partner up…*

"So, how's Freya?" Sam's voice brought the Wiseman out of his ruminations.

"Huh? What do you mean?" Brennan asked.

Sam smirked and floated so that he was right in front of Brennan. "I meant, how's Freya doing?"

Brennan cocked his head at the twelve-year-old boy, wondering how he could be so perceptive.

"I know you two have been chatting telepathically, and I suppose you would've at least tried to find out why she's so pissed off at you." As an afterthought, Sam added, "You *did* try to reach out, didn't you?"

Guess I wasn't so subtle after all. "You don't miss much, do you?" Brennan shook his head ruefully. "Yeah, I did. But it was more of what you already witnessed...Unless that's Freya's way of declaring her undying love for me, I doubt she wants to work with me."

"That bad?" Sam pouted.

"Hmm...yeah. I still don't get it myself. Why is she so against me?"

The ghost hesitated, an oddly adult look on his face. It was so fleeting, the Wiseman feared he imagined it.

Before he could probe further, Sam grinned in his usual mischievous way and teased, "Brennan, for the past two years I've known Freya, I learned at least one thing about her – she is most certainly *not* a damsel in need of rescue."

Brennan picked onto what Sam was hinting at, and winced. "She heard that... Well, obviously, since she was in the same room as me." When Sam nodded, Brennan ran a hand through his hair in agitation. "But I was joking! She must have realized it, surely!"

"Probably, yeah," Sam shrugged. "But as long as it gives Freya an excuse to keep a distance, she will hold it against you."

"But *why*?" Brennan whined.

"Because, dummy, she's very independent. That and, from what I can gather, you two are very much alike."

"So?" Brennan frowned, clearly not getting what Sam was saying.

"*So*," the spirit huffed, "Freya knows deep down that she's found someone who could be her partner in fighting ghosts. But she's been solo for as long as she can remember. She won't exactly accept a stranger coming into her life and wanting to be her partner... A stranger whose character is very much like hers and who, in Freya's opinion, is trying to get in her way."

"But I only want to help!"

"In that case, old pal, find her and propose a truce."

Brennan seemed to think about it for a second, then stood from the chair. "So, where is she?"

Smiling mysteriously, Sam said, "Come on Bren, you can figure that out!"

"And just how do I go about that?" Brennan scowled.

"Just let her energy guide you."

Brennan seemed puzzled for a few seconds, then rolled his eyes, "Right." In a few quick steps, he was heading out the door when Sam stopped him with another question.

"Why do you want to find her so badly?"

Brennan turned to Sam, once more noticing that almost adult-like expression, as though the soft blue eyes were sizing him up. He thought about it for a beat, then said, "I just want to set things right with her."

Sam nodded, seemingly satisfied by the answer. Brennan dashed out, senses alert as he scoured the grounds for Freya's vibrant energy.

Back in the room, Sam's mouth turned upwards into a knowing grin. "Either that, or you're starting to have more than platonic feelings for a certain Sage, Bren."

Laughing, the ghost dematerialized into thin air.

&&&

"Damn it! Where can she be?" Brennan grumbled as he closed the twentieth – or thereabouts – door. He'd looked into every single room in the castle, and Freya was obviously not in any of them.

He had tried searching for her sparkling spirit, but to no avail. It was as if the Sage had disappeared. Originally, Brennan had thought she had gone for a walk outside, and then would have come back. Now, he realized he was probably mistaken and she'd been heading out somewhere else, which meant he'd lost precious time.

Brennan fought the urge to kick himself, and instead turned on his heels and ran down the stairs.

Let her energy guide you, Sam's words rang in his head.

Easy to say... Brennan paused at an intersection of corridors. *Now, let's see. If I was pissed off at somebody and needed to let go of my anger, where would I go?*

His feet led him to the first floor, and a door that opened upon the castle's garden. *Probably someplace quiet, where I could be alone and no one would disturb me...* Brennan's gaze travelled around and stopped on the river far away on his right. *Somewhere where no one could enter unless they have certain powers...*

A smug expression graced his features. "Got you!"

Brennan ran towards the river, picking up faint traces of Freya's fury on his way. He was definitely on the right path, that much was obvious. When he reached the clear water, he stopped. Twenty or so meters separated him from one side of the river to the other. Brennan glanced around, desperately hoping there was some kind of passage, to no avail.

"Wonderful. You're a hard girl to track down, Freya Hayes," he muttered. "But I'm not one to give up easily. Before this day is over, you *will* hear me out."

I just hope I can pass this test without losing too much energy.

As Brennan's spiritual strength came from the inside, whenever he used it – except for telepathy – he lost some of his vital energy. It was the sole reason he avoided digging into his powers to such an extent, unless he was in deep trouble.

This time, it couldn't be avoided. A determined look in his eyes, Brennan seated himself on the green grass, legs folded Indian-style. He placed both palms face up on his knees and closed his eyes, inhaling deeply.

When he exhaled, his entire body relaxed with the air escaping, and a sense of serene peace took over. Brennan searched deep within, almost detaching himself from his corporeal form. A transparent copy of himself shimmered nearby, then travelled above the river.

His real body, now transfixed and immobile, levitated and followed his essence across. Astral projection was a skill in the works for the Wiseman, but it was the quickest way he had of passing through barriers.

Landing down, Brennan felt his pulse quicken, then slow down to nearly nothing. The ghostly version of himself was once more absorbed in his body, and he breathed deeply.

He opened his eyes and stood on shaky legs, feeling quite weak. "Never...truly got the hang of this," he muttered aloud, before falling back on his knees, barely supporting himself with his hands. "Damn it!" Brennan gasped, taking in deep breaths to calm his fast-beating heart.

He glanced at the dragon-like necklace dangling from his neck, then lifted a shaking hand to it. Once before, it had come to his aid when needed.

As soon as his fist wrapped around it, Brennan could sense his grandfather's energy all around him, comforting him. It was the same peaceful feeling from his childhood, when Thomas had taught him about his own powers as a Wiseman.

The weakness in his joints eased away, and force returned little by little. Slowly, Brennan got up and let go of the medallion. He focused on Freya's vibe, which he could clearly feel now. *She must have used the river to mask her private place.*

"The little minx," he chuckled aloud. "Told you I was stubborn!"

Without bothering to further think things through, he strode purposefully towards the trees.

&&&

One, two, and three...

Freya shouted in exertion as she again reached her target and gave it a well-placed punch in between the eyes. She then grabbed its arms and, taking support from the mannequin, Freya propelled herself in the air, flipped backwards and landed in a crouch. The ball of energy she'd accumulated in her hands left her in a whoosh and hit the dummy in the chest.

Panting, Freya stood straighter and wiped the beads of sweat from her brow. For the past half hour or so, she'd been using a different target to let go of her anger, frustration, and other emotions that might have gotten in her way during the mission.

This particular training mannequin was approximately seven feet tall and quite muscular, made of a rough wood. Freya had chosen it for its roughness and solidity, knowing that when the mannequin's head would be cut off it, then – and only then – would her blows be strong enough to break necks.

In a world full of untouchable ghosts – to most people, at least – Freya had to forge her own weapons. Logic, swiftness and agility, along with her abilities, had quickly become her best weapons.

My powers... Freya thought as she stared at the mark on the dummy's chest.

Sam had been right with his observation that Freya had grown stronger. Compared to the fight with Cadmael, her abilities had increased. With each night she perused over the dragon runes, and day she trained, the Sage was evolving. But none of that would help unless she could fully control the elements, and unleash her energy without fear of losing sight of it.

Earth, fire, air and water, she recited in her head. *The four elements. If I can mingle my powers with all of them, I could do more. So much more.... And I'll be strong enough to take on Raksh, and show Seamus I don't need Brennan's help for a mission.*

With that thought firmly in mind, Freya jumped in the air, slick as a feline. She kicked the target in the ribs, going over its head and landing behind it. Her fall was broken when she rolled over her shoulder, then got back swiftly to her feet.

From there, she made a quick escape to the left, towards the oak tree that was there. She pulled on air and earth, using the elements to enhance her abilities – and get a little help. Jumping up became easier, and one of the tree branches leaned towards her. Freya grabbed it and pulled herself up, then spun and let the energy escape her hands and hit the dummy in the head, this time leaving a hole there.

A smug smile graced her features, but was easily wiped off as she heard a light clap beneath her, then a cocky voice praising, "Impressive."

Impossible!

Freya snapped her eyes shut, as if that one action would make the impertinent voice – and the person behind it – go away.

This is impossible! There's absolutely no way that he could've passed the river! I must be hallucinating, hearing voices...from the lack of sleep and...

"Very impressive indeed, Freya."

Freya's hands curled into fists, and it was all she could do to not let the wave of pure fury overwhelm her. *How* dare *he come here? Of all places!*

Tyr's tone was cautious as it answered. *Freya, have you considered perhaps Brennan has something important to share?*

That still doesn't give him the right to come into my sanctuary, even less –

"Frey, can you come down for a sec—" Brennan didn't get to finish his sentence, as a very furious Freya jumped off the branch.

Right leg extended in a striking position, she made contact full on, then somehow hopped over his falling body and landed graciously near his head. From her crouched position, Freya caught sight of Brennan's surprised stare, and would've laughed if she hadn't been so mad.

"I thought I told you to never call me that!" she hissed through gritted teeth.

Brennan grinned sheepishly. "I never promised anything, did I?"

Freya's gaze darkened, and even her hair seemed to grow blacker than ever. Brennan couldn't help an inward pat of satisfaction. He knew just how to piss her off, and enjoyed the challenge of having to continuously fight her.

He surveyed the Sage's face, and arched a single eyebrow at her fuming expression. "Did I go too far?"

Unfortunately for him, Brennan realized at the same moment the words left his mouth that he was in a slightly disadvantaged position. Freya could've easily harmed him, as he was slightly pinned to the ground by her knee on his arm.

Furthermore, the Sage scowling at him had reached her limits, and Brennan didn't particularly want to face her wrath. He was very aware of what she could do when cornered. The recollection of a certain punch he'd received in the gut during their last mission floated in his mind.

Brennan winced as he remembered Freya's frustration with him, and he was starting to think about what he could do to try and calm the Sage down, before she either broke his arm, or... *Well, maybe I did go too far.*

Freya tilted her head to the side, thrown back by the Wiseman's silence. His golden-brown eyes glinted to something akin to regret, and it was not a side she was comfortable to seeing on the cocky teenager.

I must be losing my mind.

Her first priority had been to shut him up, in her usual way, but another thought struck. *He's trying to make me lose my cool.* The newfound realization brought on a fierce determination to win.

Resolved not to give in, Freya lifted her knee off Brennan's arm to release him and walked away smoothly. She straightened her t-shirt, reattached the string of her sweatpants and went about tidying up her loose ponytail, before finally facing the target again.

Left bewildered, Brennan slowly got up from the ground. He'd seen a flicker of something pass through Freya's eyes – annoyance, anger? – right before she'd moved off him, but he couldn't place his finger on it.

He leaned against the tree Freya had previously been in, golden eyes surveying the Sage quizzically. Without so much as a glance to him, she launched into a series of punches and well-aimed side-kicks to the mannequin.

As she faced the target, Freya's attention focused entirely on it, analyzing its strengths and weaknesses. She was decided to inflict as much damage as she could with a ghost, and at the same time put on a show for Brennan– one that left him in no doubt about the little help she needed from him.

Straightening her back, Freya inhaled deeply and tried as best she could to block out her surroundings. The blasted bond between them made her hyper-aware of Brennan's proximity and trained eyes on her, but with a few practiced breathing exercises, the Sage was able to push it to the back of her mind.

She hopped on her feet for a minute, then ran towards the target and jumped high in the air. Deflecting to the side, she landed behind the training object and joined her hands as if praying. Next thing she knew, her entire body – every single molecule in it – was concentrated on her movements, feeling them and releasing the energy they produced. The strike hit the wood, splintering the arm in pieces.

With a satisfied nod, Freya moved to the other side, alternating between keeping in movement and being able to shoot off blasts of spiritual light while so doing.

After about thirty minutes of watching Freya fight the immobile target – it seemed she had completely forgotten about him – Brennan broke his vow of silence. "Don't you ever get tired?"

Freya stopped her kick halfway through, which caused her to slightly lose balance. She regained it, however, by purposely letting herself fall forward and rolling over.

She stood up and threw Brennan a surprised glance. "You're still here?" she asked casually, hiding a grin at the answering annoyance that flashed in his eyes.

"Of course I am!"

Freya threw him an amused smile. "Well, you'll have to excuse me if I don't sit down and chat, but I need to train for *my* upcoming battle."

"Ours," Brennan corrected coolly.

Freya frowned at him, but before she could say anything, Brennan stepped up to her until he was only a few feet away.

It's now or never. I'm playing my last card... the Wiseman sighed inwardly. *I'm just hoping it'll be enough.*

"Freya," he inhaled deeply, then continued, "I get it. You're strong, you're independent, and you don't need me. Or think you don't."

When she opened her mouth as though to fight him on it, Brennan lifted his palm. "Hear me out. This isn't easy for me to say, but it's why I came here. I wanted to ask you to please let me help you. We worked well together last time, and we were able to learn things from each other. Whether you like it or not, a fight is coming, and we'd be stronger together."

Brennan paused, hesitating for the last bit, unsettled by Freya's intense gaze. She was looking at him as though seeing him for the first time, and he almost choked on the words. Before he could lose his nerve, the Wiseman rushed the last words.

"Anyway, I have one piece of the puzzle and you the other. With the medallion and the manuscript, I'm sure we'll both evolve, one way or another. There's only stuff to be gained. So, what do you say?"

Freya glanced down at his extended hand in confusion, before meeting his gaze again. Brennan's golden eyes were sincere, and something in her shifted. It was an unknown feeling, but it was enough for Freya to catch on that he was right, and the opportunity was too grand to pass up on.

In spite of what she knew of his grandfather, or maybe because of it, it was her duty to act more adult and less child-like – as Tyr continued to tell her. Nodding to herself, Freya grasped Brennan's hand in hers, and they shook on it.

Even as the Wiseman grinned at his victory, Freya returned a small smile. She wouldn't let him get away with winning so easily, as she had to ensure he could match her – in all ways.

Smirking, Freya shifted her weight on her left leg and folded her arms across her chest. "All right, Brennan. You give a great speech, but how do I know you're good enough?"

"Good enough?" He threw her a puzzled look.

"To work with me," the Sage explained. "You see, I don't want you to get in my way. So how can I be sure that you won't?"

Freya... Tyr groaned. *You are taking this too far!*

Nope.

Why can you not accept his truce offering – do not bother denying it, you know it is one – and cooperate with him?

Because, Tyr, at the end of the day, I still don't know Brennan well enough.

There was a short silence. *Come again? Freya, I specifically instructed you to stop with the games. Brennan fought by your side, he saved your life... What more do you have to know?*

How about why he was pushing to find the relics last time? Freya felt the tiger was about to retort, but she interrupted before it could say anything. *Tyr, how much do we really know about Brennan's background? Hmm?*

Silence was her answer.

My point exactly.

But Freya... We do know he was trained by his grandfather, and... Tyr trailed off, at a loss on what to add next to convince her otherwise.

Exactly.

Very well, the tiger sighed. *But do not be too surprised if your powers are of the same caliber.*

What's that supposed to mean? Tyr?

As per its latest habit, the tiger was no longer present. Hiding her annoyance well, Freya threw Brennan a challenging look. "Well? What do you say?"

Completely unaware of the exchange between the Sage and the tiger – it hadn't lasted longer than a few seconds – Brennan reciprocated Freya's smirk and held his hand out to shake again. "You're on. And when I win, no more backtalk on this."

Freya rolled her eyes, but took it. The shock she received had her yank out of his grasp as though bitten by a snake. "What was that?" She looked at Brennan's hand as if it had grown three heads. "I swear, if it was you..." Freya said in a threatening tone.

Brennan held his palms up in mock-defense. "That wasn't me! I swear it!"

After one last suspicious glance, Freya turned her back on him and walked away, with Brennan following shortly.

"So, what did you have in mind?" His question was casual, even as he threw his jacket off, now only in a shirt.

Freya stole a glance at his profile out of the corner of her eyes. Unbidden, her gaze lingered on his broad shoulders, set in evidence by the white t-shirt and the muscles underneath.

Realizing what she was thinking, Freya shook her head as if to clear it, then faced Brennan. "Well, since you've interrupted my training twice already, we can start with that."

Brennan's eyes widened slightly. "Hang on a second. You were using your powers to practice, pulling on the elements. There's no way I can compete with that, you know we get our highs from two different areas."

Freya rolled her eyes. "Yeah, I do know that. What I was trying to do has no tie-in with you, Wiseman. I only had to make sure I can both use my spiritual energy for fights *and* take advantage of the elements to give myself a boost." She shrugged, then looked at her nails. "What I need from you is your body. To practice on."

The Wiseman looked from her to the wooden target, and gulped. "Let me get this straight... You want me to take the place of your target for the next, what, few hours?"

"Yup! Of course, you'll be fighting back. Just not, you know, with your powers. Nor will I use mine."

"So it's basically a physical endurance test?" Brennan questioned.

"If you're feeling up to it," Freya's voice was deceptively sweet, eyes glinting mischievously.

Brennan was about to point out the pointlessness of the test, but bit back the words. "I feel more than up to it. Let's get started, shall we?"

"If you're sure you're ready."

Shaking his head and chuckling slightly, Brennan grinned, "Always."

As he'd already turned his back to Freya, he didn't see her look of pure shock at his remark. Without even realizing it, Brennan had answered the question just as she would have.

Freya's frowned at Brennan's back. *Maybe I should just accept his help. We're more alike than I would've normally liked, but I can't ignore that our characters are very similar.*

Brennan's next words threw that observation out the window. "Now, now, Freya, focus. There'll be plenty of time later for checking me out."

She instantly gritted her teeth. *Who am I kidding? If I really do have to work with him, then I'd better make sure he learns his lesson. That way, there won't be any misunderstandings between us.*

Freya glared at Brennan, then surveyed the space between them. She stepped back five feet, ensuring they had enough distance between them.

"Oh, and Brennan?" Freya threw.

"Yeah?"

"Don't hold back, because I won't."

The Wiseman scowled at her. "I wasn't planning to."

"Great!"

She stepped up to the left, pace swift as a feline. Not a noise was made, but in one quick movement she both planned the attack and carried it out. The strike was lightning fast, and Brennan didn't even see it coming before he was sprawled on his back – for the second time that day.

Freya had already returned to her previous position by the time Brennan overcame his initial surprise and got back on his feet. "Nice one."

"Thank you," was the automatic reply, but Brennan could see in Freya's eyes that she was already assessing the next attack.

The Wiseman decided to be quicker this time. Hastily analyzing the distance between him and Freya, he then ran to the tree on his left. Stepping on air as if it had been stairs, Brennan caught the branch closest to him and flipped over it like a gymnast once, twice, then let go the third time.

The force with which he was propelled forward was a bit more than anticipated, and he bumped straight into Freya, knocking the wind out of her. Brennan himself lost his balance and ended up on the ground once more, groaning.

As she dusted herself up, Freya was smirking. *Tyr, I think you overestimated him. If this goes on, it's going to be a piece of cake. Brennan himself may even decide he's not fit for this, and leave.*

The only problem with her statement was that, soon after she said it, Freya realized she wasn't looking forward to him leaving. Not anymore.

I really must be tired, she concluded wryly, trying to clear her head of thoughts that had no business being there.

Movement behind her caught her eye, and Freya turned. Brennan was grinning despite his missed attempt. "That was just warming up," he said.

Freya bit back a smile.

Chapter 5

They'd been sparring for a little over an hour, when Brennan finally got annoyed enough to stop holding back.

"You're really something," he muttered a particularly vicious kick from Freya, and shifted into a defensive stance.

Freya, recovering from her last strike, was about to question his state of mind. Before she could, and in a move worthy of a martial arts expert, Brennan moved.

Sleek like a panther, he evaded her offensive blow, ducking under her too-wide punch and landing a blow to her ribs. It wasn't enough to hurt, but it knocked the wind enough out of Freya, and she bent over.

"Now that's more like it!" the Sage enthused, then made a grab for Brennan's wrist.

He spread his fingers, then swung his arm upwards in a broad movement and got her off balance. Freya stumbled in his arms, and they stared at each other for a beat of a moment, both shocked at the proximity. She grasped his shirt for balance and to hold him, but Brennan escaped from her grip by flipping backwards.

The Sage had to let him go, or else fall after him. She ran to the other side of the meadow, reaching Brennan just as he landed, and punched him in the gut.

On his way down, Brennan tripped her with some fancy footwork, and Freya landed on the grass. With a soft groan, she rolled away from him and jumped to her feet, arms held up defensively for any upcoming blow.

When it looked like he planned to strike her again in the ribs, Freya glued her elbow to the side and instead angled to kick. Her foot hit his side, but was pulled forward when Brennan caught her ankle.

When he twisted it around, Freya plunged face first to the ground, luckily managing to support herself with her arms. One leg still in Brennan's hand, she used the other one to kick his own legs. Brennan lost his balance and let go of her, falling backwards.

A soft "Ow" was heard, but Freya ignored it. The two got back on their feet at the same time, both panting.

"You're good," Freya admitted.

"Ah, you're not so bad either," Brennan conceded.

Words were forgotten as Freya launched forward to punch Brennan in the gut again. He'd anticipated the movement though and grabbed her wrist, twisting her arm back. Freya was pinned to the ground in a matter of seconds.

The Sage was surprised at the change of roles, but her irritation was further stirred by Tyr's comment. *Did I not warn you?*

Warned me about what? Freya retorted impatiently.

Both you and Brennan are of equal strength, whether in your powers or your physical bodies.

That is so not true! Freya snapped back, though less convincingly than before.

Then would you mind explaining how you came to be in this precarious position? Tyr asked smugly.

Freya bit her lip, even as pain shot through the arm Brennan was holding.

My point exactly, the tiger concluded, throwing Freya's words from earlier back at her.

The Sage's scowl passed unnoticed by Brennan, as she had her head bowed, but Tyr felt her annoyance. *Very well. I will let you see for yourself.*

Before Freya could protest further, the tiger vanished. *That is not—* She bit back another comment, and instead concentrated on Brennan's pin.

The Wiseman, meanwhile, was startled as he felt an annoyance that was definitely not his. *Odd...* he thought, but Freya's next movement made him forget all about the bizarre feeling.

In a twist he hadn't predicted, the fiery Sage elbowed him in the thigh with her free elbow, coming dangerously close to a sensitive area. Grunting in surprise, Brennan's grip on her loosened. Taking advantage, Freya grabbed the Wiseman's arm and flipped him over her head, succeeding in making Brennan kiss the ground again.

Freya dropped on her back as Brennan grabbed her legs with his own in an iron grip, and pulled them forward.

As they both lay on the ground, catching their breaths, a voice echoed from one of the trees. "I would say that's a tie."

Freya lifted her head slightly, then groaned as she let it fall back on the soft grass. "Sam, go away. We're in the middle of something here."

"I would, honestly," the ghost retorted. "But Frey-Frey, that cat of yours is waking the whole castle."

"Cat?" Freya repeated, puzzled for a few seconds.

A hand entered her vision and she took it, allowing Brennan to lift her up. "Did you hit your head?" he teased, golden-brown eyes sparkling. "I'm pretty sure Sam means Artemis..."

Freya was struck for a moment by his mischievous gaze, and stared in surprise. When Brennan frowned in confusion, it dawned on her that she was ogling him like an idiot.

Rolling her eyes, she turned to Sam. "Well, Artemis wouldn't be so noisy if you could play with her from time to time."

"Actually," Sam scowled, "I think she's hungry, Freya."

Freya's eyes widened as she remembered that, due to her intensive practice since dawn, she'd completely neglected to feed her cat. The Sage almost ran out of the clearing, then turned back to Brennan and Sam.

There's really no way out of this. Groaning at the wayward fate, Freya muttered impatiently, "Congrats, Brennan, you're in. Now both of you, out!"

Shrugging at her change of mood, Sam led Brennan outside the forest. As soon as Freya was sure the two had exited her training place, she jogged ahead, used her powers to pass the river, then ran at full speed towards the castle.

She'd reached the immense building in a matter of minutes and, as expected, Freya found Artemis at the entrance, a reproachful look in her green eyes.

The furry-white green-eyed cat was Freya's most recent acquisition from England, and the sweetest thing there was. She'd grown at a fast rate since then, and was now almost full-sized. It never ceased to amaze Seamus when he saw her. Freya, on the other hand, thought it was only another sign that her kitten was special.

Usually, the Sage took great care of her – not that the independent pet needed a holding hands kind of approach. But when those emerald eyes glared at her, Freya knew she was in trouble.

Picking the cat in her arms, Freya rushed to her room on the fifth floor. She grabbed a tuna can and dropped the contents into a small bowl, then let the squirming cat down to it.

"I'm *so* sorry, Artemis," the Sage apologized, heart clenching painfully. "I was a bit busy with training since this morning. I promise I'll never let it happen again."

The kitten turned her stunning green eyes to Freya, and gave her a haughty look. Freya would've laughed, if not for a flicker in the cat's eyes that was only too familiar to her. It was an expression of pure intelligence – one she had already seen in the eyes of another feline.

However, before she could investigate it further, Artemis turned to the food and started gulping it down noisily, completely ignoring Freya.

The door to her room opened again and Freya stood in time to greet Seamus, Brennan and Sam. She scowled at them, then gestured to the armchairs near her window. "To what do I owe this intrusion in my personal space?" Her eyes landed on each male in turn, reflecting her annoyance.

O'Keeffe gave her a sheepish smile. "Sorry about that, Freya. We just wanted to let you know we're leaving in a few hours to the airport. We're taking the night flight to Spain."

Freya threw a look to Brennan, who shrugged in response. "All right," she said to Seamus. "That gives me some time to get ready."

She turned to Artemis, and was surprised to see the cat was listening intently to the conversation.

"About your cat," O'Keeffe said, misinterpreting Freya's frown, "What are you going to do?"

"Well, I was thinking—" Freya started uncertainly, but didn't finish. She'd once again seen that flicker in her cat's eyes, and this time she had no trouble placing it. Gaze still on the white fur-ball, she smiled in assurance. "Oh, I'm sure Artemis will be well off here. I'll leave her food and she can take care of herself."

Seamus stared at Freya, as did Sam. Brennan arched an eyebrow questioningly, but Freya cut them all off before they could say anything. "I should start packing, as should you two. So if you don't mind..."

O'Keeffe glanced from Brennan to Freya, unable to hide his surprise – and delight. "Two?"

"Yes," Freya rolled her eyes. "Since Sam doesn't need to pack, you and Brennan make two. He's coming, you win."

"Might I know to what do I owe this change of mind?" O'Keeffe questioned her.

It was Sam who answered, before Freya could even as much as open her mouth. "Well, after a physical endurance test between the two of them, Freya finally jumped on the band-wagon and realized that Brennan could actually help her, and allowed him to come on the mission."

Freya glared at ghost. "You need to learn to keep quiet, Sammy ol' boy. Now can you all just head out? There's too much testosterone around me, and it's upsetting Artemis."

The three men took the hint and exited the room. Freya closed the door behind them, then let the laugh bubbling escape. After she'd calmed down, she turned around to her pet. "All right, Tyr. What the hell is this all about?"

Artemis gave Freya quite the innocent look, but the Sage wasn't fooled. "Come on, Tyr. I know that look, and it was most certainly you. Now what I don't understand is how can it be you in Artemis? Whatever you did, I'm pretty sure you're not supposed to be doing. Now come on."

As the cat stubbornly kept the innocent façade, Freya grew impatient. "Tyr, don't play me for a fool. Get out of Artemis right now!"

The cat grinned at her, then bowed its head just as a familiar booming voice in Freya's head said, *To be fair, Freya, Artemis and I are one and the same.*

And then, right under the Sage's eyes, the fuzzy, inconspicuous cat transformed into a ferocious tiger with white fur and black stripes. The only resemblance was the green, intelligent eyes – now speckled with golden flecks.

Freya gaped at the tiger, who grinned back at her, the corners of its mouth pulled upwards. Startling bright fangs were exposed, easily able to tear human flesh in a matter of seconds.

Finally coming out of her daze, Freya stepped up to Tyr and knelt in front of it. "I can't... All this time..."

Tyr lay down too, its head at the same height as Freya's. *From the beginning of your mission with the Vikings, I knew I had to keep an eye on you. Thus, I allowed a part of me to turn into a white cat, which I made sure you would find. Despite my presence around you, I still could not shield you as I wished. I later on remained in the form in order to watch over you permanently, even in the human world.*

Freya shook her head in amazement. "But what about your energy? You told me the come-and-goes between the two worlds usually eat some of it."

Tyr exposed its fangs again, emerald gaze sparkling. *Animals see the unseen, living between both worlds. That is why they can see ghosts. This new body is a conduit. It is only a small part of me, thus only a tiny percentage of my energy gets sucked. In the spirit world, I barely feel it.*

Freya nodded, understanding what the tiger meant. "I'm glad you're here, Tyr."

The tiger bowed its head, so as to make eye contact with the Sage. *Listen, Freya. This mission is much more dangerous than you can imagine, which is why I have to ask you to not go into perilous places. Understood?*

"I promise," Freya whispered.

And as for Brennan, the feline went on, *trust him. He may seem arrogant sometimes, but he is very reliable. Not to mention the bond between the two of you will hardly let you separate, let alone take risks.*

"Yes, so I've noticed," Freya grumbled.

Tyr threw the Sage an amused look. *I cannot understand why you dislike him so much. I was under the impression you would miss him when you left England, and kept glancing out the window.*

A faint blush crept on Freya's cheeks, but she willed it away and raised her chin defiantly to Tyr. "Yes, well, you were wrong, as you can very well see. The only reason I'm letting him on this mission is because you and Seamus wouldn't stop bugging me if I didn't."

The tiger seemed as if it was about to say something else for a second, but it then settled for an, *Of course.*

After a short silence, Freya tilted her head to the side in almost reticent questioning. "Will you be coming?"

The tiger shook its massive head, its eyes turning serious. *No. Someone has to keep the castle safe.*

"What do you mean?" Freya asked.

Tyr glanced away for a fraction of a second, then sighed and looked back at Freya. *Only that it is better I stay here. Or at least this small part of me.*

Freya renounced at probing further, aware that Tyr wouldn't tell her more. "All right. I'll keep in touch, though, we may need your help."

Tyr nodded, then stood up. Instantly, the small white cat Freya had grown used to having in her room took the tiger's place, and Freya scowled at it. "To think you actually had me fooled..."

Tyr's laugh echoed in the Sage's head. Shaking it clear, Freya got to her feet and took a suitcase from her closet. It was time to start packing.

A short while later, after a full scan of her room, Freya inspected the contents of her suitcase. It held nothing more than what was truly necessary – clothes, sneakers, toothbrush, and some toiletries.

"What's missing?" the Sage wondered out loud.

A meow answered her, and Freya turned to her right to see Artemis clawing at her dresser. "Right!" Freya walked over to it, opened it and extracted the red dragon manuscript. "Thanks, Artemis," she caressed the cat's head gently. *And don't worry, Tyr. I'll keep in mind your warnings about the dragon runes.*

Freya placed the book in her backpack, which she'd be carrying around. She closed her suitcase, and after one last survey of her room, headed for the door. Before she exited, she turned to Artemis one last time. "Take care."

The cat nodded and as Freya walked away, Tyr added softly, You *take care, child.*

&&&

Suitcase in hand, Freya knocked on Seamus's office door, then entered. She was unsurprised to see Brennan and Sam already there, chatting with O'Keeffe at his desk. When the click of the closed door resonated in the room, they turned to Freya.

"Am I interrupting anything?" the Sage asked.

"Freya..." Seamus rolled his eyes, then pointed to the remaining armchair – which, luckily, was her favorite. "Sit down, why don't you?"

She walked gracefully to the armchair situated right beside Brennan's and plopped herself down on it. "So, what's new?"

The question had been directed to Sam. The ghost was floating by O'Keeffe's left side, not quite noticing either of them, but seemingly lost in thought. At the resounding silence, he glanced up to everyone staring at him expectantly.

"Want to fill Freya in on our destination?" Seamus pressed wryly.

"Right," Sam nodded, shaking himself out of the funk. "This might be familiar to you, Frey, but we're heading to Girona. If that doesn't ring a bell, perhaps the region's name —"

"Catalonia!" Freya gasped, and a true smile graced her features as her gaze shifted to Seamus. "You're joking, right?"

Seamus smiled in return, his blue eyes sparkling. "Not at all. Additionally, we will be staying at a hotel by the water, you are sure to enjoy the view."

Freya gaped at him for a few seconds, before closing her eyes to better savor the moment. "Pure bliss."

"Did I miss something?" Brennan intervened, glancing between the other three companions. Though he was glad for once Freya was not aiming to hurt him, this new side of her was nonetheless surprising to witness.

O'Keeffe let out a chuckle as Sam explained, "Let's just say that Catalonia is Freya's favorite place on Earth."

"And for good reason too!" Freya exclaimed. "The buildings, the people, the *food*..." She groaned, closing her eyes and inhaling deeply as though able to taste it.

"Now you're speaking my language," Brennan teased.

"It really does take you back in time," Seamus added. "Have you never visited, Brennan?"

"Unfortunately, no. My trips mainly kept me to the north of Europe. But it does sound like an adventure."

"That, it will be, you just wait and see!" Freya grinned. Then a sobering thought occurred to her, and she focused back on Sam. "Okay, so that's the good news. What's the bad?"

"Right, well..." He rubbed the back of his neck sheepishly, then admitted, "Here's the not-so-pleasant part. I located the ghosts, or at least some of those stirring up trouble." At Freya's expecting gaze, Sam revealed, "They're hiding in the Cathedral, or so we think."

"Shit!" Freya turned to O'Keeffe, ignoring his chastising glare at the offending word. "But... That thing is a maze! How the hell are we supposed to find them in there?"

A cough interrupted her. Eyes blazing, Freya turned to Brennan's pointed look. "You forgot about our powers."

Freya bit back a snappy retort, and instead said, "Actually, we can only use a small percentage of our powers in the Cathedral."

"That's impossible!" Brennan gaped. "You're telling me a *church* actually stops us from using our *spiritual* abilities to the max?"

"Yeah," Freya confirmed. "It's a place of power, blah blah...Seamus can explain it better." She gestured to the elder Sage in an unspoken invitation to fill in the blanks.

"What Freya means is that the Cathedral, being that it has stood the test of time for ages, has gathered faith of hundreds upon thousands of regular humans. That kind of energy does something to a place, same as with the Vatican. Well, when the portal opened and these ghosts appeared, something happened that turned the Cathedral into a holier place – a no man's land, so to speak. It probably affected all other religious places the same way, but we have not really had a chance to verify them all."

"Either way," Freya cut in, "that place nearly cost me my life the last time I was in Spain."

"And that was…" Brennan trailed off, hoping that Freya would complete his sentence. He was not disappointed.

"Some ghosts were planning an attack on the city," Freya explained. "And they'd hidden in the Cathedral. I rushed in with no backup and…" The Sage shrugged. "A few minor bumps and bruises, but luckily I got out of it alive. It could've turned out worse."

"Got it, so no rushing in." As an afterthought, Brennan asked, "Out of curiosity, who was the leader of the group?"

"Gustav," Freya answered, her eyes turning a dark grey at the name. "Why?"

Brennan turned to O'Keeffe. "Isn't he one of the most powerful leaders of the cliques? I seem to remember he has one of the biggest groups in Spain."

"Yes, that's true," Seamus nodded pensively. "Do you think…?"

"He might have joined the conquistador's side?" Brennan completed his question. "Yes."

"No," Sam said.

"Why not?" Brennan countered. "You said this conquistador was trying to rally all spirits, right? So why not recruit Gustav?"

"Good thinking," Sam smirked. "But still no. Frey-Frey, jump in anytime now?"

The Sage leaned back in her chair and folded both legs underneath her. "Gustav is the kind of ghost that wants to lead, not *be* led. His reputation precedes him in all of Spain. If this conquistador really is after the ghosts of Spain, then he'll leave Gustav for last."

"Because that way," Brennan caught on, "if Gustav refuses to submit, the conquistador has his army to threaten him with."

"Exactly," Freya nodded, then addressed Seamus, ignoring the spark of pride in his eyes. "Just two questions – how much time do you think we have until the conquistador rallies all his troops and what do you think he intends to do with them?"

O'Keeffe rubbed his chin pensively, and glanced out the window with an absent gaze. "I cannot say what he wants to do with over a thousand ghosts, but I can guarantee it will not be good. As for the time... I would say we have about a week, maybe less, until the conquistador tries to go after Gustav."

Freya and Brennan shared a look, trying to gauge what the best route of action would be. As if on cue, Sam intervened. "So, what's the plan?"

"First, we'll try and find out who this conquistador is, and what his intentions are," Freya started.

"Then, we'll come up with a plan to ruin his game and fun," Brennan added, smirking.

They nodded to each other, then Freya turned to Sam. "Meet us at the hotel, and from then on we'll improvise and gather information on our new enemy."

Sam agreed and hugged each one of them, before dematerializing into thin air.

Freya then turned to O'Keeffe, biting on her lower lip in thought. Her mentor's blue eyes shone softly, and she could read within his regret for their fight. She shrugged faintly, then mouthed, *I'll be okay.*

Brennan hadn't missed the exchange, but he smartly decided to remain silent. He could guess challenges would lie ahead, but at least they had a good team to fight them off.

Sensing the Wiseman's gaze on her, Freya met it head on. *Soon, I will tell him about his grandfather and what I saw. Soon...but not just yet.*

"We should get moving," Seamus interrupted their staring. "Spain awaits."

"With baited breath, I bet," Brennan muttered, earning a chuckle from Freya.

He picked up his suitcase and hers in hand, then followed Seamus outside of the castle. Freya glanced around the library one more time before stepping out into their newest mission.

As the three hopped into a car to drive to the airport, Artemis' green eyes stared thoughtfully from the tower. Once the humans disappeared past the horizon, the white cat jumped off and started her patrol.

Chapter 6

A few hours later, a plane landed at the Girona Airport in Spain. The massive metal bird, overcoming winds and having flown over seas and oceans, touched the ground with a slight bump, then came to a stop as the air currents forced it to slow down.

Brennan, Freya and Seamus stepped off it slightly tired, rumpled, but overall ready to attack the new mission. Luckily for Freya, she'd settled into a nap as soon as the plane took off, and had avoided a conversation with Brennan during the flight.

As the companions walked towards the terminal, she trailed behind, oddly put off. Something was swimming at the brink of her consciousness, like a half-forgotten dream or imagination.

Without even realizing it, Freya was soon distanced from Seamus and Brennan, lost in thoughts. She glanced out the window of the airport, at the starkly dark sky above, and shuddered. Like a dam breaking, the nightmare burst past her consciousness.

It had been the same image from Seamus' mind, but this time focused in vivid detail on her parents' pleas for help, on her own baby body at the back of the car crying out. Freya closed her eyes, trying to fight against the emotions running through her, to no avail.

Tears struck the Sage's eyes, and her chest squeezed painfully at seeing something so vivid – she could almost touch them, but was still unable to save them. Her breath was cut short and Freya had to lean against a wall to support herself.

"Stop..." Her whispered plea echoed faintly in the hallway, but no one answered.

Freya now understood what Seamus kept saying about wanting to shelter her, and his belief she wasn't ready. If the memory alone broke her so, what would the full reality of the situation do? A stab of anger at all he'd hidden flashed through her, just as quickly extinguished.

Sighing, Freya peered out the foggy glass again, thinking back to the recollection. She could almost see it playing on the window like a movie. The fire, the car, the two shapes... She was sure they were demons like Raksh, probably under his command, if only based on how the flames reacted around them.

Her fists clenched, desperately fighting the need to find out more about them, or anything really. At war with it was the responsibility weighing on her shoulders, to ensure the conquistadors didn't achieve their troubling plans.

"Freya!" Brennan's hand on her shoulder shook her out of her reflection, and she raised glazed eyes to his.

"What?"

At Brennan's concerned expression, she glanced around and noticed where she'd stopped. Before the Wiseman even had a chance to ask her what happened, she snapped, "I'm fine. Where the hell is Seamus?"

Brennan's eyes widened, even as he clenched his jaw in response. For a millisecond, Freya was sure he'd retort in the same tone, but he seemed to take a closer look and change his mind.

Ruffling his hair with one hand, he gestured vaguely in the direction of the exit. "He's with the suitcases and our car."

Freya moved ahead, delaying until she passed Brennan to surreptitiously wipe at her cheeks, and the tears she felt at the corner of her eyes. Keeping her steps fluid and graceful wasn't easy, but she achieved it, cloaking the despair underneath.

Behind her, Brennan wasn't fooled. He'd been the first to notice Freya missing and, following Seamus' insistence, had gone ahead to find her. The waves of anguish that had assailed him mere moments earlier had been a dead giveaway to her location. He'd rushed forth, thinking she was in danger, only to find her blankly staring outside.

No matter what the Sage tried, Brennan was a master of disguise as well. So despite her offhandness and attitude, he'd seen the tears on the brink of being shed. Even now, as she walked ahead, he could clearly sense her uneasiness and see the rigidity in her back muscles.

Brennan sighed and quickened his pace. Whatever upset her, Freya was most likely to open up to Seamus or Sam. However, he vowed to keep an eye on her, just in case.

The two teenagers reached the exit door, where Seamus waved them over. They hurried to him, then into the taxi standing by. Seamus got the passenger seat at the front, while Brennan and Freya took the back. As soon as they were in, the car drove off in a squeal of tires.

"Where were you, Freya?" O'Keeffe asked gently. "We were concerned when we did not see you."

"We?" Freya arched an eyebrow at Brennan.

He shrugged nonchalantly – or as much as he could. "Well, are partners now, so..." He trailed off with another shrug.

Freya threw him a curious look, then turned her head to the window. "I had to stop by the washroom," she lied to O'Keeffe.

Brennan frowned and glanced at her out of the corner of his eye, trying to be subtle about it. *Why isn't she telling the truth?* His attention was even more piqued when he caught a change in Freya's emotions... He wouldn't have felt it without the bond, but as it was, her increasing pulse registered in his mind.

Brennan had to stop himself from contacting Freya instantly and probing past her odd behavior. There was something she was hiding, some reason why she was even more closed off than usual, and he intended to find out what. After all, when he'd offered partnership, he meant it.

Tonight, he vowed, intending to catch her off guard and have a heart-to-heart.

"Ah, I figured as much," Seamus replied to Freya's comment, though Brennan detected a hint of regret in his tone of voice.

Another glance between the two proved useless, so he settled into the backseat, trying to be as comfortable as he could. In an effort to stretch his legs, his knee bumped Freya's. She turned a hollow gaze towards him, and in the obscurity of the backseat, Brennan couldn't read her expression. Nonetheless, his gut clenched painfully, only guessing at the turmoil hiding under the surface.

&&&

"Do not think about it, Tyr," Isis admonished.

The tiger glanced up at the goddess from the fireplace it had been staring into. Though Isis tried to be firm, her lips tugged into a smile.

Why ever not? Tyr's jaws opened in a feline grin.

"Those two are bound to connect as they should and were fated to... Eventually, at least. Do not intervene, when it will cost you."

A little nudge will do them good...

&&&

Back in the car, Brennan was still trying to stifle his curiosity – and failing.

This is way too weird, he mused. I don't get it. *Everything seemed fine a while ago, but...*

Why not ask Freya, Brennan? a voice boomed inside his head. The Wiseman was so startled by it that he jumped, drawing Freya's attention to him.

"A bug bit you?" she questioned, an eyebrow cocked mockingly.

"Sure," the Wiseman drawled, then turned his head to the window. When Brennan was absolutely sure Freya was back to staring outside and Seamus was deep in conversation with the driver, he concentrated. *Who are you?*

A chuckle answered him. *Are names so important nowadays? You may call me Tyr, not that it will mean anything to you. I do not mean you harm, only aid.*

And why would you be interested in doing that? Brennan questioned suspiciously.

Avoiding a legitimate response, Tyr instead suggested something else. *Ask Freya what so torments her. Be open with her, and you might just be rewarded.*

Wait! Brennan pleaded, but no reply came. Whoever Tyr was, the presence had left.

Musing over its words, Brennan thought, *Hell, I might as well give it a try. The worst she could do is throw me out of this car.*

Checking Seamus was still conversing with the driver, Brennan turned to the Sage. "So, how's it going?"

Freya hadn't moved a muscle when the answer came, oddly bored and without much energy. "What do you want, Brennan?"

Brennan hesitated, oddly aware of her distress, and not wanting to add on to it. Despite their differences, over their last mission he'd come to care for Freya, and wanted her trust, at the very least.

Willing himself to stay cool, he continued, "Hey, can't we just have a normal conversation for once?"

"No conversation with you is ever normal," Freya retorted with a scoff.

Brennan was happy with the slightly more energetic reply. Though it was not the usually spunky Sage he was used to, it was better than the hollow tone she'd used before.

Though he'd planned to be smooth and subtle, it took only a closer look at Freya to realize it was simply not in his nature. "Honestly, though, what's wrong?" he blurted.

Freya sighed and turned to face him with a visibly wary look. "What are you so afraid of?" His question came out gentle, but only seemed to piss her off further.

"Mind your own business, Wiseman!"

Brennan frowned at her, then turned away and whispered disapprovingly, "All right, Freya. But you should stop being selfish, and notice that Seamus is worried about you. And as much as I'd like to ignore it, I am too."

With the last comment, Brennan retreated, knowing a lost fight when he saw one.

To get his thoughts off a certain Sage, Brennan focused on the landscape passing by. Girona's streets were absolutely marvelous, but not even their ancient beauty could distract him. He leaned his head against the chilly glass and drifted to sleep.

Beside him, Freya frowned at her knees. Pushing Brennan away, her dismissive tone, somehow it all felt amiss. *There's just something... Times when I have to be alone...* The Sage battled with herself, excuse after excuse drifting in her mind. None helped alleviate the guilt weighing down her heart.

I understand...

The reply had been soft, and Freya turned to Brennan, gasping. He seemed asleep, and yet she was sure it had been him. "Brennan?" she whispered.

He didn't budge.

"Must've been my imagination," Freya sighed. With one last glance to the Wiseman, she rested her head on her elbow and closed her eyes, hoping for a calming nap.

&&&

O'Keeffe glanced behind to see Freya and Brennan both fast asleep, and smiled fondly. It was no surprise the two were exhausted. The sky outside was still pitch-black, and O'Keeffe could estimate the time to around three in the morning.

Seamus sighed deeply. It would take some time for Freya to actually forgive him, but he thought he was doing well. For her sake and to shelter her. *You are still so blissfully ignorant of the dangers of your past, my dear Freya.*

His memories went back to that fateful night, when Freya's parents had died. Or rather, had been killed.

Yes, Seamus knew quite well the story, having passed the last twelve years of his life relieving every torturing moment, every painful second of that night in his nightmares, always trying to find a way... Something he could have missed... Something that could have saved Mark and Evelyn.

There had not been a single day since, when O'Keeffe had not wished to have avenged his friends' death by finding and killing their assassins. But the two shapes in the fire, the two figures he knew only too well had disappeared off the face of the Earth. And without his powers... O'Keeffe couldn't hope to find them.

The old man knew, however, that Freya could. Once she became aware of the whole truth and once she was entirely ready to face her parents' murderers, he would let her. But until then, his duty was to defend her, as he'd promised his friends.

O'Keeffe tried to clear his mind. He had to keep it blank if he wanted to help Freya and Brennan win this fight. As he looked ahead, he could see plenty of obstacles for his young protégés.

"Are they dating?" the Spanish chauffeur asked in a heavily accented English.

It took some time for Seamus to realize what the man meant, but when he did, he stifled a laugh. "Who? Them?" He pointed behind to the back seat.

The chauffeur smiled, showing teeth yellowed by nicotine. "Yes, the pretty lady and the boy. Are they... How do you say...? Together? An item?"

O'Keeffe laughed aloud this time. "No. I cannot even imagine the two of them being anything other than friends. For them to be dating... It would take more than a miracle. They are quite at war with each other, you see. Well, Freya is."

The man nodded wisely. "Ah yes. But sometimes, hate can morph into love..."

O'Keeffe said nothing, surprised at the man's wisdom. The car was hushed for a few minutes, until Seamus remembered that cab drivers were always an invaluable source of information on a city. "My friend, tell me, how are the ghosts here?"

"Pfft, how I should know?" The driver shrugged, then checked the rear-view mirror and switched lanes. "Here and there, they haunt restaurants and places... Nowadays, you see them in broad daylight."

"Ah..." O'Keeffe commented. He was about to fall silent again, when the driver seemed to recall something.

"But lately," he started hesitantly, "I haven't seen as many... Oh, well! Maybe they finally turned to dust." His casual comment was followed by a laugh.

O'Keeffe joined in, though half-heartedly. *This cannot be good...* he fretted. *I cannot help but feel our time here is counted.*

Just as he thought that, they passed by the Cathedral. "Stop the car!" Seamus startled the driver, and the vehicle came to an abrupt stop.

Throwing a look over his shoulder to make sure the teenagers were still dormant, Seamus said, "Stay here, I won't be long."

There was something he wanted to check, a shape he'd seen that he could not accept. The elder Sage ran up the stairs, barely stopping to catch his breath until he was at the entrance. Within and all around himself he could sense the charged energy of the place, and the way it tugged at his powers.

He expanded his senses, already feeling dizzy with being around so much spiritual power. *I could not have seen...*

"You sssaw right," the icy voice answered from behind.

Seamus whirled around, eyes widening as they fell on the demon. "How can this be? *You*, near a religious place?"

The demon sneered, lifting a hand filled with chains made of fire. "Much hasss changed in this place sssince your last time."

Seamus clenched his fists, ready to tackle him bare-handed if need be. "You will pay for my friends' deaths!"

"I do not think ssso. You are old, and eager to attack sssomething you do not yet undersssstand."

Raksh opened his fist, blowing the chains towards Seamus. They floated in the air, and though he lifted his palms in a vain attempt to block them, they easily passed through the barrier he tried to conjure. They wrapped around Seamus, restraining him.

Whereas the professor expected burns, all he felt instead was a probing into his mind, followed by an odd dizziness. Unable to stand, he collapsed to the ground, panting.

"What is this sorcery?"

"What you call sssorcery, I call a tool," Raksh hissed. "A tool meant to get you out of the way, and unable to help your preciousss pupil. You will never be able to regain your powersss, old man. They are forever lossst now."

Seamus froze, then forced his heavy-lidded eyes to look at the demon. "What do you mean, lost *now*? They have been lost for ages!"

"Fool...They were lingering, alwaysss ready to be unleassshed. But no longer!"

His cackle was the last thing Seamus heard before passing out.

&&&

The driver gave a happy sigh, announcing, "We have arrived."

Seamus could barely nod as they pulled in front of the hotel. "Thank you," he mumbled, then turned to the back. "Freya! Brennan! Both of you, wake up! We are here."

The Sage was the first to open her eyes and groggily ask, "Say what?"

O'Keeffe smiled at his pupil's sleepy expression. "We are at the hotel. Would you mind waking Brennan up while I check us in?"

As Freya nodded, now much more aware as she took in her surroundings and stretched.

Meanwhile, O'Keeffe got out of the car. He held onto the metal frame for a moment, gathering his strength. Whatever the demon had done to him was lasting, as he could barely stand.

He could only blurrily recall dragging himself down the stairs, and back into the cab. When the driver had asked him if he was all right, Seamus had only commanded him to get to the hotel.

Shaking his head, the elder Sage inhaled deeply and moved away from the car. With slow, calculating strides, he entered the building. The taxi driver followed him carrying half of their suitcases.

Freya sighed and turned to Brennan, noticing he was frowning in his sleep, as if his dreams were not pleasant. She slowly reached for his shoulder to shake him up. Instead, her hand slipped and ended up touching the silvery dragon medallion at his neck.

Oh, shit! It was the last thought in the Sage's mind, before her inside spirit entered Brennan's dream.

&&&

Freya was surprised to see herself floating into mid-air, above what appeared to be the desert. She willed her spirit to go closer to the ground, focusing on the energy that attracted her.

She started descending and ended up five meters above Brennan, who appeared to be kneeling in front of a hawk. Neither the Wiseman nor the majestic bird took any notice of the Sage.

Freya hesitated at the familiarity of the scene. Behind the hawk was what seemed like a...lost city?

"No..." Freya squinted her eyes and gasped. It was a ruined city, completely visible to her gaze as she floated around. Entranced by the beauty of the ruins, it was with a startle that she sensed the Wiseman move.

Her eyes settled on him, noticing he was now bowing his head to the hawk. Had it grown in size? Unknown to Brennan, the bird opened its beak, apparently ready to strike and make a meal out of him. Freya didn't think, fearing for his safety.

"Brennan! Watch out!"

His head immediately went up and looked straight at her. "Freya?" She could feel his surprise, but something else held her hypnotized.

The hawk.

Or more precisely, its eyes. They were a dark charcoal, burning with an evil fire within them. Unlike Freya's grey eyes, the hawk's were not gentle. Any small glint of goodness that had once been in them was long vanished. They reflected the evil deep within its heart, and the Sage could feel the hairs rising on the back of her neck.

Freya's own eyes stared into the bird's, now unable to move. She descended lower and lower, losing from her height and decreasing the distance between them. Her eyes widened at her paralysis, unable to grasp how it was happening.

The hawk was now within striking distance, an intelligent gleam in its eyes. *Finally... After all these years...* Freya heard a steely voice say, and she had the unmistakable impression it was the bird speaking.

Just as it seemed ready to strike, its beak nearly cutting through Freya's neck flesh, a voice yelled, "*No!*"

The hawk turned to Brennan, giving a low cry in anger. The Wiseman was now standing up, his golden-brown eyes more furious than anything Freya had seen "Leave. Her. *Alone*!"

The hawk cried once again, its eyes boring into the Wiseman's. Brennan was fast as lightning. He shot a ray of light at it, then jumped in the air and pulled Freya's hand to him. "Come with me!"

Freya met his eyes, then nodded. She looked back up to the sky, and tried to imagine them awake... Waking up... Away from danger...

The hawk's angered cry echoed below them as the desert got lost in a fog.

&&&

Freya found herself back in the taxi, her hand still on Brennan's medallion, and the Wiseman still resting. No more than a few seconds had passed. The taxi driver tapped on the window, having taken their luggage out.

Brennan stirred up next to her and as if by reflex caught her arm. His eyes bore into hers once more, that same flicker she'd just seen in them.

As if suddenly realizing where he was, Brennan released her, then smiled hesitantly. "My bad. Let's go and help Seamus, shall we?"

Freya gaped at the Wiseman's back as he opened the door and walked out of the car and into the hotel, stretching and yawning as he did so. Quick on her feet, she followed him inside and grabbed his arm, tugging on it.

She dragged him to a corner and furiously asked, "What *was* that?"

"What was what?" Brennan was fooling no one with his innocent look.

Taking a deep breath, Freya folded her arms across her chest and tapped her foot impatiently. "What was that dream, Brennan? It seemed so...real."

When he didn't answer, Freya reached out to him, holding onto his forearm. He frowned down at her, thinking at full speed. *How can I trust her when... she won't tell me what she's hiding?*

Take the first step for once, Brennan, the voice advised.

Brennan did not bother answering, knowing the presence had probably left already. He opened his mouth to speak, but—

"There you are!" Seamus stumbled into the hotel lobby, using his last remaining strength to fight off the dizziness he could no longer shake off. He smiled to both of them, then addressed Brennan. "You would not mind sharing a room with an old man and a ghost, would you?"

The Wiseman forced a grin, not wanting Seamus to catch on. He didn't mind, but the moment was now broken – just as he'd been about to tell her everything.

"Not at all," he responded, trying to catch Freya's eye – and failing.

"Good," O'Keeffe smiled, then frowned as he caught sight of Freya's hand on Brennan's arm. "Was I interrupting anything?"

Freya released her grip at once and glared at Brennan. "Just a fight, as per usual." The Wiseman's eyes were trying to convey his intentions past her frustration, but to no avail. She turned to O'Keeffe, dismissing him. "Am I sharing a room with you as well, or do I have my own?"

"Your own," Seamus answered hesitantly, not entirely oblivious to the tension around the two. Had he not been so drained, he could've caught on it earlier. For whatever reason, Freya seemed even more incensed than she'd been earlier.

Freya shrugged tightly at his probing look, and held her hand out. "Can I have my key, then?"

Seamus' gaze shifted to Brennan, but he was avoiding it. Left with no choice, he handed the key to Freya. With a hasty *good night*, she grabbed her suitcase and walked away, leaving them both behind.

A confused Seamus turned to Brennan. "What happened this time?"

Concealing his hurt expression, Brennan grinned sheepishly. "Oh, you know. I just pissed her off again. Doesn't take much these days."

Seamus wasn't fooled by the words, not when Brennan's tone was so uncharacteristically heavy and full of unspoken feelings. Peering closer at him, Seamus noticed how he stared at the elevator Freya had disappeared through with a look of utter confusion and hurt.

"You might want to go and apologize," the old Sage advised softly. "It does you no good to have her mad at you. Trust me, I know."

The last sentence was barely above a whisper, but Brennan heard. He shared a curious look with the old man and caught a glimpse of sadness in his eyes. *I promise I'll find out what this is all about.*

He glanced back to the elevator, wondering whether it would be worth it to speak to Freya, or if he'd find the window of opportunity had closed. Setting his jaw, Brennan knew he didn't care if she slammed the door in his face – he had to try. Masking anything from her at this point had been complete idiocy on his part, when all he wanted was her trust.

"What room?" he asked Seamus, before he could change his mind.

"21."

Brennan reached for his suitcase, but Seamus shook his head and waved him off. With a grateful smile to the professor, he rushed up the stairs to the second floor, mulling over the right words to say – and knowing full well they would fail.

Chapter 7

Raksh stepped past the stairs and into the entrance of the Cathedral. The barrier of energy surrounding the building shimmered, then let him pass. After all, he had the protection of the gods themselves. Its pure spiritual substance was nothing when compared to what was contained in the demon's physical form.

"It will never cease to amaze me that you can enter this holy place."

Raksh turned around, smirking towards the Spanish soldier. The man was his height, dressed in all the finery of a general, sword on his hip and a hard look in his eyes.

"Then perhapsss you ssshould be even more amazed, Cortésss," he taunted. "I have eliminated one of your opponentsss from the equation, leaving only the two humans."

"I did not ask for your help."

Raksh barely contained the flash of anger rippling through him. *Humans, always so despicably proud and unable to accept what is offered.* "It isss a show of good faith, Cortésss. Take it."

The ghost said nothing for a few moments, only surveying Raksh with that unnervingly flat gaze. Finally, he nodded

– who was he to reject such help? Even if it did come with strings attached. "Very well. Which one?"

"The elder man."

A snicker escaped Cortés, before he harshly commented, "That must have been quite hard for you to do, no? A helpless, weakened human, faced with your demon powers." The mocking chuckle continued until Raksh stepped close to him, raising one ebony hand.

Chains of fire like the ones that had wrapped around Seamus appeared, and Cortés stopped laughing. His widened stare met the demon's. "What is the meaning of this?"

"You ssshould not be dismissing my help, Cortésss. If I eliminated the elder Sssage, it isss becaussse he would be the more problematic. What he knowsss, what he can get the other two to do, if he revealsss the passst to them, isss beyond your imagination."

Cortés surveyed Raksh with unfathomable eyes, then inclined his head thoughtfully. "As you say. And what am I to do with these two? Did you not warn me they were special?"

"They are. But they are children, unaware of the forcesss they play with." Raksh laughed, thinking of the Sage he had met. "One tiny dissstraction, and without the old man's guidance, they will fail."

"And I know just the bait..."

Cortés whistled and from the shadows emerged another spirit. Mid-forties, he had dark long hair and somber eyes, a jaw you could cut things on, and a muscled body. "You called?"

"Gustav, my new friend. I do believe you have some un-finished business... Freya Hayes."

Raksh grinned, pleased, even as Gustav's eyes shone maliciously.

"And you would be right."

&&&

Seamus entered his room and flopped on the bed, not even bothering with the suitcases. He would have been out like a light, if not for the teenager phantom fretting about.

"Are you all right, professor?"

O'Keeffe opened weary eyes to Sam, groaning. "I will be, once I get some rest."

The ghost drew near the bed, an anxious frown creasing his features. "What *happened* to you?"

"Sam..."

At the warning tone in Seamus' voice, Sam floated away. He waited in the corner, eyes focused on the old man he'd grown to love and respect. *Something isn't right.*

&&&

Panting slightly, Brennan walked down the hall, glancing at the numbers. *25, 23, 21...* He counted mentally. Facing Freya's door, he took a deep breath and knocked.

"Who is it?" Freya nearly growled from the inside.

Brennan rolled his eyes and answered telepathically, doing his best to conceal his nervousness. *Who else but yours truly?*

A minute later, a click was heard and Freya opened the door. Brennan noticed the same look in her eyes as before, when he'd found her leaning against that wall. "You okay?"

"Perfectly fine," she said, but her guarded tone was implying the exact opposite.

Freya met his golden-brown gaze and nodded to his silent plea. Sighing, she stepped aside to let him enter the room. She then walked ahead and stared out the window. Unsure, but sensing he had to go with it, Brennan stepped by her side.

The view from Freya's room gave onto the hotel pool. As it was still night, it was empty, only lighted by small lamps that gave it an otherworldly glow. The moon was high in the sky, making the entire landscape even more breathtaking.

"I haven't swum in such a long time," Freya whispered longingly.

Brennan threw her a curious look. "Nothing stops you from doing it."

Freya was hushed, lost in morose thoughts.

The Wiseman glanced at the pool below, quickly assessing the risk. The night manager had seemed fairly half-asleep when they'd entered the hotel, and he could see no cameras. Most of the rooms occupied were on the other end of the hotel, with the view of the street. Really, when it came down to it, they were the only newcomers in that particular part of the building – which meant, no one around to tell them no.

Without thinking twice about it, Brennan grabbed Freya's hand and dragged her out onto the balcony. The pool was underneath it, an easy jump of a few feet.

"What are you do–" Freya started, but Brennan didn't give her the chance to protest.

He wrapped an arm around her waist then pushed off the ground, slightly aided by Wiseman spirit strength. They flew in the air, Freya shrieking then shutting her eyes so she wouldn't see them splatter on the asphalt.

Laughing, Brennan used the same force to straighten their floating forms in the air, then slowly lower them to the water.

"Open your eyes, Freya," he whispered.

When she did, the grey orbs latched onto his, and he smiled. The genuine, full-blown grin hit her harder than the shock of floating in midair. Freya snapped out of the odd moment of connection and glanced at the blue water of the pool scintillating beneath them.

"You really shouldn't be wasting all this energy..." Her whisper was half-hearted.

Brennan beamed wider. "It's worth it." At her shocked look, he quickly amended, "For a bit of fun!"

His concentration lost, they both plunged into the water, and came back out sputtering liquid. Freya took one look at Brennan's wet face and burst out laughing. Then she could no longer stop, until tears streamed down her cheeks – a release of all she kept inside.

"Hey..."

Having felt the change of mood, Brennan swam through the water and pulled Freya in his arms. "I'm sorry, I didn't mean to make you cry..." At a loss on what to do, he awkwardly patted her back until the sobs quieted.

Freya froze, having only then registered she was crying in his arms. Ashamed at her loss of control, she pulled away and wiped at her cheeks. "It's not you, Bren," she muttered, using a nickname for the first time.

"Does that mean I get to call you Frey?" Brennan tried to joke.

It got a small chuckle out of her, then she splashed some water his way. "Annoying prick," she mumbled, though it was more of a tease than an insult. "Since you already got me wet, we might as well have our fun with this."

Brennan's jaw dropped at the words, *Did she...*

"What? What did I say?" Freya froze as the innuendo of her words caught up with her. Then she burst into full out laughter – no tears this time. "You're *such* a guy!"

Still chuckling, she dove underwater and swam to the other end of the pool. Brennan was left shaking his head, then followed after her.

They frolicked around for close to an hour, until their teeth chattered and their lips became blue. Then, Brennan was gentlemanly enough to lift them back up to Freya's room.

The Sage walked to the bathroom and brought out two cozy robes, which they both shrugged into, to warm up. In the silence that followed, Freya couldn't help but think how sweet Brennan had been – how completely unlike his regular self.

Could it be, this was the usual Brennan she missed out on? Not the arrogant teenager whose face she constantly wanted to hit, but rather this sweeter version with a caring side? If he was, Freya felt she might be able to trust him with what she'd learned.

Child... Confide in him... Tyr's voice soothed Freya's remaining wounds and chased her doubts away. The Sage sighed, knowing it was time to reveal what she'd seen.

"Freya, about that dream..." Brennan started.

She spun to face him instantly, her gaze intent. "So you *do* admit having had it!"

"Of course." Before Freya could reply, he went on, "And it's not the first time, either."

The Sage took a seat on the floor and motioned for Brennan to do the same. "What do you mean?"

"Only that this has to be the thirtieth time I've had this dream."

"Recurring, then?"

Brennan nodded, glancing away with a faraway look. "It always starts with a storm – a sand storm. Then, I find myself sleeping in the middle of the desert. As I wake up, there's a hawk flying towards me. For some reason, I feel an urgency to bow. I resist it for some time, but then the need is too powerful and I do so. I never got past that point... Until today." Brennan threw Freya a curious look. "Mind telling me how exactly you got in my dream and what happened?"

"I..." Freya started, then sighed. "To be perfectly honest, I'm not sure. Seamus woke me up and asked if I could do the same to you while he checked us in. I was about to shake you awake when by mistake I touched your necklace and..."

Brennan slapped his forehead and groaned. "The bond!"

Freya had to bite back a chuckle at his dismayed expression.

"Well, it might not be such a bad thing, after all," Brennan admitted, secretly hoping now would be the time for a heart-to-heart.

Freya tilted her head, assessing his expression, then smiled. "Definitely not the worst that's happened to me."

Brennan searched for something in her eyes that could tell him something – anything – about why she wasn't opening to him. No such luck. He sighed, then got up to leave.

"Where are you going?" Freya asked.

"Uh... To help Seamus... unpack," Brennan replied hesitantly. Was it his mind playing games or did he see a disappointed expression in Freya's eyes before she bowed her head and stared intently at the rug in front of her?

The Wiseman tried to decipher her expression, but the long raven hair did a good job of masking it, and he couldn't figure it out. Brennan opened his mouth to say something, but decided against it. He walked to the door and was about to open it, when Freya's voice stopped him.

"I have to tell you something... And I need you to listen to the end, and not get mad."

"I promise."

Brennan dropped his hand by his side, a small smile tugging at the corner of his lips – they were making progress in trusting each other, and he was pleased with it. He slowly turned around, registering that Freya was still starting at the carpet, seemingly deep in concentration.

What can be so bad?

"Before you came to Scotland, I had a dream. Rather, a repetitive dream. And it involved, well, your grandfather."

The smile disappeared off Brennan's face, and his eyes narrowed. "Say what?"

"Of the day he died. I think I saw it happen, Brennan."

So it's back to Brennan now, he thought wryly, before concentrating on her words. With a huge effort of will, he kept a blank expression and knelt at her feet. "Tell me everything."

Freya raised her gaze to his, then the words flowed. She explained about the demon, what she'd seen after Cadmael's death, the images in Seamus' mind and, finally, Thomas' death.

Brennan listened throughout, unflinching except for the anger slowly burning in his eyes. When Freya was done, she mumbled, "You promised you wouldn't get mad."

"I'm not mad at you," he explained, "but at that blasted demon and his cowardice!"

Having already gone through the same rollercoaster of emotions, Freya patiently waited. Unable to sit still, Brennan stood and started pacing furiously. "So he wants what we have – the medallion and the manuscript."

"Yep."

"And he wasn't above killing to get them... Your parents and my grandfather."

"Yep."

"Never mind the part where they were amazingly strong spiritual beings, probably way more experienced than we are."

"I'd say so, yeah," Freya agreed once more.

"And we definitely want revenge on him."

"Yep."

"So why the hell isn't he killing us?" He ran a hand through his hair, tugging on it. "I mean, he's got the advantage here, doesn't he?"

Freya nodded, biting her lip. "When I met him, Raksh implied that he could use us to get the relics for him."

"As if we ever would!" Brennan yelled.

Freya shushed him, looking around as if expecting to be overheard. "Calm down. It's early morning and we don't want any guests to complain of noise disturbance." She waited until Brennan nodded, then said, "You're right, we never would. But the fact Raksh even thinks we might, proves he's been keeping an eye on us. He must've known that at some point we *did* consider it."

Brennan looked at her then, his jaw clenching. "When I was trying to convince you to get them... You think he knew about all that?" When Freya nodded, he shook his head. "But how?"

She shrugged. "Demon powers, who the hell knows? Point is, we need to be really careful. We can fight him – *and* get our revenge – but we'll have to be smarter than he is."

Brennan stopped pacing, then extended his hand to Freya. "I thank you for being honest with me about this. And you're absolutely right, we'll have to be extra ingenious about this. But let's be true partners in this, not just halfway."

Freya glanced down at his hand as though it was a snake ready to bite for a moment, before shrugging off the feeling and shaking it gently.

"Great." Brennan's voice didn't sound enthusiastic, despite his words, and Freya could tell why he was masking the pain of Thomas' death.

"You don't have to hide it, Bren," Freya whispered and stood up, grasping his shoulder. "What you feel – the pain, anger, resentment, unbearing misery – I feel the exact same about my parents and what Raksh did to them. We *will* get vengeance, I promise you."

Brennan was about to nod, when a light out of the corner of his eye drew his gaze. They both glanced around and noticed it was coming from Freya's closet.

"Umm.... What is that?" Brennan asked.

&&&

Tyr was overseeing the realm of the living, checking on Freya on Brennan, satisfied at their progress together. The tiger was about to retreat when it sensed an odd energy around Seamus.

Following the essence, it entered the room in spectral form and saw the elder Sage sweating profusely in bed, tossing and turning even as a perturbed Sam watched on.

"Let me call Freya," the ghost was begging. "She'll know what to do."

"No..." Seamus grasped his hand, holding him. "It is her that he wants."

"Who, professor? Who wants Freya?"

Seamus gasped, eyes flying open. They landed on the tiger, seeing it for the first time, and the green-golden eyes, so familiar, returned his look calmly.

"You..."

"Professor?" Sam looked behind, but saw nothing where he was staring. "Seamus, you're scaring me."

Who did this to you?

Seamus' eyes widened at the tiger's voice, but he could feel time was counted.

"You know who," he muttered.

Was it the demon Raksh?

"Yes," Seamus revealed on a long exhale. He leaned back on the sheets, out of strength as though the confession had taken all he could give. "Protect... Freya..."

I will. He will not touch her.

Tyr was about to leave, when Seamus yelled, "Wait!" He was dimly aware of Sam's grip on his hand, begging and pleading for him to stop hallucinating. "There is more. See...in...me..."

Seamus then passed out, a black veil over his eyes.

Tyr stepped closer, connecting to the man's mind to see his encounter with the demon. When it caught Raksh's scent, and the reality of what he'd done to Seamus, it growled. *Enough is enough.*

The tiger knew it could not leave Seamus as such, else he could die. Breaking most rules it was attuned to, the feline let its spiritual form immerse into his body and infuse him with strength.

Though Tyr did not have the power to undo the demon's curse, it did manage to cleanse the elder Sage enough for some of his strength to return. When Tyr pulled back, he'd regained color in the pale cheeks and was breathing evenly.

"Seamus?" Sam whispered, noticing the change.

He will be all right... The voice echoed around and Sam's eyes darted around furtively.

"Are you...God?"

Only laughter answered him, then silence.

&&&

Tyr followed the scent of the demon until it reached the Cathedral. Snarling and growling, the tiger cast a net wide enough to encompass the entire place, willing to lie low until Raksh showed up.

"You cannot be here."

Tyr ignored Osiris' voice behind, instead arching its back.

"Tyr, you owe me obedience."

I owe you to rid you of a scoundrel! Why you have not yet disposed of him, is beyond me.

"There is a bigger picture you are missing here!"

Tyr turned to glare at the god, eyes shining with anger. *Then tell me.*

"Come back to our realm and I will."

No!

Osiris peered almost nervously behind, before admitting, "Raksh is only a pawn."

Who does he work for, Cortés?

"No. Someone much more powerful than that, someone who orchestrated this entire ghost mess."

The full truth, now!

"My brother, Set."

When the tiger was shocked enough to not shield itself, Osiris lifted his ankh cross and muttered an incantation. A bubble enveloped them, then they disappeared – only to reappear in the godly realm.

I hate it when you do that, Tyr grumbled.

"And I dislike not being obeyed," Osiris countered.

Isis chose that moment to enter, and calmed her husband down with a gentle touch on his shoulder. "Tyr, we could not tell you from the beginning," she said, an apology in her voice. "At first, we did not realize Set was behind this, but now... There are simply too many coincidences."

Behind what, exactly?

"Once, long ago, Set tried to kill us. He was always jealous of Osiris, always wanted what he could not have. We imprisoned him..."

And he escaped.

"Not quite," Osiris corrected. "He is still imprisoned, but the demon Raksh wants the relics of the Underworld in order to release him."

But they only give one control over all dead entities.

"Yes... And with them, Set would be able to take over my realm of the Underworld, influence his guards, and eventually escape. He is cunning, this brother of mine."

You should have told me, Tyr growled. *I would never have gotten Freya involved.*

"It is too late," Isis mumbled, averting her eyes. "Set has already seen her. And the book has chosen them to fight."

What do you mean?

"See for yourself," Osiris added, and waved his palm until the dancing fire became a mirror.

&&&

"Umm..." Freya shared a confused look with Brennan, before opening the closet door. After she moved the mountain of clothes in her suitcase, she tugged the small backpack to her – and the dragon manuscript shone brightly.

Brennan knelt by her side, eyes riveted onto it. "What do you think this means?"

"I'm not sure, but... Remember how Seamus kept going on about us trusting each other, and all that?" At his curt nod, Freya continued, "Well, maybe it picked up on that."

"Our conversation?" he scoffed, then outright laughed. "Come on, Freya, it's a damn book!"

Freya opened her mouth to retort, but already he was reaching for it. "Brennan, *no*!"

Her hand slipped off his, and they both touched the manuscript at the same time – and froze. Brown eyes onto grey, they did not dare to move for fear of triggering something.

When nothing happened, Brennan muttered, "Well, that's a downer."

As though they were the magic words, the light shone brighter, until it filled the entire room and their bodies with the glow.

"You *had* to open your big mouth!" Freya accused.

Before Brennan could retort, two blue wisps emerged from the dragon's eyes on the book. They took the shapes of mini-dragon heads, each facing one of the teenagers.

"Umm, Freya?"

"Shut up, Brennan," she scowled. "Just shut it before you do anything to make it worse!"

"Hey, I wasn't the only one touching it!"

The two dragon heads faced each other for a brief second, then their eyes flashed red and each flew into a teenager. Brennan felt as though fire filled his chest, scorching through every intestine until they were raw. He groaned in pain, bending over in an effort to make it stop.

Freya was shivering, filled with a foreign chill that was not of this world. She tried to push it away with her powers, but it burst past every barrier until her brain itself felt frozen.

As soon as it started, it stopped. The light vanished, and the dragon heads were no more. The book was a regular book once more.

Panting, Brennan raised his head off the ground, noticing Freya in a more pitiful state than him. He crawled over to her, picking her up in his arms. "Freya? Freya, wake up!"

Tears prickled at the back of his eyes, an emotion that was foreign to him. Just as he was getting ready to curse the skies for hurting her, the Sage gasped, and grasped his robe.

"Freya?"

Her eyes snapped open, but they stared unseeing. She frowned, not appearing to have heard him.

"The desert..." Freya was looking deep inside herself for a memory of that place. The power, whatever she'd received, had awoken something in her, and she wasn't sure she could control it.

Tyr! Help me! What's happening?

"I know the place, Brennan," she tried to whisper.

He bent lower to hear her words. "What?"

"The hawk... His eyes... Been there, seen it..."

As though it was too much for her, Freya went limp in his arms. "Freya!" Brennan tried to shake her awake, but it was to no avail.

He probed deeper with his spirit, and to his immediate relief concluded she was in a deep sleep. Still, as he grasped her hand in his, he noticed its utter coldness.

Professor! Brennan yelled mentally, at a loss on what to do. Though the old Sage had lost his powers, the Wiseman knew he would feel his call. He had to.

&&&

Back in his room, O'Keeffe stood up in bed abruptly, startling Sam who'd been keeping an eye out for him.

"Brennan! Freya!"

"What?" the ghost questioned, anxiety filling his eyes instantly.

O'Keeffe didn't stop to explain. He ran out of the room with Sam following closely behind, and burst into Freya's room.

His jaw dropped when he saw Brennan gently lowering her on the bed.

"Good thing you heard me," the Wiseman said, relief clearly evident in his voice.

"What happened?" Sam asked as he hurried to Freya's side.

"I don't know..." Brennan trailed off, throwing a distressed look to Freya. "One minute she's okay, the other she blacked out."

Seamus' astute dark grey eyes surveyed the room, sensing the energy vibrating just underneath the surface. "Cut the lie, Brennan. What did you kids play with?"

"I..." Taken aback, the Wiseman did not know whether to be truthful or keep lying. Freya was comfortable hiding stuff from her mentor, but in the end, Brennan found he was not. "The book."

Seamus headed to the closet he pointed to, and picked up the dragon manuscript. He glanced at Freya on the bed, then back at it.

Sighing, he dropped the book and headed back to the bed to check Freya's pulse. "Whatever you two did, and the past emotions of the day have been too much for her. Let's give her a good night's rest and she might be fine by the morning."

The elder Sage threw Brennan a stern look. "I expect a full account of what you did, once she is awake."

"Of course, but... Would you mind if I stayed with her? Just...to be here when she wakes up." Brennan was helpless against the need ingrained in him to be by her side, for support as much as safety.

O'Keeffe sized him up for a moment, then nodded wearily. "Fine. Call me if anything."

He turned to leave, but a wave of dizziness hit him. Brennan was there to catch him, barely in time before he hit his head on the nightstand.

"Seamus, are you okay?"

Sam, who'd been observing the scene in silence, opened his mouth to speak. At Seamus' stern glare, he closed it.

"Simply tired," O'Keeffe lied, then stepped out of the room and closed the door behind him.

"You'll have to be honest with them too," Sam accused, having followed him out.

The professor refused to answer, though he knew the truth of the words.

&&&

Freya was at the bottom of a hill covered by snow. Though the white powder covered her clothes, they were not damp, nor icy. This scene in her dream was only too familiar to her, as she'd been there once before.

Sure enough, when the Sage raised her head to the top of the hill, there stood Tyr. Its coat of white fur was pure with black stripes, green-golden eyes standing out even more against the frosty background.

Freya ran to the tiger and was by its side in a matter of seconds. Before she could even open her mouth, it spoke. *I know why you are here, child.*

"Brennan's dream... Tyr, there's something about it... About that hawk, about that city... It feels so damn familiar! I can't help but think it, too, has something to do with my parents."

You are correct, the tiger admitted, no hesitation showing in its voice. It knew the only way to keep Freya way from danger's path was to tell her a bit of the truth. *It does have something to do with them and your past. All of it.*

"And the hawk is the demon..." Freya trailed off, remembering those eyes.

No, Tyr corrected, its green eyes guarded and yet warm as they settled on the Sage. *He is much worse than that, and not someone you are ready to face.*

"But why is it following Brennan?"

Because the Wiseman had no one to support him, until now. I will ensure that hawk does not harm either of you any more – nor try to contact you. Swear to me you will let me know if he breaks past the barriers I have set in motion.

"I swear," Freya agreed, shivering despite herself.

As for the demon... There is more than what Raksh told you to the story. He hunted your parents for a long, long time. Seamus, too. It is why he took such care with the castle in Scotland. You need to respect that and allow him to help you.

The Sage bit back her emotions, the desire to probe for more, and settled for what she was given. "I promise. But before I leave, one more question."

Tyr watched her expectantly.

"The demon...Did he go after my parents because of the artifact they supposedly had?" Despite her bravado, Freya's grey eyes were wary of the truth that would be spoken.

Tyr was already being led away, and soon enough it had disappeared. But just before Freya left, she heard its voice in her head, answering her question with the dreaded word – *Yes.*

Now, at least, she knew part of the truth.

Chapter 8

Hours overlapped each other and passed by. Soon enough, night made way for day and a single ray of sunshine entered the room, falling on the faces of the two partners.

Freya stirred and opened her eyes. At the same time, Brennan whispered, "Welcome back, sleepyhead."

"Brennan!" Freya exclaimed, wide awake now. "You're up? What happened?"

He dragged the chair he'd spent the last few hours in closer to the bed, muttering, "You mean before or after you started blabbing nonsense?"

"That was no nonsense, Brennan," Freya denied weakly.

He threw her a wary look, all fights between them forgotten. "You're actually serious about what you said?"

"Yeah. Trust me on this, please, but that dream of yours in the desert, that hawk you keep struggling with, it's bigger than both of us right now."

"What do you mean?" He frowned, unable to make sense of the riddles.

There was no hesitation in Freya's mind as she started telling him the rest of the story. "You remember the demon you warned me about, that presence when we were hunting Cadmael?"

"Yeah..."

"Well, he's not the biggest evil around, at least not from what I'm gathering."

Brennan stared at Freya for a beat, trying to gauge how much of what she was saying he could take at face value. Thinking back to the voice he was hearing, and the way it advised him on such things, he nodded slowly. "All right, let's say that's the case. What do we do about it?"

"We can't *do* anything just yet. Whatever the book did to us will make itself shown at some point over the next few days, I guess. When it does, we'll know if we have more power to hunt Raksh down. If we do, eventually we'll come up against his master." She paused for a beat, then continued, "Do you feel any different?"

"Not really," Brennan shrugged. "But I guess you're right, we'll find out one way or another soon enough."

They paused for a beat, each lost in their own thoughts. Then Brennan recalled something. "By the way, Seamus was here... He kind of figured out what we did, and he's not too happy about it."

Freya's mood instantly changed, scowling. "He's one to talk."

"What do you mean?"

"Just that he can be a bit of a hypocrite, hiding all his secrets. Either way, he was bound to find out someday. We'll fill him in." At Brennan's odd look, Freya sighed, "Don't give me that, I'm not being insensitive for no reason. You're well aware we had a disagreement, and I know you've been wondering about that. Bottom line is, he's keeping stuff from my past, about my parents and how they died."

"Do you want to elaborate?"

Freya attempted to appear indifferent, but her eyes showed her pain. She shook her head. "Not yet... There are just some things I'm not ready to talk about yet."

Brennan smirked bitterly. "Just like me, in many ways." When Freya threw him a questioning look, he shrugged. "There are a lot of things from my past that I don't usually share. Let's just say... I'm familiar with the emotion."

"Then we understand each other."

"When you're not biting my head off."

Freya couldn't hold back a chuckle. Her face grew serious at the thought of their mission, and she stood up slowly. "Where are Seamus and Sam?"

"Probably still sleeping," Brennan guessed. "Why?"

"We should get started on gathering information. I bet anything Gustav won't be fooling around, and depending on how much he's involved in this, it'll be bad news for us."

"How good of an opponent is he?" Brennan frowned.

"Good enough," Freya said and looked away.

"How come he's not dead yet?"

"When I fought him, I didn't have the knowledge I have now. I had to beat it into him."

Brennan guessed there was more she was not ready to divulge on that particular fight, but let it go. They were, for once, conversing without arguing, and he wanted to maintain the peace. "I pity the ghost," he said instead.

Freya laughed, then stood up from the bed. "Come on, lazy, we have to get a head-on start."

As they headed for the door, the Wiseman remembered something. "We might as well start with finding out who Cortés is."

Freya stopped dead in her tracks. *There is no way I heard that right.* "Who?" She asked out loud to make sure, even as dread slowly fell upon her.

"Sam mentioned he heard those ghosts call someone by the name of Cortés," Brennan explained.

Freya's jaw clenched. "How could he *forget* to tell me that?" Without an explanation, she rushed out of the room, leaving a very confused Brennan behind.

&&&

"Do you think Freya's up yet?" Sam's childish bouncing across the room was not fooling anyone. His voice was tinged with an edge that wasn't usually there.

Seamus sighed, staring intently at the map of Spain displayed in front of him on the desk. Parts of the country were circled in red, designing the principal locations of the ghost groups. "I cannot guess, Sam," he replied tiredly. "Why don't you go check?"

A door slamming open against the wall had them both spin to face it. A very pale Freya entered, literally shaking with fury.

"Freya! You're up!" Sam said cheerfully. The glare he received in response had him shut up just as quickly, and he was left staring at the Sage in confusion.

"What's wrong?" O'Keeffe questioned, his gaze going from the bewildered ghost to the fuming Sage.

Brennan chose that moment to enter through the open door, closing it behind him. Patiently and quite calmly –

very unlike his normal self – he grabbed Freya's shoulder and turned her around.

"Cut it out, Freya!" The firm tone of his voice seemed to breach through, as she stilled. "What's this all about?"

Freya shut her eyes closed, shaking her head in reticent denial. Brennan could feel the energy rumbling underneath the surface, full of anger and fear – a *lot* of fear. When she opened her eyes again, the confirmation was in their grey depths.

But fear of what? He had a feeling he'd get the answer soon enough.

"The problem," Freya hissed, "is that we came here with absolutely no information on our enemy. We have suppositions, but no real tools to fight whatever will come!"

"I would not quite put it that way," O'Keeffe retorted icily. "It would be hard to find time to research anything, considering you two have been busy playing with that book behind my back."

Freya moved out from under Brennan's touch, stepping to the professor. "Don't you start with that, Seamus! We didn't do it on purpose – the damn thing came to *us*! And one has nothing to do with the other. Maybe it would've been a good idea to interest ourselves in this new enemy beforehand, and assess the situation properly!"

Is this really my irresponsible pupil speaking? Seamus mused wryly. It took only a closer look to see that Freya was taking the issue rather seriously, and a chill ran up his spine.

As she stopped to regain her breath, Sam intervened softly. "Frey-Frey, why are you so mad? If I didn't know any better, I'd say you're afraid."

Freya turned to him, and for a minute she looked as if she was about to faint. She then took a deep breath. "What did you hear about Cortés?"

Sam's eyes widened, and he was practically bouncing off his toes. "That's the guy I heard about! When I was listening to those two ghosts, they said something about..." He stopped to remember, then snapped his fingers. "Having to report to Cortés!"

Freya gaped at him incredulously for a moment, clenching and unclenching her fists. At a loss of words, she leaned against a wall and buried her head in her hands with a groan. "Un-freaking believable."

O'Keeffe and Brennan shared a look, then Seamus approached the Sage. "Freya, what is it?"

Troubled grey orbs met his, her tone a hopeless whisper. "You really have no idea?" When only bemused silence answered her, she shook her head. "Professor, does the name really not tell you anything?"

When O'Keeffe only stared blankly, Freya continued, "First the demon, now this guy. We couldn't have picked a worst battle if we tried." She then stood and walked towards the door, ignoring her mentor's outstretched arm.

"Wait a second!" Sam's voice stopped her. "Why are you mad at me? Can't we at least know what that was all about?"

At the childish voice, Freya turned with a sad smile. "I'm not mad at you, Sam. I'm simply disappointed in our own lack of planning." She opened the door, but before exiting, threw over her shoulder, "Seamus? I'd suggest you look up in your books the name Hernando Cortés. Perhaps that'll refresh your mind, and give you an image of who we're up against."

Before anyone could stop her, she vanished through the door. Brennan was about to run after her, when he noticed Seamus' petrified expression. Though Sam was just as confused, apparently the name did strike a chord in the old man's mind.

"What is it?" Brennan pressed urgently, his thoughts more on Freya and going to ensure her safety.

"I did not realize..." Seamus rubbed a hand over his face and plopped down in the chair as though his legs could no longer hold him up. He gestured for Brennan to sit down opposite him. "It may be time to fill you in."

As Brennan took a seat, Sam muttered, "I still don't see the big deal."

"Cortés is one of the Cursed," Seamus announced bluntly, as though that alone should have meant something. Brennan shared a confused glance with Sam, though the ghost had a tiny frown that didn't predict anything good.

"Professor," Sam started slowly, as though not quite believing it. "Are you talking about the humans that...*blasphemed* of their living?" The last part had been said in a barely-there whisper.

Seamus took a deep breath, then nodded. "A few years ago, while Freya was still unaware of her lineage, I did a lot of research on the spirits, trying to find out where they were coming from. In one of the texts from your grandfather, Brennan, I found references to what they called the Cursed Ones. Of our living, every act we do, be it good or bad, takes an imprint on the soul. When we die, it is what decides whether we move on to the next journey, or remain stranded as ghosts on Earth, phantoms never able to find peace."

"What about hell?" Brennan asked.

"There is no such thing – at least not according to the old texts. There is the Underworld, where the peaceful go to live on, or be reincarnated, or the likes. There are dark passes where demons live, where they are joined by truly evil humans. However, since the ghosts have existed only on Earth, without a way to move on – be they good or evil – it has taken a toll on these less than stellar beings."

At his meaningful pause, Brennan scowled. "Would you please get to it? The suspense is killing me."

"They are damned," Sam intervened, "and the more they do evil, the closer they get to becoming demons themselves. We all know it – all the ghosts, that is. Whispers we hear around, which is why we try to do good. But…"

"But there are those who are not deterred," Seamus continued. "On the contrary, they crave this new status of wraith. Cortés is one such phantom. No matter what, he will keep at his path, and destroy everything he can. I had not realized until Freya mentioned his first name, but he was on your grandfather's list."

"List?"

"Over the years, Thomas gathered together a list of top evil beings on Earth, many of whom he had run into personally. Cortés was one such person. Of his living, Hernando Cortés was the first successful conquistador. He ignored orders of his commandants and, as was reported later, went ahead in an act of what they called open mutiny. He took over the Aztecs at the time of the conquistadores and became rich with their gold."

Surprise was depicted on Brennan's expression, from the raising of his eyebrows to the slight gaping of his mouth. This was all news to him, and the more O'Keeffe continued, the more he grasped the danger they were facing.

"However, gold was not all he got from the Aztecs," the elder Sage was saying. "He also found an ancient sword that gave powers to any mortal or immortal. The sword made him arrogant in his own abilities, and he purposely ignored orders and led unauthorized conquests of Mexico. He lived on for many more years, until finally he left the world of the living. Evidently, that was only temporary."

"But why lie low for so long before he started to...you know, actually do something?" Brennan frowned.

Sam answered the question before O'Keeffe could as much as open his mouth. "Because of the sword."

Seeing Brennan's puzzled look, Sam said, "Cortés' weapon had certain capabilities, or so the rumor went... Dark magic, the type that was said to be able to control humans, getting its strength in the Underworld and fallen gods of the many pantheons."

"And you know about this...how?" Brennan questioned.

"Freya and I took the same history lesson. With the same teacher." The ghost turned to Seamus, eyes narrowed in confusion as though not understanding how the professor could've missed out on the connection to the name.

Brennan focused his senses on O'Keeffe, for a second fearing the enemy may have infiltrated their circle. Seamus *had* been acting strange since they'd landed, after all. However, despite all the probing, all he caught was a great weakness in the Sage, which apparently had affected his memories.

"What's going on?" Brennan leaned forward, elbows on his knees, his expression concerned. "Freya's right, you hide too many things, Seamus. If you want our cooperation in this, then it's best you come clean – with everything. And we will, too."

Seamus sighed, weary of the whole ordeal. Resting his head in his hand, he revealed what had happened. "In our last mission, I felt a great evil following us, one I had dealt with in the past. However, it never showed up to face me."

"It did Freya," Brennan divulged, not relishing the look of shock on the Sage's face in the least. "After the fight with Cadmael, Freya told me this demon, Raksh, showed up in her dream, and tried to attack her, taunting her about her parents. She escaped, but the memory remained. That's why she was so adamant about figuring out the powers of the book, especially with what little she knew of her parents' death."

"And she told *you*?" Seamus wondered, pleasantly surprised. "No wonder the manuscript showed itself, and bestowed whatever it did to you. You two are working together now, much more than in the past."

"Be that as it may be," Brennan cut, "stop evading the question."

The two stared at each other for a beat, Seamus assessing the young man's demands. In the end, he looked away and gave in once more. "When we entered Spain, on our way to the hotel I caught a glimpse of the demon near the Cathedral. I believe it was the same one Freya interacted with, on the basis of the history we share. Regardless, I went to inspect closer and he attacked me in order to get me out of the fight, I suppose – and probably affect my memories to delay us figuring out Cortés is behind this."

"Seamus was really sick last night," Sam added, "I was afraid for a moment he was close to..." He paused to catch his emotions, then sniffled and continued, "Anyway, then he was better."

"Some kind of guardian angel helped me," the elder Sage whispered, almost to himself.

Seems to be going around... Brennan reflected.

"Okay, so the demon is obviously afraid enough of us to try to pick us out one by one," the Wiseman concluded. "Which means I need to go get Freya, and soon. But first, hasn't one thing struck either of you as odd?"

"What's that?"

"First Cadmael's axe, now a sword? Since when do ghosts get magical objects that can affect humans?"

O'Keeffe seemed to think about it, then slowly said, "They would not, unless... Someone is handing them out."

"Someone like the demon."

"Yes..." O'Keeffe continued, "If that is the case, we may have some time. After Cortés' death, his sword was lost. If the demon ripped it from wherever it existed previously and re-gifted it to the conquistador, the blade may have lost all its properties. Which means it would take a certain amount of time before it regained them, once back in the world of the living."

Brennan threw a look towards the door Freya had disappeared through, slightly paling. "Are you saying that now, Cortés is in full power?"

"Not exactly," Seamus hesitated. "You see, his control over the abilities of the sword has weakened, and thus Cortés is no more influential right now than, say, you and Freya. However, the situation will not remain like this. It is only a matter of time before Cortés grows as powerful as he used to be. And when he does, there is no telling what he will do."

As Brennan processed the information, another thought hit him. "Professor..." When O'Keeffe and Sam turned their gazes to him, he asked, "Is it possible that that's why all the ghosts are rallying to him?"

"Very much so," O'Keeffe nodded slowly. "It would explain why the groups of Spain would even *think* of becoming allies."

"Then we've got both a problem and a solution. Solution because all we need to do is get rid of that sword, and Cortés isn't the biggest and baddest any longer..." Brennan clenched his fist. "But problem because with the blasted sword, Cortés can force Gustav to back him up, and rally him to his plan." He glanced towards the door. "No wonder Freya was upset!"

"True."

"Isn't there some way we can make destroying the sword easier?" Brennan asked, his golden-brown eyes concealing his fear.

"Of course there is!" Sam's eyes were eager. "You guys are strong, so much stronger than before! You're turning into legit Batman and Robin! Or Superman and Wonder Woman or..."

"That's enough, Sam," Seamus held up a hand to stop him, biting back a laugh. "However, you do have a point. I will research more on the sword, but I believe it can be destroyed by a large amount of spiritual energy. With all the changes and the book's new powers bestowed upon you, uniting your abilities may not be such a far-off objective."

Brennan's gaze went icy as he arched an eyebrow quite sarcastically. "If only I could believe that – especially coming from you."

"What do you mean?" O'Keeffe was taken aback by the hostile tone.

Sam, as for him, remembered the conversation, and he also recalled what Seamus had told him about spiritual completion... And their doubts that Freya and Brennan could ever accomplish it. He said nothing, though, instead opting to let Seamus and Brennan go on with their conversation.

"Well, let's see..." Brennan drawled. He pretended to be thinking for a second, then snapped his fingers. "I know! How about the condition you conveniently forgot to mention? The one that needs to be fulfilled in order for me and Freya to be able to unite our powers. Or did that just slip your mind?" As O'Keeffe shared a look with Sam, Brennan sighed and asked, "What is it?"

After a few excruciating minutes, Seamus finally looked Brennan in the eyes. "I am sorry to have hidden this from you, Brennan. Both you and Freya had the right to know, but I held out in the hopes you would figure it out on your own. I thought it would bring you closer... At least a bit."

"Why?" Brennan's gaze was intense on the elder Sage, not liking where the conversation was headed.

"Because..." O'Keeffe hesitated, then admitted, "In order for you and Freya to be able to unite your powers, not only do you two have to be tightly linked... You also have to trust each other completely."

"Umm... Define *completely*," Brennan offered hesitantly.

Seamus glared in irritation, then briefly explained, "From the bottom of your very hearts, you and Freya have to trust each other with your very lives."

Brennan stared at him for a beat, then sighed and stood up. "That won't be happening for a long while, professor... Neither I nor Freya are ready to share all our secrets. At least not yet." The Wiseman threw both O'Keeffe and Sam a sad look, then went on, "However, I do intend to make an effort. For the sake of whatever is on the end of Cortés' plan."

Just as O'Keeffe inclined his head in assent, Sam floated to Brennan, his blue eyes oddly intense. "Go find Freya. Wherever she went, she's not feeling too happy right now, I can guarantee that. Me and Seamus will try and find out a bit more about this sword of Cortés' and its weaknesses."

Brennan nodded and after a curt salute to both of them, went off in the city to look for Freya. As soon as he was out the door, Sam turned to O'Keeffe. "Professor, do you think they could win this?"

O'Keeffe rubbed the back of his neck pensively, but concealed his doubtful expression. He owed it to Freya to trust her with winning the fight, and to Brennan to be there to support her. Instead of shaking his head, the old Sage smiled weakly. "Even if they are unable to come together as they should, there may still be a chance."

"What's that?" Sam tilted his head.

"That they, at least, trust each other enough to combine their powers and to count on the other to be there."

"And that's actually possible? For them to go only halfway, I mean," Sam elaborated with a raised eyebrow. He knew very well, from what O'Keeffe had told him, that Freya and Brennan had once before combined their powers... In order to get Seamus back to the hotel and away from the Vikings, they'd been forced to work together. But he wasn't entirely sure that Freya would be able to go the extra step and rely on Brennan. She was far too independent for that.

"It had better be, Sam," Seamus mumbled, and stood. Oddly dizzy on his feet, he had to grip the edge of the table to remain on his feet.

His eyes drew back to the map, glinting fiercely. *They will be able to. They have to. And at least, I can do whatever I can to come to their aid in this new quest.*

"Professor..." Sam started slowly, observing the elder man. Shoulders hunched inwards, Seamus seemed unable to stand up properly, and a slight sheen of sweat appeared on his forehead.

When O'Keeffe turned to him, Sam gulped and made a conscious effort to appear calm. "How can I help? With research on the sword, I mean."

Seamus seemed to think for a minute, then pointed to his suitcase. "I brought with me an old encyclopedia of world history. If we look through it and the papers I have on the conquistador era, we might find something."

Sam nodded, then floated over to the bed to sort through the luggage.

In the meantime, the old Sage glanced once more at the map. His hand passed over it at precise places, but nothing happened. A wave of regret passed over him at Raksh's words, and all he had lost.

It is in moments like these that I wish I still had part of my powers left.

No matter how deep the longing, there was nothing he could do to get back what had vanished. Sighing, Seamus dragged himself towards Sam, ready to do some research.

Chapter 9

"What a damned mess," Freya muttered, eyes fixated on the water lapping at her feet.

Perched on a rock by a river, the Sage was reflecting on all she knew of Cortés, in an effort to be more positive about their situation. With each passing second, the impossibility of the task ahead dawned clearer.

After exiting the hotel, she'd run over to the one place peace called out from – a secluded forest on the outskirts of the city, away from prying eyes. A rather large stream passed through the magical place, and she'd taken her shoes off, dipping her feet in the cool water – if only to enjoy the sensation of it lapping at her heels.

The forest cloaked her presence, and the tree just a few feet behind had extended branches which set a welcome barrier to the sun's rays. Freya was physically comfortable as she sat there, but her mind was in turmoil.

She'd hoped the hiding spot would revive the force desperately lacking in her. With a disgruntled sigh, Freya tried to touch the water's essence as she had back in Scotland and found she didn't have the strength for it.

Scowling, she pulled her feet out of the river and retied her shoes, then brought her knees up to her chest. *No matter which way I look at it, I still feel helpless. First the blasted demon, now Cortés...* To fight a man whose sole purpose for existing was to conquer, who was decided to become a demon himself, was not something she could've predicted.

How can we fight a man who was invincible of his living? Especially with that sword...

This is not the Freya I know, Tyr's voice boomed in her head. *Neither you nor Brennan can ever give up. No matter how insurmountable it seems, you have to fight and keep going!*

Even if the cause is hopeless? Freya prompted.

Even so. The tiger paused, trying to find the right words and tone, before continuing. *Freya, despite how powerful someone seems, there is always a flaw. You have to find it and play with it. Toy with it. That is the best way to get rid of enemies. For you, Cortés may seem invincible. But I can assure you he is far from it. Though he may now be immortal, the human weaknesses of his living are still very present in him.*

As Freya pensively gazed at the horizon, Tyr pressed, *What happened to your drive to kick ghosts to the far beyond, hmm? Where is the fierce girl who would not hesitate to battle any phantom that came her way?*

"Do we even have a chance?" Freya whispered, her glazed eyes glued to the horizon. Everything seemed so bleak, as though nature itself caught her mood and reflected it.

If you believe that you can defeat him, then my answer is yes.

Tyr, how much do you know about Cortés? Freya probed rather than answering, and the tiger understood she needed more reassurance.

Only what you do, child... Plus a little interesting fact about his sword, the one supposedly so powerful.

What do you mean? Freya frowned. Her eyes followed a bird that had soared through the sky until now, and now flew down towards the water. At the last moment, it let a wind current carry it over and back towards the clouds.

Concentrating on Tyr's voice, Freya could almost see the tiger grinning as it answered, *Did I not tell you? It must have slipped my mind... The particularity of Cortés' sword is that in the living world, it is indeed strong, even more so if used by a phantom such as him. However, in the realm of the dead, it loses most of its abilities completely. When humans die, Freya, they usually get to carry one object of their desire with them... In Cortés' case, the sword was lost in the realm of the dead.*

Until it founds its way back to him, here. A glimmer of hope started to shine in Freya's eyes again, but it was driven away by her next thought. *But it's already been a hundred years. The sword must've regained its strength by now... Right?*

Not quite, came the slightly hesitant response. *You see, the blade is similar to a battery. It needs to recharge itself after a long period of being unused. If my guess is correct, though Cortés is using it to rally all ghosts to him, its capabilities are not all returned.*

You mean he's bluffing? Freya asked.

Yes.

As the information was processed, Freya let out a huge sigh of relief. *Tyr, this helps so much!*

Before the tiger could comment, Freya jumped off the rock in one swift move, turning to face the bushes behind her.

"What was that?"

Freya, is everything all right? Tyr questioned, its voice holding a hint of distress.

Yes, I... The Sage trailed off, scanning the region with her senses. *I thought I felt something.* Frowning at the silence surrounding her, Freya added, *Tyr, I'll get back to you later.*

Very well, but be careful. And remember what I warned you about earlier... Stay away from the hawk and *the demon.*

The Sage nodded, then concentrated on her surroundings. "Now what was it that I sensed?"

Her frown deepened when she picked up a presence not too far away, hiding behind the bushes. The Sage focused her powers on the barrier surrounding the intruder and pierced it, revealing a familiar energy.

He's never going to learn, is he?

Silent as a wolf, Freya tiptoed towards the bushes. She passed under one of them, stepping into the shade until she was cloaked. Freya then turned her palms to a tree about ten meters away from her, sending a burst of air towards the spot.

No more than a second later, a startled cry was heard and a familiar brown-haired Wiseman soared up in the air. As Freya stepped up to him, laughing, Brennan glared down.

"That was completely unnecessary!" he reproached, half-sulking. Freya was sure he didn't appreciate being outwitted by a girl.

"Oh, and I suppose you wanting to scare me off was?" Her grey eyes twinkled in amusement.

"Seamus sent me to look for you," Brennan mumbled, twisting this way and that in midair as he tried in vain to release himself from the levitation.

"What for?" Freya arched an eyebrow.

"To tell you about Cortés' sword and other stuff," Brennan explained.

"Don't bother," Freya rolled her eyes. "I already know."

"You do?" Brennan stopped moving, eyeing her suspiciously.

"Yeah," Freya avoided his gaze by shrugging and checking out the surroundings instead. "I did some research long ago... Either way, I know how his weapon may have something to do with the rallying of all the ghosts of Spain."

Judging by his smug expression, Brennan had no problem being cocky – even upside-down as he was. "Well, mayhaps I could interest you in some *other* news. Your mentor got his ass kicked by the demon we both hunt, I've explained about the book, and we also figured out Raksh is the Good Samaritan doling out weapons of mass destruction amongst the ghosts."

His grin widened when Freya gaped in mute shock. Surprised at the words delivered, she lost focus and Brennan dropped on the ground with a thud.

"Ow! Dammit, Frey, would it kill you to be careful with my backside?" He stood up and rubbed said part of his body, wincing.

Freya didn't react to the taunt, instead stuck on one thing. "Raksh attacked Seamus? Is he okay?"

"He's fine," Brennan reassured, his gaze softening. "I also told him about the demon having contacted you."

That got Freya's full attention – and annoyance. "You had no right!"

Brennan rolled his eyes at the predictable response. "I beg to differ, but I did. It's past time you two stop hiding stuff from each other. No one benefits from it."

"Whatever, you still had no right," Freya retorted, but her tone was gentler. "Anyway, here's something for you," she started, decided to have the last word on the Cortés discussion. She was about to go on when Brennan's gaze went straight to something behind her, and a slight crease appeared on his forehead.

Freya spun around, all senses alert. In tune with their bond more than he would've liked, Brennan stepped to her side.

"Are you catching anything?" His mouth was by her ear, and the whisper caused Freya to shiver.

She shook her head, intently spreading her energy to cover the full area. If Brennan used his spiritual strength for something so mundane, he'd weakened and she didn't want to risk it.

Despite her best efforts, a soft zap echoed in the air. Freya turned to Brennan, eyes narrowed. "Stop it."

"Stop what?" His innocent expression didn't fool her in the least.

"Whatever it is you're doing, Bren, it's sucking up your energy."

The Wiseman bit back a grin at the nickname, instead shrugging good-naturedly. When Freya's glare didn't ease off, he pet her head condescendingly. "Relax, it's only a precaution. Invisible barrier to stop all supernatural attacks – just in case."

"Really, Brennan, stop it."

"No need to. I'll be okay, promise."

"Brennan..." Freya trailed off, a warning edge in her voice.

He threw her yet another smug look. "Don't worry that pretty face on me. I'm the king of trouble, and trust me when I say that nothing's going to weaken me anytime soon."

"Fine," Freya spit, knowing when to give up. "But don't fall on me when you pass out."

"Please!" Brennan chuckled. "I won't."

Freya was about to comment, but movement ahead caught her eye. She shared a look with Brennan, then slowly started to advance forward.

Is everything all right? Tyr asked.

We'll find out soon enough...

Brennan's eyes were locked to Freya's moving form, oddly aware of her. He'd chalked it up to the bond, but now... Another noise up ahead made him snap out of his thoughts, alert for any sign of danger and ready to defend her. *I just hope the barrier will hold in case of trouble.*

Take care of her, Tyr urged.

Brennan did not bother to answer, sensing its presence no longer. Even more, another movement had caught his attention. "Freya, watch out!" In three quick steps, he'd caught her arm, angling his body to push her behind him.

However, Freya shook her head and resisted. Her action surprised Brennan enough that he let go.

"It's not an enemy," the Sage said softly.

"How—" Brennan started, but was interrupted by a ghost emerging from the bushes.

He surveyed the newcomer warily – about five feet nine, lanky bordering on skinny, raven-black hair and onyx eyes. At first glance, he seemed no more than fifteen years old. He was dressed in old-school pants and some kind of shirt that was partly open at the collar.

The dark eyes fell upon them and the ghost floated closer, an apprehensive look on his face. In that moment, Brennan backtracked his original observation. The spirit was not young – he was at least his age, if not older. His features, now tight in a mask of suspicion, spoke of aristocracy and money. The only thing that contradicted that conclusion were the clothes he wore.

In a few quick strides, he reached Brennan and Freya, piercing them with his gaze but still maintaining a distance. "Who are you? *Qué quieren?*" he grunted – almost barked.

"Watch your –" Brennan growled, but already Freya stepped around him, a timid smile on her face.

"I'm Freya, and this is my friend Brennan." She'd spoken in Spanish, the words melodic from her mouth, and the Wiseman caught himself staring – again. There was nothing confrontational in her tone, and even her body posture was neutral as she let the ghost size her up. Only the smallest rigidity in her pose told Brennan she was determined not to back down.

Not about to be outdone, Brennan butted in, "*Somos turistas aquí,*" informing the phantom they were tourists.

The boy's gaze flicked to him, then back to Freya. "*Americanos?*"

Freya responded with a tight smile. "*Británicos*."

The ghost surveyed her for a long minute, as if attempting to figure out if she was telling the truth. Freya used the time to assess him warily. *He's Spanish, that much is obvious with the Catalan accent. And yet he's not with his clique... Coincidence?*

Or maybe he's not on speaking terms with them? Brennan suggested.

Before they could debate further, the spirit threw one last wary glance to Brennan, then nodded. A bright smile crossed his face as he switched to English, speaking the language with only a slight accent. "You speak Spanish very well for Englishmen."

"I would expect to," Freya smirked, "after all those lessons."

Something about her calmness irked Brennan. He wasn't stupid – evidently Freya was trying to butter up the newcomer in order to gain something out of it. What, he had no clue. But did she have to be so *nice*?

"I'm sorry, I didn't catch your name," Brennan interrupted, stepping as close as Freya had.

She threw him a warning look, sensing his stiffened muscles and rigid stance. Keeping her face inscrutable, she concentrated on Brennan's energy. *Don't be aggressive. I have a gut feeling he can help us somehow.*

You're kidding! Brennan retorted, and Freya heard the disbelief in his voice.

The ghost smiled to both of them, completely unaware of what was happening underneath the surface. "Emmanuel," he said.

"No last name?" Freya questioned.

For a brief moment, a shadow seemed to flash across Emmanuel's face, but he soon dismissed – or hid – it with another bright smile. "Not important."

Recalling Brennan's demeanor when they'd first met, Freya raised an eyebrow sarcastically and half-glared at Brennan. *Why am I not surprised?* Ignoring the near-snort escaping him, she addressed the spirit again. "Are you from around here?"

Emmanuel shook his head slowly. "Not particularly, why?" He was intrigued by the girl, and in spite of himself, his thoughts went back to the time he'd been alive... To his sister and the girlfriend he'd left behind. He concentrated back on the raven-haired girl and on the man by her side. They were spiking his curiosity, and he was aching to find out more about them.

"Just wondering how come a ghost would prefer the loneliness of the hills to the noise of the city, that's all."

Emmanuel shrugged. "In summer, Girona is very popular with tourists. Some ghosts like to stay in the city to remember the old times, when they themselves were alive. I, personally, find it depressing and would rather spend the season in the quiet of nature."

"That makes sense," Freya nodded, then cocked her head as if thinking about something.

Brennan groaned by her side. *What now? I know that look...* To Emmanuel, he said, "Fair warning, she usually gets like that when she has a new idea. Most of them haven't turned out too well for us."

Contrary to what Brennan was thinking, Freya heard him and met his gaze, grey eyes shooting lightning warning. "Just what are you going on about?"

"You know..." Brennan full-on smirked as an idea formed in his mind. "Let's see. Thanks to you, we got lost, we nearly starved, and did I mention we got *lost* countless times?"

As Freya threw him a puzzled look, Brennan tried to be less obvious. *You said he could help us, right? You meant guiding us in the city... Here's your chance.*

At once, realization dawned and Freya caught on to the play. Not missing a beat, she pouted. "Yes, well, none of that would've happened if you'd known the city half as well as you promised!"

Brennan felt like he'd been kicked in the gut at her playful expression. Sure, they'd joked around and fought multiple times, but this was an entire side of Freya he'd ignored existed. A softer, mischievous, *gentler* side...

His eyes dropped to her stuck out bottom lip, and he gulped. *What the hell is wrong with me? This is Freya!*

Though only a few seconds had passed since the Sage's last retort, Brennan willed himself to snap out of his stupor and get back in the game. "Yeah, well, need I remind you that we're tourists? The whole purpose of this trip was to discover new places!" The scowl on his face was not faked, annoyed as he was at his own haywire emotions.

"Perhaps I can help you," Emmanuel interrupted their fake-bickering. When both Freya and Brennan turned to face him, he went on, "That is to say, I know the city very well, having grown here. If you wish so, I could be your guide."

Freya pursed her lips thoughtfully, then threw Brennan a falsely-annoyed look. "I'm pretty sure you can't do worse than Brennan."

"Hey, I resent that!" the Wiseman retorted, completely out of character and forgetting about the plan. "I was doing a very good job in the first place!"

"Perhaps this is a good a time as any to let someone else take your place and show you the many marvels of Girona."

Brennan glared at Emmanuel, no longer playing. The glint in the ghost's eyes was much too eager. Despite the obvious benefit of the offer, and the evidence he was dead and had no chance in hell with Freya, Brennan backtracked.

"Thanks, but we can manage on our own."

Freya's eyes nearly bugged out of her face, unaware of his seriousness.

"Aw, come on, Brennan," she cajoled, placing a hand on his arm. "Don't be such a party pooper. I'm sure Emmanuel's right."

At the same time, her voice rang in Brennan's head, *Don't do or say anything that can give us away!*

Brennan froze, his brown-golden eyes darkening at the panic in hers. When Freya turned her full-watt smile to Emmanuel, he snapped. *Oh, don't worry, I won't. But you might want a drool check.*

Freya spun around, eyes blazing. Before she could do anything, Emmanuel intervened, completely unaware of the tension in the air. "So, what parts of the city would you two care to visit?"

Freya felt a familiar rage settle on her shoulders at Brennan's disconcerting attitude. Every time they were close to some sort of peace, he went and ruined it. He blew hot and cold too many times, and it was a rollercoaster she couldn't get used to.

Despite it, she took a deep breath, in an effort to keep herself calm. *No need to lose it. He's not going to have the pleasure.*

As Brennan observed his partner, he caught a whiff of the anger emanating from Freya as if it was his own. The wave of fury passed like a tornado, destroying everything in its path. A hint of satisfaction surged through him, since she was now completely ignoring Emmanuel and focused on not losing her cool – because of him.

He glanced over at the ghost, noticing his bemused expression as he took in Freya's rigid stance and tightly shut eyes. Before Brennan could help it, laughter bubbled out of him, and next thing he knew, he was on the grass, clutching his sides and having a riot.

"Are you feeling all right, Brennan?" Emmanuel raised his eyebrows at him.

In response, the Wiseman held his hand up – still mid-guffaw – to indicate he needed five minutes to calm down. Out of the corner of his eye, he noticed Freya was clenching her fists. *Ah, I really know her too well.*

Breathe in, breathe out, in and out... Freya recited in her head. The mantra seemed to at least block Brennan's laughter from her ears, and the Sage calmed down slightly.

Freya, why are you so upset? I can feel your rage all the way across the realms! Tyr warned.

Breathe in, breathe out, and breathe in and out...Slowly... No use getting all worked up.

The tiger paused for a second, then it all clicked. *Ah, I see now...*

Slowly... See what*!?* Freya snapped.

Tell me, Freya, is Brennan in the vicinity?

How'd you guess? Was her sarcastic reply.

Well, you do have this habit of losing your cool around him... Seems he has quite a gift of getting under your skin.

Freya took yet another deep breath and forced the fire inside to diminish. It didn't last long, however, and burst even higher, anger reaching its peak.

Freya... Freya! That is enough! Tyr ordered.

The Sage exhaled slowly, forcing herself to get a grip on her emotions. *Do you see why I didn't want to do this mission with him? I knew he'd end up pissing me off! What is it with him that can get the worse out of me?* Freya ranted. *Normally, I can control myself perfectly fine, but with Brennan... Ugh!*

Child, take a deep breath now, Tyr instructed. *Forget about him, and his taunts. Try it, and you will see, control is not that hard.*

Slightly wary at the amount of energy the Sage was about to unleash, the tiger reached across the realms and blew a soothing breath. The volcano inside Freya, which had been slowly rising to epic proportions, was put to rest. The Sage felt as though she'd dunked her head in a waterfall of cool water, and emerged refreshed.

Freya's anger calmed down, until only ashes were left. *Thanks, Tyr.*

You are welcome. It seemed like you needed it. Now please, do your best to keep him from riling you up again.

Freya mentally rolled her eyes. *I promise I'll try.*

She then raised her head, reconnecting with the world around her. Only a few minutes had passed, and she saw Emmanuel looking at Brennan, perplexed. The Wiseman's laughter reached her ears, but this time it didn't trigger anything – much.

"Oh, *do* grow up, Brennan!" She glared at him, not that it did any good.

Emmanuel gave her a questioning glance. "Tell me, does your friend always go into bursts of laughter at random times?"

"Only when he's being an ass," Freya winced. When Brennan kept going, she grimaced in sympathy towards Emmanuel. "Please excuse me." She then walked over to the Wiseman and smacked him over the head, effectively ceasing his fun.

"*Ow*!" Brennan yelled, rubbing the back of his head and straightening up. "What was that for?"

Freya leaned down and hissed, low enough so Emmanuel wouldn't hear her. "Brennan, get me one more time this mad, and I swear to all the heavens you'll find yourself with a very nice black eye."

Under Brennan's slightly admiring gaze, she straightened her back and offered the most superficial smile ever, despite the annoyance burning in her eyes.

Brennan peered past her to Emmanuel, semi-smug at having been able to get a reaction out of her. "All right. No need to get so touchy, Freya."

He was about to place a friendly arm around her shoulders, but Freya ducked and turned to the ghosts. "You were asking earlier what places we'd like to visit. Is the Cathedral in this region?"

What are you doing? Brennan's asked, this time in a slight panic.

Trying to see if normal ghosts noticed something weird going on, that's what! Freya answered curtly.

Emmanuel seemed surprised. "Well, yes. How did you guess?"

"I've been here before, but never had a chance to visit it all." She smiled, this time a warm smile, and Brennan clenched his jaw reflexively. "This time, I intend to see all Girona has to offer."

"You definitely won't be disappointed!" Emmanuel agreed enthusiastically – a little too much, for Brennan's taste.

"It's a shame we're here on business," the Wiseman commented. *Thank the heavens Freya doesn't need to see this guy again after this, I don't trust him.* He tried to focus on the sobering thought, and avoid losing his mind over how she was acting.

However, Brennan's impression was shattered when Freya shot back, "That won't stop me from visiting the city."

Brennan remained stubbornly mute as Emmanuel described the charms and old streets of Girona. Freya's retort had felt like a slap, and he barely held back a scowl towards Emmanuel. He was not a jealous person by nature, but something about Freya brought out his worst qualities at times.

Without thinking, he mocked, *And I suppose you'll be doing this with your new boyfriend?*

Brennan, shut it! The warning was crystal clear, but lost on her partner.

As Freya pretended to be intently listening to Emmanuel, Brennan went on, *Hey, maybe I'll tell Sam to chaperone you two.*

"That's *it*!" Freya yelled out loud as she turned to Brennan, her hair swirling in the wind, eyes aflame. She'd tried her best to dismiss it, but the Wiseman seemed intent on taking the joke overboard and there was only so much she could take and not fight back.

Without warning, she grabbed Brennan's forearm and twisted it in a semi-circle roughly. Their bodies slammed together, sparks flying as their incensed gazes collided – and Brennan smirked victoriously.

Shouting in anger, Freya forced him off-balance, extending her wrist and dragging him with her. Before Brennan knew it, he was on a knee, pinned down by the Sage's iron grip and unable to escape it.

"This is your last warning," Freya hissed in his ear. "Drop the cocky act, or *else*!"

Just as suddenly as she'd grabbed him, Freya released Brennan and straightened up, then smiled forcefully at Emmanuel. "Sorry about that. He tends to...piss me off sometimes."

Emmanuel glanced between the two, lips twitching in amusement. "I see..."

Freya walked to him smoothly, even as Brennan said from behind, "Aw, come on, Freya, just admit I was right."

On some subconscious level, Brennan knew it was time to bow out graciously – and shut the hell up. He was well aware of it. But knowing and doing were two separate things.

"You're going to ignore me now?" he teased, focused on Freya's rigid back.

I'm reaching new immaturity levels... He shook his head internally at his own reaction.

Emmanuel gave both of them a puzzled look, but Freya had her eyes shut in an effort to stop the avalanche from starting – again. Brennan's next words, however, effectively ruined her efforts.

"Freya and Em—" he started in a singsong voice, but didn't get to finish before Freya spun around, cheeks rosy in anger.

"Brennan, you're the most infuriating guy I've ever met!" She then started to stomp towards him angrily, but a hand caught her arm. "Let me go!"

Surprisingly enough, the grip lessened, and Freya peered up to notice Emmanuel staring at her wide-eyed.

"Oh, shit!" The muttered words escaped her before she could stop them.

What happened to not doing anything to give us away? Brennan asked, adding fuel to the fire.

The Sage threw him a look, and he smiled sheepishly.

How are we going to pull this off? Freya wondered, her gaze locked with Brennan's. All fight was forgotten as they tried to find a way of getting past the new hurdle. A ghost ally was not something they could squander, and an additional enemy was definitely not something they needed. Especially if said phantom was aware beings such as them existed and were in the city.

Start by explaining, I guess, Brennan suggested, jerking his chin to emphasize the suggestion.

But... Brennan, he's a spirit! I don't think he'd enjoy finding out we have the power to, uh, send him back to his grave.

Yeah, I guess you're right. He sized the shocked Emmanuel with a speculative glint in the eyes, before correcting, *Go with half the truth then.*

Freya couldn't help but roll her eyes. *Typically predictable of you to say that.*

And, uh, Freya? Brennan ignored her comment, trying to get more important words out before he chickened out. *I'm sorry about earlier. I did go a bit overboard.* He read the surprise in her eyes, and shrugged, *What? I can admit when I push some limits...*

Freya simply nodded, too preoccupied with their current dilemma to be as upset as she wanted to be. *You're forgiven. Besides, I have a short temper.* She then turned to Emmanuel and started hesitantly, "Emmanuel, there's a plausible explanation for what just happened."

"I know," the phantom replied quite calmly, a small smile playing on his lips as he glanced between the two of them.

Freya hesitated, sharing an uneasy look with Brennan. "Say what?"

"You're a Sage, aren't you?"

"I..." Freya trailed off, gaping at him.

Brennan, who'd joined her side in three steps, surveyed Emmanuel suspiciously. "Just how do you know that?"

Emmanuel, still grinning, started explaining, "I have a friend who is friends with a Sage. He told me a bit about them... you."

"Well, that's a surprise," Freya commented.

"So the whole bit about you two looking for a guide was only an act?" Emmanuel asked, not missing a beat.

"Sorry, but yes, it was." Brennan didn't sound the least bit apologetic, as he was looking forward to getting rid of the ghost. However, Freya didn't seem to think along the same lines.

"Actually, Emmanuel," she started, "we do need a guide. Not that I don't know the city, but there's places I'd rather not get lost in."

Brennan observed her, and bit back a sigh. Unwilling to have a repeat performance of before, he pushed back the clenching in his gut, instead clearing his expression of all emotions. "What do you say, Emmanuel? Would you mind showing us around?"

"Not at all," the ghost grinned, looking beyond happy.

I hate this... Brennan ruminated darkly, but didn't share the sentiment with Freya. Against all odds, in the half an hour the encounter had taken, she'd come to like the ghost. Rather than make him feel better, the realization only worsened his mood.

"Good," Freya smiled. "Why don't you come with us back to our hotel? I have a friend who'll be happy to meet you."

Emmanuel agreed cheerfully, and Freya addressed Brennan with a pleading expression. "Tell me you came here in a car."

He smirked and dangled the keys of the rental in the air. "Sweet!"

About thirty minutes later, the three entered the hotel and headed straight to O'Keeffe's room. Freya went in first, and Sam ran into her arms as soon as the door opened.

"Frey-Frey!" he whined, blabbing in his usual childlike voice. "You won't imagine what Seamus made me do. It was so *boring*!"

"I know that voice..." The surprised whisper came from behind Brennan.

The Wiseman turned to look at Emmanuel, thus clearing the path and Sam entered his sight. The look of shock was mirrored on the two ghosts' expressions, and words died on their lips. To say they looked dumbstruck would've been the understatement of the year.

Chapter 10

"Sam?" Emmanuel finally whispered, getting over his initial stupor.

With a happy cry, both ghosts rushed in each other's arms for a hug. Normally, they would've been unable to have direct contact. But Brennan's, Freya's and O'Keeffe's presences in the room filled it with such an aura that the two spirits were instantly solidified.

Completely oblivious to their audience, they hugged like old friends – which, they were.

As Emmanuel pulled away, he grinned at Sam's slightly shorter frame. "Well, well, well... Look what the plane flew in!"

Sam chuckled, then his boyish face was lighted by a huge grin. "Still the same as ever, huh? So how are things over here?"

A few years earlier, while Freya had been kicking Gustav's butt, Sam had met Emmanuel and the two had quickly become friends. Their friendship, despite its strength, had been roughly tested when Emmanuel's loyalty had been called into question. Ever since then, they'd remained the best of friends, and Sam visited when he had time.

However, because of what he'd found out about Emmanuel during their last time in Spain, Sam had kept his friendship with the other spirit hidden, and neither Freya nor O'Keeffe had been aware of his secret.

Emmanuel's face grew dark at Sam's question, but he forced a smile and waved it away with his hand. "We'll have time for that later."

Sam threw him a troubled look, but decided to drop the issue for the time being. He knew his friend well enough to catch on that he carried bad news. Once they were alone, he'd bet Emmanuel would tell him, so he shrugged all worries off for the time being.

"So this is the friend you refused to tell us about," a voice suddenly brought them back to reality.

Sam faced O'Keeffe, whose eyes twinkled in amusement. His must have shown panic, because Seamus' expression softened. "If you are wondering how I knew about this, it suffices to say that not many things escape me. I trust you had your own motives not to share – Emmanuel, is it? – with us."

Freya, quiet up until then, stepped closer and glanced between Sam and Emmanuel, then grinned widely. "So let me guess – *you*'re the friend Emmanuel meant, the one who knew a Sage."

Sam nodded in response, oddly shy.

As he was behind the youngsters, O'Keeffe felt another dizzy spell hit, and he swayed on his feet. Barely catching himself in time, he concealed the weakness before they noticed. Clearing his throat, he said, "You will have to excuse me, I feel rather tired from the day's research. Would you mind heading to Freya's room, to continue catching up? This is certainly a moment in no need of an old man."

Freya turned towards him in surprise, eyes gravely following her mentor's hesitant steps to the desk

Behind her, Sam and Emmanuel already floated through the door into the hallway. Brennan paused in his tracks with his hand on the knob, then met Freya's eyes. "Go on."

Freya shared a charged look with the Wiseman, registering the mental push he was aiming her way. Biting her lip, she nodded and tiptoed towards the desk, before she could change her mind. Behind her, she heard the door close as Brennan left.

"Seamus?"

The elder Sage lifted his head from his hands. Freya noticed the exhausted gleam in his eyes, the ashen color of his skin. She recalled Brennan's admission before they'd met Emmanuel, and winced.

"Brennan told me, about the demon...Raksh."

O'Keeffe surveyed her quietly for a few moments, then inclined his head wearily. "I truly believed I was keeping you safe. I never meant my silence to be a burden, or hurt you."

As his voice broke on the last words, Freya crossed the remaining distance and hurled herself in his arms, hugging him tightly. "I know," she murmured in his chest, taking comfort when Seamus returned the embrace.

After a few moments, she pulled away. "You need to rest. The research is important, but leave it to us four. I don't want whatever he did to you to harm you further than it already has."

When Seamus seemed ready to contest it, Freya warned sternly, "I mean it."

Shaking his head, the old professor chuckled. "Since when did you become the bossy adult?"

Rather than answer, Freya helped Seamus to the bed and tucked him in. He was asleep before his head hit the pillow, and she watched over him. After a few long moments, she stepped out and returned to her room.

&&&

Sam noticed out of the corner of his eye that Freya and Brennan weren't around, and figured it was as good a chance as he'd get. He pulled Emmanuel through the wall and into Freya's room.

"What's going on?" he asked his friend, keeping a low tone.

"The city has much changed since your last visit," Emmanuel responded with a wary glance to the door.

"I guessed as much. I saw Raoul."

"When?" Emmanuel hissed, fear clouding his gaze.

"When I first found out about all this mess, and went to get Freya and Seamus...." Sam trailed off as the expression on Emmanuel's face hardened with panic.

"Sam, these are dangerous waters. I am afraid for your friends."

Sam's eyes flickered to the Wiseman who'd just entered the room, then he grinned reassuringly. "Don't be, they can handle themselves."

&&&

Freya walked in shortly after and joined Brennan. He was frowning, watching the two ghosts chat in a corner. "Cat got your tongue or something?"

Brennan shrugged, then addressed Sam loudly. "Tell me again why you didn't say you had a friend in Spain?"

Sam glanced between him and Freya, and the Sage frowned at the look in his eyes. Sam was usually a ghost that could be read easily, but in that particular instance his expression was guarded, even with her.

"Well... It must have slipped my mind." He shrugged sheepishly, then rubbed the back of his neck awkwardly.

Was it just my imagination...? Freya wondered. *But no... No, I know Sam, and right now he's hiding something.* Her gaze flicked to Emmanuel, and something instantly clicked in her mind. *Whatever it is, he's doing it for his friend. And considering how much he's done for us, I can allow Sam to have this one secret. If complications arise, I'll deal with them then.*

The question was, would Brennan be as lenient?

Freya peeked at the Wiseman, subtly trying to probe past his aura to guess at his emotions. She need not have bothered – fists clenched at his side, jaw equally tense, he was the picture of confrontation ready to strike.

Cool it, she whispered his way.

When Brennan said nothing, Freya reached out and touched his back, rubbing in what she hoped was a soothing way for a few seconds. He froze, but it was a different type of rigidity, born out of shock.

Sure enough, when his golden-brown eyes met hers again, they were wide with confusion and a swirl of emotions.

Better? Freya smiled, removing her hand.

Brennan gulped, then nodded briefly. The distraction had worked, and he was now grounded again. Smugly satisfied with herself, Freya folded her arms and mockingly glared at her friend. "Sam! Is there anything else that you forgot to tell us? Besides, you know, that your friend knows Girona like the back of his hand and that Cortés is the bad guy?"

Oblivious to what had transpired, and apparently relieved that he'd eluded them, Sam grinned. "Nope, but I'll let you know if I remember something."

Freya muttered something under her breath, then walked to the desk and took a seat on the chair. Brennan followed shortly, though he was lost in his thoughts.

His partner's touch was burned in his back, a tingle still running across where she'd rubbed. Something about the connection had split through his jealousy and foolhardiness, and instead calmed him down enough to think clearly.

As he sat in a chair facing Freya and watched the two ghosts floating between them, Brennan's gaze remained glued to Emmanuel. Though Freya had not noticed it, he'd seen the grim expression that gripped Emmanuel's face once Cortés' name was mentioned. It didn't take a genius to realize that what he saw on the ghost's face could only mean trouble.

What the hell is this all about? Brennan was about to voice his thoughts, when the same voice he'd been hearing for the past hours stopped him.

Do not ask anything out loud, or you risk scaring away a potential ally.

More riddles? Brennan questioned.

Wiseman, let Freya handle this because, no offence, but sometimes you are not the most diplomatic person around.

Oh, and she *is?* Brennan's voice dripped of sarcasm. *It's because she lost control that Emmanuel found out first hand that she's a Sage.*

A laugh echoed in his head and Brennan narrowed his eyes. *What's so funny?*

You will find out soon enough. Perhaps it would be time for you and Freya to start working together.

With that fair advice, Tyr left Brennan to ponder its words. *I would if she'd stop trying to beat me up.*

As soon as the words actually registered with his brain, Brennan marveled at his own hypocrisy. Based on the night they'd spent talking together, he readily concluded that Freya would give him a chance if he wasn't so keen on pissing her off.

In an effort to show his good intentions, he resolved to turn the immaturity level down a notch. One way to do that was by setting his emotions aside and being nice to Emmanuel.

Nice... Brennan had to stop himself from making a face. However, he had no choice. Sighing, he got up and walked behind Emmanuel. Placing a hand on the ghost's shoulder, he casually asked, "How did you two meet, anyway?"

Emmanuel jumped at the contact, startled by it, and turned to Brennan wide-eyed. "You're a Sage, too?"

Brennan bit back the retort about to escape him. He glanced at Freya, whose hopeful eyes were settled on them, and instead replied, "My question first."

Emmanuel held his gaze for a beat, then said, "I was roaming the streets when I ran into Sam. He seemed to be in need of something. Since I knew the city well, I provided him the information he needed."

"At no cost," Sam grinned. "Em didn't know I had more than one question, and I bet he soon regretted it... But he kind of became my go-to guy."

"So *that*'s how you were so useful back then," Freya muttered jokingly.

Sam threw her a mock-offended look, then shrugged. "May have been. Either way, once Em helped me out, every time I was in the area I'd stop by and we kept in touch."

Brennan had been watching the newcomer carefully, trying to read past the façade.

"Now your turn," Emmanuel taunted. "An answer for an answer."

"I'm no Sage," Brennan smirked – he actually wanted to sneer at him, but caught himself in time. Before he could continue, Freya stood up and walked over.

"Nope, Brennan's something else entirely. Meet my Wiseman partner, who has the bad habit of pissing me off."

Emmanuel gave her a puzzled look, even as Sam chuckled at the introduction.

He then turned to Emmanuel and explained, "Wiseman are much like Sages – they also fight ghosts. However, as I told you long ago, a Sage's powers come from the four elements. Well, a Wiseman's powers come from his internal emotions. More so, their energy gets sucked when the spiritual powers are used, which makes the whole situation a bit dangerous."

"But doesn't that make it hard to fight?" Emmanuel pointed out, then glanced at Freya. "Or do you let your girl do the fighting for you?"

Brennan was about to retort something, but Freya beat him to it.

"First off, I'm not *his* girl, thank you very much. And second, are you saying girls can't fight?"

The Wiseman was gleeful at her sharp tone, and Emmanuel's stricken expression. Sam looked from one to the other, then laughed awkwardly. "Come on, Frey, Em was joking! He has no filter sometimes."

Emmanuel seemed to snap out of his surprise, then grasped Freya's hand in his, bowing over and kissing it. Brennan nearly gagged. Freya, on the other hand, blushed at the gesture, before pulling her hand away.

"Don't think some old-school romance trick is getting you out of this. Well?"

Emmanuel laughed good-naturedly, then admitted, "I am sorry, I did not mean it such. Of course girls can fight, sometimes they are much better at it than men. I meant no offence, to either of you."

Freya squinted at him for a brief moment, then nodded, seemingly satisfied. Biting back a comment, Brennan intervened, "To answer you, I do fight my own battles, don't need powers to do that. But I do avoid using them unless absolutely necessary."

"That explains the whole Wiseman thing," Emmanuel mused aloud after a brief moment of reflection. "You had me confused for a second there."

Freya observed them, thinking that Emmanuel could really help them. It must've been a real stroke of luck that he'd landed in their path – and that not many explanations were needed. She wanted to ask Tyr about it, but the entity seemed mighty busy these days.

Brennan, on the other hand, had difficulties controlling his reaction to the ghost. There was something about Emmanuel, a shifty quality to his gaze that warned he was not to be trusted. Plus, there was the way he kept looking at Freya like the sun rose and set with her.

Ugh. Get a grip on.

Brennan gritted his teeth, resolving to stay in control. Despite his best intentions, the itch couldn't be scratched, and he gave in. Since Freya was not paying attention to him, he closed his eyes and forced every single ounce of jealousy to the back of his mind, burying it there for good.

Though most guys were capable to compartmentalize emotions, he was able to quite literally control them. Brennan took the little green monster and literally locked it shut, where it was to remain for the next foreseeable time.

When he opened his eyes, he felt considerably better and was able to look at Freya without betraying himself.

"So you were mentioning the Cathedral earlier..." Emmanuel was asking. "Why?"

"The bad guys may be hiding in it, and we wanted to check it out. But we can't use our powers inside of it." Brennan was trying not to reveal everything, but if he really wanted the spirit to be able to help them, sooner or later he knew he would have to trust him.

Better later than sooner, he mused darkly.

Emmanuel shared a look with Sam, who gave an almost imperceptible nod. Almost, because Freya caught it out of the corner of her eye, just before the ghost said, "I think I know why."

"Care to share?" Freya questioned, forgetting all about what the two might hide.

Emmanuel hesitated for a fraction of a second, before revealing what he knew. "Well, the Cathedral is a center of energy on Earth, nourished by the faith of humans. Because of it being a spiritual go-to place, no power can be used inside of it. If anyone should try to, then it would be instantly absorbed by the Cathedral."

"So there's no hope of me and Brennan being able to use our abilities on the inside?" Freya was disappointed, as it was much the same information she knew from her last time, and what Seamus had told them.

"I'm afraid no," Emmanuel shook his head. "Unless the surge of power can be greater than that of the Cathedral, then it is a definite no. But still, I think you may be right about the ghosts hiding in there."

As Emmanuel chatted, Brennan's powers were growing at their max. *This is my chance, he's too busy to notice anything.* Fixating his gaze on the ghost as though in deep listening, he told Freya telepathically. *Keep him busy, I want to check his aura a bit.*

Much like living humans, ghosts carried an aura that held their history and ancestry. As a Wiseman, Brennan was most well suited to read it properly. His uncanny people skills came with the internalization of the abilities he was gifted with. Though it was not something he used much –

sometimes he saw too much in a person, and could not unsee it after – Brennan felt the need to push past the limits just this once.

Though Freya's facial expression hadn't changed, Brennan could tell she was irritated in her reply. *Why? He's Sam's friend, and I trust him.*

Perhaps you do, but I don't, was the only answer he was willing to give – but didn't. Instead, he took a deep breath and said, *I've been warned to be careful on this mission, and I intend to be.*

Warned by whom? Freya probed curiously.

Brennan was evasive in the response. *Someone* I *trust.*

The Sage was silent for a few seconds, eyes on Emmanuel as he talked about the odd behavior of the Spanish groups for the past weeks. *All right. But make it short and don't lose more energy than necessary. I plan to check the city out later and you'll be coming with me.*

Got it, partner, Brennan teased, then cut contact as he concentrated.

An expectant fire burned at the pit of his stomach and he smiled inwardly. He mentally looked through a list of emotions and focused on what he felt at the moment which was...nothing. Well, there was the jealousy he'd hidden, but releasing it would mean two things. First, Freya would definitely get a whiff of it thanks to the bond. And second, there was a chance he'd lose control of it this time.

Better not risk it, Brennan decided, and instead looked over his other options. After five minutes of frustration, he was losing his calm. *All right. So no other emotion that I feel is strong enough...Damn!*

The Wiseman was about to give up, when a thought struck him. It took every ounce of self-control he had to avoid jumping in the air and yelling his victory. Instead, he jubilantly glanced at his partner. *My emotions aren't strong enough, but Freya's anger was, and for a moment I felt it as my own. So, technically, nothing stops me from using it. All I'd have to do is relive that emotion and use it to activate my powers.*

Satisfied with his more-than-brilliant idea, Brennan took three breaths, exhaling slowly. He turned to the window of the room and pretended to be interested in the landscape.

When he was sure Emmanuel's attention was on Freya and Sam who were now taking turns explaining to him their presence in Spain, Brennan closed his eyes and touched the dragon medallion around his neck.

His senses focused on Freya, so close to him – then he recalled the emotion to his mind. The anger boiled in his blood, nearly overwhelming him. Brennan kept it in check as he used it to access the fireball at the pit of his stomach. The stronger the emotion, the longer he could keep going.

And this is no simple aura check-up.

Using the rage to his advantage, Brennan unlocked the power within and let it fill him slowly. He sent a small parcel of it to circle Emmanuel which, of course, passed unnoticed by him and Sam, but not by Freya.

From head to toe, Brennan examined the ghost as fast as he could without forgetting places, knowing that his time was limited. However, his intended search didn't give the results he'd been expecting.

Brennan had been hoping to find at least a small part of the living Emmanuel, but it seemed luck wasn't on his side. Suppressing his disappointment, the Wiseman continued his analysis. In spite of starting to feel dizzy, Brennan knew his gut instinct never betrayed him, and it was telling him that there was something about Emmanuel that both he and Freya had to know.

After another few minutes of a futile search, Brennan had to admit he might've been mistaken. He was about to end the process, when Freya's voice rang in his mind.

There, Brennan!

She'd shadowed his search, tapping it with hers, until both their spiritual strength had unearthed something. A part of Emmanuel's aura was lighted, and Brennan focused on it. He let the parcel of his energy confound itself with the small part of living essence. The energy he instantly felt was unknown to him, but it seemed potent.

I know this... Freya mumbled, vaguely aware of Sam's continued conversation with Emmanuel.

Whose is it? Brennan asked.

I can't... It's odd, but I can't place my finger on it. But it's definitely someone I know or... knew.

Brennan was about to question Freya further, when he sensed a tug from the connection. Before he could react, a wave of weakness washed over him. He dropped to the ground, unable to support himself standing any longer.

&&&

Tyr snapped to from its nap, and stepped closer to the fire. Linking across the distance to the two teenagers' minds, it caught Brennan's loss of energy, and its cause. There was something about the ghost the Wiseman picked up on.

With its additional senses, Tyr was able to pinpoint it was related to Emmanuel's history as a human, and his associations. Unable to get enough information by simply reading the aura, Tyr decided to follow the grain of memory to its source.

The tiger's attention was taken away from the teenagers as it followed the source to its root.

In a secluded part of the city, near what appeared to be a large warehouse, was the ghost Gustav and the demon Raksh. Tyr tuned into their conversation in time to hear the last of it.

"I am telling you, I felt something. Those two will be a nuisance."

Despite Gustav's threatening tone, Raksh only stared back affably. "It isss your problem, not mine. You chossse that boy of yoursss."

"Demon!"

"If I tap into it, they will feel me. The girl already wantsss my blood, and the Wiseman will sssoon follow." The demon scowled. "I need them both alive, but unaware."

Gustav's fists clenched, then unclenched as he maliciously whispered, "Very well. But then I get to have my fun with Freya. We have unfinished business since –"

Raksh lifted a hand, effectively silencing him. "Sssilence! We are no longer alone."

Though the tiger should have been invisible to his eyes, the wraith looked straight at Tyr. His lips moved into a chilly sneer. "You again..."

Feeling the tendrils of darkness eagerly move forward, Tyr broke the contact in time, and was back in the palace of the gods.

"That was foolish!" Osiris admonished, having sensed the disturbance in his realm.

Tyr turned around, eyes shining with anger. *You did not tell me everything. That demon is much too powerful. To see me when I was cloaked in your protection? He may serve a master who is imprisoned, but you are done fooling me.*

Isis, never far from her husband, intervened before the situation got out of hand. "We suppose Set is somehow feeding it, but we cannot –"

Show me the god.

"Tyr, really!"

Show me Set, in his cursed cage, otherwise you are done using these two youngsters as bait!

Isis bit her lip, dark eyes shining with conflict, then shrugged. She lifted a hand and an orb shone in it. Within its foggy depths an image developed, more vibrant with each passing second. Tyr stepped closer, and saw indeed a cage. Trapped between the metal bars was a darker version of Osiris, with eyes that glinted like coal.

As though sensing he was being watched, Set lifted his gaze to the ceiling. "You can keep me here for as long as you wish, brother. I will eventually escape, and you will rue the day you imprisoned me!"

Guards with jackal heads stepped to the bars, tapping them. Electricity rang through them and the earth, and the god dropped to the ground in pain.

Set's face, contorted in fury and hate, was the last thing Tyr saw before the orb disappeared.

"Satisfied?" Osiris asked.

Not nearly... Your brother is dangerous.

"Don't we know it," the god muttered morosely.

You know he is reaching out to Brennan and Freya in dreams. He is no longer blocked, but getting stronger every day.

Isis shared a tormented look with Osiris. "Tyr may be right."

What will he want, if he escapes?

"Power," Osiris answered without hesitation.

Since he is the one behind these ghosts getting weapons they can use to hurt humans, there must be something else... Why pick the conquistador?

Another glance between the gods, another hesitation. It was Isis who whispered, "Cortés is a Cursed One. He blasphemed so much of his living, that in death his soul is twisted. Soon, he will become the demon he was meant to be. As for what Set sees in him... He needs someone to link ghosts. Set does not have Osiris' dominion over the dead, nor his strength. Because of that, he is looking for a stronger phantom to achieve it for him."

And the demon cannot?

"Raksh is a pawn, easily disposable and swayed," Osiris snorted. "Set would want someone more like him – and Cortés fits the description. He think an army ruled by the conquistador would help him obtain the relics."

Tyr paused, mulling over their words. Then, it inclined its head in deference. *Thank you for being truthful with me.*

"What will you do with the information?" Isis asked.

Ensure it falls into the right hands, Tyr retorted, then turned back to the fire where it could observe Freya and Brennan. *What now?* it wondered quizzically.

Chapter 11

Everything happened fast after Brennan tapped into Emmanuel's aura. The room around him started spinning, and he dropped to the ground. Dimly, he could hear noises around him, and his partner's anxiety washed over him in repetitive waves.

"Brennan!" Freya rushed and knelt beside him, placing a hand on his shoulder.

"What's happening?" Emmanuel asked, confused.

"Are you okay?" Sam added, moving closer.

"Stay away!" Freya warned, pulling the Wiseman more towards her. The two ghosts watched, agape, as she grasped his hand, trying to peer under his bent head to meet his gaze. "Bren, come back to me."

With his remaining energy, Brennan recalled his spiritual force to him. Like a magnet, it was stuck to Emmanuel's aura. For a brief moment, he could almost see a string linking them both, and no matter how much he tugged, it wouldn't come loose.

The Wiseman's eyes started to close and his breath grew shallower. Strength escaped him in huge bursts. Eyelids heavy, he was ready to pass out. Freya's voice was muted, as though they were separated by thick walls, despite her being close by.

Unwilling to let him lose consciousness, and pushed by pure instinct, Freya reached out for the medallion. The instant her fingers clasped it, a blue light enveloped them both, and she felt a wave of energy pass from herself to Brennan. She started to struggle against the pull, but Tyr's voice stopped her. *No! It is the bond, Freya. Let it be.*

As suddenly as it had appeared, the light dimmed and Brennan opened his eyes, gasping for air. He raised his head and his forehead nearly collided with Freya's, whose hands tightly gripped his shoulders. She blinked dazedly, then realized their precarious position and quickly pulled away.

Brennan thought over what he'd just sensed – while Freya's energy was being transferred to him, he'd caught something... Another energy mingling with it. He couldn't identify the source, but he'd never sensed anything quite as potent before. All Brennan could determine was its purity, and the lack of evil within it. Wisely, he decided against asking Freya about it – for the time being.

"Are you all right, Brennan?" The Wiseman broke the eye contact with the Sage and looked up to see both Sam and Emmanuel peering at him. Brennan had hoped the glow of the medallion passed unnoticed, but their curious gazes quickly dispelled the notion.

Smiling reassuringly, he came up with an easy lie. "Sure, was just testing Freya on this new trick we learned."

"Some trick..." Sam muttered, but shut up with a glare from Freya.

She stood, then offered Brennan her hand and he got up to his feet as well. Freya took one look at him, then turned to the ghosts. "We're going to do some research of our own. Let Seamus know we'll be meeting him at dinner time with our results."

Sam nodded, then he and Emmanuel floated to the door. As they were about to pass through it, Freya called out to them.

"Don't go too far, Sam, if you go out. The streets aren't safe. Gustav's people probably know we're here by now."

Sam nodded, but the minute he and Emmanuel were outside of the room, he grabbed his friend's forearm. "We need to get more info."

"Sam..." Emmanuel groaned, but half-smiled. "You don't change. You really are the perfect informant for the Sages! But you heard Freya, and she is right."

"Yeah, yeah, but we'll be careful. Any information we can gather, especially on how Gustav's mixed in all of this, can be useful to them."

Emmanuel hesitated, then carefully agreed. "Very well, my friend. I will follow you."

The spirits dematerialized, only to reappear on the steps of the Cathedral. The moment their phantom forms had completely shown up, a strong wind picked up from the ground.

"Uh oh..." Sam muttered, glancing around.

"Sam!" Emmanuel warned, pointing towards the doors of the Cathedral. The younger boy's eyes widened as they registered the group facing them.

&&&

Tyr pulled back from Freya's mind, finding Isis still in the surroundings.

The goddess next to the tiger and caressed its fur. "Why the torment?"

What do you know of the dragon manuscript, and its powers?

"Why do you ask?"

For once, I wish I could get a straight answer from you, Isis, Tyr grumbled. *Freya and Brennan were affected by it, and now I sense a much deeper connection between them. Not only can they feel each other's pains and emotions, but their powers are linked as well.*

The goddess hesitated for a beat, before pointing out, "It is not that much different than when they fought the Vikings, and Brennan saved her with his vital energy."

The tiger shook its head, adamant. *Perhaps, but it grows stronger, and they cannot control it as they should.*

Isis frowned, then murmured, "To answer you, I only know the book grants the guardians who protect it shelter. For Freya's parents, as you well know, it also connected them."

I do not wish that same connection upon Freya... It was a blessing, but also a curse.

Isis softened her gaze, reassuring, "This is not something you can choose for her, Tyr. Much as you may see it as a threat, Brennan and Freya will grow to use it properly. In their case, they will be able to reinforce each other by adding to their powers. Freya will be able to use some of Brennan's, and vice versa."

Emerald-golden eyes glinted in frustration, and the tiger growled softly. *I still do not like it.*

&&&

After Sam and Emmanuel left, Freya walked over to lock the door. Then she turned to Brennan, her eyes blazing with suppressed anger. "What was that?"

"I don't—" he tried, but Freya cut him off.

"I told you not to take any chances, Brennan!"

"I *didn't*!" he protested, eyes wide and honest. "That's what's odd... I honestly didn't take any risks."

Freya crossed her arms over her chest, pursing her lips. "Then what happened?"

"I think... I think it was what you showed me – that small area that echoed of the past. Speaking of which, how did you know about that, and what I was doing?"

Freya gave a small snort and the gleam in her eyes calmed somewhat. "It was impossible for me *not* to feel anything. Honestly, Brennan, you're lucky both Sam and Emmanuel have no powers."

"Why?" he asked, obviously puzzled.

Freya rolled her eyes. "The anger was cracking through the air like static. Even Seamus could've sensed it, and he doesn't have quite the same abilities anymore!"

Brennan's eyebrows rose way up, then he bit his lip with an amused expression.

"Why are you so smug?" Freya wondered warily.

"Because, Freya, that rage you felt...was yours."

Her jaw dropped, and for a beat she was silent. Then she narrowed her eyes on him. "You used *my* emotions to give you access to your powers?"

Brennan could see the fire lighting her eyes and decided to intervene before it was too late and he found himself kissing the ground – again. "I couldn't use anything else at the moment, and it was crucial that I analyze Emmanuel." Without giving her time to interrupt, he went on, "Besides, you didn't answer my question. How were you able to keep up with the process?"

Freya's eyes slowly returned to their normal gleam, and she shrugged. "Aside from all that static? The bond. Seems it's a bit more intense than either of us suspected."

Brennan recalled the fight with Cadmael, and how the connection had been forged between them. Like lightning striking, he realized a piece of the puzzle they'd missed back then.

Freya saw the look of realization on his face and jumped on it. "What is it?"

"You know... I think I just understood it better."

"How so?"

Brennan gestured to the armchair and, as Freya sat down on it, he dragged a chair to face her and took a seat. There was a tiny pause as he gathered his words, then he admitted, "That link is here for a reason – to protect us both."

"I thought that was a given," Freya said.

"Yeah, but why? Why is it important we're protected?" Brennan waited until realization dawned on Freya, before saying, "Exactly! Because we're both guardians of an artifact. Think for a second – if one of us loses energy, the other will provide it whether he wants to or not. That way, we're linked telepathically and can not only feel each other's emotions when they're potent, but if we concentrate enough, we can find out the location of the other."

"But what about the manuscript and what it caused?"

Brennan mulled it over for a few moments, then said, "I think, because we were trusting each other and opening up, the book decided to do the same. It opened to gift us something – which, we already established we won't know how powerful it is until we test it. But the bottom line is, both these objects are attuned to us. During our last fight with Cadmael, the medallion reacted to each wanting to defend the other, and it provided us with the link. Now, the book sensed this..." He stumbled for a minute, then caught himself, "new development, and also upgraded us."

"You make it sound like a superpower," Freya chuckled.

"Isn't it?" Brennan smirked.

"Mm, in a way I suppose it is." The Sage chewed on her bottom lip thoughtfully. "All right, I see where you're going with it. But what does that have to—"

"—do with Cortés?" Brennan finished her sentence. "Everything! You see, there's one thing Seamus hasn't told you. When you left this morning, I got it out of him."

"And what was it?" Freya raised an eyebrow curiously.

"Do you remember, before the battle with Cadmael, that Seamus was talking about how uniting our powers would make us extra strong?"

"Yes..." Freya nodded, trailing off as her curiosity was awakened even more. "I also recall you mentioning that Seamus kept something from us."

"And I was right," Brennan agreed. "It's the key to uniting our powers."

"Oh, stop with the drama act, and spill already!" Freya rolled her eyes.

"All right," the Wiseman grinned and leaned against the back of his chair, a lock of hair falling casually in his eyes. "In order for our powers to unite, we have to not only be tightly connected, but also have complete trust in one another."

Freya's eyes flickered for a second, but Brennan couldn't guess what exactly it was that he'd seen in them. He tried to catch the Sage's emotions, but found himself cut off from her.

"So we basically have to trust each other with our lives?" Freya tried to confirm, her voice guarded.

Brennan inclined his head in assent, eyes never leaving her tight expression.

It was if he'd just pronounced a death sentence. Tears filled Freya's eyes, and her shoulders slumped. She sighed heavily, then passed a hand over her face in a gesture of total hopelessness.

Freya then stood up from the armchair and walked to the window, feeling Brennan's intent gaze on her. She could also sense the recollection of that night crawling back to her, wanting to infiltrate itself in her mind again. *No! That's enough!* Taking a deep breath, she murmured, "Brennan, I... I can't. I'm sorry."

He frowned, though she couldn't see him. However, as the image tried to forcefully return to her, Freya had let her guard down a little and Brennan became aware of her sadness and weariness. "Freya, unless I'm mistaken," he said gently, "this is the only way to get rid of Cortés. Our united powers would be enough to destroy that sword. And Cursed One or not, he'd be lost without it."

"I know, but... Just give me some time," Freya's voice was strained. "My past is complicated, as is yours, and neither of us is ready to share everything, not to that extent. Not yet, at least." She turned to him, her eyes pleading. "The image I last saw of my parents still bothers me. I need to somehow over-rule it, or else I won't be able to focus on this mission. And this is *so* not the time to have a fit."

Brennan nodded at her, his eyes sympathetic. Inwardly, he wished he could help out more, but as long as she wouldn't reveal everything, there was no way he could. *Until then, I'll have to help her from afar,* he thought. "It must be hard for you, but I get it. And you're entirely right. As much as we both want Cortés gone once and for all, I'm not exact-ly ready to go down memory lane either."

Freya gave a small laugh at his expression, and Brennan cracked a grin. "Now, enough yapping, I think it's time for some action," he smirked.

The Sage rolled her eyes and muttered something that sounded suspiciously like, "Boys and mood swings."

"Look who's talking!" Brennan scowled at her, having heard quite clearly. "Just who wanted to kick my ass not even two hours ago?" Despite his words, he was happy of the lighter tone of the conversation.

Freya smiled innocently, but soon dropped the act. "Well, I had a good reason to. You were being incredibly im-mature!"

"Right..." Brennan trailed off, not wanting to start another scene, but then his curiosity got the best of him. "So I
was wrong about you and Spanish guy?"

"Actually, he asked me out when you weren't listening..."

Brennan gaped in shock, unable to tell whether Freya
was joking or not. When she merely met his gaze unflinch-
ingly, an odd sinking sensation stirred in his stomach. He
looked away to hide it, but Freya snickered.

"I can't believe you, Bren!" The Wiseman narrowed his
eyes, but the twinkling in her eyes clued him in that he'd
been fooled. "Of course you were wrong!"

He shrugged nonchalantly, managing yet again to conceal his feelings. "Well, you never know... Girls are weird that
way."

Freya scowled, her fists automatically clenching at the
tone of his voice. "I'll never understand how you can turn
from a sweet guy to an impossible one the next!"

"Wait, you think I'm sweet?" Brennan's jaw dropped,
even as the sensation in his stomach turned into something
else. After a split second of staring in shock, he shook his
head and went back to his regular self. "If you want to know,
that's part of my charm!"

Freya leveled an incredulous look on him. "More like
split personality."

Brennan was about to retort, but she was no longer paying attention. "Did you hear that?" Freya was glancing
around the room, eyes narrowed suspiciously.

"Hear what, exactly?"

"That..." Freya trailed off, biting her lip. *Was it just my
imagination? But I was sure I heard a cry for help...* Her frown

deepened as she scanned every nook and cranny of the room, trying to determine whether the shout had come from within the hotel or outside of it. Her gaze landed on Brennan, who was watching her attentively. "You seriously didn't hear that cry?"

"No, but I can feel someone's distress close by." When he tried to probe further, the energy eluded him. "Do they sound familiar?"

Freya closed her eyes and her spirit spread in an attempt to find the source. Oddly enough, she couldn't. "It's weird, Brennan, but I can't. It's almost as if it disappeared off the face of the Earth."

After a moment of pondering the matter, Brennan stood up from his seat. "Watch the master at work."

Freya arched an eyebrow in silent inquiry, but the Wiseman was already acting. His gaze clouded with the strength of the spirit used, and the room fell away to the background. Brennan let the power fill him as before. Latching onto the bond with Freya, he used it to track the essence she'd sensed, sending it as far as it would go.

Within mere seconds of venturing outside the hotel walls, the energy returned to him like an elastic band snapping back into place. The sheer force of it caused Brennan to lose his balance and stumble to the floor ungracefully.

Freya snickered. "What part of that was I supposed to watch again?" She nevertheless offered him a hand and helped him up.

"Whatever it was," he said, ignoring her remark and dusting himself off, "I'm pretty sure it's gone."

Tormented by an odd instinct, Freya was unable to agree.

You are right to doubt it, Tyr whispered. *Try again – but with your powers.*

But I already have, it was useless!

Sometimes, what you can do and achieve needs to be triggered or activated by another person. In this case, Brennan's.

So you're saying that he may have uncovered the source of the cry? Freya asked. She took the silence that followed as confirmation and shut her eyes again.

Using the breeze she felt coming from the open window, Freya let her power mingle with its essence and fill her wholly. She then accessed the trace of the cry she'd felt, and was surprised to find it. Not willing to linger further, she sent a nudge to find its origin.

Brennan, now sitting on the bed, was observing the Sage. He was concerned at the familiarity of the vibe he'd caught, as though it was someone they both knew.

But who?

He was pulled out of his ruminations when Freya's eyes snapped open. "I know where it's coming from!"

"What? Where?" Brennan questioned, but the Sage was already out the door and he had to hurry to catch up with her.

"It's no wonder your energy was slammed back into you," she said to Brennan as he jogged by her side. "There's a barrier surrounding the place, and nothing can get in or out. Nothing spiritual, anyhow."

Brennan tried to mask his concern – these were words he'd heard once before. Nonetheless, he shadowed his partner as they exited the hotel through the back door and broke into a run, the wind slapping against their faces. "So where is the place?"

"Can't get a clear read, but we're heading there," Freya said. "I'm keeping in contact with the vibration emerging from it. We're in the right direction."

Brennan could only nod as Freya picked up the pace through the city's streets. The sun was rising, bathing everything in a warm glow, and the sheer beauty of it was distracting. Just as he was about to ask the Sage again about their destination – seeing as he was starting to get breathless – Freya turned a corner, then came to an abrupt stop.

"Oh, no..." she whispered.

Brennan followed her gaze with his own and groaned when it landed on the Cathedral. *Figures.*

Even in the light of the day, the building still had an eerie air about it. Freya couldn't help the shivers running down her spine and the hairs on her neck rising as those of a hissing cat.

"Emmanuel was right," she admitted, breaking the silence with an odd tone. "There's no way we can use our abilities in there. I can feel it all the way to here, much more than I did in the past."

"That may be true, but I wouldn't let it deter us. We can still try, and I bet a solution will be revealed in time." Whatever else he would've added was lost when the voice reappeared in his mind.

Do not enter that building, Brennan, it warned. *It is too dangerous for both of you. Make sure especially to keep Freya out of it for the whole duration of your stay in Spain.*

Why? Brennan asked. *The bad guys may be hiding in there, and we'll have to fight them eventually.*

Not in the Cathedral, I can guarantee it.

How can you be so sure? the Wiseman questioned, getting just the teensiest bit annoyed by Tyr's confidence.

First, because Cortés will not want to confront you on a territory where his powers do not work. And second, because you two will choose the place of the final fight.

Brennan restrained himself from gaping, *And just how are we going to do that?*

He received no answer back. After delaying for a few more seconds, he finally sighed and addressed Freya. "This is where the cry for help came from?"

The Sage nodded, her gaze still glued to the Cathedral. "Yes, I'm sure. But how..." She trailed off, overwhelmed by the building's simple presence.

"More like *who*," Brennan corrected. "Say, Freya, are you sure the voice didn't sound familiar?" She shook her head in response. Brennan cocked his head at her, his mind racing as he thought of who might've called Freya. The explanation that struck him chilled his blood.

Damn! If this is a trap, we walked right in it!

He voiced his realization out loud, but Freya didn't seem fazed by the news. "I already thought about that, but I don't think so. I mean, why would Cortés want to fight on a territory bad for all of us? It would be a lose-lose situation."

Brennan pursed his lips, Freya's reasoning making sense. Tyr's warning echoed in his mind, and he saw the opening as an opportunity to share with his partner what he knew, without telling her how he had come about the information.

"Freya..." He paused until she turned to him. "If we can't fight Cortés here, then maybe we could lead him to a place that would favor us."

Freya seemed to consider the possibility, then slowly nodded. "Yeah, that's a good idea."

Her tone was a bit surprised, and for some reason, Brennan couldn't stop himself from retorting, "Well, what do you expect? I am, after all, the best Wiseman there is."

"Oh, really?" Freya muttered sarcastically. "Gee, that's news to me."

Shaking her head, she faced the Cathedral again. Raising his eyebrows at the dismissal, Brennan decided to show her that he didn't enjoy being ignored. "Well, you know, I'm thinking that maybe I should be the one making the plans around here from now on."

That got Freya's attention, and she faced Brennan with a glare. "What was that?"

He ignored the warning that flashed in her eyes. "I'm a guy, after all, and we were born take things in charge."

"So that you can save damsels in distress?" Freya retorted glacially.

"Precisely."

Setting her jaw firmly, Freya stepped up to the Wiseman and buried her fiery grey eyes into his sweet golden ones. Being a few centimeters shorter than him didn't seem to affect her. "Listen here, Brennan, because I'll only say this once. Before you came, I could very well take care of myself and fight the ghosts by myself. And I still can! I'm not some weakling teenager that pleads for mercy, nor do I need saving. I could've done this mission all by myself, but since Seamus didn't give me a choice, I had to accept having you as a partner. However, you will *not* take charge of the situation. Not unless I die! Is that clear?"

Hmm... I went just a teensy bit too far this time. Brennan had the foresight to realize it and mumbled, "Crystal."

Freya opened her mouth to add something, but in that moment a ghost passed through the nearest wall. They turned their heads and recognized it immediately: it was Emmanuel.

"Thank the heavens I found you two!" he breathed out in relief as he floated to them.

"Emmanuel? What are you doing here?" Freya asked, her grey eyes returning to their normal gleam.

The ghost glanced between them both, an edge in his voice. "I was about to ask you the same."

Brennan shrugged, oblivious to the relief on Emmanuel's face. "Freya heard a cry for help and using our powers we tracked it here and—"

He was interrupted by the Sage, who stopped scouring their surroundings, her body oddly rigid. "Where's Sam?"

No... Freya attempted to quiet the fast beating of her heart, but found she couldn't breathe as easily any longer. *It couldn't have been!*

Emmanuel seemed close to tears when he answered. "That's why I was searching for you two. Sam's been kidnapped by Gustav's men. He's being held hostage inside the Cathedral."

Chapter 12

As Freya froze by his side, Brennan was busy sizing up Emmanuel – and warily thinking they'd concerned themselves with the wrong enemy.

The ghost's head was bowed in – one could only suppose – shame. Brennan's eyes were glued to him, attempting to figure out what kind of game he was playing. *This is definitely not good.* Despite his best efforts, he couldn't get a proper read to see if the emotion was faked or genuine.

Before he could use his spiritual strength, Brennan caught a different sensation. His heart raced and fury spread in his veins, overwhelming his peaceful state of being.

These aren't my feelings, he realized with a sinking feeling.

It didn't take more than two seconds to pinpoint whose emotions he was attuned to. He turned to his partner, whose own head was bowed, fists clenched and white-knuckled by her side. "Freya," Brennan said gently. "Freya, are you all right?"

She didn't answer. Desperately trying to find Sam's energy, the Sage was deaf to anything else. Her efforts were trampled by the barrier around the Cathedral, and after a few tries, she had to stop. At a loss on what to do, but refusing to give up, the Sage appealed to the tiger that was her guardian.

Tyr! Tyr, please do something!

The answer came almost immediately, tinged with regret. *I cannot, Freya. I know what you ask of me and I feel your pain. Listen to my words, and do not ignore their wisdom. That Cathedral has become a powerful anchor, one that could deplete me of my energy if I went in. For yourself or Brennan, it would cause you to be extremely vulnerable to ghosts. Sam is safe in there, as his essence is pure. Nothing will harm him.*

Tears stung Freya's eyes. *You're telling me to leave him? Tyr, he's like my younger brother! You know how much I love him! I can't leave him there... Not without trying to save him first!*

I understand your concern, child, but you are of no use to him dead, Tyr tried to reason with her, in vain.

Freya wouldn't give up easily, prepared as she was to risk her life in order to save Sam. Tears poured out of her eyes unreservedly. *Tyr, Gustav kidnapped Sam for a reason and—*

—it was in order to attract you and Brennan into a trap. And to get revenge on you for having defeated him previously.

Freya let the words sink in, strong with the confirmation that Tyr was right. Gustav had sunk low instead of confronting her, and it couldn't mean anything good for her, Brennan and Seamus.

Freya, heed my words, the tiger pleaded. *Use your powers. Can you not sense the evil lurking in the Cathedral? Can you not feel the eyes set upon you three? You are surrounded, and the ghosts are lying low, ready to capture you. Please do not give in and put all your lives in danger.*

The Sage didn't bother with a response, fully aware of how the place would block her powers. After all, it wasn't so long ago that she'd been in danger grave enough to lose her life. She couldn't ask Brennan to risk himself for her folly, and Emmanuel couldn't help any further.

Then I will go in alone, she decided.

Freya, no!

She'd already made up her mind, and resolutely blocked her mind. Freya felt an odd zing in her veins, almost as if something clicked in place, and faintly wondered if her ability to do so was due to the new powers the manuscript had gifted her.

Removing the thought from her mind, Freya wiped at her cheeks and raised her head, her expression determined. "I'm going in."

"What?" Emmanuel's shocked stare shifted between Freya and Brennan. He was looking at the Sage with wide eyes, not believing what he was hearing. But just as he started thinking about ways to stop her from entering the Cathedral, Brennan moved.

He was by Freya's side in a matter of seconds, holding onto her arm to immobilize her. "You're not going in there," he half-growled, meeting her gaze straight on.

Freya glared back, chin raised defiantly. "You have no right to tell me what I should or shouldn't do. I make my own decisions, Wiseman, and I'm going in to save Sam."

Brennan couldn't accept what his ears were telling him. He was staring at the Sage he was holding onto, taking in the determined gleam in her eyes, the need to save her friend. *Is she nuts!? She can get killed!*

Part of him understood what was pushing her to act in such a way. If anything was to happen to Sam, Freya would never forgive herself when she'd had a chance to save him.

That still doesn't mean I'm going to let her risk her life by walking straight into a trap and get captured. Not if I can help it.

Brennan couldn't fathom where the sudden urge to shelter Freya had come from, and he wasn't about to start looking for ways to explain it. Only one idea looped in his mind – there was no way he was letting her enter the Cathedral.

"Oh yeah?" Brennan's eyes hardened as he clenched his partner's arm tighter. "And how will you save him? By sacrificing your own life? You're no use to him dead, Freya!"

"He's right!" Emmanuel agreed and Freya turned her gaze to him. The ghost gulped when he saw the ardent gleam in her eyes, but nevertheless went on with a tone that wanted itself pacifying. "Whatever happened to him, Sam would not want to put you in danger, Freya."

Brennan gritted his teeth at the ghost's intervention, but as long as his words kept Freya away from doing something foolish, he'd restrain himself from punching him.

Movements in their vicinity drew his attention. Brennan extended his senses, trying to see if any ghosts were trying to attack. Out of the corner of his eyes, he kept an eye on Freya, hoping his and Emmanuel's words had gotten through – and that she'd changed her mind. Or at least that she was willing to listen to them.

His hopes were shattered when Freya released herself from his grip, avoiding his eyes. "I refuse to do nothing while Sam's in trouble. I'm going in, and that's final." With that,

Freya turned her back on them and broke into a quick jog toward the Cathedral.

Crap, now she's done it! Brennan muttered as he extended his senses instantly. He had to keep an eye on the Sage and their surroundings, if only to make sure the ghosts currently observing them would stay away.

"Brennan!" Emmanuel called to him.

What does he *want?* Brennan gritted his jaw, unwilling to deal with the spirit. Nonetheless, he turned a frosty gaze to him. "What?"

"You have to do something!" Emmanuel was saying. "She's going to her death!"

Brennan averted his eyes from him, not wanting to say something he'd regret. A bitter remark still escaped past his lips. "And I suppose you'd know all about that."

Emmanuel looked as if he'd been slapped. He opened his mouth to say something, but couldn't. Finally, the words came out in something merely above a whisper. "I... I did not... Brennan, I had nothing to do with this!"

The Wiseman sized up the ghost, then turned away dismissively. "Forget it. Just keep in mind that I'm not as easy to fool as Freya might be, Emmanuel." His eyes zeroed in on her shape in the distance, getting much too close to her target. "And as for Freya, you heard what she said. She won't listen to me."

"So you're just going to let her get killed?" Emmanuel asked incredulously.

Use your powers, Brennan, and stop Freya from getting into that Cathedral, Tyr's slightly panicked voice ordered. *Push your pride away, and do not let harm come to her!*

I would, but I don't think I have enough energy, Brennan admitted slowly.

The reply did not delay. *I will second you if I have to, but stop her from going in!*

"Listen, Brennan, I don't know why you don't trust me, or whatever I did that makes you so keen to hate me. I'm sorry, for whatever it was that I did. But please, stop Freya from entering that building."

Brennan shook his head and said in a bored voice, "Save it." He then sighed and clapped his palms together, tightly joining them. He drove them apart until they looked as if they were holding a ball of air.

The trick itself, if he was quick about it, would ensure he didn't faint while using spiritual energy. Plus, there was the added benefit of Emmanuel's shock as he stared, in awe with Brennan's powers.

Using his annoyance at the ghost, and his fury at Freya for not listening to him, the Wiseman used the force spreading in his veins out of his body and into the ball, creating an energy sphere.

"Wow..." Emmanuel remained speechless as Brennan went on with the operation.

He focused on the ball, which was now of a silvery color, and transferred his request to it. Slowly, it escaped the Wiseman's fingertips and raised itself in the air, where it dissolved into tiny particles, similar to a sand storm.

A wind picked up, carrying the remnants of the orb on its swift wings. Stronger with each passing second, it blew in Freya's direction.

&&&

Hang in there, Sam, Freya pleaded mentally with her friend. *I'll be there shortly.*

As she ran, the Sage remembered all the good times they'd shared, the silly things they'd done together, the missions they'd experienced together...

Tears brimmed in her eyes, blurring her vision, but Freya wiped them away furiously. *This is no time to get emotional. I'm coming, Sam!*

"Just hold on," she whispered aloud, pushing past the ache in her legs and running faster, driven by the urge to save her friend.

A shiver at the back of her neck had the Sage come to a sudden stop. She could sense an energy coming towards her from behind, a determined intent behind it. Tyr's words resonated in her head, warning her about the trap.

"What the –?" Freya muttered as she spun around, looking for the source.

Her eyes landed on the far-away forms of Emmanuel and Brennan, but could notice no danger. It wasn't until the wind blew in her face that the warning sensation became stronger. Freya's eyes flashed dangerously, settling on the Wiseman.

Brennan! Freya yelled mentally, but got no answer. Just as she was about to use her spiritual force to retaliate, bits of energy appeared around her, sparkling like diamonds – or rain drops.

They remained suspended in midair, even as Freya gaped. It didn't take a genius to figure out that Brennan was very keen on stopping her from entering the Cathedral, and that he was ready to do so at any cost.

"Brennan, stop this!" Freya yelled, but to no avail. The particles in the air started pulsating, emitting a low vibration that ran across her body, numbing it. Her limbs got heavy and her eyes clouded, and before the Sage could stop herself, she fell smoothly to the ground.

&&&

"Freya!" Emmanuel yelled as he saw the Sage paralyzed, eyes widened in shock and fear.

Brennan didn't waste any time. He started running to the Sage, with the ghost floating closely behind. They reached Freya as her body dropped in slow motion to the ground. Brennan grasped her by the waist right before she hit the cement, cradling her against him.

Ignoring the rightness of having her so near, he surveyed their surrounding warily. They were too close to the Cathedral, and he could sense the hidden phantoms, prepared to attack. He called once more upon his powers and let an invisible barrier surround Freya, himself and – after a second's hesitation – Emmanuel.

Brennan then bent his knees and picked Freya up in his arms, straightening up. His jaw was clenched, determined to bring her away from harm before anything else happened. He glanced down at her peaceful face, unsurprised she weighed no more than a feather.

"Is she going to be all right?" Emmanuel asked, true distress in his voice.

Brennan peered once more around, distractedly mumbling, "Angry at me, but perfectly fine otherwise. However, we won't be able to say the same thing if we don't get out of here."

"You're right. Follow me, please. I know a faster way to the hotel."

The Wiseman hesitated, still debating on trusting the ghost. However, realizing they had no other option, he nodded and trailed behind Emmanuel.

Neither saw the pair of eyes following them, then dematerializing into nothing.

&&&

O'Keeffe stared at the sheet of paper in front of him, tiredly rubbing his forehead. For the last few hours, he'd been sitting at the desk in his room, reading through books until he found mention of the conquistador. He picked up the latest text and reread it for the hundredth time.

"This is impossible," he muttered, throwing his head back and looking at the ceiling. "If it's true that Cortés loved power this much, there is absolutely nothing that can guarantee us that he has changed. And that means... His target will be of great importance."

Sighing, O'Keeffe closed his eyes for a few seconds. The dizziness was bothering him – he wasn't used to feeling helpless. Furthermore, he hadn't heard from the four teenagers since he'd left them. It struck the elder Sage that now might be a good time to check on them.

Before he could get to his feet, the memory assailed him – of the night when Freya's parents had been killed, the night that he'd sacrificed...

"No!" Seamus stood, shaking his head. "This is no time to start thinking about that. Cortés may have rallied all ghosts to him... If I do not soon find a flaw beside the sword he has, we cannot win this fight."

Seamus knew that the only other way to conquer was if Freya and Brennan united their powers. From observing their relationship, it was well apparent they were on the right track, but hadn't reached spiritual completion. Rather disturbingly, they were still far from achieving the goal.

Realizing he'd yet again derived from the subject, O'Keeffe exhaled heavily and ran a hand over his face. *This... Something has to give.*

At that moment, there was a knock on the door. Raising an eyebrow, O'Keeffe walked over and opened it. Emmanuel and Brennan faced him, and the Wiseman was holding what seemed like an unconscious Freya in his arms.

Seamus's eyes widened as they landed on the Sage. "What happened? Is she hurt?" His gaze flicked between the two teenagers.

The Wiseman smiled reassuringly. "Not to worry, professor, she's perfectly fine, only resting."

O'Keeffe stepped aside to let them in, and Brennan walked to one of the beds and placed Freya on it. He then motioned for Seamus to close the door.

Emmanuel was glancing from Brennan to Freya, looking as though he wanted to ask something. Finally, he said, "Shouldn't you wake her up now?"

"Not yet, or else she'll have my head on a silver plateau." Brennan turned to Seamus and went on, "I hope we didn't interrupt anything, but I had to leave Freya somewhere and since she couldn't tell me where the key to her door was..."

O'Keeffe waved the matter away impatiently. "Yes, yes, I understand. But what happened? And where is Sam?"

"Well..." Emmanuel's confession was halting, with an undertone of remorse vibrating through. "Sam's in the Cathedral. Gustav's men have him."

O'Keeffe's eyes showed his surprise, and before the barrage of questions took place, Brennan quickly caught him up to date.

Having learned what had taken place in the last few hours, Seamus dropped in an armchair and held his head in his hands. Brennan ignored the look Emmanuel was throwing him and approached the old Sage. "Professor... Seamus, please, you have to pull yourself together."

O'Keeffe raised troubled eyes to him, but slowly nodded. "Yes, you... you are right, Brennan." Clearing his throat, he asked, "How did they capture Sam, exactly?"

Emmanuel hesitated, and Seamus's gaze intuitively searched his. Biting his lip, the ghost then started telling his tale. "Well, I and Sam went to check out the surroundings. He wanted to find this one person, Raoul, whom he'd seen a few days back before warning you. We went by the Cathedral..."

"I thought I told you all quite clearly not to get near that building," O'Keeffe whispered under his breath.

"There was no changing Sam's mind," Emmanuel said. "When we appeared, the ghosts were expecting us. They knew we were coming, and a wind pulled Sam close to them like a magnet. I... I was held in place, and when Gustav showed up, Sam yelled for me to go get Freya. I did..."

Brennan frowned, but said nothing out loud. Thus far, the ghost's story seemed plausible, and he had no doubt that it would keep on being so. Despite it, he wouldn't trust the ghost completely until he had proof of his innocence.

O'Keeffe stood and placed a hand on Emmanuel's shoulder in unspoken support. "It's all right. There is nothing you could have done, in any case. You did the right thing, because you are now here with us and could tell us what happened. I would say, even more, that it was quite brave of you to go and look for help, regardless of how much you wanted to help Sam."

Brennan kept his opinion of how brave he thought Emmanuel was to himself, and instead glanced over at the dormant Freya on the bed. "Right," he cleared his throat, and O'Keeffe directed his attention to him. "I'm going to take my chances now and wake up Freya."

"What exactly happened?" Seamus asked.

Brennan threw him a sheepish look. "Well, she was going to go in to after Sam, so my only chance to save her was to, uh, force her to sleep."

O'Keeffe shook his head and a chuckle escaped him.

As he took yet another long look at Freya, Brennan's courage seemed to fail him, and he tried to delay the incoming disaster. "Umm, so Seamus, did you discover anything new?"

The elder Sage was not to be fooled, only smiled knowingly. "Brennan, wake Freya up." As the Wiseman groaned and gave him a pleading look, O'Keeffe shook his head again. "Do not fret, she won't be too mad."

"Yeah, right!" Brennan muttered under his breath.

Emmanuel threw him an amused look. "A bit of courage, *compadre*. She can't be that bad..."

Brennan didn't reply, instead moving closer to the bed. *I guess I can only hope that she'll be too sluggish to be angry.* He closed his eyes and concentrated hard on the Sage's energy, then called mentally, *Freya! Freya, wake up!*

His voice broke through the barrier that surrounded the Sage and she stirred awake, instantly aware of the Wiseman by her bed.

Groaning, she sat up in bed, clutching her head. "What the hell hap—"

Freya stilled as she recalled the last events – Sam kidnapped in the Cathedral, herself running towards it to free him, then Brennan's powers causing sleep. Freya's fists clenched in anger and a wave of rage unlike any other passed over her. It was enough to make her want to roar like the fiercest of lions.

Chapter 13

B rennan gulped, more than familiar by now with the signs of an incoming fight she displayed. He turned a pleading look to O'Keeffe, who only shrugged in response. Swallowing hard, Brennan cleared his throat and started hesitantly, "Uh... Freya?"

She was deaf to his plea, instead staring intently at the blankets in an effort to calm her powers. *Tyr... I can't control this...* Freya whimpered mentally.

The tiger's voice came almost immediately, concerned. *Calm down, child. Take a few deep breaths, but do not lose control.*

Freya tried to do as Tyr suggested, and through her efforts she heard O'Keeffe's voice. "Freya! Freya, are you all right? Answer me! Freya!"

Tyr! the Sage called.

Do not panic. Try to take a deep breath... Freya, no! Freya!

The Sage had turned deaf to its cries. A volcano erupted in her, controlled only by anger. She stood up with flaming eyes and lunged at Brennan, pinning him to the wall by the throat. Wrath strengthened her spiritual energy and physical endurance, transforming her grip into an unmovable one.

"What the *hell* did you think you were doing!?" she hissed furiously. "Sam's like my brother! Now, because you wouldn't let me go and save him, he may forever lost to us!"

"Freya, calm down," Seamus entreated as he hesitantly approached her, palms raised in a calming effort.

"If you had entered the Cathedral," Brennan wheezed past the choke hold, "you could be dead by now! Gustav wanted *you*! Don't you realize what that means?"

"I. Do. Not. *Care*!" Freya shrieked, and the calm light in her eyes had completely disappeared by then. Just as suddenly, lightning struck outside, near the hotel.

Brennan's gaze remained focused on Freya, while his powers were searching her, trying to find a way to put a stop to her tantrum. *Now would be a good time for you to appear,* Brennan begged the voice. *My partner seems to have lost control, and I'm honestly a bit scared right now.*

Nothing answered for a few seconds, then, *Freya's wrath is controlling her. You will have to try to breach her walls and wield control over the emotion.*

What? I've never done anything like that to another person!

You are a Wiseman, it is in your nature. Do not fear it, the bond will help you. Whatever you do, do not upset her more.

Very reassuring...

Brennan glanced outside out of the corner of his eye. Rain had started pouring down non-stop, hammering the ground fiercer than the Wiseman had ever seen. He couldn't help a frown at the sudden change in the atmosphere. His attention refocused on Freya, whose hair was whipped against her face furiously, entangling itself.

"Freya…" By Brennan's side, O'Keeffe was still approaching the Sage cautiously. "Brennan was right to stop you from going inside—"

"What do *you* know?" Freya asked furiously, spinning around to face O'Keeffe, while still keeping her hold on the Wiseman. "My parents are dead and you won't tell me what the hell happened! You always hide whatever is most important from me, and now Sam's been kidnapped! I refuse to leave him when I know I can help!"

Seamus narrowed his eyes and clenched his jaw. "You are acting like a selfish brat, Freya. If you had attempted to save him, you could have been killed!"

"You know *nothing*!" Freya yelled, and the window blew open and an icy wind swept in.

Realization dawned on Brennan at once, and the magnitude of what was happening sent chills down his spine. Forgetting about the hate he had towards Emmanuel, he turned to the ghost and firmly commanded, "If you value your existence, dematerialize and go elsewhere, now!"

After a first surprised look to Brennan, then a troubled one to Freya, the spirit nodded and disappeared.

"I know what she's doing!" Brennan shouted to be heard above the noise. "The elements!"

"Explain," Seamus commanded.

"You said a Sage's powers come from the four elements – fire, water, earth and air, right? Freya's unleashing them all! Water is the rain, air is the wind, and now all that's left is fire and earth!"

You have to stop her before she frees them, Brennan! Tyr warned.

Gee, you think so? the Wiseman retorted. Using all he could feel at the moment, Brennan let the strength of his spirit fill him wholly, ready to focus it on stopping Freya.

However, it seemed that not only were her powers out of control, they also enabled her sensitivity, sharpening the Sage's senses. She spun to Brennan, having felt the power surge within him.

"You have no right!" she shouted, and a lamp exploded near the curtains, flames soon licking the wall. Luckily, the wind and the rain that kept entering the room extinguished it before the fire alarm started.

Brennan realized at once that if he didn't act soon, Freya could do something to hurt them all – whether she was conscious of it or not.

&&&

Raksh stepped away from the Cathedral, glancing towards the hotel where the elements seemed to have converged. He used his darkness-fuelled senses, sending them to scout the area.

When they returned in moments, reporting on the Sage's loss of control and extensive display of energy, Raksh sneered. "So she has learned to use the book, and does not even know it."

His mind slithered towards his master, whispering, *She is the one who can free you. We are closer than we thought!*

There was no reply for a moment, then a growl rumbled through him, *Good...*

&&&

I have no choice.

Brennan thought back to how he was able to compartmentalize his own feelings for guidance, hoping something similar would work on his partner. He stretched his free hand to touch Freya's waist, his closest point of contact, thus grounding their connection.

The bond he always sensed around them, which had become part of him, seemed to centralize with clarity. After a slight hesitation, Brennan pressed through in Freya's mind, throwing himself in the midst of the chaos dominating her.

The hand pinning him shook as she sensed the intrusion, then their eyes locked and he read the confusion.

"Brennan?" Freya murmured, her voice tiny and afraid.

He took advantage of the distraction and grabbed her wrist, twisted it and released himself from her grip. He then turned Freya around, wrapping both arms around her tightly.

"Let me go!" Freya yelled, straining against his grip, but Brennan held good.

Calm down... The tone in her mind was peaceful, though his heart beat wildly in his chest. *This is not you, do not let it control you. Breathe, Freya. Breathe with me.*

He imagined a bubble of energy surrounding the chaos in her mind, capturing it, and holding it at bay. Brennan then pictured the sphere being squeezed like a deflated soccer ball, and the air escaping was the anger evaporating.

In his arms, Freya stopped struggling, and instead took a deep, shaky breath.

"That's my girl," Brennan murmured, not completely aware of what he was saying. "You can do it... In and out, Freya, in... And now out..."

Listening to his calm voice, the Sage was able to inhale, and the wave of anger receded until none was left. As she came back to, she realized Brennan had been able to use their link to tap into the fury and calm it down.

Huh… Guess having a Wiseman around is useful, after all.

Slowly, the wind retreated through the open window and before long, the sky outside cleared up and the rain stopped.

O'Keeffe shut the balcony door, then turned to Brennan. "It's all right now, you can release her."

After a slight hesitation, Brennan let Freya out of his arms. She leaned on the wall to remain standing, as if unable to rely on her legs. He had to fight the urge to keep her close by, if only to linger on the feeling of rightness that had come over him.

Brennan threw her a slightly apologetic glance. "Freya, are you okay?"

"Oh, she is perfectly fine!" O'Keeffe snapped bitterly. "She would have been fine even if she had kept awakening the elements." Noticing the Wiseman's confused look, Seamus said, "Brennan, would you mind leaving us? I think it's about time me and Freya had a heart-to-heart discussion."

Brennan nodded uncertainly, and left the room. As he closed the door behind him, he connected with Freya's energy and asked, *Do you want me to wait for you?*

Her reply was tired. *No. Just go, Brennan.*

Hesitantly, the Wiseman walked away from the room, but remained nearby. The energy he'd dispensed had somehow not tired him, perhaps because it had been more of a transfer through their bond than anything else.

Nonetheless, a very strong part of him wanted to make sure Freya was all right. Brennan stopped around the corner and slid down the wall, extending his legs and leaning his head against the wallpaper.

&&&

Back in the room, O'Keeffe had started pacing in silence. "I cannot believe you could act so foolishly!" he finally burst. "You placed us all in danger!"

Freya raised a hard stare towards him. "Oh? And you're not doing the same by not revealing my past?"

"I thought we had settled this, Freya," O'Keeffe's gaze gentled. "I am doing this to shelter you, for your own good!"

"Don't even give me that!" the Sage said as she stepped away from the wall. "You lied about my parents asking you to keep the secret. Do you even know how hard it is to not know where you come from? All my memories of those four years are gone! *Gone*, do you hear me!?" Tears streamed down her cheeks like rivers of diamonds, and she was unable to stop them.

O'Keeffe looked at his pupil helplessly. "Do *you* know how hard it is to keep all that from you? I am not your enemy."

Freya shook her head in denial, even as more tears followed. Without knowing how it had happened, she found herself in O'Keeffe's arms, crying her heart out. Time passed by slowly, and in her mentor's safe embrace, Freya let go of all her emotions.

Finally, after what seemed like forever but had only been an hour, Freya whispered, "I'm sorry, Seamus. I went a little overboard with everything."

"A little?" Seamus chuckled. "I would say so." He gently pushed her away and smiled down at her. "I apologize as well, for not being able to tell you all that I want. I promise, one day, that time will come."

"I know."

Freya smiled at Seamus, then said, "I'll go wash up, and meet you and Brennan for breakfast tomorrow morning, all right?"

O'Keeffe nodded and watched her leave the room. Then, he passed a hand over his face and sank in an armchair. "Mark, if there's one thing I can say is that she's got your temper. Definitely." Chuckling, O'Keeffe then picked up a pile of papers and started rereading them.

&&&

How could I have been so careless? Freya wondered. *I've never lost control this way.*

Maybe it's the stress of not being able to measure up with me, a teasing voice came.

Ha, ha. Very funny, Brennan, Freya retorted sarcastically, but couldn't help the smile from spreading on her face, bringing a twinkle that hadn't been there before back in her eyes.

Thank you, I do try, Brennan said. After a few seconds of silence, he said, *Open your door.*

Freya stepped over and did as he asked, surprised to find him there. Little did she know, the Wiseman had observed from afar as she left Seamus, and had felt her sorrow the entire time – unable to distance himself from their connection long enough.

In the end, he'd given in to his basic instinct and headed her to the room. *Only to make sure she's okay,* he tried to convince himself.

Despite the wry grin, Brennan's golden-brown eyes were filled with concern. "How are you feeling?"

Freya cringed in response, leaning against the door for support. Her recent flirt with unleashed spiritual energy, then the emotional backlash, had left her feeling wiped. "I'm...okay, I guess."

"You don't sound too sure," Brennan pointed out, frowning.

"Is that worry I hear in your tone?" she teased.

Relieved at the mischievous glint back in her eyes, Brennan shuffled his feet. "Now don't go getting any ideas. I'm allowed to be concerned for the sake of my partner."

"Thanks. I'll be all right as time goes by."

"Will you be able to focus on the mission?" Brennan asked, at the same time nearly smacking himself over the head for his loss of tact.

Freya shrugged, unfazed for once. "Of course! Who do you take me for?"

"I was just making sure. But really, Freya, try not to lose control like that again. You scared the crap out of me."

"Yeah, right," the Sage scoffed. "The mighty Brennan Dublin, winner of the Prize for Cockiness, grandson of the greatest Wiseman yet, *scared*? Don't make me laugh."

"It was worth a try," Brennan snorted. "You sure you don't want to chat?"

"In the middle of the night?" Freya chuckled easily, then rolled her eyes. "Thanks for coming by, but I was going to take a nap. Maybe later, if you don't turn into the other Mr. Dublin in the meantime."

Brennan gave her a long look, then nodded. "All right, then. Enjoy your rest."

He seemed like he wanted to say more, but instead bit his bottom lip thoughtfully. Freya hesitated for a brief moment, before stretching on her tiptoes and kissing his cheek.

"Thanks for what you did," she whispered in his ear, then pulled away quickly and closed the door.

Brennan was left, jaw hanging open, staring in shock for a few moments. Eventually, he raised a hand to his cheek, then shook his head ruefully. *This girl...*

Inside her room, Freya hit the bed with a groan, trying to ignore the odd sensation in her stomach. "He's my friend," she grumbled to the darkness, as though trying to convince it. "He's too annoying to be anything else than that."

Nonetheless, the feel of his arms around her as he'd calmed her down, his soft voice and serene demeanor had shaken her. Thinking back over her assessment, Freya snickered. *Serene? Brennan? I must be high.*

Freya turned to the side, curling up on the mattress and falling asleep almost immediately. She never caught sight of the closet door opening, and the soft glow escaping from the manuscript...

Chapter 14

Tyr was staring pensively at the fireplace when the gods appeared by its side. Their gloomy faces predicted nothing good. Warily, the tiger stood to its full height and leveled a curious gaze on them.

What is it?

"Your protégée," Isis explained. "When she was chosen to guard that book, much like Brennan with the medallion, we did not think of her youth."

And now you do? Tyr snorted, unable to stop. *What changed your mind?*

"Her slight instability a few moments ago, for one," Osiris cut in.

Freya is affected by the manuscript, you know that as well as I do! The powers that object decided to bestow on them, and has been sharing with Freya, alter the way they perceive the world and their own personalities.

"That may be so... But if she cannot handle it, we need to find another way."

What is that supposed to mean? Tyr growled.

"No need to get aggressive, my friend," Osiris lifted a palm pleadingly. "We will not harm Freya, but we may have to take the manuscript away."

A connection has already been established. Breaking that may have consequences neither of you can foresee.

"Perhaps," Osiris mused pensively, "and perhaps not. We cannot risk Set being unleashed."

Tyr paused in its next words, tilting its head to the side. *What does Freya's lack of control have to do you with your brother?*

Isis shared a warning look with Osiris, pursing her lips. "We might as well," she whispered, then addressed the tiger. "The demon Raksh sensed Freya's powers, and presumes he may be able to use her to release Set."

But he cannot. He needs the relics of the Underworld, as you explained.

"Yes…" Osiris trailed off for a moment, as though carefully choosing his words. "However, the unification of the Sage and Wiseman's powers, along with Freya's boost in abilities, may breach the prison in such a way it gives Set something to work with."

You are saying that Freya can help him escape, but the relics would actually release him from the imprisonment.

"Yes," Isis nodded.

Tyr glanced between the gods, noticing their seriousness. *I will keep an eye on Freya to ensure this energy she now has does not get out of control. You do not have to worry, Brennan did a good job helping her calm down.*

"Do as you will, Tyr," Osiris warned, "but if Freya loses control like this again, we cannot risk having the manuscript guarded by someone like her."

The tiger was about to answer, when a tug on its mind pulled it towards the fireplace. *Not the damn book again!*

Helpless, it watched as the glow from the book imbued Freya, and her being shone once more with whatever upgrade it had bestowed upon her.

"Be careful," Isis entreated once her husband had vanished. "The medallion may focus their link, but the manuscript is more fickle. Over the ages, these objects have developed their own conscience, their own way of connecting to their guardians."

Tyr could only exhale heavily, desperately trying to find a solution. If the book was removed from Freya, no one could tell what would happen next.

&&&

Brennan stood by Freya's closed door for a few moments longer after she went back in. Though he knew the Sage was shaken up, he was also mildly content that she'd sorted out the issue with Seamus. Nonetheless, confusion stirred underneath the surface of his thoughts.

The main reason for it was the intricacy of their bond, and its recent evolution. At any given moment, they could sense each other's emotions profoundly, and powers, without even trying. Brennan hadn't realized up until that very day how much it would come to change both their lives.

Ruefully shaking his head, the Wiseman moved down the hall, heading to the lobby of the hotel where he hoped to rest. Seamus was still slightly agitated, and the young man needed a few moments to himself. He surreptitiously glanced around at the staff, but it seemed no one had heard the commotion in the room.

As he rounded a corner, a wave of something hit him and he stumbled, leaning onto the wall for support. The medallion around his neck shone softly, and the Wiseman felt a surge of energy, uplifting him until he was a few inches off the ground. Just as he was about to lower himself back down, the glow stopped and he landed.

Brennan peered around once more, ensuring no one had seen anything – thankfully, he was alone and there were no cameras in the old-fashioned building. *Now what the hell was that about?* Guessing it must have been a type of after-effect to his previous actions, he started walking again.

Reflecting over the past few years of his life, Brennan concluded he hadn't amounted to much. Ever since his grandfather's death, he hadn't returned to the small village in Wales where he'd been born in, and had instead preferred to live in London. It wasn't because he was ashamed of where he came from, either. The problem was that he was no longer wanted there.

Sighing as he sat down in a much too comfortable armchair, Brennan rubbed his eyes and stared out the window of the main lobby. In the end, he was glad for the connection between him and Freya. No matter how much they fought, they could always rely on each other for help.

And a friendship is quite important for you, is it not? Tyr probed, trying to get to know the young man that was becoming a big part of Freya's life.

Brennan held back from rolling his eyes, and instead leaned his head against the armchair and closed his eyes. *It's true. And Freya... Well, I just never get bored with her. Not to mention we equal each other in skills and power.*

It must be fate, Tyr commented smugly.

What is? Brennan asked.

Before he could be answered, a wave of light penetrated him like a knife and he had a vision of Freya opening the dragon manuscript, her eyes glazed almost as though she was sleepwalking. His breath got caught in his throat for a second, and he had to fight the urge to panic. The sensation disappeared as soon as it appeared, and Brennan was left in turmoil.

"*Señor, estás bien?* Are you okay?"

Brennan blinked and his gaze landed on a young waiter who was watching him attentively.

"Yes, fine," he responded curtly, then caught himself and smiled.

After a slight hesitation, the man apologized for disturbing him and returned behind the counter, leaving Brennan to his thoughts. *Can't I take a nap around here without causing a stir?* Brennan was amused at the fast reaction. He picked up a magazine and pretended to be engrossed in it.

His brain was racing miles, thinking of what he'd just witnessed. Biting his lip slightly, Brennan decided to check up on Freya.

Frey? he mentally asked, using the nickname he knew would cause a spark. Silence was the only answer, and Brennan started panicking, fearing for the Sage's life. *Freya!*

Freya, if you don't say something, I swear I'm capable of breaking your door down. Freya, answer me!

She cannot respond, but do not fret, Tyr spoke softly. The being seemed to have a knack for always appearing when Brennan had questions or needed guidance.

What do you mean? What happened to her? What was it that I saw? When the only reply was a hesitant pause, Brennan grew impatient. *Listen, I have a right to know, she's my friend! And if she's in danger, I want to help out!*

She does not need your help, Brennan, please trust me.

Brennan gritted his teeth. There were only so many riddle-like comments he could take, and he'd had enough of them for the past twenty-four hours. *What are you getting at?*

Freya is all right. She will feel weak, but that is because of the new legacy she has accepted.

It took a while before the words registered and it suddenly dawned on Brennan. *You mean... The book is... And Freya... She got more new powers from it?*

Yes, same as you with the medallion, Tyr confirmed.

So that's what that was earlier... Are you sure she's all right? Brennan questioned yet again.

Positive. Before the Wiseman could demand more answers on the subject, Tyr went on, *Now, about what happened before, when Freya lost control –*

How did you find out about her anger? Brennan interrupted suspiciously.

There was a silence again. *I have my resources.*

Brennan scowled at the magazine he was still holding. *And you say you're not an enemy? For all I know, you could be getting your information from the bad guys.*

And tell me, were there any bad guys *around who could have known about Freya's outburst?* Tyr purposefully chose to avoid informing Brennan about the demon.

Right, touché, Brennan muttered. *But still, whenever I ask a question, the answer is always vague. I'm tired of secrets!*

When he got no reply, the Wiseman sank deeper into the chair. His first instinct was to focus on Freya's energy, devoured by an uncanny desire to make sure she was all right. He located the Sage shortly up in her room, and could not help a sigh of relief escape him. *I don't know just why I care so much, but I sure as hell don't want her hurt. I haven't had my share of friendships in life, which is probably why ours is so important to me.*

As Brennan set the magazine away, decided to get his share of rest, he caught a glimpse of something out of the corner of his eye. "What—" As he turned to look out the window, he recognized Emmanuel leaving the building.

Brennan remained speechless for an instant, undecided about whether he should follow the ghost or not. He'd promised to give Emmanuel a chance, but... *I didn't say I would trust him. And now's my chance to see if he's as innocent as he looks or if I was right all along.*

Without further thinking the plan through, he stood up and exited the hotel at once. Remembering the small part of energy he'd felt in Emmanuel's aura, Brennan decided to stick behind the phantom and follow him to wherever he was going.

Quickening his pace so as not to lose sight of him, Brennan turned a corner around a street, ensuring he maintained a safe distance at all times. He raised an eyebrow as he realized that Emmanuel was headed to the savage region of the city, towards the same place they had all met.

What's this all about? Brennan wondered.

When Emmanuel stopped in mid-air, the Wiseman called upon the power of his necklace and the pit of fire in his stomach. Rooted to the ground, he delayed until he heard the audible zap in the air, a sign that he was now cloaked from curious gazes.

Not even a second later, Emmanuel turned and checked his surroundings, frowning. He inspected the area, but seeing no trace of anyone in his trace, shrugged and continued on his way.

Brennan exhaled in relief when Emmanuel turned away. Still keeping the shield up, he trailed the ghost through the streets. It wasn't long before he had to tap into his spiritual strength to keep track of Emmanuel and his random zigzags.

A faint sheen of sweat appeared on his forehead after another few kilometers of a walk. Brennan was aware that, at the rate he was going, he wouldn't be able to last much longer before fainting. *If I keep this up, I won't have much energy left. But I have to see what's happening.*

Quickening his pace so that he was only a few feet behind the spirit, Brennan thought over the way he and Freya had met Emmanuel. The ghost had been in the same area then, and they hadn't thought much of it. Now, he was second guessing it – especially in light of Emmanuel's odd aura.

One that sucked my energy, he reminded himself. Had not it been for the bond, he could've died from the loss of vital energy. *But Freya saved me by lending me her energy... Which I can't let happen this time.*

Brennan had realized as soon as he had started following Emmanuel that it would be a solo assignment. Aside from Freya needing the overdue rest, she'd also gained new abilities, which meant she was weak. If he was in a tricky position that once again required a transfer of energies, it was not a risk he was comfortable taking.

No problem then, Brennan resolved bravely. *All I have to do is not lose too much vitality. Piece of cake, I'd say.*

He quickened his pace once more to keep up with Emmanuel, but at the same time scanned the surroundings for signs of other presences. *I wonder what he's doing here... Or who he's going to meet.*

Lost in his thoughts, Brennan was more than surprised to see that, while he'd lost touch with the world around him, the landscape had turned from city to rural. He observed the new environment with a new eye, but tripped over a rock when he wasn't paying attention.

Emmanuel immediately turned around, alert. Brennan stilled, not daring to breathe despite the invisible shield. After one last darting sweep, the ghost continued on its way, unsuspecting.

This is getting odder by the second... We're back to where we first met Emmanuel, but why? I'm starting to think I was right, and this Spanish guy isn't as innocent as he seems.

Brennan was startled out of his musings by a sudden movement he perceived with his powers more than with his senses. He had to blink forcefully to maintain his eyes opened, and it dawned on him that he was now losing too much energy.

Since he couldn't exactly lose track of Emmanuel in the open space, Brennan removed the tab he'd been keeping on the phantom and let go of the connection.

Now, back to that move— Brennan's breath was cut off suddenly and he dropped to his knees. It returned just as soon, and the Wiseman had to double check to make sure his shield was still working.

Once that was done, his eyes turned dark with worry. *Freya, whatever's happening, I just hope you're all right.*

Dismissing that thought for later, Brennan got back on his feet and followed Emmanuel, bridging the last remaining distance between them. As he was walking, Brennan kept glancing around, in search of what had caused the movement he had perceived. *What could it be?*

He extended his senses as much as he could, but didn't get more than the energy of living creatures. *If it's another ghost, I should still be able to feel it,* Brennan frowned.

His train of thought was interrupted brutally by the appearance of a six feet tall Spanish phantom. Brennan narrowed his eyes as he took in the newcomer's appearance – black hair, heavy eyebrows, casual but formal clothes, spade, he looked like...

A conquistador's soldier? Brennan's eyes widened. *A Spanish soldier, here? And with Emmanuel, to boot.*

His gaze immediately went to Sam's friend. Though he'd been expecting it, Brennan was still stunned to see Emmanuel's face didn't hold any fear or surprise, only recognition.

"*Hola*, Raoul," Emmanuel said to the ghost, his eyes gleaming with indifference, his face now impassable.

Brennan stepped closer until he was only a few feet away from the two ghosts, gaping at Emmanuel. It was shocking to be right, and he still had a hard time accepting. *He... All this time... He's with them!?*

Before he could explore the thought further, Brennan's vision blurred and his head started spinning. The loss of energy was expanding, and the Wiseman knew he was reaching the end of his reserves. He looked around, trying to see if there was any place he could hide and still eavesdrop.

"It is time to step back into the fold, Emmanuel," Raoul was saying in Spanish. "Cortés' power is greater than what you can imagine. He's got all other—"

"I do not care about Cortés," Emmanuel interrupted frostily. "Where is Gustav? I asked to meet him."

Gustav? Brennan repeated, growing more panicked by the second. *So he* did *have something to do with Sam's kidnapping!*

Having spotted a tree near Emmanuel, Brennan moved towards it softly, swift as a feline, and climbed up. He spread his weight equally on the large branch. Pressing his chest to the wood, the Wiseman leaned his cheek against its coolness, barely able to remain standing any longer.

His new perched spot permitted him to hear the conversation, but also remain out of sight if – *when* – his energy would run out and he passed out. Though his ears opened wide to catch every tidbit of the conversation, Brennan strained to also maintain the invisible barrier for as long as he possibly could.

"You know he's busy," Raoul was saying. "He asked me to come and speak with you."

"What for?" Emmanuel questioned icily. "I told you before, I'm not interested in helping Gustav."

"He's your ancestor, Emmanuel. Don't you think you owe him that?"

Whatever Brennan had been expecting, this had most certainly not been it. Not only was Emmanuel meeting with their enemies, he was furthermore the descendant of Gustav, one of the leaders of the cliques!

This is... Can't be true... In danger...

Brennan's thoughts mingled together, forming a huge ball of confusion. He shook his head to clear it, and having partially succeeded in doing so, focused on the discussion again.

"Do you think I care?" Emmanuel was asking ruefully.

"You helped us by telling us about those Sages..." Raoul said suggestively.

No! Brennan's silent scream was lost on the phantoms, and his body went limp, completely hugging the branch. Only one thought was keeping him from losing consciousness. *I have to... warn... Freya...* He took a deep breath to try and gain some control, but to no avail.

In a last attempt to warn the Sage, he yelled mentally, *Freya! Don't trust him! Don't trust...*

Darkness closed around Brennan before he could finish what he wanted to say. The last thing he heard was Raoul saying, "You're one of us, Emmanuel." Then, he fell into darkness' expecting arms.

Chapter 15

Unaware they had company, Emmanuel gave Raoul a cold stare. "I never was and never will be one of you. I'll help the Sages win the battle, if it's the last thing I do."

"You won't change your mind?" Raoul asked.

Emmanuel thought he'd heard, for a fraction of a second, pleading in his voice. But not even that would have changed his stance. He shook his head resolutely. "The way of life you have chosen is not mine. I may be dead, but I, at least, still have my values."

"Oh? And what are those?" Raoul questioned. "What's so important you're ready to throw up the chance of a lifetime?"

As he looked at the one that had been his friend, Emmanuel pitied him. The moment evaporated, and he smiled sadly. "Friendship and justice," were the three words he said solemnly.

Raoul stared at him, as if not believing his ears. Then, he laughed dryly. "You live in a dream, Emmanuel. And when you wake up, it will be too late."

"On the contrary, Raoul, it is you who lives in a dream. And you know what the worst part is?" When nothing but silence answered him, Emmanuel said, "It's that until quite recently, I shared the same dream."

Raoul's facial expression didn't change, but Emmanuel noticed a flicker in his eyes that betrayed his emotion.

I have to give it another try, the ghost thought. *For the sake of old times.*

"Raoul, don't fall in his trap. Cortés is out for power, and he'll do anything to get it. Whatever he has told you, Gustav will, sooner or later, rally him."

His words reached empty ears and Raoul only grinned manically. "And when he does, it will give us all more power. Emmanuel, his sword is... unbelievable. Don't miss out on this!"

Emmanuel shook his head, then turned his back to his old friend and walked away. A few steps further, he sighed, "I am sorry I ever trusted you. As of now, we are enemies, Raoul."

His friend's last words were toneless. "Then there is no need for me here."

Emmanuel felt the air changing, and when he glanced back, Raoul had vanished. The phantom sighed and raised his face to the moon, his eyes mirroring his sorrow. "No, indeed, Raoul. And there is no need me for me to wait any longer. I have chosen my path, and you yours, my old friend. Now, we're on opposite sides of this battle. And I'll fight you if I have to."

Exhaling heavily, Emmanuel dematerialized back to the hotel. He was still completely unaware of the unconscious Wiseman in a tree, his energy drained – and no defensive barrier whatsoever around his body.

&&&

"It will not work."

Gustav turned around to face the demon, masking his surprise. When he'd entered into the devil's bargain, he'd not signed up to have his every movement be spied on. It was fast becoming annoying.

"What?" Gustav questioned the wraith, scowling.

"Emmanuel will not join, I have told you before to ssstop wasssting your effortsss."

"I will not!"

"Why do you insssissst on one puny child, when Cortésss will soon link all ghostsss to himssself? It will be more power than you can imagine, and more sssoldiersss to pick from."

He will never understand.

"It is not a soldier I am looking for. It is someone to leave my legacy to."

"Yoursss?" Raksh snickered. "Do not get ahead of yoursssself, Gussstav. We have a deal."

"*Sí*, I realize that," the Spanish soldier muttered in a bored voice. "You came to me, remember? Asking me to join Cortés, to offer him the sword from you as a gift of loyalty. You told me it was to gain land, to become a great nation again."

"Why do you sssound doubtful?"

"Because for days now, all you care about is the girl!"

Raksh grinned evilly. "And you do not?"

"With a difference. I do not want to use her, as you do. I want to hurt her, make her feel pain, get my revenge – then kill her."

Raksh's eyes shone ferociously of a red glint. "And you can do all that," he growled, "once I am through with her."

Their frosty stares met and held defiantly, each battling for dominance. In the end, Gustav inclined his head deferentially. "As you wish..."

When the demon turned to leave, he lifted his gaze, shining maliciously. *I will get my revenge on Freya, with or without your help.*

&&&

Freya... Child, wake up! Tyr's gentle voice penetrated through the thick fog surrounding Freya's thoughts. Her eyes fluttered open and she slowly stood up on the floor, her back sore and her heart pounding.

"What happened?" she wondered, trying to sort through the muddled thoughts in her mind, and failing. Freya attempted to stand up, but found herself kissing the ground in mere half seconds, a sharp pain lightning through her. Her head was spinning and she felt weak, more than she'd ever been.

She called upon Tyr, anxious over what was happening. *What is this?*

Do you not remember?

Freya frowned, trying to recall what the tiger was referring to, when it dawned on her. She'd been gone to the world, or so she thought. She heard a song, went to the closet, touched the glowing book and...

A tingly feeling rolled in the pit of her stomach. *I... Tyr... What exactly happened?*

Freya could hear the smile in the tiger's voice when it answered. *I would have thought you recognized this by now.*

The Sage tried to get to her feet again, but to no avail. Her body felt as though it had been run over by a train, time and time again, and had no forces left. *You mean I got new powers?*

Yes, child. You were ready for them, and the manuscript – or rather what is in it – knew it. You will be weakened for some time after this, maybe a few hours or days, depending on your recovery period.

Freya's eyes widened at the news. *What? Tyr, Sam is being held captive at the Cathedral. I don't have any time to waste!*

Tyr's voice came commanding. *You will not go anywhere near that place, do you hear me? I cannot help you in there, Freya!*

The Sage gritted her teeth and anger washed over her like a hot shower – a very familiar and tempting one.

Do not! Tyr yelled.

Freya was so startled by the tiger's outburst that she momentarily forgot her frustration. *What is it?*

Nothing, only... The reply came hesitant, and Freya knew at once that the tiger was hiding something. *Do not let your emotions control you again.*

Though she understood what Tyr meant, Freya had the uncanny feeling that it wasn't divulging everything in order to shelter her. *What else is there?* she asked.

What do you mean? Tyr's wary tone confirmed her suspicions.

What else aren't you telling me? Freya repeated.

The manuscript affects you, and not just your powers. When you and Brennan touched it and the new abilities en-

tered you, they also changed your previous capacities. Your emotions can now easily get out of control and influence the environment – the elements. Brennan, on the other hand, can control feelings, or anything internal.

Freya was dumbstruck at the information, but before she had a chance to comment, Tyr continued, as though in a rush. *Heed my warnings, child. These novel abilities may be tempting and seducing, running through your veins as they are, but you cannot use them yet.*

Why not?

The four elements need time to adapt – and so does your body – to the overwhelming energy running through you. When it sensed the Sage's indecision, the tiger went a step further in its lesson. *Think of it as a shiny gadget with untested batteries. If the batteries have the wrong voltage, it will ruin the toy.*

It took a moment for Freya to follow what Tyr meant, then she gulped. *And in this example, I'm the gadget?*

Precisely.

Freya chewed on her bottom lip, letting the information sink in. The new powers could help her win against both Gustav and Cortés – once she could dominate them, rather than the opposite.

At a loss, she switched topics. *Hey, Tyr... Any news of Cortés' plans?*

Not particularly, but –

Before the tiger could finish, the Sage was hit by a particularly strong wave of energy loss.

Freya!

&&&

The Sage gasped in pain and dizziness at the large amount of energy she was losing. The ceiling was spinning, when a soft silvery light appeared out of nowhere in the middle of her room and Tyr stepped out of it, rushing to the teenager.

The tiger touched Freya's cheek with its muzzle and immediately the Sage felt a cooling sensation spread to her, keeping her grounded and protected.

The attack against her disappeared shortly after, and Freya was left panting for breath. When she finally got a grip on her lungs, the Sage wrapped her arms around Tyr's wide neck. "Thank you... For coming."

The tiger smiled at her, but Freya could see the perturbed gleam in its eyes.

"What was that?" she wondered, even whilst she scanned the hotel for signs of the only person whose emotions she could've sensed so vividly. Not finding him, she frowned and raised her eyes to the tiger. "Tyr, where's Brennan?"

The tiger shook its massive head. *I do not know. I tried to—*

Its voice was cut off by a much stronger one – Brennan's. *Don't trust him! Freya, don't trust...*

The words died away before the sentence could be finished.

Brennan? Brennan! Freya yelled mentally. *Brennan, answer me!* Nothing responded, and she gnawed on her bottom lip worriedly. *Come on, Wiseman, you can't do this!*

An eerie silence echoed in her mind, and Freya turned a concerned gaze to Tyr's. Before she could voice anything, the tiger confirmed, *I heard it too. His vibration is very faint, but I will find him, and let you know. Take care in the meantime, and stay out of trouble.*

Tyr waited for Freya's reluctant nod, before inclining its head in a gesture of goodbye. A glow appeared once more behind it, and the tiger disappeared through it.

Freya sighed and raised her gaze to the ceiling. "Please be all right, Brennan."

A few moments later, the Sage's senses picked up Emmanuel's energy. Not even a breath afterwards, he entered her room, face grave and pensive.

When he saw the pale-looking Sage on the ground, Emmanuel hurried to her, fearing she'd been attacked. "Freya! Are you all right? What happened?"

"I'm fine, don't worry," she waved him off. "I'm just..." As she tried to stand up again, Freya plopped once again on the floor, scowling at it.

"Weak?" Emmanuel suggested.

"Guess so," Freya muttered, deciding to stay where she was for the time being.

Emmanuel bit back the string of questions he had, settling instead for a simple one. "Is there anything I can do?"

"Not really, but thanks for offering."

Already, Emmanuel was glancing around, scanning the room for her partner. "Where's Brennan? I was hoping to speak with both of you."

"I don't know," Freya's eyes clouded. "I haven't seen him since last night, and our last contact was brief and...odd. I'm not sure what's wrong."

"You don't think he's in trouble, do you?" Emmanuel frowned.

"I hope not." Shaking her head as if to clear it from negative thoughts, she asked, "Anyway, what is it? Did you find anything new about Cortés?"

"No..." Emmanuel suddenly looked uncomfortable. "Actually, I wanted to speak with you about, well, myself."

Freya raised her eyebrows, surprised in spite of herself. "You?" At the ghost's hesitant nod, she continued, "What about, exactly?"

Emmanuel looked at her uncertainly, then around the room. He wasn't quite sure about his decision of revealing everything to the Wiseman and the Sage, but so far it was all he had.

Thinking over his meeting with Raoul, Emmanuel knew he'd made the right choice. There was no other way to help both Freya and Brennan in winning this fight. *That, and Gustav also has Sam held captive, and he is my friend.*

Emmanuel's gaze finally locked with Freya's expecting one, though his words were halting and unsure. "Well, it's got to do with my ancestors. Or ancestor, actually."

"Ancestor? What do you mean by that?" Freya tilted her head to the side, eyes narrowed as she tried to catch his meaning.

"Sam did not have the time to tell you, and I did not want him to either at the beginning but... I think now would be the right moment."

"Tell me what?" Freya pressed.

Emmanuel took a deep breath, then met her gaze frankly. "I am a straight descendant of Gustav. My last name is Rodriguez."

Freya's eyes showed her surprise, but she didn't say anything, expecting Emmanuel to continue. When the spirit didn't, she prompted, "That's it?"

Emmanuel stared at her for a few moments, before stuttering a small, "Y-yes."

Freya folded her arms across her chest and chewed on her bottom lip thoughtfully, not once removing her gaze from his. Other than her perusal, her face was an impassable mask.

After a few moments of the painful silence, Emmanuel asked, "Aren't you... surprised? Mad? Angered?"

"Surprised? Yes. But angered? No." Freya shook her head. "It makes sense now."

"What does?" It was Emmanuel's turn to seem puzzled.

"Brennan scanned your aura and found a small part that's still the same as it was of your living," Freya explained. "That part was familiar to me when he showed it, but I couldn't figure it out at first. Now, I get why – it resembled the same energy I'd felt around Gustav."

Emmanuel gaped at her for a few seconds, then asked to make sure, "So you really aren't upset?"

"Why would I be?" Freya shrugged, never once losing eye contact.

"Well, because I'm..." Emmanuel trailed off, obviously at a loss of words and confounded by Freya's reaction – or lack of it.

"Related to Gustav, one of my enemies?" Freya filled in. When Emmanuel nodded, she shrugged once more. "You can't control your inheritance, Emmanuel. It's not your fault who you're related to. Gustav is my enemy, not you. Besides, Sam trusts you, and so do I. I'd like to think I would've known if you had any ill intentions when I met you."

Emmanuel smiled, relieved beyond words. "I'm glad you think like that, but before you grant me your full trust, you have to know that Cortés knows you are here, you and Seamus, because of me. Indirectly, but it is still my fault."

That drew Freya's attention. "Explain."

"When Sam told me he was friends with a Sage, I was at the time friends with Raoul, one of Gustav's best lieutenants, and I shared the information with him. I did not think about the consequences of my act, and the result was that Raoul told Gustav. Ever since your battle against him, Gustav has been keeping people of his own at the airports to alert him if you ever set foot in Spain again. When you arrived, you can be sure he has been notified by it and used this tidbit to provoke Cortés."

"What do you mean?" Freya frowned.

Damn, this was unplanned, she mused thoughtfully. *Gustav, I can deal with that... But now I'm going to have Cortés' men on my back too? Well, considering Gustav's background and his loud mouth, I shouldn't be that surprised... I really ought to teach him a lesson soon.* Freya then concentrated on what Emmanuel was saying.

"I've been on his trail, following him when he's too busy to notice," the ghost admitted. "When they met three days ago, Cortés threatened Gustav by telling him all ghosts have rallied to him. To show he was not afraid, Gustav told Cortés that two persons would be sure to oppose him and that he'd would never join him. I'm not entirely sure about the truth of the last statement."

Freya was lost in reflection long after Emmanuel was done with his story, her gaze on the rug underneath her.

Emmanuel took her silence as disapproval and pleaded, "I really am sorry for my part in this. I acted foolishly and I understand if you cannot trust me, but please let me help. I want to be as much help to you as possible in finding Sam and rescuing him."

"Good," Freya declared, then raised her gaze to meet his. "At least we're on the same train of thought."

"Excuse me?" Emmanuel was perplexed – again. Whenever he thought he had the girl figured out, she surprised him.

Freya smiled mischievously, not a stranger to his thoughts. "I want to find Sam and rescue him too, and I know he's your friend. I don't care about Gustav, I can take him on now. You made a mistake, so what? I make plenty every day. Some people – namely Brennan – will be sure to tell me that trusting you is yet another one of my naïve traits. I say, *I don't care*. You cannot control your blood, Em, and I have faith in you anyway."

The ghost's face was lighted by a grin so big Freya couldn't help the laugh that escaped her. When Tyr's words came, they only confirmed she'd made the right decision.

He is not a bad ghost, Freya, and he will not betray you.

Chapter 16

Back in the wilderness, Brennan stirred on top of the branch, groaning in pain. He was slowly starting to come back to himself. His fingertips moved, and no more than a few moments later, his eyes snapped open.

Immediately, the Wiseman jerked and tried to stand up, but realized he was too dizzy to do so. After a few minutes, he started moving inch by inch, until he was straddling the branch. Gritting his teeth, the moved one leg over it and hopped off.

He dropped to the ground with a thud, swearing at the pain in his shoulder, and feeling as though stars exploded behind his eyes. After a few deep breaths, he rolled on his back, biding his time until the spinning in his head ceased.

The Wiseman's thoughts were still very much in disorder, but if there was one thing he knew for certain, it was that Emmanuel couldn't be trusted. He sighed and leaned his head against the trunk of the tree – all the thinking was making the light-headedness even worse.

He mentally scanned himself to ensure he wasn't hurt in any way, then extended his senses to see if he was alone. Satisfied, Brennan closed his eyes, trying to gather all his forces. "Now, if only I could get up…"

When he tried to force his legs to move, the Wiseman only slipped and fell back down ungracefully. *Crap. Guess that's that for now.* He was stuck for the time being, whether he liked it or not.

At a loss on what to do, he tried to connect with Freya's energy, but not even that was possible. It seemed that, apart from using his spirit to scan himself and the surrounding woods, Brennan's batteries were completely drained. *Great.*

"Wow…" Brennan muttered incredulously, mad at himself. "Great job, buddy. You really did it again! It's a wonder I didn't need an energy transfer again…"

You did require one, Brennan, but Freya was shielded from it, Tyr reproached.

All color drained from the Wiseman's face at the thought of hurting Freya. *Is she all right?*

Yes, was the monosyllabic answer.

Brennan felt his gut churning at the thought of what could've happened to Freya. If her energy had been taken away while she'd been in an already weakened state… *I didn't… Oh, God, she could've…*

Yes, she could have died, Tyr said impassibly, apparently determined to make Brennan understand that nothing came without a price. If their bond was to remain, both the Wiseman and Freya should be careful not to drain each other to death. *Luckily for both of you, she was shielded from the bond and now all right. However, the consequences…*

"I know!" Brennan snapped. He was only too aware of the risk he'd run, and of what could've happened. Distantly, the clenching of his heart and the pain in his chest registered.

If Freya had been hurt because of his lack of judgment, he would've never forgiven himself. *Look, I don't have to justify myself to you, but I didn't mean for that to happen. My powers got drained sooner than I expected them to, and I was taken by surprise.*

You should first learn to recognize signs of weakness before you go on an errand all by yourself! Tyr scolded Brennan.

How could I know my powers wouldn't last as long as I wished them to? I thought I had enough force to make them work! The Wiseman trailed off again. After a small silence, he asked, *How long until I can use them again?*

A few hours, no more, Tyr grudgingly admitted, and Brennan sighed in relief.

Good, because I have a feeling I might need them sometime soon.

The being did not answer, instead saying, *Would you mind telling me what exactly happened?*

You first, Brennan demanded. *I have delayed asking you for too long. Are you a friend or a foe? And why did you choose me to guide?*

Brennan could've sworn he heard a heavy sigh, and imagined Tyr was getting annoyed with his constant questions. But he had to know. Ever since Tyr had shown itself, Brennan had never picked a negative vibe from it. Not that he had ever tried scanning it as he'd done with Emmanuel.

For some reason, the idea hadn't even crossed Brennan's mind. Now that it occurred to him, the Wiseman wondered why that was. *Especially considering my track record.*

After his grandfather's death, Brennan had grown to be quite a suspicious person, and he'd proven as much when he'd first seen Freya at the airport. Rather than be upfront and trust her, he'd chosen to follow her and Seamus for hours before finally revealing himself.

It begged the question then, why didn't he have the same amount of distrust towards the new presence? Was it because the tiger had had countless occasions to hurt him, and never did? Or because it always seemed to be around and save his butt out of trouble?

I am a friend, Tyr finally said, startling Brennan out of his thoughts. *I have told you before, I do not mean you nor Freya any harm. I speak to you because, out of all the people Freya is friends with, you are the one that can most help her win this fight.*

You've got to be kidding me, Brennan groaned. *You've seen how bad I can piss her off… Not to mention she gets angered really easily.*

Yes, I know all that, Tyr admitted in a patient – and amused? – tone. *But I also know that you can be there for her when she needs you and that, in spite of Freya getting mad at you so easily, she appreciates you being here with her.*

Yeah, sure, Brennan snorted.

You doubt my words? Then tell me, if she did not, why did she let you come to Spain in the first place?

Well, because... Brennan racked his brain for an answer. Unable to find a satisfying one, he had to recognize Tyr had a point. *All right, maybe, but...*

But what? Tyr questioned.

Brennan bit his lip, deep in thought, but no matter which way he reflected on it, Tyr was right. Though Freya often got upset at him, the times when she didn't yell at him, she seemed happy enough to have him as a friend.

Brennan also recalled something else... He'd pointed out to Freya, not too long ago, that they were the same, even in their way of thinking and sometimes distrusting each other. If that was true – and he had no doubt it was – then the Sage had been lacking friendship too, and this was her one chance to actually battle the ghosts with a bit of help.

But why doesn't she trust me with her secrets, with her past? Brennan asked himself.

Tyr's answer was quick this time. *For the same reason as you keep yours under wraps, Brennan. Because she is not yet ready. Just like you, there are parts of Freya's past that haunt her more than anything else...*

"Even more than the battle she's supposed to fight," Brennan whispered to himself.

Yes, Tyr agreed. *And she has to first deal with those things before she can share them.*

I understand. In many ways, we're only a mirror of the other. That was when Brennan realized Tyr still hadn't answered one question. *So I'm supposed to have faith in you just because you don't wish us harm?*

For that, you will have to find your own answer, Brennan. I cannot force you into trusting me and I cannot give you advice if you do not.

Brennan said nothing as he bowed his head. What Tyr said was true – it was his choice to make, whether to trust it or not. But given Emmanuel's betrayal and all that had happened since they'd arrive in Spain, Brennan couldn't make up his mind.

It was then that he remembered a thing his grandfather had told him, a long time ago. "When things get the most confusing, just follow your heart and you're bound to end up right," Brennan whispered the words out loud, giving them a new meaning.

Tears stung his eyes at the thought of Thomas, of all the times he'd taught him from sunrise to sunset, and sometimes even after midnight. Then Brennan remembered the events that had followed his grandfather's death and his own decision to leave his village to a place where he'd be welcomed.

Brennan sighed heavily and, pushing those memories to the back of his mind, concentrated on the issue at hand. If he trusted Tyr, he'd receive good advice and they could probably need its help. *Plus, Tyr could prove to be a valuable ally.*

On the other hand, it could also prove to be an enemy, the way Emmanuel had, and Brennan would've been mistaken. Even more, he would be placing Freya, Sam and O'Keeffe in danger, too, if he became reckless.

But Brennan had already made his decision. Sure, there was a risk that he could be utterly off base and in that case everyone would get hurt, but Tyr had proven its loyalty so far.

Not to mention that Tyr may be my only way of connecting with Freya for some time... Brennan mused.

Am I to guess that your choice is made?

Brennan smirked and leaned his head against the rough surface of the tree. *You may say that.*

You will not regret it, Brennan. You will come to see, in time, that I am truly no enemy to you.

Brennan nodded, then a thought struck him. *Hang on... Since you know so much, maybe you can clarify something for me.* Ever since Freya's outburst, he'd been wondering, but seeing as he couldn't ask anyone, he'd pushed the thought to the back of his mind, promising to investigate later. But since the chance came, why not take it? *Since Freya can unleash her powers when she's mad, does that mean I can do the same?*

Silence followed Brennan's question, and the Wiseman guessed Tyr was pondering the matter over, until it wasn't anymore. *Freya's powers come from the four elements. When she gets mad beyond her control, all four different sources mingle together, forming a sort of energy shield around her that in turn influences everything around her.*

How so? Brennan frowned.

Well, a slight breeze can turn to a full-blowing wind; a slight rain will turn into pouring, or even a storm; a spark of light can produce, in a few seconds only, a fire large enough to bring down a house; and as for the earth... Well, if she really unleashes her powers, she could cause an earthquake or who knows what else?

Brennan absorbed the information in silence, realizing just what they'd been playing with. He had no doubt the book affected Freya, much as the medallion had increased his own strength over the months.

It was a sobering conclusion that if the Sage got really upset, she would hurt not only herself, but ultimately other people around her, though unknowingly. The Wiseman was more or less sure that during Freya's outburst, the Sage had lost all rationality, controlled by her anger. If that was true, then he was better off not crossing certain lines in the future.

While Brennan was mulling that over, Tyr went on, *For you, it would be different. Your powers are the source of your emotions, thus meaning that your own spiritual energy comes from inside of you. Every time you use them, it touches your vital energy, which is why you get so weak. With that in mind, the same thing that happened to Freya* could *happen to you...*

But? Brennan pressed, feeling a mixture of emotions at the news. On one hand, it meant that he was just as strong as Freya was when she lost control. But on the other, the potential scared him. He'd seen that she couldn't dominate it, and wasn't sure he'd fare much better.

But not unless, Tyr was saying, *your emotions all mingle together to form that same ball of energy as the four elements have formed in Freya's body.*

What would happen then? Brennan asked, fascinated that such a power could exist inside both him and Freya.

If would burst, as it did for Freya. Only...

Only what? Brennan demanded impatiently.

Only instead of influencing the elements around you, it would affect the people *around you.*

At once, Brennan fell dead silent as the shock of the news hit him. *What...?*

Yes, Tyr confirmed. *Such a burst of energy from you could influence the emotions of those around you. Do you realize now how powerful you and Freya could be if you trusted each other completely?*

The Wiseman was unable to answer, stricken as he was by the images in his own mind.

Think for a second, Brennan. Imagine you were in the middle of a battle and you both reached your peak. Freya's abilities would cause chaos, while yours would affect every ghost in the vicinity and be able to command them what to feel. They would be at your mercy.

Brennan was gaping, not trusting himself to speak. Then, he whispered a small, "Wow... I... Wow..."

He heard a chuckle, then Tyr repeated, *Indeed, wow. You remember Seamus telling you and Freya about the unity of the powers of a Sage and a Wiseman and how potent that could turn out to be, right?*

Yes, I do, Brennan nodded. *But he also didn't tell us that we'd have to put our faith in each other unconditionally for that to happen.*

Very true. But there is also another way to get at least half of that same influence. You and Freya have combined your abilities before, yes?

Surprised that Tyr knew about that, Brennan confirmed, *Yeah, on one occasion – when we materialized back at the hotel...* When Tyr stayed quiet, he questioned, *Why do you ask?*

Because I believe that if you and Freya do it again while fighting Cortés, it would be enough to assure your victory.

Brennan's eyebrows rose way up. *Really? But Cortés' power is still greater than ours!*

It is no match for the powers of a Sage and Wiseman, even if only combined, Tyr declared solemnly. Something in its tone irked the young man, almost as though the being itself spoke from experience.

Brennan tapped his fingers impatiently on his thigh, pondering the entirety of the information he'd just received. To say he was stunned was an understatement.

Tyr took him by surprise when it announced, *You can stand up now. You may still feel a little bit dizzy, but you will be better soon.*

Brennan got to his feet and stepped away from the tree, realizing that he could, indeed, move about without fear of passing out.

Go back to the hotel and try to get some sleep, Tyr recommended. *But do not waste any spiritual energy unless absolutely necessary.*

Half-grumbling, Brennan agreed and started walking into the darkness, knowing he had a long way to go.

Chapter 17

B ack at the hotel, Freya and Emmanuel were deep in conversation, despite the hour that had long since moved past midnight. The ghost had just related his last conversation with Raoul, and Freya was intrigued.

"But Em, what did you mean?" she asked, using his new nickname. "When you said that you'd both been sharing the same dream?"

Emmanuel shrugged, smiling bitterly. "Raoul and I were best friends of our living. When I found out about Gustav being my ancestor, Raoul thought I should go and meet him. I was not too *de acuerdo* with that, but I agreed nonetheless."

Freya waited patiently as the phantom collected his thoughts enough to continue. "Gustav... Well, ghosts don't usually converse with humans, though they can be seen by all. But if, say, a human is their descendant – direct one, in my case – they will interact. That's what happened with me."

Emmanuel's eyes glazed over, as he recalled the story that would become his life's biggest mistake. "Shortly after I met Gustav, he asked both me and Raoul to join his group, saying that I could be of use to him as his blood relation. I suppose he saw part of himself in me... I felt special because of the attention, and agreed. My parents had died long before, and I had lived with Raoul, my sister and a girl I knew on the streets ever since I could remember. Gustav was the first person who showed real interest in me and, like I said, I felt unique."

Freya gritted her teeth, already guessing at Gustav's ulterior motives. The man had never done anything for someone other than himself, thus it was no surprise when Emmanuel's story came to its unhappy ending.

"At one point, Gustav demanded that I and Raoul to go into unfriendly territory to get some information on one of the rival cliques. He explained everything about them, and how cold wars often started between the groups. We agreed and, well, we died. A huge wood board hit us over the head during the mission and, next thing we both knew, we were no longer part of the living."

"Go on," Freya entreated gently.

"Of course, it just so happened that we transformed into ghosts...and were never able to leave this plane of existence, like the others."

Probably because of whatever Cadmael activated when he came here, Freya mused as she remembered the Viking ghost.

Uncaring of the consequences, the old leader had been thirsty for power and returned to the world of the living, opening a portal. It not only released him, unfortunately, but the rest of the phantoms as well. Despite the newfound knowledge, Freya had still not figured out if the process could be reversed. Seeing as Emmanuel had been honest, she only thought it fair to return the sentiment.

"I know why your souls were stuck here," she said softly.

When Emmanuel gave her a questioning look, Freya told him about Cadmael and the portal. After she was done, the ghost nodded pensively. "That explains the barrier," he whispered, almost to himself.

"Barrier?" Freya repeated, bemused. *Tyr?* she called softly to attract the tiger's attention.

I am listening, was the reply.

Emmanuel changed his position, floating in mid-air with his legs crossed underneath him Indian-style. "When I died... There was this moment when I left my body and I felt I would be shattered in a million pieces by the slightest wind. I could not help but think about my sister and the girl I then knew, and had to come to terms with the fact that there was nothing I would be able to do for them again. I resolved to stay away from them just in case others planned to use them to make me rally Gustav's clique."

He paused, lost in the pain of being away from his loved ones for so long. "In any case," he ended up clearing his throat. "When I died, after the original shock of the death itself, I ascended towards the sky and a glow appeared out of nowhere to guide me. I felt warm and serene and I floated towards it... Upwards, I think. I had nearly reached it when..." His fine eyebrows narrowed in a slight frown as he finished, "I never got to the light."

"Why?"

"A wall stopped me. I had not seen it until I bumped into it. Its force was so great it blasted me off. The radiance disappeared, and I was back on Earth, in the exact spot of my downfall."

Freya took a step closer to the young man, placing a hand on his shoulder reassuringly. "I'm sorry, Em."

The ghost smiled gratefully, but it felt forced. Freya left him in the memory of the moment, instead turning to the window and redirecting her thoughts towards the tiger.

Did you know about this, Tyr?

&&&

In the realm of the gods, Osiris appeared next to the entity. "What will you tell her?"

I was going to tell her I knew nothing of the sort, but now I am second guessing that statement based on your reaction, Tyr retorted. *Let me guess. Another connection to Set?*

Osiris pursed his lips, unwilling to reveal more than he already had, but also unwilling to lose the one ally he had. In the end, he sighed. "When the ghosts appeared on Earth, I and Isis suspected something more was going on. We used our godly influence and investigated, and were led back to my brother, yes."

How unsurprising.

"We do not know what exactly he did, but a void opened from the other side, forcing these phantoms onto Earth. When we reached it, the hole was growing, and we were afraid soon demons would enter the peaceful territory as well. In an effort to stop it, we forced the portal closed."

And why could you not send the ghosts back through it?

"Because if we opened it again, we risked destabilizing the Underworld, where my brother is imprisoned. Such a thing cannot be unleashed onto Earth." Osiris' tone was firm, but regretful at the same time.

Tyr paused, thinking over before asking, *What shall I tell Freya?*

"The truth – that she cannot do anything about it."

With a displeased grunt, the tiger focused back on its charge.

&&&

I presumed something like that existed, but I did not want to reveal it unless I was absolutely sure, Tyr said in a slightly resigned voice.

Why not? Freya asked.

Because I knew you would want to do something about it and I want you to concentrate on Cortés... At least for the time being.

Freya thought of a way to press for more information without upsetting her guardian. *Is there anything I can do?*

Tyr sighed heavily, rumbling, *No, Freya. For that barrier to disappear, all ghosts would have to, as well. Which is an impossible feat.*

Why not? Freya continued stubbornly. *They don't have to pay for the mistake of one stupid Viking. They deserve to rest in peace... So why can't it be possible?*

The tiger wanted to correct her badly, but could not afford to under the god's perusing gaze.

Because one human alone does not have the required power, however strong they can be. When Freya started to protest, Tyr retorted, *We will leave it at that, Freya.*

But why, *Tyr? Why is it you can't tell me more?* the Sage whined, sensing it was withholding information.

Freya, I know you want to help nearly everyone. Even while you are supposed to be fighting Cortés – or at least think-

ing about the battle and planning it – you also want to help Emmanuel, and I admire that, but you cannot.

Freya remained silent, fully aware the tiger was entirely right.

So there's really nothing I can do? she attempted one last time, though her tone was resigned.

Not for now, child, Tyr admitted gently.

Sighing heavily, Freya ended the connection and raised her gaze to Emmanuel, whose own was glued to the ceiling once more. "Em?" She waited until he faced her to continue. "I'm sorry," Freya said, and she meant it with all her heart. "There's nothing I can to do withdraw that barrier. Trust me, I'd try if you want me to—"

"Wait," Emmanuel stopped her by holding up his hands. Registering the look of surprise on Freya's face, he continued, "You think I want you to lift that barrier?" At her slight nod, he narrowed his eyes in confusion. "*Porqué*, Freya? Why would you conclude that?"

Freya frowned slightly, her forehead creasing as she answered hesitantly, "Well, I guess I just assumed..."

Emmanuel's warm smile and slight chuckle cut her off. "*Es un malentendido.* You have *completely* misunderstood me."

"What—" Freya started, but the phantom cut her off again.

"I did not tell you about my experience in order to beg you to do something about it. From what Sam told me, I know that not even your great prowess would be capable of such a miracle. And I don't want you risking your life when

I'm already dead, because that would be an incredibly selfish thing to do, Freya. And I'm not Gustav."

"I know that," the Sage said softly.

"Besides, we'll need you for something else," Emmanuel smiled. "Namely, the battle against Cortés and saving Sam."

"We'll do that first," Freya nodded determinately. "Save Sam, *then* battle Cortés."

"Somehow, one will come with the other trailing close behind," Emmanuel warned. "And you'll have to be ready for the ultimate confrontation. Gustav will not play fair, not with that cursed sword."

"Sword?" Freya repeated, tilting her head to the side. "I thought it was Cortés'."

"In the legends, *sí*. But it was also lost, and that man did not find it on his own." Emmanuel rubbed the back of his neck contritely, before revealing, "Raoul told me a few weeks back about this weapon Gustav randomly came upon, which gained him Cortés' favor."

"What!?" Freya gaped. "So he's the one who gave it to that conquistador?"

"*Creo que sí*," Emmanuel admitted believing so.

"But why? Why would Gustav want to do that?"

Emmanuel shrugged, muttering, "His mind is a thing I do not pretend to understand."

"Well, whatever the case, I wasn't afraid of the Viking Cadmael and I was more inexperienced then. I sure as hell won't cower in front of Cortés and Gustav now that I have a few more aces under my sleeves."

"You shouldn't be."

Freya's eyes widened as they landed on Seamus dragging himself in the room, holding onto the wall for balance. "Are you okay, Seamus? I'd stand up but... Kind of weak myself."

"Seems to be going around like the plague," O'Keeffe grumbled, before dropping onto the ground next to Freya. "What happened to you?"

"Book..." Freya mumbled, looking away and expecting a lecture.

To her surprise, Seamus only nodded thoughtfully, then said, "Might be for the best. If it's another upgrade you received, you will need it. I could not find anything that made sense on Cortés and these ghosts. So I looked into something that did."

At Freya's blank look, Seamus glanced towards Emmanuel. He peered at the youth pensively, assessing whether he could speak freely, then continued, "The relics of the Underworld."

Freya straightened, all attention focused on him. "What of them?"

"We thought originally there are two objects of power related to them, to create a map. The truth is, there are five."

"*What*?" Freya exclaimed for the second time that night.

"The manuscript and medallion are the positive forces. To oppose them were created three others – an axe, a sword, and chains."

Freya gaped as the truth of the matter sank in. "We need to tell Brennan! That means these weapons the ghosts got...Seamus, then what Cadmael and Cortés are trying to use, it's all related to the relics!"

"Yes," Seamus nodded. "And who do we know that wants the relics?"

"Raksh," Freya responded immediately.

Emmanuel looked between the two of them, then muttered, "I don't suppose I'm meant to understand any of this."

"Nope," Freya answered distractedly. She chewed on her bottom lip, then said to Seamus, "This is bad. *Really* bad. There's a much bigger picture here than we all realized."

"Yes, there is. I will continue to research the matter, since I cannot do much else." O'Keeffe glanced around, oddly preoccupied. "Where is Brennan?"

"We don't know... He hasn't come back," Freya revealed. "After I recover my strength, I wanted to go search for him."

"Good plan," Seamus whispered weakly, then got up with a groan and exited the room. "Be safe, please. It is obvious we do not know as much as we should. And until we do..."

Freya nodded in agreement, then bit her lip, deep in thought. She glanced at the watch by the bedside and saw it was nearly three in the morning. A plan slowly started forming in her head, and she let it unfold for a few moments, like a map appearing little by little. Once she was satisfied, she stretched her muscles and stood up.

The Sage sighed in relief at the realization her physical strength – at least – was back. It would be enough to get her through at least half of her makeshift idea. As for the other part... *I'll worry about that when I get to it,* Freya resolved.

"What are you doing?" Emmanuel prompted her.

Freya threw him a challenging look, defying him to try and stop her. "I can't stay here when Sam is in grave danger.

This Raksh guy is way more dangerous than Gustav and Cortés, and being around him could mean certain death. I can't – *won't* – allow that to happen."

Emmanuel's eyes widened in horror, but he still kept his sangfroid. "But Freya, you can't risk going to the Cathedral... You've heard what Seamus, and even Brennan said."

Freya shrugged, an ironic gleam in her eyes. She was decided, and no one would keep her from doing what she was determined to. "I don't care. I'll be careful, but I don't want to risk losing Sam, not while I can do something to stop it."

With those last words, Freya was out the door and on the road in mere seconds. After a quick look around, she broke into a jog towards the Cathedral, breathing in deeply the chilly night air.

Still in the Sage's room, Emmanuel shook his head. *That's one stubborn* muchacha, he thought.

Realizing that he may not be of much help, but still wanting to aid the Sage in her plan to release Sam from the conquistador's grip, Emmanuel decided to go and help out as best as he could.

If all goes to hell, he reasoned, *I can alert Brennan or Seamus.*

With that thought firm in mind, the ghost dematerialized into thin air, until nothing was left of him but brilliant shards of crystal.

&&&

Tyr ran through the halls of the palace, calling onto the gods, snarling in near rage. It had followed Freya's conversation until Seamus's revelation, and the surprise alone had struck it dumb. Now, the tiger was on a quest for answers.

When Isis showed up in its path, Tyr came to a dead stop. *You should have told me. Five objects! Not three, but* five!

When the goddess only stared, contrite, Tyr shook its head. *And here I thought you wanted to defend Earth.*

"It was not us who created the other three objects. Set did, and he gave the chains to the blasted demon!"

Which Raksh used to hurt Seamus.

"Yes... unfortunately."

I have stood by for too long, this cannot continue.

Isis' eyes glittered dangerously. "Focus on your protégée, and leave Set to us." She spun on her heels and disappeared down the hallway, leaving Tyr to pace.

&&&

A few minutes further from the hotel, entering the city from the savage part of the region, Brennan panted as he dragged one foot in front of the other. His body was yelling in pain at the physical effort it was being submitted to, but still he wouldn't stop.

"Somehow, I doubt I'll be able to get out of bed tomorrow," Brennan muttered. He could clearly picture soaking into a hot tub filled with ice, then letting his muscles relax and getting a good night's rest.

A few more minutes passed by, and he was getting closer to the center of the city. The Wiseman had to stop for a short minute to lean against a house and regain his breath.

Note to self – never enter a mission solo in the future, he mentally chastised himself. No matter how many times his grandfather had warned him against it, he'd still thrown away all precaution and nearly got himself drained of all his powers. Even worse, his mistake had nearly cost Freya her remaining forces, as well.

More for the need to chat than to actually be yelled at, Brennan asked the presence, *No more reprimands?*

You are doing a good job yourself. To his relief, Tyr's tone was light and amused this time.

Brennan bit his lip as he steadied himself and started walking once more. By that point, his limbs felt like they were ripping apart, yet somehow he blocked the agony until he was numb. The less he felt, the more he could concentrate on each step.

As Brennan raised his head, he could see against the dark light the outlines of the hotel, further in the distance. "Nearly... there..." he muttered out loud. "Few... more... kilometers."

Brennan! Tyr's urgent tone sent shivers down his spine.

It also started the Wiseman and he stopped dead in his tracks, senses alert for an imminent danger. Instinctively, he went to reach for his power, but realized it hadn't yet returned. "Great!" His sarcastic whisper echoed in the night, soon followed by a heavy sigh.

What's wrong? Brennan asked the tiger, in a slightly less hostile tone.

Freya! She and Emmanuel left the hotel and their energies have completely disappeared from the building!

Brennan's eyes went wide, even as he clenched his fists in anger. Multiple scenarios started playing in his mind, lighted by a spark of anger. *I have no time to think about this.* If there was a slim chance to still catch Freya before she was out of his reach, he had to take it.

Ruled by an intense feeling of panic, Brennan broke into a run towards the hotel. Ignoring the protests of his muscles and entire body, the Wiseman jogged towards the building as fast as his feet would carry him.

He burst open the doors and ran up the stairs to the floor where both Freya and O'Keeffe's rooms were. Heart pounding in his chest, Brennan fervently prayed that she'd be where he'd left her, exhausted by the new powers received. Every particle in him was focused on her safety.

As he reached Freya's room, Brennan slowed his pace down and approached it cautiously. As an afterthought, he couldn't help wondering if this was perhaps a trap, courtesy of Emmanuel and his friends.

Unable to use his senses and not knowing what was on the other side of the room, Brennan turned the knob and the door swung open without resistance.

The room was empty.

Chapter 18

"N̶o, no, *no*!" Brennan exclaimed, desperately scanning the place for a sign of his partner, all physical pain forgotten in detriment to his heart.

He entered the room, locked the door behind and frantically checked every nook and cranny, though he was positive Freya was no longer there. He was ready to bet Emmanuel was, at the same moment, leading her somewhere as part of a master trap. But where? And was Freya a captive or was she free?

As he made his way to the bathroom, his muscles gave way and Brennan collapsed on the floor, groaning as pain hit him. The numbness disappeared and agony returned with a vengeance, causing the Wiseman to drop his head onto his knees, panting heavily.

"Where the bloody hell could they have gone?" He smacked his fist against the floor, desperate to find Freya before trouble did.

It should not be too hard to guess, Tyr intervened, its tone tense.

"Hold on..." Brennan said as he raised his head up. "You don't think she would actually attempt to rescue Sam on her own?"

When all that answered was complete silence, the Wiseman clenched his fists in despair.

"Damn it!" The curse escaped him unbidden, his voice resonating strangely in the empty room. Brennan got up slowly, testing his muscles, and realized he was capable of walking – for the moment.

I wonder how much this'll hold, the Wiseman thought bitterly, annoyed at his own weakness and how it prevented him from moving freely.

You alone are at fault, Tyr reminded him.

"I know!" Brennan snapped. "And the worst part is that because of me, Freya is probably being led in a trap by that traitor, and no one's there to stop her."

You have to go after her.

"I would, but unfortunately, my physical strength is far from being back to normal. I would most probably get in Freya's way of escaping, if she can."

Hoping at least the telepathic part of his powers worked, Brennan closed his eyes and tried to reach out. *Freya?*

His hopes were crushed when only silence answered. He tried a few more times, with the same result, and had to admit defeat. "I have to do something... Why does she have to be this stubborn?"

If you find the answer to that question, do share, the entity responded.

Brennan bit his lip, mind racing as he thought of ways to save Freya, and potentially help out Sam. Unfortunately, none of the options he came up with could be accomplished as long as he was still useless from the loss of energy.

His only hope, therefore, was Seamus. Despite his lack of spiritual power, the elder Sage was a never-ending well of knowledge, which meant he might have a magical solution.

I can't shake off this stupid feeling we're running out of time... Brennan shook his head, trying to get rid of the morose thoughts. He had to focus, and that meant being open to any other way of helping Freya.

Brennan stumbled to the door, about to head out, but hesitated with his hand on the knob. *What if he thinks this is all my fault?* The last time they'd spoken to the elder Sage together, he'd been none too impressed by the secrets they hid. Brennan was afraid that if he was seen in the weakened state, Seamus would have reason to pinpoint the blame on him.

After a few more moments of second-guessing, the Wiseman concluded Freya's safety trumped everything else, and stepped out of the room. *She matters more than my ego,* Brennan thought resolutely.

In front of Seamus' room, he lost some of his nerve. Inhaling deeply, he knocked and waited with baited breath. When no one answered from within, Brennan searched in his pocket for the spare key and inserted it in the lock.

It clicked softly and the door swung forward, granting Brennan entrance in the darkness.

Is he there? Please confirm he did not join them on the suicidal crusade, Tyr muttered.

Brennan entered the room and closed the door behind him, then switched on the lamp closest to him. A dim glow lighted the room and Brennan's eyes landed on the desk and the person sitting in front of it, his head asleep on a multitude of papers.

He's here, he said.

His golden-brown eyes surveyed Seamus, taking in his hollow features and the dark circles under his eyes. The old Sage looked exhausted, more so than the last time Brennan had seen him.

From the looks of it, O'Keeffe had spent all day getting information on Cortés. On a map of Girona, he'd circled in red the possible places the conquistador could be hiding. The Cathedral was one of them, which made the Wiseman frown. *I thought Gustav alone was hiding there.*

Brennan gently picked up a sheet of paper and read the beginning, his eyes scanning the page quickly. It was giving an account of Cortés' achievements of his living, several of which Seamus had underlined in red. On the margin, Seamus had written a quick note – *thirst for power.*

What is it?

The Wiseman suppressed a snort for fear of awakening O'Keeffe. Instead, he settled for reading mentally to the being constantly in his mind. When he'd finished, there was a short silence, then surprising words.

To be fair, the observation does bring up a good point.

"What?" Brennan questioned.

Well, of course Cortés has an insatiable appetite for influence. The real question, though, is what does he want now? Of his living, he conquered the Aztecs... What is his goal now, especially with that sword?

"I bet you anything Emmanuel the Traitor probably knows," Brennan grumbled.

Do not judge him yet, Brennan, Tyr warned softly.

"Why not? There was hardly room left for interpretation from what I witnessed."

And what if there was something you missed? Something you did not hear?

"I can't believe you're taking his side!" Brennan accused, frowning at the piece of paper in his hand. He placed it back on the desk, then picked up another. This one, oddly enough, was referring to the relics of the Underworld.

I am not taking sides, Brennan, Tyr corrected. *But you should give this ghost the benefit of doubt.*

"Emmanuel doesn't deserve it. He betrayed our confidence and Sam's, and he's no better than Gustav." Keeping his anger in check, Brennan warned low, "I swear, if he dares to hurt Freya, I won't be happy until I track him down and make him pay."

You are impossible sometimes! Tyr said, annoyed at Brennan's refusal to listen to any other opinion but his own.

"I have every reason to be," Brennan snapped back, no longer keeping a tight rein on his tone. "He's been playing us for fools, and I have no mercy for his kind of folk."

When only silence answered him, Brennan realized through the hazy fog of frustration that Tyr had vanished. He clenched his fists, grunting in annoyance, and tightly wound with the fear of losing Freya. No matter what this all-knowing being said, his gut instinct warned him against Emmanuel, and he intended to listen to it.

Granddad... Brennan felt a wave of loneliness hit him, as he realized just how alone he was in the mission. Freya had Sam and Seamus, but he had no one. *It's at times like these*

*that I need your guidance. Why did you have to leave when I
needed you most? When I... When you knew that mom wasn't
there anymore and dad didn't understand?*

Tears stung the back of Brennan's eyes, and dread filled
him all over again. He was concerned for Freya and he
couldn't stand being unable to help if she was in trouble. He
considered it his duty to be by her side every step of the battle, to aid her in the fights, and strengthen her when needed.

Brennan bowed his head and dug his nails in his palms,
attempting to push the sensation away, in order to focus on
what truly mattered. Instead, an unbidden warmth rose in
his chest, almost pulsing against his skin.

The Wiseman reached under his shirt and pulled out the
dragon medallion Thomas had gifted him. It glowed faintly, vibrating against his hand with almost a steady heartbeat.
What the....

Before he could finish the thought, the necklace emitted
a pale light that started to crawl on Brennan's hand, then
body, getting absorbed into it. As it did so, it spread through
his veins, sending a message of love and caring straight to his
heart.

The Wiseman did nothing to stop it, able only to stare
wide-eyed. Through the hazy daze surrounding him, he
heard O'Keeffe ask him something, but could only shake his
head in response. Then another voice resounded in his ears,
one so familiar he could recognize it in a million.

You still have my guidance, Brennan, never forget that, it
reassured.

Granddad? No response came and the warmth slowly
disappeared, as did the glow. It left Brennan with an uncanny

feeling of belonging, and the message of love imprinted on his heart.

"Brennan! Brennan, are you all right?" Seamus's troubled tone broke through his thoughts and the Wiseman started as O'Keeffe touched his shoulder.

He raised a slightly confused look to Seamus, then blinked out of his stupor and let go of the medallion. It took a moment to feel grounded again, as though he'd been floating.

"Yes, I'm...fine, I think," Brennan admitted with a soft hesitation, still amazed by what had just taken place.

O'Keeffe squeezed his shoulder, scanning Brennan's features piercingly. He'd been sleeping peacefully when a surge of power had woken him up, and a voice he thought he'd heard saying that his guidance was not lost. When he'd fully awoken, it was only to see Brennan surrounded by a golden glow, holding onto the necklace he permanently wore. He'd tried getting his attention, but it seemed the Wiseman was in a trance. Now, however, he was coming back to himself.

"What happened?" Seamus prompted gently.

"I don't really know..."

Frowning, the Wiseman did a quick scan of his body with senses, then stopped in shock, realizing what had just happened. "My powers! I've...They're back!" He glanced down, sensing the small ball of energy within as surely as the air entering his lungs.

"Brennan, what are you referring to?" Seamus' contrite tone brought down his exuberance, realizing the slip of the tongue.

O'Keeffe wasn't yet aware of what he'd found out, and thus didn't know about Emmanuel and his betrayal. *Natu-rally... While he's here actually doing something useful for the mission, me and Freya keep looking for trouble.*

Without delay, he told O'Keeffe all that had taken place since they'd last spoken. He revealed everything he could remember about Emmanuel's conversation with Raoul, and about him being Gustav's descendant.

While he recounted the tale, Seamus sat down, resting his chin on his tented hands, eyes on the piece of paper still in the young man's hand. He bid his time until Brennan was done with the story, then said, "So you've been away from the hotel this entire time?"

The Wiseman nodded warily at the odd tone the pro-fessor was using. Seamus paused for a long moment, analyz-ing the youth in front of him, before asking, "How long has the bond been present between you two – with this type of strength?"

Brennan gulped, as it dawned on him neither him nor Freya had truly been truthful with O'Keeffe about that part. "Umm..."

"No lies."

At the firm tone, Brennan rubbed the back of his neck sheepishly, then mumbled, "Since the victory over Cad-mael."

Seamus stood abruptly, and took the piece of paper from Brennan's hand. "Like Freya's parents...."

"Professor?"

Seamus turned around, then sighed. "Mark and Evie, Freya's parents, were guardians of the book. A bond was forged between them as well, one that could let them feel each other's presence and abilities. It was a lot more than that, but that's the gist of it. It is a powerful thing, but also fickle."

"Yeah, we noticed," Brennan grumbled. "When either of us is weak, the other is called upon to substitute a surge of energy."

"That's how you helped Freya after she defeated those ghosts."

Brennan didn't bother commenting. Instead, he pointed to the page in Seamus' hands. "What's that about, the relics?"

"Freya did not tell you?" At Brennan's confused look, he summarized, "There are five objects. Two good – the medallion and book. Three evil – an axe, a sword and chains. During my conversation with Freya, we theorized the demon is at fault for these ghosts coming upon the weapons."

Brennan mulled it over, then nodded thoughtfully.

"You do realize how much danger you were in, during your solo mission?" Seamus pointed out wryly. After a slight hesitation, Brennan inclined his head in assent, fully expecting a lecture. All he received in response was a chuckle. "Well, you and Freya certainly deserve each other as partners."

Brennan was about to ask what Seamus meant by that, but he didn't have to. Having seen the interrogating gleam in his eyes, O'Keeffe gave him a tight smile.

"I meant you both have the same character, and the same heroic gene. But I won't go into detail now on that, there are other much more important things to concentrate on."

"Namely, Emmanuel?" Brennan questioned.

"Yes. What you revealed, it could be problematic. He was there through my chat with Freya. I simply cannot accept that he would betray us..." O'Keeffe frowned. "Are you sure—"

"Yes!" Brennan interrupted firmly. "Listen, Gustav is Emmanuel's ancestor. He would be much more likely to stand with him than with us."

O'Keeffe rubbed his jaw pensively, then gave a single shake of the head. "I will not judge him until I speak with him myself."

Wisely deciding against contesting that, Brennan instead asked, "What else did you figure out about Cortés' plan?"

"That he is too big of a fish to settle for something as small as rallying the ghosts under him. Especially not with that sword."

"And if someone else is pulling the strings..." Brennan trailed off as a thought struck him. "Seamus, you know how I and Freya can feed off each other?" When the old man nodded, he continued, "Can ghosts do that?"

Seamus was about to deny it, but recalled something. He turned back to the desk, pushing papers aside until he found the one he was searching for. He glanced up from it, mouth agape. "They could. With that blasted weapon, Cortés can link them to him."

"Shit."

They shared a look, then Brennan muttered, "Still doesn't explain Gustav's role in all this. If he gets tied in, then he loses his independence. And you've all been saying he's not the type to follow, but to lead."

"Yes," Seamus agreed, "that is true. However, this would grant Gustav the type of protection he never would have on his own. He is a cunning one, if nothing else."

"So what if he's not just smart, but also a wild card?" Brennan reflected aloud. "His main goal has been trying to get Freya, maybe he's just piggybacking on this whole plan until he gets what he wants."

Seamus looked at him in horror. "If that is true, Freya is in much larger danger than she knows! Brennan, if she's going to the Cathedral, whether she's following Emmanuel or not, she will be on their territory. She will be unable to defend herself properly, and without you around as backup, Gustav could very well defeat her!"

They both stared at each other, bodies tense with realization.

"You think, as I do, that she may be with Emmanuel, then?"

O'Keeffe narrowed his eyes. "It is possible, yes. Freya is cautious when it comes to phantoms, but if Sam trusts Emmanuel, then she will stand by his side until she is convinced he is an enemy. Brennan, are you strong enough to use your telepathic bond?"

The Wiseman hesitated, still bitter at the failed attempts from earlier. "It didn't work before, but I can try. Or, I could just go after her! I've gotten the knowledge I needed from you now."

"No," Seamus shook his head adamantly. "We are guessing that they are headed to the Cathedral, but if you are right about Emmanuel, he may have led her into another part of the city. We have to find out where she is first." He ran a hand through his hair in agitation, then added, "I know this may be useless against Freya's stubbornness, but try and convince her to return to the hotel. Tell her we have new information, and we can come up with a better plan to get Sam back, together."

Brennan hesitated, then concentrated on the familiar energy of the Sage. At first, he didn't catch anything, only echoes of her aura. Then, a trail blazed in his mind, and he was able to feel the click of the connection. Almost sighing in relief, Brennan wasted no more time.

Freya? he asked telepathically.

Nothing answered.

Freya? Brennan asked once more.

Still nothing.

Freya! His mental yell had more force, and this time produced an answer.

Brennan!?

The Wiseman told himself the relief at hearing her voice was mainly due to friendly concern for his partner. That the way he sagged against the wall in gratitude, raising his eyes to the ceiling to thank whatever gods existed, was also due to the same fact. The lie worked – for the time being.

No, Santa Claus, he retorted sarcastically. *Of course it's me!*

Well sorry mister, but I've been busy while you were out doing...what, exactly?

I was on a mission, Brennan admitted shortly. *And do tell me what's so important.*

As if you don't know already, Freya scoffed.

Brennan gave a mental growl then, repressing his annoyance, replied, *You're right, I do know. Just like I know that you've got new powers.*

There was a short pause, then Freya asked, *How did you find out?*

Brennan evaded that particular can of worms, and instead continued, *And there's another thing I happen to know – Emmanuel betrayed us.*

A pause, heavily telling, followed.

Freya, you have to get out of there if Emmanuel's with you, Brennan tried to reason with her. *We can come up with a better plan to get Sam! That guy is a traitor and he's luring you into a trap.*

When only silence answered again, Brennan panicked. *Freya, come back here, now!*

What did I tell you about giving me orders? Freya retorted icily.

A knot formed in the Wiseman's stomach at the realization she wouldn't listen. Worse, somehow she'd already taken sides, and ended up opposite him.

And plus, Freya added, *you're mistaken, Brennan. Emmanuel's with us.*

I heard it myself, he's Gustav's descendant, for crying out loud! Brennan tried to make her understand, but she was deaf to his pleas.

I know he is! Freya snapped back. *And I trust him because he had the guts to be honest with me and told me himself. He would've told you, too, had you stuck around instead of being a lone wolf.*

Ignoring the pique, Brennan's tone hardened. *You're too naïve, Freya. Emmanuel's most likely just as* **bad as Gustav!** *Think about it, he's your enemy's descendant!*

Freya's voice was equally frosty as she accused, *You don't know what you're talking about.*

Why can't you just face the truth and listen to me!? Brennan yelled. *Damn, Freya! We've been partners for a bit, we faced enough foes together. You should be able to trust me by now!*

And you *should be able to trust* me, Freya bit back. *You refuse to admit you're wrong!*

Because I know I'm not. Raoul told Emmanuel he's one of them, he affirmed it! Don't you see? He can't be on our side!

Maybe not on your side, but he is on mine, Freya retorted determinately.

Brennan's face drained of color. *What's that supposed to mean?*

It means that unlike you, I take the time to get to know people, and not make judgmental calls. If I have to stand up to you, make no mistake, I will.

The Wiseman was quiet as the blow took some time to get over. *You're unbelievable! If you had as much faith in me as you do that damned ghost, we wouldn't be in this mess! We could've gotten rid of Cortés from the get-go.*

Well, you've got no one to blame but yourself for that.

What's that supposed to mean!? Brennan pushed back, but Freya didn't reply. *All right, I can take a hint. You're on your own there, Freya.*

With that said, Brennan cut the connection. Clenching his fists, he bit back his frustration and hate of Emmanuel.

He was already regretting the words spoken in anger, but he was too proud to take them back. The hurt from Freya's words threatened to suffocate him, he pushed it to the back of his mind, setting it aside.

He turned to O'Keeffe, ready to admit failure in the one simple task he'd been asked to do. But the elder Sage's dark grey eyes were gentle and full of compassion as they caught Brennan's.

Seamus raised a hand up in silence. "It is quite all right, Brennan, I guessed as much. Freya can be much too stubborn sometimes." Taking a closer look, he added, "She can say hurtful things, but eventually will come around. If you can, all I ask is you keep an eye on her from afar... Let me know if whatever she does gets out of control. There is nothing we can do at this point but wait."

After a slight hesitation, Brennan nodded. "Fine, but it might be best if I'm surrounded by her things." When Seamus didn't contest it, he left and returned to Freya's room.

Taking off his shoes, he laid down on the bed, arms crossed under his head, staring at ceiling morosely. After a few moments, an overwhelming need to nap washed over him, and he closed his eyes.

Left in the room alone, Seamus frowned as he recalled the glow and the medallion that had woken him up, as well as the voice. "Are you truly dead, Thomas? Or simply disappeared?" His words lingered in the empty room, but the answer he sought eluded him.

&&&

A few kilometers away, in front of the Cathedral's steps stood a fuming Freya and a determined Emmanuel.

Freya's anger had nothing to do with the barrier that was surrounding the church. Rather, it had everything to do with a certain Wiseman who was getting on her nerves. Though Brennan's words had hurt more than Freya would admit, she preferred fury to sadness.

How dare he assume he knows everything? Freya gritted her teeth. *He knows nothing of what Emmanuel had to put up with after his death!*

Freya, keep your temper in check, Tyr recommended.

The Sage was about to retort with a nasty comeback, but instead started taking deep breaths, inhaling and exhaling out slowly.

Next to her, Emmanuel surveyed Freya out of the corner of his eyes.

After joining her outside the hotel, they'd jogged up to the Cathedral at a normal pace – Emmanuel mostly floated. It was when they'd nearly reached it that Freya had stopped dead in her tracks, frowning. When the spirit had asked her what was amiss, she admitted having felt an unusual warmth in her chest for a split of a second. He'd been about to call the whole thing off, but after Freya's reassurance, decided to keep going.

Minutes later, they reached the Cathedral and found a spot where they could observe the entrance without being seen in return. They settled at a distance from the building for the time being.

At some point during their watch, Freya jumped next to him. Emmanuel had rightly guessed – from what Sam had told him about telepathic conversations – that Freya was mentally conversing with someone. He'd observed as she'd been first overjoyed, then shocked and, finally, angry... Until the moment she closed her eyes as though fighting back tears.

Emmanuel took yet another peek at Freya out of the corner of his eyes. She took another breath to calm herself – or so he guessed.

Unable to stand by quietly any longer, Emmanuel turned to her. "What happened?"

"Hmm?" The Sage's eyes were slightly misty, but she blinked and focused on him.

"Well, you were chatting to somebody just now, who obviously pissed you off. I wanted to know if I could help with anything."

Freya raised an eyebrow mockingly, her anger now vanished. "And just how did you know that?"

"A good friend of mine told me about the wonders of telepathic conversations."

The slight smirk on Freya's face was immediately wiped off her face as soon as she heard mention of Sam.

Emmanuel bit his lip, but got past the hesitation and asked, "Out of curiosity, was it Brennan you were conversing with?"

Freya did not reply immediately, her gaze wandering at the still dark sky. "Yeah," she eventually admitted, a bitter edge to her voice. Thinking over what Brennan had said, she knew he was wrong. Utterly so.

I trust your judgment on this, Tyr said.

"He doesn't trust you, Em," Freya sighed, deciding to be truthful. "He thinks you're leading me into a trap, straight to

Gustav." The Sage was now staring away from Emmanuel, towards the Cathedral.

She could feel the ghost's eyes on her. "Do you... Do you think so, too?"

"Of course not. You've been more than truthful with me, and I value honesty. I trust you, and will continue to do so until you prove me otherwise."

The ghost nodded, Freya's words touching him profusely.

He was surprised when the Sage frowned and asked, "Still, do you happen to know how Brennan could've found out that you're Gustav's descendant?"

Emmanuel shook his head in answer, thinking that there was no possible way that the Wiseman could've known that. He stopped mid-motion, though, when something struck him. The last time he'd met Raoul out of town, he'd been suspicious of being followed. The impression had been forgotten when Raoul showed up, but now...

"Freya," his admission was soft-spoken, and slightly contrite. "I think Brennan followed me when I went to meet Raoul."

Chapter 19

Freya narrowed her eyes and stared at Emmanuel for a long time, mulling over his words. In the end, she shook her head with a pained expression on her face.

"That is so typical of Brennan," she muttered, adding the pieces of the puzzle together based on what she knew of the Wiseman. "He probably saw you leave the hotel and since he had an issue with you from the beginning, he decided to see where you were going. Still," Freya's frown deepened. "From what you told me, you made it clear to Raoul that you weren't on his side. And yet Brennan was adamant that Raoul said you were one of them."

"He must have been missed the rest!" Emmanuel's eyes widened. "It's the only logical explanation. If he'd heard everything, he would not doubt me."

Freya nodded slowly, but surprisingly, it was Tyr who came up with the missing part. *Something did happen then, that would account for the missed conversation. Brennan used too much of his powers. Like you, because of the new abilities gifted from the book, he should have rested. When he did not, he was quickly exhausted.*

But then he's being stupid! He knows he hasn't heard every-thing! Freya protested.

She was answered by a short silence, then Tyr added, *I do not think he realizes it.*

What do you mean, Tyr? Freya questioned.

Only that Brennan drew his own conclusions. His judgment may be hasty, but it is clouded by his distress for your well-being.

Freya felt a lump in her throat, and had to swallow past it. She furiously blinked back the tears threatening to over-whelm, and sighed loudly in annoyance. *Then Brennan's being an idiot, Tyr. And that's too bad if he thinks Em's a traitor, because I don't agree.*

I support your decision entirely, Freya, Tyr tried to placate her. *I do not, however, agree with you being so near that cursed place.*

Too bad. I need to see if I can pick up Sam's trace, maybe get him out of here.

And I would feel better if you could put more distance be-tween you and that spiritual place.

When Freya refused to reply, the tiger growled. *Very well, I see I cannot change your mind. Do not be a fool, do not go in-side it. That place can be your tomb if you do not listen to me.*

Freya thought it over for a second, then finally allowed, *All right, Tyr. I promise.*

When the connection had ended, Freya turned to Em-manuel. "Let's take a look around without entering the Cathedral."

The ghost nodded, but a worried look crossed his fea-tures. "As you wish. What about Brennan?"

"What *about* him?" Freya retorted curtly.

"Well..." Emmanuel hesitated. He would've felt a lot more secure if the Wiseman was there to help the Sage in case any unforeseen problems arose. "Is he coming?"

Freya's eyes darkened with unspoken anger, even as she clenched her fists. "No," the answer came through gritted teeth.

"Why not?" Emmanuel probed, tilting his head to the side. Sure, the Wiseman didn't trust him. But he would've thought his concern for the Sage overbalanced the dislike.

"Because he's an idiot," Freya muttered. She seemed ready to add more, but only exhaled heavily in the end. "We can do this on our own, so let's get to it. Sam's been captive for too long."

The ghost nodded gravely, getting the hint – she was done sharing. Whatever had happened between the two, no matter how serious, would remain a mystery.

He hurried to float to the Sage's side, who was already heading out. When he neared her, Freya stumbled and had to take a hold of Emmanuel's arm to steady herself as a wave of weakness passed through her. *Probably still the after effects of my new powers...*

"Freya! Are you all right?" Emmanuel asked fretfully. He scanned the Sage, whose eyes were shut tightly in an effort to regain some countenance.

Finally, the world stopped spinning and Freya was able to stand without support. She pushed herself away from Emmanuel and smiled weakly. "I'm fine, don't worry. Just a bit dizzy because of the lack of sleep."

She then turned to her left and took one last look at the empty street, half-expecting Brennan to come running from nowhere and apologize, then admit he was ready to kick some ghost butt.

Nothing happened though, and the street remained desolated.

Freya bit back the threatening tears, refusing to show any sign of weakness. Especially not this close to the mission.

You could make the first step, Tyr suggested hesitantly.

Freya clenched her jaw in response. *No.* Brennan's words had hurt her in a way nothing had ever done, but pride stopped her from letting go of the sorrow. Instead, she did the only thing she could – turned the aggression towards the mission, and the bad ghosts. It was a therapy far more helpful than crying.

He said what he thought, and I told him my opinion. And he's right – we're not as similar as we both thought. We're two totally different persons, Tyr.

Freya... The tiger trailed off, at a loss of what to say. *I know his words hurt you... But have you thought that your words may have hurt him even more?*

Freya mentally snorted. *Please, Tyr. As if I'd believe that. Brennan cares more about himself than any other person in the world. If he took any offence to what I said, it's only because I bruised his ego by taking Emmanuel's side.*

Tyr's voice was strangely sad as added, *You may be surprised to find out that his ego is not all that suffered...*

Before Freya could question the tiger further, the connection was broken. The Sage gave one small shrug. *Just as well, I've got a mission to focus on.*

With one last look at the street, she turned to Emmanuel. "Let's go."

&&&

Brennan's eyes snapped open as a pang of weakness hit him. He stood up on the bed and turned his gaze to the window outside, eyes narrowed in concentration.

Though he refused to acknowledge it, everything in him was pushing for contact with Freya. Wanting to apologize, to take back his words, to help her in whatever crazy mission she was out there fulfilling on her own.

Through the window, the Wiseman could see the darkness envelop the whole city. An envious moon looked coldly upon the world of the living and the stars watched the souls of the dead.

He thought of Freya, and how she'd be fighting Gustav alone if he ambushed her. Some part of him relished the satisfaction he'd feel when she would return and reveal that he'd been right, that Emmanuel had betrayed them...

But what if she doesn't? A tiny voice at the back of his mind asked. Indeed, what if the Sage didn't survive? What if he was mistaken? Or worse, what if because of his stubbornness, she got killed?

Brennan sighed heavily, shutting out similar thoughts. Freya had chosen to stand by Emmanuel no matter what, and he wasn't about to beg her to listen.

Before he closed himself off, the Wiseman tugged at the link, and could sense Freya was weak at the moment. She was still getting over the upgrade in her spiritual energy, and the urge to contact her persisted, if only to ensure she was well.

In spite of his best judgment, Brennan closed off the connection between them and unglued his eyes from the window. *Freya made her choice.* With that thought firmly in mind, he lay back on the bed, arms crossed under his head once more.

No matter what would happen, one thing was sure – he needed to replenish his forces. And the best way to do so, at the moment, was rest.

"Please be all right, Freya," he whispered to the darkness, then let sleep carry him off.

&&&

A few kilometers away, Freya and Emmanuel had finished checking the surroundings of the Cathedral for any signs of ghosts. Not having found any, they both returned to the rendezvous point fairly quickly.

Freya leaned her back against one of the small houses and took a deep breath of the fresh night air.

"No sign of Gustav or any ghosts," Emmanuel reported with a hint of tension in his voice.

Freya didn't say anything, simply nodding her head curtly to acknowledge his words. Her grey eyes scanned the Cathedral, all senses alert, but she couldn't find a hint of the phantoms. She had a feeling the power of the Cathedral was cloaking them, and she did not like it.

Finally, the Sage turned to Emmanuel. "Same here. No sign of any ghostly presence other than your own. But that doesn't mean they aren't here... The energy barrier around this place is strong. It's harder to separate it from what I'd normally be looking for with Sam – his soul-like quality."

Emmanuel's eyes glanced to the Cathedral, then back to Freya. "But then... That means it would apply to the other ghosts. So they could be hiding in there right now, observing us. We could be sitting ducks!"

Freya shook her head, her raven locks swinging around her face, and folded both arms across her chest. "They wouldn't be that stupid, to be so close within view. But as for the other part, I'm sure they're in there. Sam's trace led me right here... I'm one hundred percent sure he's inside."

Emmanuel nodded gravely, knowing not to doubt the Sage's powers. But that only made it harder, knowing that Sam was almost within reach yet they could not go in to rescue him.

As if reading his emotions, Freya whispered, "What if we went in?"

Had he been alive, Emmanuel's heart would've stopped in panic. As it was, he could only hope the Sage didn't mean what he thought she did. "*Qué quieres decir?*" he asked, just to make sure.

Freya met his gaze, chewing on her bottom lip. "What I mean is, we're going in."

"No!" Emmanuel shook his head. "Trust me, I want to rescue Sam, but Freya, from what O'Keeffe and Brennan have been saying, it really isn't a good idea to go in by yourself."

It was her turn to frown. "You're wrong if you think I'll let you go in alone, Em. I'm not the type to sit around and watch. I plan to get Sam back, no matter the risks and what everyone's been saying."

Emmanuel gave her an annoyed look, knowing only too well that Freya would not make things easier. He wondered if it was better to convince her of the futility of her actions before she got hurt, or simply to go and find Brennan. He settled for the former, seeing as the Wiseman probably hated him even more than he had at the beginning when they'd met.

The ghost was no fool – he'd seen the hostile glares from the Wiseman. It was clear he didn't trust him, but what was even more crystal was that Brennan didn't fear for his own life. He feared for Freya's. Which was why he was so protective of the Sage, even if she wasn't aware of it.

I should remember to do something about it... Perhaps Sam can help, Emmanuel mused mischievously.

"Freya...." Emmanuel tried to reason with her. "Just think this over for a second, please? The Cathedral's huge amount of energy can either totally waste your own energy or render you powerless. None of which will help Sam. Besides, it would be complete madness to go in there in your weakened state."

She seemed to ponder his words for a moment, eyes shifting around and scanning the area. Emmanuel was left with a slight hope that she'd take his advice. However, when she finally turned back to him, her eyes glinted with something akin to excitement.

I don't like this...

"Why do I have the feeling that whatever I just said passed through one ear and escaped through the other?" he asked warily.

"That's because it has," Freya's didn't bother denying it. "Before you start, I have a plan. It'll work for both of us, and I assure you it's a win-win situation. We won't go in the Cathedral, we'll just get closer to it. Enough to see if I can pick any vibe from Sam."

Emmanuel cocked his head to one side, intrigued and slightly fearful of where she was heading with the idea.

"See those stairs?" Freya pointed to the long marches leading to the church. When he nodded, she said, "We'll go up them until we reach the entrance to the Cathedral. From there on, if I don't pick anything strange, then you can go inside for fifteen minutes – no more – and check it out, see if you can find anything. If not, we'll improvise then. So what do you think?"

"I think you're *loca*," the spirit muttered truthfully.

Freya let out a chuckle. "You're not the first to call me crazy, Em. I meant about the plan."

Emmanuel hesitated, partially wanting to believe the Sage would hold her promise, but still knowing she probably wouldn't. *It's not like there's much choice left,* he reflected. *If I don't go, she'll do it anyway.* He decided to accompany the Sage, at least that way he might be able to help.

"Fine," Emmanuel nodded towards Freya. "But how can you be sure this idea of yours will work?"

With a shrug and a toss of her ponytail, the Sage pounced ahead before the question was fully phrased. "Because it's foolproof," was all she threw over a shoulder.

"It had better be," Emmanuel added gravely.

"Don't be such a spoilsport! Come on!" She then broke into a run towards the dreaded building.

Emmanuel could only follow her, floating.

&&&

Sighing heavily, O'Keeffe got up from the bed and took a seat by the window, unable to rest. His thoughts were swirling in a pool of confusion, awakening memories in his mind that he hadn't dared remember for many years.

He looked up at the bright full moon and the clear night sky, at the sparkling stars, and closed his eyes. The armchair was comfortable and, lulled by the sounds of the night, he drifted to sleep.

In his dream, O'Keeffe found himself in a place of glory, a circle of power like the Stonehenge stones. However, it was not that particular one.

"Seamus!"

The old Sage turned around, shocked to find his Wiseman friend just mere feet away. "Thomas!" he breathed in shock.

Hair slightly greyer than he remembered, brown eyes just as smiling, the man grinned. "Long time no see..."

Seamus crossed the distance and pulled him into a hug, patting his back before pulling away. "I have missed you, my friend!"

"And I, you. But we do not have much time. You are focusing on the wrong thing. Forget Cortés, focus on the demon. There is something more behind him. Look at the story of Isis and Osiris. Read of Set..." When Seamus only stared back in confusion, Thomas added, "It will all make sense when you follow my instructions."

"What will?"

Lightning crossed the sky, and ominous thunder beat in the darkening clouds. Thomas glanced up, fear crossing his face. "It is time I leave."

"Wait, Thomas!" Seamus tried to grasp him, but woke up.

The old Sage's gaze went to the mountains of papers on his desk, surveying them all. He then stood and rummaged in his suitcase for the old text he always brought around, containing the mythology of the world – the *real* one.

Having long since accepted his calling as a Sage, Seamus had been trained in all aspects of it. One such part was being aware of the reality that was the world at some point. Gods fighting each other, creatures of dark and light existing, parallel dimensions, even. It had blown his logical mind when he'd learned everything, but eventually it became common knowledge among his peers, and he'd grown accustomed to it.

Skimming through the old book, Seamus found the part referring to Egyptian gods. He hastily read the story, eyes widening throughout. As he stood to pace, something fell out of the book – a piece of paper, with Thomas' scrawling on it.

Seamus dazedly picked it up, recalling his friend had once borrowed the book, months before his death. The elder Wiseman had always been sensitive to vibrations, and could even read certain things off them, similar to prophecies. He always tended to write them down. Most were cryptic riddles, but the particular one in his hand was clear as crystal.

Isis and Osiris imprisoned Set in the Underworld, hiding him from all mortals' eyes. Guardians keep the gate, but the dark god is not yet done. His powers still immense, he constantly wishes for escape.

Next to it, Thomas had added a warning:

The relics of the Underworld can help him. They cannot fall in his hands.

Seamus looked up from the last piece of the puzzle, his eyes widening in horror. He quickly double-checked his information and, realizing it was only too correct, gave a small incredulous sound. "This isn't... If this is true..."

O'Keeffe got up from the chair and dashed for the door, knowing he had no time to waste.

&&&

Freya panted as she climbed the stairs leading to the Cathedral, her eyes taking in the imposing gothic structure of the building. She glared at Emmanuel, who was floating effortlessly ahead, the use of his muscles not required to climb the monstrous staircase.

Feeling a slight pain in her side, Freya paused. "Em, slow down a second, will you?"

The ghost smirked as he floated down to Freya. "Don't tell me you're tired already."

She waved him off. "You don't have to climb these stairs, you can just float above them!"

Emmanuel smiled wryly, "Indeed, I don't." His deadness was not lost on him, and the reminder stung. To gather himself, he turned away from Freya and moved further up.

Realizing she'd hurt him without meaning to, the Sage sighed and apologized, "Sorry. Some situations just get the worst out of me."

The ghost glanced up at the sky, an oddly nostalgic look on his features. *What is done is done.* Resolving not to linger on it, he faced her once more. "Don't worry about it. I'm not one to hold grudges."

"Yet another difference between you and Gustav," Freya panted, climbing to be at his level. "You're entirely sure you're descended from him?"

Emmanuel chuckled, a sad undertone to his voice. "Unfortunately. Now come on, Sage, we still have a bit to go."

Freya straightened and pulled at her loosened ponytail, puffing out a breath. With deft fingers, she re-tied her hair and moved forward. "All right, let's go."

Emmanuel lingered behind this time, his eyes scanning the Cathedral and its imposing structure. He frowned slightly, unable to view it as anything other than a menace.

I wonder if perhaps my subconscious is trying to warn me about something...

Emmanuel knew that being Gustav's descendant, he could sometimes feel whether his ancestor was around or not. Usually, it was an instant sensation that alerted him. Sometimes, it took a few seconds to realize it, but it was never confusing. *Not this kind of confusing.*

The phantom's eyes stopped wandering across the building, and landed instead on Freya. The Sage had paused midstep, body wired tightly.

All of Freya's senses yelled in alarm at what her subconscious perceived. Freya shut her mind off to better pick the vibration. She pivoted around, taking in everything around her, every single ounce of vibration, but what she was looking for had long evaporated, as if it hadn't been there at all. Oddly enough, she was gathering more in her sweep than she usually did.

The Sage was left with a bitter taste in her mouth. What she'd felt, even if only for a second, awakened echoes of a past battle at the back of her mind. *A battle with a formidable foe...*

Freya frowned as her gaze landed on Emmanuel. The ghost seemed to be asking her something, but she couldn't hear him.

As she stared dazedly, Emmanuel floated until he was in front of her, and touched her shoulder gently. "Are you feeling all right?" he repeated.

The Sage bit her lip. *Am I? There was something... For a mere second, I thought I picked up another vibration, but... Nah, it was probably Emmanuel's. I must be getting rusty.*

Freya shrugged, willing herself to sound reassuring. "Sure. I was waiting for you to catch up."

Emmanuel gave her a mocking look. "Yeah, right!"

"Okay, okay," Freya admitted. "I picked up a vibration, but it must've been a fluke. It was gone shortly after."

Emmanuel arched a fine eyebrow. "Are you sure? Because if you aren't, Freya, I consider it my duty to call this off and get you back to the hotel before it's too late."

"Are you doubting me? I told you, it must've been nothing." They stared at each other for a few moments, until he glanced away, mumbling something under his breath.

"Great, so let's go," Freya rushed on. "The sun will rise soon, and we don't want to be here when people arrive."

Emmanuel rolled his eyes, but followed after her. The end of the staircase was drawing nearer by the second.

&&&

Since he'd woken up, Brennan hadn't been able to fall back asleep. He'd tried to convince himself it would pass, but he knew better than to accept his own lies.

Restlessness, he was used to when not in constant action. But the sensation of his heart being tight in his chest, almost making it hard to breathe, was not. With each passing moment, the knowledge he'd let Freya face peril alone weighed more and more.

Unable to fall back asleep, Brennan replayed his last conversation with the Sage over and over in his head. He desperately wanted to feel some resentment towards her for choosing to stand by Emmanuel rather than by him, but he was unable to.

What was worse, Freya's judgment was starting to make sense, even to him. Despite it, he refused to contact her.

Why do you have to be so damn proud? Tyr growled. With being stuck in the godly realm, the tiger had no choice but to push the Wiseman to act. Unfortunately, it had forgotten how complicated mortals were.

"I am not!" Brennan retorted aloud.

Really? You could go and help her, and it would only cost you some of your pride.

"Need I point out I still don't have my full strength back?"

Tyr sent a surge of power through their link, and watched in satisfaction as Brennan was blasted off the bed to the ground, and left panting.

Now you do.

"Why the hell didn't you do that before!?" Brennan questioned the empty air, lifting himself in a proper sitting position.

Because what you felt now is only an awakening of what was already returned to you. Now go to Freya!

"No!" Brennan burst, surprising both himself and the voice. "She wouldn't listen to me about Emmanuel. Too bad for her."

I was mistaken, apparently, Tyr muttered, sounding disappointed.

"About what?"

You are not proud, but an egotistical teenager. Freya was right to keep you from interfering with her mission.

"What? I'm not, she—" Brennan tried to protest, but the words soon trailed off.

This is not about Freya making the right decision, Tyr went on, pitiless. *This is about her picking Emmanuel over you, about bruising your ego!*

"I... That's utterly—"

True, the being finished. But at the same time, it picked something else in Brennan's feelings. The reality of it caused a slight softening of its tone. *It may be time for you to face your feelings, but you will have to wait until after the battle. For now, go and apologize to Freya!*

"I said no already," Brennan said stubbornly. "She can go on without me. Hasn't she been singing that song ever since

Seamus told her I was coming on the mission? Besides, if she's in trouble, Emmanuel can get her out of it."

You know you do not mean that, Tyr said, its tone conciliatory. *And besides, what if she was right and you were wrong? What would you do then? I would guess probably run away, go back to England and pretend your feelings do not exist.*

"What's that supposed to mean?" Brennan frowned. Only silence answered, and he was left to ponder the words.

Frustrated, Brennan got up from the bed and started pacing in the room. He was so lost in his own thoughts that the knock on the door took a few seconds to reach his brain.

When it did, Brennan headed over. "Who is it?"

"It's me, Seamus."

Relieved for the distraction from his ruminations, the Wiseman opened the door at once. "Professor," he greeted the old Sage.

O'Keeffe entered the room like a whirlwind, turning to Brennan with panic glinting in his grey eyes. "I hope I'm not waking you up, but I had to come here immediately."

"Not at all, I was having some difficulties falling asleep." Choosing not to elaborate on his last statement, Brennan gestured for him to sit. "What's so urgent?"

O'Keeffe took a deep breath and lifted the old text, his voice shaking as the words poured out.

&&&

Freya placed her hands on her hips, craning her neck to look up at the Cathedral. On her right side, Emmanuel followed her gaze.

"Intimidating, isn't it?" he whispered.

The structure loomed like a large, gothic monster in the midst of more modern buildings. The moon shone on it, giving it an almost eerie glow in the darkness. Light bounced off the dome, glinting in the night.

"Just a bit," Freya laughed nervously. "I'll check for signs of ghostly presences, all right?"

When Emmanuel nodded, Freya closed her eyes, tuning out all other senses except her spirit, which she let roam free to sweep around the church. For a few seconds, she received nothing back. Then, that same vibration she'd felt earlier appeared, followed by Sam's.

"Sam!" Freya breathed out, then blinked in shock.

"He's in there? You felt him?" Emmanuel asked.

"Yes," Freya nodded. "Him and someone else, but—" She didn't get to finish her sentence.

At that same moment, a familiar voice yelled from deep within the Cathedral. "Help!"

"That's Sam!" Freya exclaimed, unconsciously stepping forward.

Emmanuel grabbed her by the arm and locked gazes with her. "No, Freya. You're *not* going in there."

The Sage's eyes turned blazing, a flame burning deep inside them. "Watch me!" she muttered in a low, threatening voice. Releasing herself from Emmanuel's grip, she ran to the great doors.

Freya paused in her movement, scanning the new obstacle. The fury and fear for Sam's well-being filled her, and she lifted her palms towards the entrance. Her spiritual energy vibrated around her, and the Sage centralized it on the element of air. With one push of her hand, a blast of energy hit the wood, and the doors flew open.

"Wow," she breathed in amazement. "So this must be what the book gifted us with...The ability to overpower places of power."

The Sage quickly reached another conclusion – however temporary, her new capabilities would function within the church. Unwilling to waste further time to analyze what it meant, she rushed in.

"Freya, *no*!"

Ignoring Emmanuel's calls, the Sage disappeared in the darkness.

The phantom was about to rush in after her, when he realized that was what expected – by whomever was awaiting them within the Cathedral. *I cannot give them the satisfaction, and leave her defenseless. That leaves me with one choice....*

With one last troubled look to the doors, Emmanuel started dematerializing, planning to get help as soon as possible. Unfortunately, nothing happened and he found himself at the exact same place, his eyes widening incredulously. "What is the meaning of this?"

It didn't take him longer than a few seconds to realize the energy emanating from it was stopping him from dematerializing. *Which means, my only choice is to go in.*

However much he was aware entering the Cathedral was going to his doom, Emmanuel nevertheless floated towards it until he reached the huge oak doors. He glanced one last time behind, actually hoping for Brennan's aid, then floated within.

Chapter 20

Raksh turned away from Gustav's ranting, facing the other way of the hall. The Cathedral was a maze, but the demon could sense the Sage's entrance.

"Ssshe isss here," he murmured in awe.

The wraith could almost taste Freya's hope of saving her friend, then something else registered – her new powers. Whereas before the Sage had been strong, now her aura radiated hotly even across the distance. *The fool! She does exactly as I had predicted.*

"Who is?" Gustav questioned.

"Freya."

The phantom clapped his hands together, rubbing them eagerly. "Finally!"

"Do not be ssso hasssty!" Raksh warned, grasping him to stop him from going ahead. "Freya is more capable than the lasst time you have fought, much more. Do not underesssti-mate the young one."

Gustav snorted, evidently not believing his words. "You've done your part," he lifted his middle finger, and the ruby ring adorning it. "This will be enough to provoke her, so thank you for your gift. Now let me do my business."

"All you need to do isss make her lossse control," Raksh repeated. "I want that energy within her."

"Whatever you say, boss-man," Gustav muttered, then turned and left. He would get the demon what he wanted – *after* he was done torturing the little witch.

Raksh watched the leader's departure, eyes narrowed pensively. Once he had Freya out of control, he could harness that energy and use it to burst the gates of the Underworld and help Set escape. *A simple enough plan, but effective.*

Somehow, he doubted Gustav would pay attention to his words. He'd known the man was a wild card when they got into business, but it was getting tiring.

No matter. One way or another, I will get what I need.

He dematerialized to go to the other part of his plan, and Cortés' new location.

&&&

Damn it, Seamus and Tyr were right! Freya swore mentally.

Arrogant in the new use of her powers, she'd chosen to ignore their warnings of staying away. Now that she was fully immersed in the Cathedral's spiritual energy, Freya could sense her new abilities waning. Even something as simple as running on straight, even ground required more focus.

She was regretting not having listened to the old Sage, but remained adamant on not going back. *Since I'm here anyway, I'll find Sam. Might as well.* A fierce will to find her friend fuelled every step, even if the way to escape out of the Cathedral was blurry.

The Sage kept running forwards, deeper in the labyrinth of columns and halls. At the same time, she was reflecting on the situation and attempting to find a solution – before she was in graver danger than at the moment.

Freya was no fool. A trap awaited her somewhere between the stony walls, but it was useless to let it trouble her. As long as it helped Sam get free, she would worry about her own safety later, when she had time for it.

As she turned a corner, the Sage bumped into Emmanuel. Since the ghost was solid whenever he approached her, it resulted in Freya losing her balance and falling on the floor. She accepted his hand and propped herself back on her feet swiftly, brushing a lock of hair out of her eyes.

"What are you doing here?" she whispered, wanting to avoid an echo at all cost.

"I wanted to go and alert O'Keeffe or Brennan," Emmanuel replied back, hushed. "But I could not dematerialize."

"You mean the barrier works for spirits too?" Freya frowned. When Emmanuel nodded, the Sage bit her lip. Someone was messing with the spiritual energy of the place, enough so to make it go haywire. Since Gustav was only a pawn, that left one being who could do such a thing.

That damned demon is here.

Tyr's words of warning came to her mind unbidden, as did the suggestion she needed Brennan to win against Raksh. A shiver crossed Freya's spine, a sense of foreboding and peril that left her antsy.

Gulping past the irrational fear, she mumbled, "Plan A won't work, then."

"Plan A?" Emmanuel questioned.

"Getting you and Sam to dematerialize while I hold the ghosts off."

Emmanuel stared at her for a beat, then cursed something under his breath. He floated away for a moment almost angrily, before spinning back to her. "And pray tell," Emmanuel started sarcastically, "how were *you* going to escape?"

Freya shrugged nonchalantly. "A bit of fighting here and there and I'd make my out to the exit somehow. Seems that's not possible, though."

"Clearly," Emmanuel commented evenly. He couldn't comprehend the Sage had such a disregard for her own safety – no matter how well she was able to defend herself. Willing himself to drop the attitude at the risk of alienating her, he asked, "So... Do you have a plan B?"

Freya glanced around, absentmindedly adding, "Yeah. Find another exit from where you and Sam can escape outside."

"I'm not leaving you here," Emmanuel declared. "And neither will Sam."

"Let's talk about this later, shall we?" Freya said. "For now, finding that exit is a priority."

Without further comment, the Sage walked away. She quickly swept their surroundings with her senses, but nothing came back to indicate ghosts were around. Satisfied, Freya jogged along the maze.

After a slight hesitation, Emmanuel followed her, and soon they were wandering in unknown territory, completely unaware their every move was being watched.

&&&

In the palace of the gods, the couple appeared near Tyr. "The stars have changed their story," Isis started. "Your protégée will not harm the book and medallion, she will continue on as a guardian."

Tyr only watched the two, unwilling to respond.

"We apologize," Osiris started. "And as a show of good faith, please look at this."

Tyr peeked towards the fire where Osiris was pointing, and saw a map of Spain and France. On its border were red dots... Many of them.

What is this?

"France. Cortés' army of the joined cliques is aiming to take over it and force their ghosts under submission."

Why bother?

"Because the demon speculated France is where he can find clues to the location of the relics," Isis revealed softly. "With the entire country under the command of his puppet Cortés, Raksh will strive, feeding off the chaos."

"And he plans to use the sword for the takeover," Osiris added.

I have to warn Freya! Tyr muttered, and tried contacting the Sage. To its utmost surprise, the attempt bounced back.

The tiger turned to the gods. *Consider your apology accepted. Now where is she?*

Isis shared a contrite glance with Osiris. As their forms shimmered to disappear, she replied, "Where you cannot reach her."

&&&

Back at the hotel, O'Keeffe had just finished revealing Brennan his findings, and the Wiseman was staring in shock.

"This is impossible... Seamus, you're describing fables and myths!"

"It is very much true. It was your own grandfather that led me to it." At his confused look, Seamus elaborated, "I had a dream of Thomas, telling me where to look and what to find." He left out his own suspicions about the man's death, and instead continued, "It is true information, Brennan. Set is imprisoned, and those relics can release him. The coincidence is too grand."

"That's why Raksh is on our trail?"

"Yes."

"And Freya doesn't know about this..." Brennan trailed off as something else struck him. "Gustav must be in league with the damned Raksh. He wants Freya so bad, who knows what else the demon has allowed for?"

"All very true," Seamus agreed anxiously. "It explains why he wanted me out of the game so early on. It took us this much longer to figure out the real plan. He must have realized during our last mission that my strength lies not so much in my brawn, but in my brain."

Brennan clenched his fists in anger. "If I get my hands on that thing..."

"Forget the wraith for now. Where exactly is Freya?"

Forgetting all about his resolution, Brennan tried to contact Freya immediately, but found his attempt unsuccessful. When another attempt failed, he panicked. That soon turned into despair when he used his senses to locate Freya's energy... Straight inside the Cathedral.

Brennan's golden-brown eyes met O'Keeffe's grey ones and he whispered, as if not believing it himself, "She went in that blasted church."

"No!" Seamus protested weakly, dropping in the armchair and grasping his head in his hands.

NO! Tyr boomed in Brennan's mind. *She promised she would not go in there!* A painful roar filled Brennan's mind at once, nearly bursting his head open, then disappeared as if it was never there.

Brennan bowed his head as he recalled the last fight with Cadmael. When Freya had released her powers and banished the Viking chief, Brennan remembered having seen a white tiger behind her. At the time, he'd thought no more of it, believing it to be an illusion. Now, the Wiseman realized it had been very real indeed.

So all this time, I was guided by Freya's protector... And I'm ready to bet she wasn't even aware of it.

As Brennan reflected on the new revelation, he also came to terms with another epiphany. He *had* been foolish and arrogant in his pride, and should have listened to the tiger. Because of him, Freya was facing great risks, alone.

But I plan to change that.

"If we fight, we fight together," he declared resolutely, then met Seamus' gaze. "I need you to stay here. I'll go and bring her back safe, I swear to you."

When the Sage nodded, Brennan grabbed a spare shirt to pull on, his sneakers, and ran out the door.

&&&

"Where are we?" Emmanuel asked for the hundredth time as he glanced around, not recognizing anything. It seemed they were moving in circles.

"I've told you before, I have no clue," Freya answered. "This place is a maze. But there's at least one good thing..."

"And what's that?" Emmanuel's tone was all but happy at the news.

"Well, if someone's following us, they're just as lost as we are," the Sage said. *Unless, of course, they know this place like the back of their hand,* she thought, but didn't it repeat out loud.

Barely a few moments later, the ghost spoke again, this time with a slight tremor. "Hey Freya, do you think we're ever going to find a way out of here?"

Freya stopped walking and turned to him, plastering a knowing look on her face. In all truth, she couldn't answer the question. But since she felt responsible for Emmanuel, she also had to reassure him.

Reading the anxiety in him, she placed a hand on his shoulder and smiled. "Of course we will. We'll find Sam and then we'll be out of here in no time."

Emmanuel nodded, feeling slightly better, and they started walking again. To where, none of them could say they knew for sure. As they passed what looked like a statue, Freya heard someone call out – a very familiar voice.

"Freya? Freya!"

She turned around, as did Emmanuel, and gaped.

"Sam!"

The younger boy was merely feet away, staring back as though not believing his eyes. In seconds, she crossed the distance separating them and hugged the twelve-year-old ghost like mad, tears forming at the corners of her eyes.

After a few moments, she reluctantly stepped away from Sam and inspected him from head to toe. He and Emmanuel greeted each other with a manly hug.

"Are you all right?" Freya questioned, ready to kick butt if the answer was negative.

"Yeah, weirdly enough," Sam sounded puzzled. "They didn't harm me. As soon as they brought me here, I was free."

"Free?" Emmanuel frowned, and shared a side-glance with Freya.

"Mhmm," Sam nodded. "I mean, I can't leave. There are always guards here and there towards the exits, but they didn't hold me locked in a cage or anything."

"No wonder," Freya snorted. "This place is a labyrinth. There's no way you could've gotten away from here. Not if you didn't know your surroundings."

Emmanuel was still fixated on Sam. "I'm sorry they captured you. I swear, I had no idea Gustav would go that low to—"

The ghost stopped talking as he saw the alarmed look Sam gave him. When he realized what it was for, he merely waved his hand. "Don't worry, I told her."

"If you're worried about me freaking out from finding out that Emmanuel's ancestor is Gustav, don't be," Freya smiled, though her gaze was questioning as it met Sam's.

The younger spirit grinned a boyish grin. "Sorry for not telling you, Freya, but I promised Em and..."

"It's all right, Sam. He revealed the truth once he figured it was the only way to help us win the fight."

Sam nodded, then bit his lip and turned to Emmanuel. "And I'm not holding you responsible for my capture, Em. I know you'd never betray us."

Emmanuel gave Sam a grateful smile, then the younger boy asked, "So what are you two doing here? I thought Seamus was against you risking your life, Freya."

The Sage cleared her throat and chewed on her bottom lip thoughtfully, before whispering, "Well, you see, my dear Sam, Seamus doesn't... exactly..."

Sam's eyes widened, then he glanced from her to Emmanuel in disbelief. When both only shrugged sheepishly, he shook his head. "He doesn't know, does he?"

"Define *know*," Freya countered.

Sam laughed outright at her attempt to appear less than mortified. "You're *so* going to hear it from him when we get back to the hotel."

"I tried to stop her," Emmanuel interrupted. "But it seems the stubborn gene is way more amplified in Freya than in any other person I know. Including you, Sam."

They all chuckled at that, then looked around quickly, fearful of having been overheard. The shadows were still as dense – nothing moved, no eerie glows.

Sam's glanced around and behind Freya, as if expecting another person to show up. When all he encountered was empty space, he asked, "Where's Brennan? I suppose he, at least, tried to stop you from— what?" Sam's look went from the Sage to Emmanuel, who was giving him a very obvious *Don't ask* look. "What did I miss?"

Freya cleared her throat of the lump forming again, and managed a small, "Brennan's not here."

"What?" Sam frowned. "What do you mean?"

"Brennan distrusts me," Emmanuel elaborated, then went to give Sam a short summary of how the Wiseman had found out about Gustav being his ancestor. He finished with, "I did not realize he was following and... Well, the thing is, I lost whatever bit of trust he had in me."

Sam narrowed his eyes, then turned to Freya just in time to see her wipe at her cheeks. "Frey-Frey?" When she met his gaze full-in, Sam saw in her expression the hurt, and guessed – rightly – that she'd fought with her partner. "Freya... Whatever he said, Brennan didn't mean it! I know him, he's not a bad guy. You guys were probably just really upset and as usual hurled things at one another without thinking them through."

Despite the truth of the words, Freya's gaze hardened at the memory. "Trust me, Sam, he meant every single word. But whatever. I don't need his help to get you out of here."

At the change of subject, Sam could only shake his head. *I'll fix this once I'm back at the hotel.* Out loud, he said, "Then what are we waiting for?"

"Pack whatever bags you have," Freya teased lightly. "And let's go."

The three shared a smile, and were about to walk away when they heard mock cooing from behind. A gravelly voice echoed all around, wiping the smugness off their faces.

"Very touching. Very touching indeed..."

Freya's throat dried and her blood froze at the sound. She knew the owner only too well. For many nights after their last encounter, it had been the voice of her nightmares.

Chapter 21

When they'd met, Freya had been in the beginning stages of her Sage training. After Seamus had revealed her lineage, and she'd a few months of training under her belt, they met Sam, then continued with smaller missions.

Girona had been their first larger such operation. Sam was sent ahead to check out the enemy, while Freya and Seamus followed in a plane. From the first moment she'd set foot in Girona, Freya had fallen in love with the city and its ancient buildings. When not busy casing out the hiding place of evil ghosts, she'd be out walking the streets with Sam.

Freya's first ever encounter with Gustav was at night, near the Cathedral. From their hotel, she'd sensed the hum of the building, and wanted to have a closer look. Reckless and unable to sleep, the Sage ventured out at night – alone.

Arriving near it, Freya decided to meditate for a while. Seamus had started teaching her the art of relaxation, and after the last few days of constant movement, she felt the urge for peace.

The Sage had sat by the bottom of the stairs and cleared her mind. She'd fallen deep into a trance, when pain exploded behind her eyelids, and she was startled out of it.

Gustav had appeared out of nowhere with four other ghosts, and attacked her from behind. Despite the major throbbing in her head, Freya started to fight back. She was new enough in her abilities that she didn't know how to harness them, and had not yet built up her physical resistance.

A few moments into the confrontation, she realized it was a lost cause. Two of Gustav's ghosts grabbed one arm each, and she was immobilized.

Freya could still recall Gustav's cold gaze travelling up and down her body, his mouth twisted in a sneer. When he spoke, bile rose in her throat, but then she felt dizzy with fear as he touched her cheek.

"*Preciosa*," he whispered, caressing her skin. Then his hand roughly gripped her hair and pulled her head back. Freya had gritted her teeth against the pain, refusing to scream, instead meeting his gaze head on. "A fiery one, are you not?" he taunted, smirking arrogantly.

It took a second for Freya to realize he was stronger. It took another second to calm her mind against the sheer panic threatening to overwhelm. Once she had, a deadly serenity descended on her, and she stopped struggling against the other two phantoms.

"My name is Gustav, little one," he introduced himself in that same tone. "A name you will learn well this night. You have caused quite some trouble running around, trying to change things from the way they have always been."

The grip on her hair tightened, but still Freya didn't utter a single sound, gritting her teeth resolutely.

"You will pay tonight," he promised lethally.

Determined not to let him touch her, Freya spit at him. Out of pure shock, he let go and stepped back. His features contorted in fury, and his punch was strong enough to send her flying backwards.

But Freya no longer cared about the lightning pain in her cheek. She was free of the binding hands, and ready to fight back. She stood, turning to face Gustav.

"And *my* name is Freya," she said. "A name you'll remember before the end of the night."

As they came at her, the Sage reached deep within for the spiritual energy like Seamus had taught her. She built a shield around her, so that none of their blows could abuse her body. Instead, she was the one putting them in pain.

With every strike of her glowing fist, they groaned and grunted in pain. With every kick of her swift feet, they yelped. By the end of the hour, the ghosts were unconscious, and Freya had escaped, returning to the hotel.

Gustav, however, had loathed her since. Their strained relationship had escalated into a full-blown fight by the Cathedral mere days later. Despite her lack of powers near the building, the Sage had delivered a humiliating defeat to Gustav in front of his men – and three leaders of the larger cliques. Her only injury had been a broken arm.

Impressed by her show of force, the three major leaders submitted to the Sages' new rules. As part of the truce, they forced Gustav to drop his plans for a takeover. The man's hatred of Freya had only grown with each passing day.

&&&

Emmanuel's eyes widened as they landed on the ghost behind Freya. There was no mistaking his ancestor's dark gaze, hateful expression and built body. And he'd brought company, too. Roughly thirty-something phantoms stood behind him, lingering about for his orders.

Sam glanced from Freya – who'd closed her eyes – to Gustav – who was watching the Sage with nothing but hatred in his unfathomable black orbs.

The memory of that night, of their first battle and her fear, pulsed through her fiercely. Freya clenched her fists, unwilling to give in to weakness. *Not tonight. Not ever again.*

A slow smirk graced Freya's features as she realized the irony. She had cemented her friendship with Emmanuel at the exact same place as she'd encountered Gustav, but the difference between the two meetings was certainly enormous.

What a coincidence, indeed, Freya reflected, amused. *I gained a friend at the same place I left behind an enemy. And my new* amigo *just so happens to be a descendant of my nemesis. Life is indeed amazing...*

Freya's ruminations took a whole different route, and she had to admit she missed Brennan's steadfast presence, and knowing he had her back. *You're on your own, Freya.* The Wiseman's words rang like an echo in her head, and the Sage bit her lip.

I guess this is fate then, she thought encouragingly. *I'm meant to face Gustav alone, and finish what I started long ago. This time, with no personal injuries.*

Freya then focused on the recollection of her last fight with Gustav, and let the emotions invade her. She was determined to give the ghost a battle he wouldn't soon forget. One that would equal – if not surpass – their first.

As Sam observed Freya, he could see her knuckles had grown white from the force with which she was clenching her fists. He didn't need special abilities to see the red aura surrounding her, depicting her anger.

Sam almost felt bad for Gustav – almost. He'd witnessed the times when the Sage had lost control in fights, and what had followed hadn't been pretty. He was about to reassure Emmanuel that Freya had the situation under control, but found him to be watching the Sage with an intensity akin to worship.

Before Sam could say anything, Freya shifted. It was not an obvious movement, and he almost missed it. But a soft breeze blew around them, and her ponytail escaped from its hold, the raven locks falling around her face as though to obscure it. The clenched fists relaxed, but another tension altogether seemed to fill her and imbue the air around her.

"At my signal," Freya's whisper was both commanding and even, "run and find another exit. Be careful." Sam and Emmanuel both nodded, signaling they understood and would do as told.

"Well, Freya, I see we meet again," Gustav spoke again, spitting the Sage's name. When she answered nothing, his mouth turned into a grimace, features taut with anger.

One of the ghosts took a step forward, as if to walk towards her, but Gustav held up a hand and stopped him. His narrowed gaze didn't waver from the Sage, not acknowledging his descendant. "What is it? Are you too afraid to face me now? After our last battle together, I would understand it."

Freya turned around slowly, and managed with an effort to maintain a façade of relaxation. "If I recall correctly, Gustav, you were the one kissing the ground and begging for mercy."

The leader's expression darkened at the memory and the teenager's attitude.

Freya grinned confidently, raising her chin in a defiant gesture. She then directed her gaze in turn to each ghost behind Gustav, giving them a chance to disappear. Four of them were familiar to the Sage, a remnant from that long ago night, and she let her gaze linger on them longer.

She then met Gustav's fury with a smirk tugging at her lips, mocking him. "So how's business around? I hear you've got some competition. Cortés, is it? It's a wonder you're here. Aren't you supposed to be groveling at his feet?"

Gustav's face contorted in anger, but he attempted to sneer. "Cortés is not my master."

He then glanced behind her, a brief telling sign that she almost missed. But she didn't, and the recollection of his tendency to cheat was still firmly ingrained in her mind. With a quick sweep of her senses, Freya ensured nothing was trying to attack her from behind. Satisfied, she focused on the ghost's words.

"Your days are numbered," Gustav warned. "This time, when we fight, I'll win. And you will join your ancestors."

"Oh, so now you're a seer, too?" Freya wasn't fazed at the barely disguised threat. She shifted her weight on her left leg and crossed her arms, her entire body posture challenging Gustav.

Come get me.

"When we last came to blows, you left me with a broken arm. Unless my memory is failing me, I recall leaving *you* with your head through the sand. This time, I won't go that easy on you."

"You bit more than you can chew, Freya," Gustav chuckled darkly. "You see these guys?" He jerked a thumb at the phantoms behind him and a predator's smirk crossed his face. "You aren't getting out of here. Especially not with my newly found gifts."

New what, now? From whom? Freya wondered internally, but kept an inscrutable mask.

Across from her, Gustav shot his left arm at Sam, but did nothing else. In mere seconds, the pale glowing aura around Sam's body diminished as he solidified.

Freya noticed the ruby ring on the leader's finger, and the odd energy emanating from it. It was reminiscent of Cadmael and how Sam had been captured back then, and held immobile. Refusing to give the man satisfaction of causing her distress, Freya resolutely kept an unfazed expression.

Though he was used to being solid whenever around Freya, O'Keeffe, or – more recently – Brennan, Sam couldn't help a gasp escape him as his spirit was forced into it. Freya's quick glance was the only thing that calmed him.

So much as he wanted to yelp and give in to the anxiety, Sam forced a chuckle. "Is that all? You bad guys need a new trick, this is getting old."

Emmanuel had to hold back the smug look threatening to creep on his face as he saw Gustav's disarmed one. Clearly, his ancestor had expected more of a reaction.

"You'll have to do better than that if you expect me to shiver with fear," Freya mocked. "Trust me, I've *seen* better."

Gustav clenched his fists by his side, clearly on the verge of losing his cool. "I can also make your friend disappear, Freya."

The Sage's eyes glinted in response, but still she didn't move. "Really? What a coincidence. So can I."

In the split second following, she faced her palms to a spirit behind Gustav. She remembered what Emmanuel had told her about an energy that was stronger than the Cathedral's barrier, and she used all her anger at Brennan, Gustav and herself to drive her powers to the edge of unleashing them. She then recalled the fight with Cadmael, and extended the energy towards the ghost with a grunt.

The specter stumbled back as a gust of air hit it. The following instant, its mouth opened in a wordless scream, and it disappeared – vanished into nothingness without so much as a sound. And Freya didn't feel a single ounce of remorse.

Gasps were heard among Gustav's ghosts, and even the leader glanced around himself, trying to find the missing ghost.

"Oh, don't bother looking," Freya added. "He's long past your reach." The satisfaction she felt at the naked fear on their faces could not be described in words.

"How did you do that!?" Gustav burst, all self-control disappearing. He recalled the demon's words of warning, and barely repressed a shudder.

"The same way you would have, Gustav. Unless, of course, you were only bluffing?" The Sage widened her eyes mockingly in surprise, then gave up the pretense and snickered. "Well, now you know *I'm* not."

The leader glared back as if wanting her instantly dead, but Freya leveled a cool expression his way. *He will not get to me.*

"You still live in the past," Gustav said menacingly. "Thinking this will be an easy victory. I am much more powerful than two years ago, Freya, and you'll see just how much soon enough. You will regret having picked this fight."

Once more, the question of where Gustav had his powers from came to the Sage's mind, but she dismissed it impatiently. Much like Brennan had, he was getting under her skin. His constant word vomit of warnings and not-too-subtle threats was wearing her patience thin.

Responding to the rising tide of her wrath, the spiritual energy within Freya stirred to the surface. Her calm demeanor was replaced by fury – eyes burning, hair swishing around her face, the Sage was the picture of an avenging goddess. "And as usual, you're mistaken, Gustav. *You* will be the one with regrets. You look at me and see easy prey, but I'm no longer the Sage-in-training you met before, either. I can safely say that my abilities have – shall we say? – evolved."

"They won't serve you here," Gustav grinned with a mean look. "The barrier will prevent you from using them here."

"And yet, I just did," she pointed out. "You say I'm powerless? I beg to differ." The flame of a candle off the wall instantly disappeared, reappearing in Freya's hand. The fire itself reflected the ardent look in the Sage's eyes.

Emmanuel shared a look with Sam behind her back.

"Gustav is so busted," Sam whispered.

Emmanuel nodded, then focused his gaze on Gustav. He knew his ancestor better than Sam and perhaps even Freya, and he had a hint that once he was cornered, cheating to win wouldn't be far off his mind.

As if on cue, Gustav narrowed his eyes at Freya, a mean look buried deep in them. He expected her to drop the act and recoil back in fear.

However, the Sage looked back with only hatred and disgust in her eyes. The flame in her hand seemed to grow, hotter than ever. Yet Gustav couldn't see any sign of suffering on Freya's face. All he could observe was a deep desire to kick his ass.

And *that* frightened him. He'd counted on being able to manipulate the Sage by showing off his new abilities and threatening to make her friend disappear. Apparently, he'd misread her.

A lot.

It didn't take long for Gustav to register it had been a grave misstep on his side. The demon had been right. Underestimating Freya was what had brought on his defeat the first time around, and he was now making the same error.

This might turn out harder than I thought, the leader mused.

Chapter 22

M iles away from the Cathedral, Brennan was running as fast as he could towards it. His feet pounded the pavement as if his life depended on it, blaming himself for having delayed for so long.

As he kept the pace, thoughts swirled through his mind. The least of them was that he hadn't eaten anything for thirty-six hours. His strength was back, strumming through his veins. Also, he was finally toying with the idea that perhaps he'd judged Emmanuel too fast.

That still won't help me get there in time, Brennan thought sourly as he quickened his pace even more.

What concerned the Wiseman more than being unable to contact Freya was that it seemed their bond was broken. Ever since he'd last spoken to her, he hadn't felt any emotion that was not his own, and it troubled him more than he was ready to admit.

That can't be possible, Brennan told himself, frowning. *A bond like ours is indestructible. It cannot be undone!*

Even as he reflected on that, the Wiseman felt fury spread through his veins at once. The bubbling rage was *definitely* not his own.

He had no problem recognizing it, having felt its effects no sooner than a few hours earlier. A smirk graced his features and his golden-brown eyes regained their twinkle. It seemed that whoever was on the receiving end of Freya's anger had better look out, for they were in huge trouble.

"Thank the heavens you're alive, Freya," Brennan murmured out loud. "Angry, but alive."

Now I just have to hope she can stay out of trouble for a few more minutes. He started running with a renewed energy, the Cathedral already looming in sight.

As he crossed over the remaining distance, he mulled over the idea that he would probably get punched as retaliation for how he'd acted. Though aware he would deserve it, the Wiseman was still willing to take the risk as long as it meant he could get there in time and fight by her side. And, perhaps, redeem himself a little.

As for Emmanuel, Brennan was still deciding. He was willing to admit that maybe he'd made a mistake, but not until he had real proof that the ghost was on their side. And, even then, Brennan wasn't feeling too keen on being friendly with him. He hated to admit it – and would never do so in front of Freya – but he was starting to feel jealous of the attention she gave Emmanuel.

The Wiseman was only too conscious that it was partially his fault, but that didn't stop him from wishing they'd never met Emmanuel.

Brennan stopped dead in his tracks, astounded by his own train of thought. *Is this really what I want?* Analyzing his feelings, the Wiseman was forced to realize that, indeed, Emmanuel was not one of his favorite persons on Earth.

Shaking his head, Brennan sighed heavily and sprinted off once more. "I've got to keep my head in the battle, not outside of it."

The Wiseman's gaze travelled up the long stairs leading up to the entrance. Heaving a sigh, he started taking them two by two, dismissing the burning of his muscles with renewed determination.

I'm coming, Freya.

&&&

Back inside the church, Freya felt the power grow and spread through her, and the fire in her palm emitted a soft energy. She glanced at Gustav and registered he was ready to make a move. Though she showed nothing of her feelings, the Sage knew she could get outrun by thirty ghosts, plus the leader.

Would she have been alone, it wouldn't have mattered. But Sam and Emmanuel were with her, and Freya's first priority was to get them out of the Cathedral. Her only chance was to hit Gustav first and then delay him and his goons while Sam and Emmanuel ran for it.

If only I could sense that blasted exit!

The following second, the flame died in her palm, no longer giving Freya energy. She'd lost focus and the anger no longer nourished her powers to the point of exploding.

"Oh, shit!" Freya swore as she remembered what Tyr had told her. Though more powerful, her new abilities wouldn't last long in the Cathedral unless she was able to keep borrowing energy from the elements.

Gustav's face turned almost joyous as he taunted cruelly, "Well, well, look who's powerless now. Unfortunately for you, *my* strength will last for longer than yours, Freya. Prepare to meet your doom."

At that, Gustav extended his arm and pointed to her, a very satisfied smirk on his face.

I have to get Sam and Em out! Freya resolved fiercely, the only thought giving her all the boost needed. She called the elements to her, gathering a spiritual blast in her palms.

Whatever Gustav planned to do next, he never got to, because Freya turned her palms to him. A blinding energy escaped them and hit him in the chest, blasting him off in the air and into a wall.

In the split second that followed, Freya turned to Sam and Emmanuel and yelled, "Now! Find the exit! Hurry, I'll hold them off!"

The ghosts nodded and, after one last look to the Sage, took off. Freya was about to trail behind them but she heard Gustav yell in Spanish, "What are you waiting for, fools? Go get Emmanuel, and bring him here! Leave the girl to me."

Freya stopped dead in her tracks at Gustav's command. *Emmanuel?* At once, she realized what Gustav had been after.

The phantom soldiers passed her without so much as a glance, rushing after Emmanuel and Sam. She whirled to face Gustav, who was merely a few feet away from her.

The ghost cackled, his yellowed teeth showing. "Don't tell me you thought this trap was only for you, Freya. Poor, poor, baby. I had a score to settle with you, yes, but my true target has been Emmanuel all along."

By then, all the specters had vanished and it was only Freya and Gustav left facing each other. The Sage cringed, reprimanding herself for her own naivety. *I should've realized that Gustav wouldn't give up on Emmanuel so easily and would do everything in his power to get him back... Whether Em agrees or not.* Blackmail was only one of the tools at Gustav's disposal, if he so wished it.

"What about Sam?" Freya probed through clenched teeth. That was the only part of his plot that didn't fit.

"I kidnapped him to get Emmanuel to come to me," Gustav revealed as if it was the most normal thing in the world. "When I saw he brought you too, it was the best moment yet. Killing two birds with one stone – the perfect hit."

Freya clenched her jaw, trying as much as possible to mask her fury. Keeping a steady voice, she asked, "Why? Why do you need Emmanuel?"

Gustav gave a laugh that made Freya dig her nails in her palms to avoid yelling obscenities at him. The ghost was badly getting on her nerves, and she wasn't sure how much more she could take without losing her cool with him.

Freya knew that if she unleashed her powers as she'd done when Brennan set her off, she could easily get rid of Gustav. Though the prospect was tantalizing, the certitude she would lose control was enough to shatter the illusion. *I risk doing more bad than good.*

"I don't *need* him," Gustav answered in a bored tone. "But I do want him by my side. Emmanuel's a bright boy, and my blood relation. I want him to follow in my footsteps. He has such a potential for the evil side, it would be a shame to waste it."

Freya let a short laugh escape her, despite the situation being the farthest thing removed from amusing. "You're an idiot, Gustav. Em doesn't want to stay by your side, and I'll do everything in my power to make sure his wishes are respected. You won't force him against his will, not if I have anything to say about it."

"You are powerless in front of me," Gustav glared at her. "Do you really think you can stop me, you foolish mortal Sage?"

Freya only shook her head, determined not to let the specter get to her. "I may not have my full powers, but you can be damn sure I will try regardless!" She meant every word, firmly determined to defend Emmanuel and Sam from whoever tried to hurt them.

Protect the weak. Destroy evil.

Gustav's icy gaze landed on Freya's and she held it defiantly. "Very well, you've asked for it. Not that I would have spared you anyhow. I have counted the days for this moment."

"And what moment is that?" Freya's fingers twitched with the urge to hit him.

"The one when you finally join your ancestors by my hand," Gustav savored each word.

Freya glared at him. "Oh yeah? Well, turns out I've waited way too long for this."

"For what?" Gustav asked, frowning.

"The opportunity when I finally shut your mouth forever!" Freya yelled and launched herself at Gustav, fists balled and ready to fight.

The ghost, too astonished by Freya's fierceness to move, received the punch in full gut and found himself sprawled on the tapestry.

Gustav soon got back on his feet and faced Freya, an ugly scowl on his face. "I would recommend you give up now and enjoy the last seconds of your life. You don't have a chance against me!"

"Watch me!" Freya growled and she jumped in the air, extending her leg. It connected with Gustav's jaw so hard his head whipped around and he hit the ground – hard.

Freya landed behind him, rolled on her shoulder and was instantly up, blocking his punch. Gustav was forced to back up to avoid Freya's knee from hitting him in a very sensitive area. Hateful gazes collided with despise and tense limbs interlocked with intent to harm.

Gustav missed Freya's head by little as she ducked his arm just in time. She then retaliated with a punch of her own, striking his shoulder this time.

As Gustav once more backed away, a cry for help was heard throughout the Cathedral. A desperate one, too. Freya stilled, her fist clenched but as of yet unwilling to release.

"I wonder what that could be," Gustav mocked. "You hear that, Freya? That's your dear friend begging for help. It seems my men caught up with him."

Freya glanced over her shoulder, then back at the leader – in time to duck out of the way of another fist aiming for her head. She set her jaw firmly, mad beyond words at the double game. "You're a cheater, Gustav. We're not done yet."

She was about to run to Sam, but Gustav grabbed her arm and twisted it around, pinning Freya to the ground. Mastering the power she knew was still inside her, Freya pushed it to the limit as she placed her free hand on Gustav's forearm. The blast that escaped her was strong enough to send the ghost flying in the air, hitting a wall far away and groaning in pain.

"You're no more than a puppet, Gustav," Freya said distastefully. "And I don't lose my time with the likes of you. We'll settle this another time, on my terms."

Her threat delivered, she took off on a run. Following deeply embedded instincts, the Sage felt attracted to one particular point of the Cathedral and headed there. As she turned one last corner, she gasped. The light of the new day filtered through the church via the open doors through which Freya had entered. It also illuminated the scene behind them.

About thirty meters away from the exit, the phantom soldiers stood in a circle around a trapped Sam and Emmanuel.

"Damn it!" Freya swore under her breath. From the looks of it, the two ghosts had been incredibly close to getting away.

Emmanuel seemed to have felt he was being watched, and he turned towards the Sage a pleading look. He couldn't shield Sam alone. Freya nodded in his direction to signal she had everything in hand.

She didn't, but Freya was not about to let her friends down. "Hey, you there!" she yelled with her hands cupped around her face for better effect.

Half of the ghosts turned to the Sage, their gazes sparkling of evil. "Why don't you pick on someone your own size?" Freya taunted.

She then used a rope that was swinging nearby to propel herself in the middle of the circle. Swinging precariously, she managed to hit a few ghosts in the process, before landing in front of Sam and Emmanuel with a fierce look in her eyes.

"Stay behind me, I'll keep these guys in check," Freya said in what she hoped was a reassuring voice.

Thirty ghosts to fight all by myself, while defending Sam and Emmanuel is going to prove to be harder than I thought...

The soldiers weren't wasting time, either. As soon as Freya was immobile, they started closing the circle around the three, limiting the fighting space.

For the next few minutes, Freya threw punches to whoever was approaching too close, and kicks when she could. At times, she could force her power out and some ghosts would get blasted. But most of the time, she was forced to fight with her bare hands – and legs.

As sweat made its appearance on Freya's forehead, she realized she couldn't keep the fight up for much longer. The lack of sleep and food were kicking in, and her vital energy was getting dangerously low.

As she struck yet another phantom, and in turn got kicked in the shin, Freya was hitting an all-time low. *Crap. As much of a jerk as he is, it's at moments like these I wish Brennan was around.*

"Did I hear you call my name?" The cocky voice came out of nowhere – and everywhere at the same time.

At first, Freya thought she was hallucinating.

"Freya..." Sam whispered, a certain awe in his tone, "Look up!"

In spite of her best judgment advising not get false hopes, Freya raised a tentative gaze to the ceiling. Brennan was perched on the same swinging rope she'd used, grinning down at her. A sigh of relief escaped her, and Freya forgot all about their fight. "Nice of you to show up!"

Brennan jumped and landed by her side in the middle of the circle, a smirk on his face and a relieved look in his eyes. "I see you've made some friends."

As their eyes met, the same look in both of them, Freya started, "Brennan, about earlier..."

He shook his head, touching her hand gently. "It wasn't just you, it was my fault as well. We'll have time for it later, all right? Right now, we've got a battle to win."

Freya opened her mouth to add something, but the words wouldn't come out. Instead, she nodded and squeezed his hand in return, before stepping away. Brennan did the same and blocked a ghost's punch, then threw him over another two. Three more specters launched at him, and his focus turned to battling for survival.

"I'll go watch the other side!" Freya yelled over the noise of the fight.

Brennan nodded as he kicked yet another assailant, then avoided one that planned on hitting him over the head.

"This had better work," he murmured, concentrating on Freya's energy and connecting with her. *Yes!* He couldn't help a victorious mental shout as the link fell into place.

Brennan? It's working? Freya asked, slightly incredulous.

Sure seems so. I'm betting anything it's mostly due to the bond. It's what keeps us tightly knit and what led me here in spite of the barrier concealing your energy.

Silence was all that answered him for the next few moments, and Brennan grew anxious. *Freya? Are you okay?* Since he was busy with the ghosts constantly on the offensive, the Wiseman couldn't turn around and check with his own eyes.

Sorry, Freya's answer came a bit strained after a few moments. *Bit busy here.*

Brennan chuckled as he once more ducked a hit and retaliated with a punch, then passed onto the next phantom as the previous one fell. *With what? What are you complaining about? I've got my hands full!*

No shit, Sherlock, Freya retorted sarcastically. She kicked out to a much too eager soldier that was trying to grab Emmanuel.

What exactly are they after, besides you? They seem way too determined.

Knowing his distaste for the ghost, the Sage debated for a brief second on what to respond. In the end, she settled for the truth. *They have strict orders to grab Emmanuel.*

As predicted, Brennan was quiet. A quick peek over her shoulder confirmed he was in the midst of an intense confrontation with a larger-than-life ghost. Once he finished the opponent with a combination of punches to the gut and throat, the Wiseman mumbled, *Figures. Always comes down to him.*

Brennan...

It's okay, forget I said anything. A pause, then, *So I guess now would be a bad time to fill you in on something important?*

Probably, Freya agreed. *But try me anyway.*

Gustav is only a puppet, as is Cortés.

That's no news, Bren... Anything else?

Yeah. The demon isn't their leader, either. It's Set.

Silence lengthened, and he caught sight of Freya tackling a ghost. After a brief wrestling match, she ended up victorious and got back to her feet, throwing him a look.

Who, now?

Set! Isis and Osiris, Ancient Egyptian mythology, that *Set.*

You're joking, right? Freya asked, trying not to panic.

I wish I was... But it's true. Seamus and I went over this. Apparently he had some dream of my granddad, putting him on the right track. Either way, it checks out.

Brennan took advance of the silence that followed and threw a burst of power at the specters around them, pushing them back and knocking them out. It wasn't enough to buy them a lot of time, but it did get them a few spare seconds. He crossed the distance to Freya, his earnest expression meeting hers.

"It's all true. They've been behind Cadmael. Long story short, Set is imprisoned, and the keys to the map we now protect will help him escape."

Freya muttered some choice cuss words, and Brennan lifted his eyebrows in surprise. "Wow. Good vocab," he teased.

"Not funny," she glared back. "How are you taking this so calmly?"

"No idea. I think I've just stopped being surprised by all this."

"So...what now? How exactly do we fight a god?"

"We don't, Freya. We just make sure he can't escape by taking out his puppets and demon."

"As if that's going to be any easier!"

Brennan glanced over her shoulder, noticing the approaching ghosts. He side-stepped Freya, placing his body between her and them as a shield. "We're back on. Let's chat more at the hotel."

Nodding, Freya moved into a fighting position by his side. She lifted her forearm in time to block someone attacking with a sword. She managed to disarm the soldier before he did any damage.

What did you do to these guys to make them so angry? Brennan asked.

Might've knocked Gustav unconscious, Freya answered, smirking as she kicked another furious ghost.

Right. Well, at least he's gone, Brennan tried to light the mood.

"Get her, *now*!" a furious voice echoed in the Cathedral.

"You *had* to jinx us," Freya groaned aloud.

Chapter 23

"Oh, shit!" Brennan swore. "Who the hell's that? Clearly *not* a friend."

"Obviously," Freya retorted, voice dripping with sarcasm. "Brennan, meet Gustav, my nemesis."

The Wiseman tried to take a look over the head of one of the ghosts, but was punched in the stomach. He doubled over in pain, then forced himself to get up and kick the assailant, sending him flying into two others.

After avoiding another well-aimed fist, his eyes rested on Gustav. Finally able to catch a glimpse of the ghost filled him with rage, and an urge to further shelter Freya. The leader had onyx eyes, black hair, and resembled Emmanuel – only about twenty years older.

As their eyes met and held, the leader saluted him tauntingly, then moved to the side. Brennan's attention was pulled by something else his senses caught, and he gulped at the realization. He returned to fighting in a frenzy, needing to get rid of as many soldiers as possible, before it was too late. *Freya, sorry to break the party, but I'd say it's about time we left.*

You think I don't know that? she retorted, placing herself in front of Sam. She then released a blast of energy to the five ghosts that were coming a bit too near for comfort.

Anytime now, Brennan added urgently.

Why are you in such a hurry, anyway? I thought you enjoyed a good challenge, Freya pointed out, trying to lighten the mood.

Her inattention for a fraction of a second cost her to lose sight of the ghost that was about to strike. Barely a breath later, Freya found herself on the ground, clutching her stomach in pain as a throbbing sensation shot through her.

Calculating his move, the specter had hit Freya with the butt of his sword in a very sensible spot right below her solar plexus. The contact had been forceful and heavy, making the Sage feel double the pain of a regular strike.

"Freya!" Brennan yelled as, he too, felt an echo of her agony in his abdomen. He tried to search for the Sage, but was unable to with the soldiers blocking the way.

As a last resort, he turned to Emmanuel, who had stuck by his side. "Where's Freya? What's wrong with her?"

The ghost frantically looked around and spotted the Sage on the floor, surrounded by a crowd of phantoms that looked particularly angry. She didn't seem to be in that good of a shape, coughing and holding her stomach. Fearing for her safety, Emmanuel grabbed Brennan's shoulder. "She's hurt. They're closing in on her, you have to do something!"

Brennan went pale as he heard the news, and he directed a good kick to one of the assailants. "Where's Gustav?"

"Nowhere I can see."

Shit.

The Wiseman was torn between his need to help Freya, and his duty to keep Sam and Emmanuel safe.

Once more, he was grabbed by the arm, this time by a troubled Sam. "Brennan, something's not right. Go get Freya, now!"

Brennan forgot about everything else, turned around and made his way through the ghosts, battling them like a maniac. It wasn't long before he reached Freya, sporting a few more cuts and bruises. A specter had grabbed a fistful of her hair back and was holding her, immobilized, while another raised his sword.

Freya's hands were holding onto her stomach, and Brennan felt her agony more potently with each step closer. Snarling, he launched at the two soldiers, punching one in the face, then pummeling his fist into the other until he dropped.

The Wiseman then helped Freya to her feet. Her strength had weakened and she stumbled, trying to hold onto him. He framed her face with his hands, searching her eyes deeply. "Freya, look at me. Come on, don't pass out. *Look* at me!"

The Sage had her eyes open, but judging by the knife-like sensation cutting through him, Brennan guessed she was suffering a great deal. He pressed a palm to her stomach, half-lifting her t-shirt up to see a largely forming bruise.

Startled eyes rose up to the Sage's glazed ones. "Freya, you're bleeding internally! How did this happen?"

She mumbled something, her head falling back, and Brennan tightened his grip on her, heart beating wildly.

"Knife, I think," she mumbled, before going limp in his arms.

Brennan had never panicked as he did in that moment. The soldiers were advancing, now within inches of them, and Sam and Emmanuel were about to be captured. Yet nothing else mattered, safe for the unconscious girl in his arms.

Tightening his hold on her further, Brennan scowled darkly at the incoming assailants. In that moment, the spiritual ability that had been out of reach while in the Cathedral became only too accessible, almost pulsing and begging to be used.

With an angry wave of his hand, he sent a sweep of energy towards the ghosts, knocking them all out. Sam and Emmanuel moved closer, both shocked into silence.

Ignoring them, the Wiseman scanned Freya's body, all the while pleading to the one person who could come to their aid. *Please, I beg of you, you helped me once before. Granddad, what do I do?*

At once, he felt an odd warmth on his chest, and grabbed the medallion that was tucked under his t-shirt. It was glowing once more, this time of a white, pure light. Brennan didn't know what he was doing, but he grabbed one of Freya's hands and made her hold onto it. "Freya, it's going to be okay. Just let it work, all right?"

Burying his head in her hair, Brennan barely saw the radiance that enveloped the Sage. Her body vibrated in his embrace, and all the while be bit back tears of helplessness. His jaw was clenched, almost unyieldingly so, with the effort it took to maintain control.

When he heard her soft gasp against his chest, it was like music to his ears. He glanced down and sure enough, Freya's eyes fluttered open, clear of the suffering gleam that had been in there moments before.

Realizing the position they were in, she was able to push away from him gently, though still maintained a light hand on his shoulder.

"You're okay!" Sam enthused, throwing a grateful look to Brennan.

"What happened?" Freya asked him instead. "I don't feel the pain anymore."

Brennan simply smiled his relief, pulling her into a hug once more. "Call it a favor, all right?" When she nodded in his embrace, he pulled back reluctantly. "I hate to bring this up, but we still have a battle to fight. Will you be okay?"

"Yeah, I will," Freya confirmed.

With a last glance over his shoulder, Brennan returned to the other side of the circle. Some soldiers had come back to their senses and were aiming straight for Emmanuel. Ignoring the Spanish guy, the Wiseman jumped head first into the line of ghosts moving to attack, but still made sure to keep in contact with Freya.

The Sage, meanwhile, went on as if the incident hadn't taken place. Her kicks and punches became more determined, packing more energy. *No more damn mercy,* she vowed, before turning her attention to her partner. *So, you still didn't answer my question.*

I do enjoy a good challenge, Brennan answered sourly. *But not with over a hundred ghosts!*

Freya momentarily stopped fighting. *What are you talking about?* Silence answered her. *Brennan? Last time I checked, there were only thirty ghosts, ten of which were unconscious. And then these few extras.*

Before answering, the Wiseman took a look around, and his suspicions were confirmed. Stepping out of the shadows at the end of the building was Gustav, and a fresh army of ghosts.

Yeah, well, you'd better look again, Brennan suggested. *I caught their presence earlier, and I'm pretty sure the situation evolved. .*

Frowning, Freya punched a ghost straight in the jaw, then extended her senses. With a shock, she realized Brennan was right. Her powers alerted her of Gustav's arrival, and of a refreshed contingent of ghosts.

A look of despair crossed Freya's face for a second, but she disguised it and faced Sam and Emmanuel. "Prepare to run for the exit and dematerialize as soon as you're away from the Cathedral."

"But Freya—" Sam started.

"No, Sam. I'm not letting them get you back. Now get ready!"

"I'll get him out, you have my word," Emmanuel promised, his gaze meeting the Sage's for a split of a second.

Freya nodded gratefully, then turned back to the line of specters in sight. She cracked her knuckles, then smiled maliciously. "Brennan, I'm going to need your help."

"Go on," he stepped closer, intrigued.

"At my signal, be ready to blast your powers to clear the way to the exit for Sam and Emmanuel."

"Then what?" Brennan asked.

"Then..." Freya hesitated. "Try not to get killed."

"All right."

What else could he say? He'd known, ever since he'd arrived in Scotland, that the mission would not be easy. And each time it seemed it could get better, something worse happened.

Each and every single time, Freya seemed to be reborn out of her wounds. Like now, for example. All that had taken was a little healing power from... Well, Brennan wasn't exactly sure where from, but at least it had worked. At least enough for the Sage to be ready to kick some butt.

Nothing surprising about that, Brennan reflected. *She's a born fighter.*

"Better start focusing, Brennan," Freya warned, though he guessed she was smiling. "Here it comes."

The Wiseman spun around, grabbing in the process a soldier's arm and twisting it so that he ended up on his knees. He glanced Freya's way and saw her levitate ten ghosts on top of twenty others, then dropping them.

She then turned around and caught his gaze. One second was enough, and Brennan was ready. He knocked the ghost by hitting his neck with the side of his palm, then faced the exit and the phantoms that were blocking it.

"Now!" Both he and Freya yelled at the same time and directed their blows to the center of the line.

The remaining soldiers received their blasts full-force and full-frontal. They were sent flying out of the Cathedral like mere flies, thus freeing the way for Sam and Emmanuel to make their escape.

"Go!" Freya ordered her friends, though it was no longer necessary. The two ghosts already had a head start. *Please get there in time.*

All around the Sage and the Wiseman, transparent bodies filled the floor, and a few started getting up, looking for a second round. Freya turned to them and impatiently blasted them off, wanting to get it over with.

"No!" Gustav was heard yelling. "Get them, you fools! Don't let them escape or else I'll have your necks! Get them *now*!" Though the specters barely spoke English, Gustav's tone of voice left no doubt on his orders.

Emmanuel and Sam were now only a few meters away from the exit. *Four... Three... Two...*

At the last possible moment, five new soldiers appeared out of nowhere and stepped in front of the younger ghosts, their massive bodies blocking their path. Emmanuel avoided them, but Sam was caught in the middle.

"No!"

Freya bit back further screams of despair, unwilling to give Gustav the satisfaction. If she helped Sam escape, Emmanuel would be caught, and she knew that was what the evil mastermind wanted. At the avid glint in the leader's eyes, a shiver of foreboding ran up her spine.

If he gets Em, his plan is set.

The realization didn't make her decision any easier. To condemn her best friend to more time in the Cathedral, in the arms of her enemy... Glancing from Sam to Emmanuel, it dawned on Freya that she had no choice.

Get Emmanuel out of here, Brennan! Freya demanded mentally. She could feel the Wiseman's incredulous look on her, and turned his way. "Just do it!"

Brennan took one look at her torn and vulnerable expression, saw the unshed tears in her eyes, and nodded. He ran over to Emmanuel, nearly tripping over his own feet. With a determined shake of the head, he set aside the dizziness from the spent energy.

As he moved forward, out of the corner of his eye he noticed the phantoms were getting up. *Clear the way,* he asked Freya.

The Sage didn't answer, only released the energy once more, turning this way and that with her upturned palms. Wave after wave of spirits were blasted out of the Cathedral, until Brennan safely reached Emmanuel.

Freya was grabbed by the arm and spun roughly around, losing sight of her companions. Instead, she was face to face with Gustav.

The leader had an evil glint in his eyes, sneering down at her. "Don't even think about getting Emmanuel out of here. Neither of you will escape this place. Ever."

Freya raised her knee and kicked Gustav in the groin, causing him to bend over. She then grabbed him by an arm and swept under his leg with her own. Gustav dropped down with a heavy thud, and the Sage moved to lock his arm in place under her knee. Immobilized as he was, he could no longer inflict damage.

"What's your game, hmm?" Freya bent over and hissed in his ear. "Why rally this many ghosts? What does Cortés plan to do with them? I know you've met him, Gustav, you have to know *something*."

The specter met her eyes darkly, then chuckled maniacally. "*No sé de qué estás hablando*. You make no sense. I did not know you have grown delusional since the last time we met. Or maybe it was your friend's capture that made you lose your mind?"

Freya pushed Gustav harder in the ground, half-growling, "You're lying, Gustav. I bet Cortés hasn't told you a thing about his plans. And why would he? He has no counts to render to a mere second-grade ghost."

Gustav froze, and that in itself should have been enough warning. Freya was distracted by voices she knew only too well, and in that moment, the leader underneath her moved. Before she could register what happened, she was on her back, and Gustav was free, looming over her.

As she jumped to a defensive stance, Freya recognized what had distracted her – Brennan and Emmanuel were arguing, and still very much present in the Cathedral.

Get him out of here! Freya yelled in frustration, even as she ducked one of Gustav's punches.

I would if he'd let me! Brennan snapped back, equally frustrated. For the last few minutes, he'd tried to reason with the ghost, and when that hadn't worked, he attempted coercion.

To his utter surprise, nothing worked. It seemed Emmanuel was much more stubborn than Brennan had originally thought. He didn't want to leave Sam behind, and instead preferred to stay with him, even if it meant his own capture.

How is that for proof? The voice of conscience at the back of Brennan's mind quipped. He ignored it, and concentrated instead on getting the brat out. "Listen, Freya told me to get you out of here, which is exactly what I plan to do."

"I'm not leaving Sam!" Emmanuel huffed.

Freya! Brennan pleaded for help from the Sage. Spirits were moving closer and they would be stuck if they were surrounded. *Stuck and powerless, since any extra movement threatens to leave me toppling to the ground.*

Brennan turned his head towards the Sage and found her busy fighting with Gustav. *Need any help?* He could sense the hate radiating from the phantom even across the distance.

Just give me a few seconds, Freya retorted.

Brennan did. He watched the Sage duck a strong punch and kick Gustav in the chest. She then grabbed his arm, twisted it over her head and had him pinned with his back to her once more.

The ghost kicked backwards and got Freya in her solar plexus, cutting her breath. She fell to her knees, blood seeping from the corner of her lips, and a raging gleam in her now darkened eyes.

Brennan took a step forward, concerned that the hit would induce a relapse from the internal bleeding. Words thrown in his direction firmly stopped him in his tracks.

Don't! This is between me and Gustav.

Brennan clenched his jaw, and quickly scanned their surroundings instead. The ghosts were still moving closer, slow like zombies, awaiting their leader's ultimate command.

As Gustav moved to place in another punch, Freya got up and hit him straight between the eyes, blurring his vision.

She then grabbed him by one arm and threw him in the air, using his force against him. When the ghost's back hit the wall and he slid to the ground with a groan, the Sage sighed in satisfaction.

In the same breath, she turned towards Brennan and Emmanuel. A distance of at least twenty meters separated them, and Freya knew her hit would have to be perfect.

Brennan, step away from Emmanuel, she ordered calmly.

He frowned. *Freya?*

Just do it, please, she repeated tiredly.

Brennan took a step away, then two, his gaze glued to Freya, who was now raising her palms. *What are you going to do?*

I have to get him out of here. At all costs.

A slight hesitation crossed her mind when her eyes met Emmanuel's, then Freya whispered, "I'm sorry, Em, but it's necessary."

Before he knew what was happening, a blast of light escaped Freya's palms and hit Emmanuel in the chest. Its force propelled him up in the air and out of the Cathedral in an incredible flash of light.

Chapter 24

Brennan gaped after the ghost, then turned to Freya. He was going to yell something among the lines of *What the hell?* but was met with a strong punch on the jaw and found himself sprawled on the floor, ten ghosts circling him.

He rolled away from the assailants and jumped back on his feet, adopting a fighting stance. As one of the phantoms went to strike again, Brennan grabbed another one closer and used it to deflect the blow, before knocking it unconscious.

Brennan turned to his left just in time to duck a punch directed at his gut and counterattack with one of his own. Someone grabbed his arm from behind and twisted it at a mean angle, but the Wiseman backwards-kicked him before he could do more damage.

He rubbed his arm, scowling. "Now, now, boys, play nicely."

A few Spanish insults echoed from the remaining ghosts. Incidentally, they were still advancing.

"Double shit," Brennan swore as he once again started to defend himself. The Wiseman cursed his inability to use his powers correctly in the blasted church. Having been able to blast those ghosts to clear the way had been a miracle in itself. Freya, however, fared much better off. *At least her abilities are useful.*

He took a brief second to pull himself together, then rerouted his frustration on the ghosts. Soon, the numbers around him diminished, mostly due to the fact he could use one to hit the other. It was all a matter of timing.

However, more appeared, and Brennan groaned, fatigue finally catching up with him. *This is such a déjà-vu, Frey. How do you always get in these situations?*

A commotion behind forced him to finish up his opponent quickly, and take a look. Freya was battling three soldiers at once. Under his stunned gaze, she pulled a sword out of one's hands, and used it to strike the other two, then the former owner until he dropped too.

Damn, girl, no need to be so violent, Brennan chastised mockingly.

Freya met his gaze, and grinned. Something about the comfortable way she did it, and the unspoken understanding in the depths of eyes, struck Brennan deeply. He jerked his chin, and she headed over to his side, until they were back to back against the remaining phantoms.

"Ready?" Freya asked out loud, a small smirk playing on the corners of her lips.

"Always," Brennan grinned.

They still had too many ghosts to count, a daunting fact not lost on either of them. With their physical capabilities on the decline, time was counted.

Piece of cake, Freya said telepathically to avoid being overheard – even if the specters didn't speak English.

Sure, Brennan agreed.

Both knew, however, that it was a lie. The ghosts were by far more trained than Cadmael's had been, and harder to overcome. They attacked in the blink of an eye – five to one, it was hardly a fair match. But both teens were grateful the odds were not ten to one.

The only thing that kept their numbers down was the tightness of the circle. By refusing to separate and fight individually, the two companions coerced the ghosts to attack in smaller packs.

Freya and Brennan fought viciously, knowing that they only had one chance at escaping. Their plan was so simple, they did not even need to compare notes – find Sam's captors wherever they'd hidden, somehow rescue the boy, and get out.

It's a story we're familiar with, Brennan pointed out tiredly. *If we don't do this quick and get out of here soon, we won't be able to move and we'll get captured.*

There's no way I'll let that happen, Freya thought determinately as the options passed through her head.

Me either, Brennan agreed while kicking a ghost. "Learn to keep your distances, buddy!" he yelled.

Both the Sage and the Wiseman returned to fighting the ghosts harder than before, counting on the opportunity they could feel creeping closer. Though Freya was terribly distressed about Sam, constant movement was a must if she wanted her friend back.

As she escaped a particularly vicious ghost, Seamus' face flashed in her mind. Her heart clenched when she imagined his worry – and probably fury. Then she thought of Tyr and the words she'd so easily let slip, then so quickly took back.

The promise... Freya thought nostalgically. She wished she could've kept it, but there was too much going on at the moment to leave her time to think about it. The Sage promised to apologize to the tiger as soon as she was out of the Cathedral.

"If..." Freya muttered out loud as she barely escaped another punch, before knocking the offending ghost to the ground.

Interpreting her sadness correctly, Brennan tried to reassure, *We'll get Sam back. And if something goes wrong, we'll come back. Over and over again. Hell, we'll come with an army of our own if we have to. Plus ladders and canons.*

Another smile cracked on Freya's lips. *We will, won't we?*

You bet! Brennan promised, knowing he would do his utmost to help Freya out.

When he sensed his partner's moody energy dissipate, he allowed a grin to grace his lips. Finally, he'd done something right.

The feeling was soon squashed when a sinister laugh echoed, and all fighting stopped. The ghosts stepped away from Freya and Brennan, leaving the two standing alone close to the exit of the Cathedral. They glanced at the doors, then at each other.

"What the hell—" Freya started.

"—is this all about?" Brennan finished.

They slowly turned towards the ghosts, and were met with quite an unlikely sight – Cortés was holding Sam prisoner. To make matters worse, Gustav stood by his side with a victorious smirk on his face.

Freya frowned as she took in the two leaders, then her gaze moved to Sam and his abnormal immobility. A brief moment later, once she'd taken a step to the side, she figured out why. The tip of Cortés' sword was touching Sam's back, and some type of shield had been thrown over him, effectively freezing him.

The Sage could see the atmosphere ripple in transparent waves, but knew without even trying that her powers were no good against it. The effect was similar to Cadmael's axe, but much more powerful. Her jaw clenched at the thought of the demon who had returned it in the conquistador's possession.

After another quick glance to Sam, Freya's eyes rose to meet Cortés' steely gaze. Something about the man struck her as odd – he didn't inspire fear. With Cadmael, she'd immediately sensed the Viking's ruthlessness. Perhaps because of it and what she'd already affronted, the new threat didn't seem quite as daunting.

You're joking, right? Brennan intervened, having followed her train of thought. *I can feel his wrath all the way over here, Frey.*

Mmm, was all she answered, gaze still glued to them. The Sage took one step forward, but stopped in her tracks when Sam's eyes widened in restrained pleading.

"One more step," Cortés warned in a rough and deeply accented voice, "and your friend here is done for."

"You don't scare us, Cortés," Brennan said icily.

"Perhaps," Cortés' aristocratic face was adorned by a very cruel and hawk-like smile. "But I do not think you want this *chico* to suffer in your stead." He deliberately let a pause settle in before he asked, "Do you?"

Freya set her jaw firm and asked through gritted teeth, "What do you want?"

"Already down to negotiations?" Cortés laughed deeply. "No, I think not. First we introduce ourselves, like polite people do."

"Why, you—" Freya stepped forward, but Brennan's hand on her arm restrained her in time, resting calmly as he conversed with her telepathically.

Don't play his game, Brennan advised. *Go with the flow until we get an opening.*

Freya didn't reply, but she did relax slightly, though her muscles remained tense.

"Wise decision," the conquistador smirked. "Now, you seem to know my name, but what are yours?" When he was met with a hostile silence, his stare narrowed. "No? Gustav, step forward and introduce us."

Double trouble, Freya thought.

We can beat them, Frey. For once, she didn't bother correcting Brennan on the nickname.

As Gustav moved, she could feel Brennan's barely held back fury. Out of the corner of her eye, she saw his glare settle on her nemesis, and her chest warmed at the obvious defensive stance he took in front of her.

Gustav introduced them with curt words, giving each a despising look – returned tenfold by the pair.

"*Muy bien*. Now that the introductions are out of the way, we can get to important things," Cortés announced.

"Release Sam. Now." Freya's order came through tightly gritted teeth, unable to make do with niceties any longer.

The conquistador tilted his head to the side. "And if I do not, how exactly will you make me?"

"We'll fight you, make no mistake," Brennan warned, his golden eyes turning dark brown with anger.

"Oh, I doubt that very much," Cortés laughed. "I have over a hundred ghosts here, ready to launch at you on my signal, and another few thousands expecting my orders. You are only two in number."

Freya clenched her fists, but before she could say anything, Cortés had broken eye contact with her. Dismissing them both, he turned to the specters awaiting his command. "Get them. And eliminate them at once so that we can go on with the plan."

The soldiers stepped forward like automatically guided robots. Freya and Brennan shared a look, not having expected the new battle.

Tell me you have a plan, Freya urged.

I thought you did! Brennan shot back.

Very funny. Now really, what is it? the Sage questioned impatiently.

I told you – I don't have one, the Wiseman answered.

What kind of rescue mission is this? Brennan...Shit! Freya swore as the ghosts advanced further. No matter which way she tried to turn it, a solution eluded her.

Then, as if by miracle, her senses picked up a presence at the gates of the Cathedral.

"Is that—" Freya didn't dare continue the phrase.

When a magnificently roar echoed in the Cathedral, though, the Sage turned to the door, as did Brennan. Her eyes turned watery as relief spread through her. "Tyr!"

Brennan extended his hand as if to blast it, but Freya grabbed it. "No! The tiger's on our side!"

The Wiseman looked down at her, and she noticed his expression. Hope emanated from his features, and pure joy and relief was in his eyes. "I know." He, too, had recognized the roar and identified it – rightly – as the voice that had been guiding him along ever since their arrival in Spain. The same being that was Freya's protector.

"What is that?" Cortés was heard yelling furiously.

"I do not..." Gustav's hesitant response trailed off.

"You said she had no other allies than this Wiseman!"

"She doesn't! I mean, she did not!" Gustav went on pitifully.

Freya glanced behind and saw Sam still at the edge of the sword, the barrier surrounding him in an iron grip.

Cortés noticed her gaze immediately, and he pushed the tip harder into Sam's nonexistent flesh. "If you want your friend, call the tiger off!"

The Sage paled. She knew she had to save Sam somehow, and if Cortés was giving her an opening... There had to be a chance to free him!

"Tyr..." Freya started as she turned to the tiger.

Do not! It was an order, and Tyr's golden-green eyes bore deep into the Sage's. *If he is starting to negotiate, it means my appearance has made its effect.*

"Freya," Brennan interrupted with a rush of adrenaline. "We can take him on. Together. Now."

The tiger roared again, though this time Freya knew it was to express its disagreement to Brennan's plan – which it had heard. The bond connected the three of them, enabling each one to hear what the other said.

Why not, Tyr? It's a good plan! It will free Sam!

NO! The tiger denied fiercely. *You are in enough trouble as it is and not ready to fight Cortés with your new powers. Both you and Brennan are disadvantaged in the Cathedral, while Cortés and Gustav are not, on the contrary. If you fight in here, it will be the end of you both.*

The words were like a death sentence to Freya's ears. She'd prepared herself to the eventuality of leaving Sam behind, but it was still not a decision she was comfortable with.

But Sam— Freya started.

Brennan caught what she was saying. *We'll come back for him. I promise, we will.*

"No!" Freya protested and she turned to face Cortés – and his army. Brennan grabbed her arm and started pulling the Sage towards the doors, away from her doom.

"Running away, I see?" Cortés yelled. "Your friend will pay for this!"

"No!" Freya yelled. "Don't you dare touch him, Cortés!"

"We shall see about that," the conquistador smirked evilly.

"He's bluffing!" Brennan assured the Sage. "You know his sword doesn't have all its abilities back. He's just trying to make you stay, Freya."

The Sage nodded softly, then turned her back to them and ran away with Wiseman. Ghosts followed in their footsteps, trailing closely behind. Freya focused on putting one foot in front of the other, gripping Brennan's hand tightly in hers. With the specters hot on their trail, the oak doors seemed all the more inviting in the morning light.

Freya turned at one point and shot one more blast to their stalkers, delaying their advancement. She and Brennan could distinctly see Tyr pacing outside, silently urging them to hurry up. The two teenagers picked up their pace, and soon they had reached the exit.

Freya stopped and turned around one more time. The ghosts were no longer running, now that the pair was in safety outside of the walls of the Cathedral. They knew a certain death would be the price if they stepped too close to them.

Scowling at their escape, Cortés threw Sam to Gustav, who dragged the ghost behind him and into the darkness. Even in the distance, she caught Sam's eye, and tears rolled down her cheeks.

"I'll come back, Sam, I swear," she promised.

Brennan grabbed her arm and tugged on it gently. "It's time to go, Freya. We'll return. Now come."

She wordlessly let him pull her away. It was time to plan Sam's rescue.

Chapter 25

B rennan glanced at Freya by his side, biting his lip in thought. Since they'd run down the stairs of the Cathedral, and finally slowed down to a walk, she hadn't said a word.

Freya's shoulders were curbed inwards, and what he could see of her gaze was dulled. The bond between them echoed with sentiments of regret, helplessness and above all, guilt. Though he wished nothing more than to take it away, Brennan knew her well enough by now to realize no words would help.

Ahead of them floated Emmanuel, equally quiet. They'd found him at the bottom of stairs, getting up and meeting their gazes as they approached. At his stricken expression when he realized Sam was not with them, Freya had only been able to shake her head and mutter an apology.

Closing the walk was Tyr, its beautiful feline coat glistening with the rising sun. They had passed some regular humans on their walk, but none seemed to notice the animal. Brennan figured it was due to a type of cloaking method used, but above all he was grateful for its presence.

Their walk had so far been in silence – or almost. The moment the tiger had started speaking, it appeared nothing could make the lecture stop.

Brennan could hear Tyr address Freya, but remained out of the conversation, only heaving a sigh.

Freya, for the last time, I simply cannot understand how you could break your promise! You could have died! Did not you learn anything from your encounter with Cadmael?

"Tyr, I said I was sorry," the Sage answered in a tired voice. "Sam was calling out for help. I couldn't just stand by and do nothing."

The feline said nothing for a moment, then stepped in between Freya and Brennan. *I understand that, child. And I can also feel your guilt. Why?*

Instead of answering, Freya simply stared away, her eyes dark with unspoken emotions.

"Freya," Brennan couldn't stop the words any more than he could avoid breathing. "Why would you feel guilty? You did all you could, taking unlimited risks even!"

She turned a haunted expression to him. "No, I didn't. I could have rescued Sam even when Cortés had him—"

"Cortés!?" Emmanuel turned around, features tight with panic.

Freya's glance settled on him, as did Brennan's. "Yeah."

"He was there?" Emmanuel seemed like he was about to throw up.

"Yes, he was," Brennan confirmed, not understanding the ghost's reaction. "Why?"

Still walking – floating in Emmanuel's case – the spirit revealed, "Then that means Gustav joined him. I've known my ancestor to be a coward, but I never thought he would be a traitor to his own people. Not to mention a hypocrite," he added under his breath.

He peered over the horizon, lingering in perusal for a few moments. When neither Freya nor Brennan said anything, Emmanuel turned to them.

The Sage's features hardened, resolute with a determination of some kind. "Even if you had seen Gustav for what he was from the beginning, you still couldn't have escaped him finding you. So don't think about it, Em."

"Maybe you're right, but... Sam. We'll get him back, won't we?" he asked hopefully, looking a lot like Sam at the moment.

"Yes," Brennan answered instead of Freya, and she turned to him at the sure sound of his voice. "We will."

Emmanuel nodded, then his gaze landed on Tyr, who had been quietly observing him the whole time. "He helped you escape?" He pointed to the tiger.

Freya cracked a smile. "I'm not sure if Tyr is a he or a she, but the answer is yes."

Emmanuel cocked his head at the tiger, then smiled. "It is nice meeting you, though I honestly admit I have no words to thank you for helping my friends escape."

Tyr merely bowed its head, then touched Brennan's hand gently with its muzzle.

Startled by the softness, Brennan looked down at the tiger. His golden-brown eyes met the deep green ones, and Brennan could sense that if only he tried, he could read deep inside those orbs the secrets of the other world. The Wiseman could feel them within his grasp, on the edge of his conscious self, but even as he tried to catch them, they flew through his fingers.

The times ahead will be dangerous, both for you and Freya.

At this, the Sage diverted her attention to them. "If you mean Cortés, Tyr, I'm going to defeat him, no matter what. With what the book gave me—"

Freya, it is time stop speak in "I" and focus on "we". Those new powers, you cannot use them yet, the tiger pointed out.

"What are you talking about, Tyr? Of course I can! I did it at the Cathedral, didn't I? Overruling the influence that energy barrier had on me, I used my... What?" Freya asked as the tiger shook its mane.

That had nothing to do with your new abilities, child, Tyr said.

"You mean she was using those she already had?" Brennan asked, perplexed.

Not quite, Tyr said. *Think of it as a tornado. It all starts with a tiny wind, then builds up in intensity. Freya was starting to use the new energy, but only a small percentage of it. Child, when you will activate the entirety of your spiritual potential...* The tiger paused as if to gather its thoughts. *When you learn to use that whole power, then you will be unstoppable. No conquistador will be able to oppose you.*

"What do I have to do for that?" Freya asked.

Tyr smiled, its fangs showing. *You will find out soon enough if you look deep inside yourself.* The tiger then looked at Brennan. *And that goes for you too, Wiseman.*

Seeing that they'd reached the hotel, Tyr stopped. *Work together and you will win this fight.* It had barely finished speaking, when a light appeared behind it. For a second,

Freya thought it was the sun, but the glow was much softer and whiter, enveloping the feline until they could no longer look at it.

Both humans blinked, and Tyr disappeared, returning to the realm it belonged in.

Freya bit her lip, staring at the spot it had vanished through, then hesitantly turned towards Brennan, sensing his gaze on her. "What?" She was confused by the concern she read in his gentle hazel gaze.

"You have no reason to feel guilty, you know," Brennan said. "We'll get Sam back soon, I promise."

Unwilling to argue, Freya could only incline her head in assent. "I'll, uh, go and get some sleep."

Emmanuel floated to the two, sensing their goodbyes. "I will head on to Seamus's room, if that is fine with you both?" At their mute nods, he added, "See you later."

Both teens watched the ghost take off, then hesitantly turned to each other. Brennan shuffled his feet, hesitating, then reached out and pulled Freya in a hug. She stiffened at first, not used to the contact, but then his heat alone permeated her cold skin and she relaxed.

As she dared return the embrace, Freya became distinctly aware of how comfortable and safe his arms felt around her. She snuggled deeper, burying her head in the crook of his neck, inhaling –

"I'm sorry," Freya pulled away, blushing crimson at her behavior. "I'm really tired, and you, well…"

"Smell nice?" Brennan questioned with a slight smile, though his eyes were unreadable.

At a loss, Freya could only shrug. She was saved from further embarrassment when Brennan chuckled, then tucked a stray strand of hair behind her ear. "It's all good. Go get some sleep."

About to run away, Freya nonetheless turned back to Brennan. "I'm not sure how much I will, what with it being day already but... You should get some, too."

Eager to escape his perusing golden-brown eyes, Freya turned on her heels and walked away towards the stairs. As she started climbing them, Brennan's voice stopped her. "Freya?"

She slowly turned around to face him, fearing another bombardment of questions. But Brennan only added a soft, "Good night."

Taken aback and more than a little thrown off by this side of him she wasn't used to, Freya offered a weak smile in return. "Good night, Brennan. And thanks...for everything you did in the Cathedral."

She then quite cowardly sprinted away, unwilling to test fate any longer. Back in her room, Freya rushed through taking her clothes off, then took the quickest shower in history. Not bothering to dry her hair, she dressed in an old t-shirt and shorts, then slid into bed and closed her eyes, sighing in satisfaction.

The blankets hugged her form, and as she snuggled deeper, Freya could almost swear she smelled Brennan's scent – of pine and fresh air, reminiscent of never-ending mountains and valleys, far away.

Sleep came by seconds later, taking her on a tour in dreamland.

&&&

Fire was everywhere, creeping closer and crackling in warning. Freya could hear voices around as she stared at the ceiling of the car. Then, a pair of arms grabbed her and held her tight, whispering soothing words in her ear.

Time passed by, and they waited. She could sense two persons in the car, but couldn't see their faces. Then, someone called out to them.

A man appeared from the fire, and Freya was handed to him. His tears dropped on her forehead as he promised to care for her, and defend her with his life.

And then they were running, on the hill and away from the explosion... And suddenly they came to a stop. Her grey eyes took in the fire, then the huge explosion that followed...

And then more tears fell onto her face, and she looked up at the man that held her, to see his grey eyes filled with sorrow and sadness. "Farewell, my friends," he whispered, then kissed her hair.

She turned once more to the flames, but they were now morphing into something else.

Freya was in the desert, all alone, desperately glancing around...

And then something soared from the sky. A bird. It was coming closer, and closer, and closer... Its steely eyes captured hers, and Freya was lost.

She was unable to move.

&&&

A few doors down the hall, Brennan entered O'Keeffe's room, to find Seamus sitting on one of the beds, with Emmanuel floating in front of him. The ghost's head was bowed, not meeting the elder Sage's eyes.

Brennan arched an eyebrow when they both turned to him. "Who died?" Brennan asked mockingly.

"No one..." Emmanuel turned his gaze back to the floor. "...yet."

O'Keeffe and Brennan shared a look, and the former shrugged. "He's been like this since he got in."

Brennan frowned and stared hard at the ghost, then started at O'Keeffe question. "Is Freya all right? And who is this tiger I hear about?"

"She's fine," Brennan answered. "As for the tiger, that's Freya's friend. Came just in time, too." When O'Keeffe gaze did not waver, instead became more probing, Brennan simply shrugged. "We'll give you a full account in the morning."

O'Keeffe seemed about to say something, then settled for a curt nod and a head motion to Emmanuel.

Brennan sighed. He was in no comforting mood, especially not to the ghost, but since he had no choice... "Listen, Emmanuel, whatever you're thinking, don't feel guilty. Freya chose to rescue you instead of Sam. I suppose she had her reasons – most of which are tied to Gustav and him wanting you on his side. I'm not saying I agree, but just compose yourself. We can turn this around by working together and saving Sam."

Emmanuel's gaze nearly made Brennan flinch. "Will you *let* me help you?"

"What's that supposed to mean?" Brennan asked. He was getting tired of innuendos.

"You do not trust me," Emmanuel noted. It was a statement, not a question. "Why would you let me help you if you cannot trust me?"

Brennan gave Emmanuel a hard stare, all warmth having left his golden eyes. "We need all hands on deck. Now if you don't mind, I'm going off to sleep."

Ignoring O'Keeffe's look, Brennan changed in a brown t-shirt and a pair of boxers and slid in bed. A few moments later, he heard O'Keeffe do the same and all lights were shut off.

The only illumination left was Emmanuel's pale lighted form against the shadowy night. Brennan sighed and drifted off to sleep.

&&&

Brennan hadn't closed his eyes for more than a few minutes when images of another's dream interrupted his rest. Though it looked like the deserted landscape he usually found himself in, the Wiseman realized this particular vision was not his own.

Odd feelings ran through him, but it was the aftertaste of guilt, bitter on his tongue, that woke him up. His eyes fluttered open, then stared unseeing at the ceiling, fear gripping his heart.

More at odds than before, Brennan could sense Freya's distress. He wondered if he should go and check on her – if she would allow comfort – or if he was better of trying to go back to sleep.

The decision was made for him when the calling intensified.

Though Freya wasn't saying his name, it was as good as. Brennan got out of bed, almost pulled forward by the need he felt through their bond. Without overthinking it, he pulled on a pair of faded black jeans.

Brennan could feel Emmanuel's eyes on him, and he turned to the ghost. The two shared a long look. The Wiseman was trying to control his feelings, whereas the ghost's gaze was defiant.

Finally, Brennan took a deep breath. "If I don't return by morning, tell O'Keeffe that I and Freya will join him tomorrow for breakfast." As an afterthought, he added, "Please."

The phantom didn't react at first, only glared back. In the end, he nodded and Brennan turned to leave. He slid across the floor without much noise and exited the room, then hurried across the hall barefooted.

When he arrived in front of Freya's door, his heart beating a mile a minute, he didn't bother to knock. He knew what he would find inside.

Brennan's hand touched the doorknob and he twisted it. A soft click echoed in the night and he pushed the door open, stepping inside and closing it behind him. Freya was on the floor, her back resting against the bed, head thrown back and staring at the ceiling.

"Freya?" he inched closer, calling her name out softly. She didn't give any sign of hearing him, rather maintained her perusal of the wall.

Brennan went and sat down next to her, leaving a slight space in between them. He mimicked her stance and also threw his head back.

They both remained in that position, in silence, for what would later on seem like hours. Then, Freya drew her head back and cleared her throat. Brennan followed her cue and cocked his head in silent question. Freya's profile was partly shadowed, especially by her hair, but the part of her face he could see was lighted by the moon's soft glow.

When she spoke, her voice was hoarse with emotion. "When I was four," Freya started softly, "me and my parents went to the countryside, in England. I used to live there before... Before everything." She gulped past the lump in her throat at the recollection, then continued, "We planned to have a nice picnic, just the three of us, and then my mother promised she'd help me catch a squirrel. We were all excited to have a day off from the normal noise of the city, and we were singing and laughing. After the accident, I buried those moments deep at the back of my mind, never wanting to see them again. It hurt too much. But then... Seamus's memory brought it back and..." She took a deep breath to calm the sobs that were trying to escape, then continued with the story. "The car was filled with our joy," Freya recalled. A single tear peered at the corner of her eye, and got stuck on her eyelash.

Brennan waited patiently for the rest of it. Though his demeanor didn't change, his insides clenched in agony for his partner.

"Then, at once, the laughter stopped," Freya went on. "The joy was filled by an imminent sense of danger. I could feel it. I knew something was coming. My parents shared a look, but they couldn't make it out for what it truly was. But

I could. I wanted to yell, tell them to stop the car and run... But my voice failed me."

Silent tears rolled down her cheeks, shining like diamonds in the moon's glow. Brennan felt a pang in his chest. He knew what was coming. And sure enough, he was right.

"Suddenly, there was this explosion right near the car. I remember hearing a scream and a screech of breaks, then..." Freya dropped her head in her hands. "I remember seeing Seamus's face and... and then a huge explosion and... I can't remember anything before that, Brennan! My memories are all blurry. I can barely recall my parents' faces!"

Brennan was startled to see Freya with the haunted look, so vulnerable, when he was used to the strong Sage that was always battling him. His emotions couldn't be put into words – and they would be useless to her grief. Instead, he simply wrapped his arms around her, pulling her so she was tucked against his side, and let her cry her heart out.

"He won't talk about them..." Freya sobbed. "I've been begging Seamus ever since that day, but he won't. And I feel so alone when I see other people with their parents and..."

Brennan tightened his hold, wanting to take away the pain. But he knew it was impossible, and that the most he could do at the moment was to hold her and listen. That was why she'd called him. And Brennan was ready to be whatever she needed him to be.

"He's saying he can't tell me because he swore to protect me, but I need to know, Brennan! And what I witnessed, through his eyes... Seamus has no idea how much it shook me."

Brennan held her still, resting his chin atop her head. Finally, after what seemed like hours, Freya pulled away from him gently and rested her back against the bed once more. He fought the urge to keep her in his arms, instead taking a breath to steady the new sensations swarming in his head.

"I'm sorry I let go like that, but... I just..." she trailed off, meeting his gaze.

"It's all right, Freya," Brennan murmured, caressing her cheek. "I know how it feels when you put on a strong face and keep bottling feelings inside until you can't anymore..." He trailed off, already getting a faraway look in his eyes.

Freya wiped away the remaining tears and turned to Brennan to listen to his story. Wordlessly, she knew they'd reached the point of no return – sharing their deeper selves. Surprisingly, there was no fear to hold her back from it, only relief.

"You remember how I told you that a Wiseman could supposedly not marry because he'd lose his powers? And how my grandfather Thomas did, in spite of everything?" Brennan asked.

"Yeah," she nodded. "And you told me he hadn't lost them and that he trained you afterwards."

Brennan sighed as the memories he'd been trying so hard to forget washed over him like an icy shower, bringing back the ghosts of the past. Phantoms the Wiseman had tried to suppress for the past years. He closed his eyes and let the recollections fill him, remembering everything that had happened and all that he had lost. All the years of practice and rancor from his people, when he was the only one who believed...

Believed in his grandfather and his abilities, in all that he'd been told... And dared to dream that he could be just as strong.

And then all his training, the years he'd spent living with his grandfather... All the obstacles he'd overcome to finally master his own powers, even if sometimes he still couldn't.

A small smile tugged at the corners of his lips when he recalled the trouble he used to create in his grandfather's house – broken windows, plates, armchairs and whatnot – and how the old man would scold him before laughing out loud at his nephew's mishaps.

"He was disgraced," Brennan whispered.

"What?" Freya frowned.

"For having married, for having chosen love over power..." Brennan opened his eyes, deep hate burning in them. "He had a son – my father – who turned out to be just as powerful as him. Because they lived outside of the main village, they rarely interacted with other Wisemen. Unaware of the Code, my father eventually married, as well. Occupied with raising a young boy, he forgot all about his uniqueness – not that he ever cherished the special abilities he'd been born with, anyway. If he hadn't he could've found a Wiseman to train him, to eventually share his powers with him." Brennan shook his head in disgust. "But then, one man from the village told him about the Code of the Wiseman, and my father got it into his head that he'd lost his chance at being a Wiseman because of what my grandfather hadn't revealed. That because he hadn't known Wiseman had to be hermits, now he was tainted, and could never be one. Rather than blame himself for having taken a wife, he blamed his father."

Brennan's jaw clenched at the memory, and a hardened glint appeared in his once-soft eyes. "He took me and mom to the village, where I grew up with another brother and sister. My mother, my father, my siblings... They all treated – and spoke of – my grandfather as if he was mental."

"Were any of your siblings...?" Freya trailed off, unsure of how to phrase the question.

"Yes, they had the ability. But it was not cultivated by my father, and they only see it as an odd blessing. Sins of the father and all. I was – am – the only one who knew the truth. The only one Thomas told everything. And the only one who accepted him. When my grandmother died, he retreated in the mountains, in an old cottage, far away from our town and the people in it. One day, I couldn't stand it anymore and followed him there. I was sick of the whole village and I missed my grandfather. I joined him in his refuge and there, he started teaching me."

"Teaching you?" Freya repeated, already drawing a parallel between her own younger education with Seamus, and Brennan's with Thomas.

"Yes. He was my mentor in many ways. It was through him I learned the ways of nature, the languages of Earth. Thomas instructed me about a Wiseman's powers and how they should be used... He taught me how to use my emotions – or those I can capture, in some cases – to nourish the power I have in myself."

Brennan paused again, and it gave Freya a moment to reflect. *Who would've thought we really do have so much in common?*

With each passing day – hell, hour even – the Sage had to admit that Tyr had been correct. Their strength built on their similarities and differences, and their potential remained untapped. Even in that instant, sitting within an inch of the Wiseman, she could sense a hum of power in the air between them.

Freya shook her head, trying to clear it of the odd thoughts. "Go on," she encouraged him.

Brennan glanced her way, as if pulled from some deep thought, then cleared this throat. "Right. Well, Thomas was disgraced. By following him in the mountains, I was cast off, too. But I didn't care. Not at that time. I had a grandfather to teach me to use my powers and we lived joyfully in our retreat in the mountains. But then..."

Brennan clenched his fists at the memory of that day. "Thomas always used to say that a healthy mind lived in a healthy body. In order to keep that balance, I exercised daily. I took long walks outside in the moonlight or at dawn and once I became too tired I used the emotions I felt to exercise my powers. After strenuous hours outside, I'd return to the cottage where my grandfather always had questions for me. One day, though, everything went haywire."

Freya's heart beat faster in anticipation. Due to the bond, she could feel Brennan's emotions just as well as he could hers. In that moment, the Wiseman was burning not only with rage, but also with the pain of the recollection.

Understanding what he was going through, Freya placed a hand on his gently. "You can stop if you don't feel like going on, Brennan."

He turned his head to her, and their gazes locked. Grey boring into golden-brown, they stared at each other for long seconds, communicating with no need of words. Their shared pain was almost palpable, as were the memories of their past. What they'd done, what they had lived through, had shaped the versions of themselves currently existing. Both were aware of the truth, yet both were also tied in to the past.

Brennan could see in that moment, clearly more than ever, Freya's thirst for vengeance in the death of her parents. It was tied in to a deep need of belonging, and getting justice for a crime committed.

From her end, Freya could feel that same yearning for revenge in the Wiseman, but without the quest for identity. Brennan knew who he was, and his strength in that regard was something she could draw power from.

Wordlessly, he squeezed her hand. "When I went back to the cabin, Thomas was dead. He looked peaceful and asleep, but I knew he'd been killed. Since then, I've vowed to find his assassin and demand justice. When you told me it was Raksh…" His eyes were burning, features set in determination. "I swear to you, Frey, I want to help you get him. For both of us – he needs to pay."

Freya said nothing, for she knew exactly how he felt. She wanted her parents' killers dead. And she yearned to be the one to whom they would look on their last breath. Freya planned to get to that as soon as the mission was over.

"Brennan," Freya started. "What about your dad? Did you… Did you tell him?"

All color that was left on the Wiseman's face drained as it all came back to him. "Oh, yes. I went to the village that same night and explained what happened. He couldn't even look me in the eye, and said only one thing – *Leave. Leave and don't come back here, ever.* I did as he wished, and never returned."

"Oh, Brennan," Freya sighed. "I'm sorry. I know they're empty words most of the time, but I really *am* sorry. Fathers shouldn't act that way."

Brennan shrugged, despite the ache of the memory. They remained in silence for long minutes after, each taking in the confessions of the other. Their hands stayed tightly clenched, basking in the comfort of the understanding.

A glow lighted the room, and they both jumped, their hands disjoining.

"Brennan, your medallion!"

He glanced down at the tell-tale radiance against his chest, then saw something out of the corner of his eyes. "Your book!" Brennan exclaimed, pointing to the closet.

Eyes wide, Freya stood and went to grab the manuscript. Brennan, having followed, knelt next to it and Freya. As he did, the leather cover shimmered, showing a locket.

The Sage's stunned grey eyes met his, almost silver in the light. "Your necklace fits perfectly in there," Freya pointed out.

Brennan took it off without hesitation and placed it in the new space. The book glowed blue, then an image of a map floated out of it. It was almost multi-dimensional, showing full hills, mountains – a path mapped out.

The two teenagers stared in shock as under their eyes, the map broke into two. Each side rolled up, until it became a dragon's head again, and entered each one of them.

They were left gasping, though not in pain like last time. Then, a voice echoed, *You are the guardians of the map now. No matter what, keep it safe with your lives. It will show you the path to the relics when you are ready.*

The illumination of the manuscript ceased suddenly, and the medallion popped out of its spot the following instant. Brennan reached for it carefully, but its surface still felt smooth when he touched it.

Stifling a relieved sigh, he took it and placed it around his neck with trembling hands. Then he met Freya's pensive expression.

"Was that what I think it was?"

"The map to the relics..." Freya said wonderingly. "You know what this means – the demon will *really* be after us."

Brennan nodded grimly, as the possibilities echoed in his mind. Then another realization followed, just as sobering. "Frey... It also means we can bait him."

They stared in silence, barely able to contain their jubilation. Finally, there was a way to get what they both wanted.

"We should try and get some sleep..." Brennan finally whispered.

"Probably...."

As he got up to leave, Freya added, "Hey, Bren? Thanks for listening."

The Wiseman nodded to her. "You too." He hesitated, then pulled her into another hug. "Good night, Freya," he whispered in her hair, then left before she could return the sentiment.

As she climbed back into bed, Freya's mind was racing with ideas. She wouldn't have thought it would be easy, but exhausted from the night's emotions, she succumbed to sleep.

Little did both know as they drifted off to sleep, that night would change their rapports forever.

&&&

Far, far away in another world, on top a high hill, a majestic white tiger with deep green eyes watched the sun to rise.

Its triumphant roar filled the night, scaring away the darkness and welcoming the light. It had sensed the change in the teenagers' emotions – but not the new gift they had been dealt.

Chapter 26

Morning light filtered through the window, achieving to wake Freya up. She opened her eyes and squinted against the sun's rays. A glance at the alarm clock on the bedside table confirmed less than four hours had passed since her morning chat with Brennan.

"Not enough freaking time to sleep," Freya grumbled with a huge yawn. A morning person, she was not.

Rubbing at her eyes tiredly, she decided to contact Tyr, without whose help neither she nor her partner would have gotten alive out of the Cathedral.

"Tyr?" Freya whispered into the morning air.

Yes, child?

"We'll get Sam back, won't we?" Despite Brennan's encouragement the previous night, she needed reassurance from her protector, as well.

I believe so, Freya. There was a slight pause, then Tyr continued, *You two crossed another milestone last night. I could feel it even in the spiritual realm, and it warmed by heart. Thus, my answer is yes, you can save your friend – together.*

The Sage then thought about her partner, and a suspicion crept on her. "Tyr, you've been chatting with Brennan telepathically, haven't you? That's how you knew a lot of things."

The feline hesitated, then admitted, *Yes, but he was unaware who I was. I only happened to be around whenever he needed guidance.*

"Just promise me you haven't revealed things I'm not ready for," Freya pleaded.

No.

Freya nodded, satisfied by the categorical answer. She then got out of bed and went to the bathroom. As she passed in front of the mirror, the Sage stopped and took a long look at her reflection.

Surprisingly, she had no dark circles under her eyes, though her grey orbs did look tired. Freya picked up a hairbrush and quickly brushed her raven locks, then piled them in a high ponytail. She splashed some water on her face and brushed her teeth, all in less than ten minutes.

As she did so, she reflected on the meeting with Gustav, and what Brennan had revealed about the demon. The same wraith that'd killed her parents. The need for vengeance was a white-hot blaze in her veins, and she gritted her teeth against it.

"I have to get a grip on myself," Freya said to her reflection as dreams and memories threatened to overwhelm her. "I can't let my past rule my future. I have to turn the page over it...for now."

Sighing, the Sage exited the bathroom and opened her suitcase. Grabbing a pair of blue dark jeans and a violet t-shirt, she got dressed, picked up her leather jacket and headed out the door. Her feet automatically took her to the dining place downstairs, where she was to meet O'Keeffe, Brennan and Emmanuel. As she turned the corner, Freya was surprised to see Emmanuel and O'Keeffe already at a table for four, a breakfast for three steaming enticingly.

Emmanuel was the first to wave her over. She settled in a chair near the ghost and opposite Seamus, happy to know that no one else except the four of them – if Brennan finally decided to show up – would be in the room, since breakfast time had passed and it wasn't lunch yet.

"Good morning, Freya." There was an odd note in her mentor's voice, but Freya pretended to ignore it.

"How did you sleep?" Emmanuel asked with an edge in his.

"Good morning to you both," Freya smiled brightly, then turned to the spirit. "Pretty well, actually." Eyeing the goods on the table enviously, the Sage muttered, "So, where's Brennan? I'm starving."

"He was still sleeping when I left," O'Keeffe said. "I decided to let him rest some more."

"Well, I'm hungry." Pursing her lips, Freya concentrated on her partner's energy, then announced, *Time to wake up, Brennan.*

When only silence answered, Freya's scowl deepened. *Brennan! Wake up!*

Huh— What? Where's the danger? His voice was groggy and she could almost imagine the Wiseman trying to chase the sleep out of his eyes.

Hilarious, really, Brennan. Get your butt down here at once, I'm famished.

So go ahead and eat without me then! the Wiseman retorted.

Do really you want me to? There's yummy bacon, omelet, pancakes... Freya trailed off at his annoyed sigh.

Ugh, stop already! All right, all right, I'll be down in a few minutes.

Ten. Hurry up.

She blinked out of her daze and met Seamus' gaze, finally noticing his frustration. Her stomach knotted uncomfortably, and she dropped the piece of toast back on the plate. "Em, give us a sec, would you?"

When the ghost floated away around the corner, Freya sighed. "All right. Yell at me, get it out of your system."

"Do you think this is a game?" Seamus started, his voice low and furious. "You were incredibly irresponsible to act as you did!"

"How so?" Freya challenged. "I had new powers. I had backup. And I *am* alive."

Seamus gritted his teeth, leaning forward. "Your powers were useless. Your backup was in the form of a phantom who was more of a liability than anything else. You are lucky Brennan was able to get there in time!"

"That's what it comes down to, isn't it?" Freya pointed out bitterly. "Brennan saving the day."

Seamus' eyes widened slightly, then his look of frustration eased. "No, it does not. I know you are more than capable of holding your own against the bad guys, but I do wish you would stop taking risks."

When Freya only clenched her teeth and stubbornly looked away, Seamus reached over the table and grasped her hand in his. "I worry for you, my dear. When I die, there will be no one around to share this responsibility with you. Yes, I am happy Brennan is around to help out. It does not mean I doubt your abilities, please understand that."

Freya glanced at him, noticing the honesty in his eyes. The fight went out of her, and she nodded. "All right." A pause, then, "I'm sorry about rushing into the Cathedral. My worry for Sam overtook everything."

Seamus pulled back, leaning against the chair again and signaling for Emmanuel to join them. "I know," he said as the ghost neared. "We are all troubled for Sam, but we will figure out a way to get him back, safely."

Freya smiled at his attempt to reassure. The food aroma tickled her nostrils, and her stomach growled in response. Groaning, she folded her arms across her chest and leaned back in the chair, gaze glued to the entrance through which Brennan was supposed to be coming in. When he was still missing once the ten minutes had passed, she was about to call him again. Before she could, he rounded the corner, a sour look on his face.

"Finally!" Freya exclaimed in delight.

Brennan sat next to her and Seamus, and opposite Emmanuel. He took a long look at the food, then started to fill his plate without further ado. Freya followed his example, leaving O'Keeffe to stare at the two in wonder.

"That was so unnecessary," Brennan complained. "I could've slept a bit more."

Freya mock-glared at him. "Not only am I hungry, I'm *starving*. So if you don't want to see me grumpy for the rest of the day, you'd better just start eating."

She hid her smug grin when the Wiseman only muttered under his breath about girls and eating habits. For the next few moments, both teenagers devoured their breakfast in tandem. They bit into the food at the same time, drank their drinks together, all until the content of their plates had vanished into the endless pit that was their stomachs.

Once they were done, both Freya and Brennan pushed away their plates at the same time and leaned back against their chairs. They were met with O'Keeffe's stunned look.

"What?" Brennan asked.

Emmanuel pointed to their empty plates. "You both just ate at the same rhythm enough food for six people, all of it without taking a breath in between. Correct me if I'm mistaken, but that's not normal."

Freya arched an eyebrow, not impressed. "No duh! We've barely eaten since we landed and last night – well, morning actually – after escaping Cortés, we went straight to bed, too exhausted out of our minds to even think about food."

Now that's a lie if I ever heard one, Brennan commented smugly, the recollection of the previous night still very vivid in his mind.

Freya hid her smirk by drinking some more juice. *Honestly, Bren, I was speaking generally.*

Brennan's gaze and Emmanuel's met across the table, and he saw the ghost was aching to say something about what Freya had just stated. However, the Wiseman's glare stopped him from doing so.

O'Keeffe narrowed his eyes at Freya's statement. "You fought Cortés?"

Brennan rubbed the back of his neck sheepishly, not in a mood to get Seamus overly anxious. "Well, not exactly, but we did face him... We just couldn't confront him directly since he was holding Sam at the point of his sword and threatening to, uh, get rid of him."

"Wait," O'Keeffe interrupted, holding up a palm. "You're telling me that even though Brennan came after you to stop you from facing Cortés and his ghosts, you were still in the Cathedral when he joined you?"

"Well..." Freya shared a look with her partner. "Seamus, it was bit hard to get out, even with Brennan to help. The ghosts were surrounding us and you know how Gustav is. Besides, I already apologized for this."

"Freya," Seamus rubbed the center of his forehead as though plagued by a headache, "has Brennan filled you in about Set?"

"Yes," she nodded. "How you think he's behind all this, and that Cortés and Gustav are pawns. He mentioned also the objects of power you think Raksh has been handing out as gifts."

Seamus pinched the bridge of his nose, seemingly fighting off a headache. "This is turning into a game neither of us want to be part of. The gods are fickle, and dangerous. I do not want to put you any more in the path of danger than before. Once we get Sam, we should retreat to Scotland and plan from there."

"What?"

Brennan caught Freya's shock through their bond, and grasped her hand in his under the table. *Chill. No need to get upset yet, let me handle this.*

She threw him a fiery look, but remained silent.

"Seamus, I don't think that's a good idea. If we do that – and I say *we* because obviously I'd come with – that places your castle in danger. Raksh will stop at nothing until he gets his slimy paws on the manuscript and medallion." He shared a secretive look with Freya, then added, "We're best off not leaving here until we deal with these ghosts."

"So that Freya can do something even more perilous than what she already did?" Seamus bit out.

Freya could no longer retain a scowl. "Yes, it's true that I entered the Cathedral, dragging Emmanuel and Brennan in with me. But Sam called out for help, and I couldn't just ignore him. Plus, I held my own against Gustav – not that it's anything new. As for Cortés, we could've handled him if he hadn't been using Sam as leverage."

And the hundred plus spirits helping him out, Brennan added mentally, but wisely did not mention aloud.

"Oh right," Freya continued without missing a beat, "and we confirmed that Gustav joined Cortés."

O'Keeffe went pale as a ghost, his face holding an incredulous look on it. Hearing the full account, he couldn't conceive that his pupil had been crazy enough to face such obstacles, and still live to tell the tale.

"But I was never in danger," Freya finished with a shrug.

"*Never* in danger?" O'Keeffe murmured, apparently still in shock.

Brennan intervened before the situation got out of control. "Freya's right, professor. Tyr was keeping an eye on us three."

"Tyr?" O'Keeffe narrowed his eyes at Freya. "Would you mind explaining to me just who this *Tyr* is?"

Freya shared another look with Brennan, realizing it was time they put all their cards on the table. *Please, Tyr, can you come?* Freya called.

Though the Sage received no answer, a few seconds later a blinding light came out of nowhere, and Tyr stepped through it. The tiger was more majestic than ever, its white fur reflecting the radiance, green-golden eyes vibrant.

The feline stepped out of the illumination and it diminished soon after, leaving behind only the glow visible around its body. Tyr then turned its enormous head to Seamus, who was all wide eyes and gaping mouth.

"Who—" Seamus began, but a voice in his head immediately interrupted his thoughts. Its warmth and casual tone immediately calmed his heart, and he was filled with a sense of peace.

My name is Tyr, the feline declared, meeting Seamus's gaze with a frank one of its own. *But long ago you knew me under another name, Seamus.*

O'Keeffe's eyes widened in disbelief. "Who are you? How can you converse telepathically when I—?"

The tiger's fangs revealed as if it was smiling. *I know the obstacles you encountered by protecting Freya, and I am infinitely grateful to you. To answer your question, I can support both of us communicating, but only for a few minutes. My stay here is limited, since my last incursion took too much of my energy.*

Noticing all the questions in Seamus's eyes, Tyr shook its mane. *Another time, perhaps. For now, know this – I am no enemy. As I mentioned, you knew me under another name long ago. Freya called me a few weeks ago, just before she fought Cadmael. I have been helping her ever since and keeping an eye on her and, most recently, Brennan.*

"And you came to their aid in the Cathedral?" Seamus whispered wonderingly.

Yes. Though I could not enter the church, Cortés would never have been able to hurt Freya. The powers she holds now are too grand to defeat, even for him. Do not chastise her further, I took care of that and she understands her mistakes. This does not mean that if she had the chance to redo it, she would not do things the same way.

Tyr glanced to Freya, knowing full well she was following the conversation, as was Brennan.

That is Freya's way and you have to trust in her. Do not lose any more time, and start planning how to defeat Cortés. I have come upon new information that he is trying to take over France... For a last battle place, I would suggest the City's Historical Museum. It would be a great trap for the ghosts.

At that, the tiger's eyes gleamed. *Do not underestimate Cortés, or that cursed demon. He has sensed Freya's immense abilities when she gets mad, and will try to capitalize on it.*

Tyr turned and started to walk away towards a light that had already appeared.

Wait! O'Keeffe yelled mentally. Tyr stopped dead in its tracks, then slowly turned around to face Seamus expectantly. *It was you, wasn't it? Who healed me after Raksh's attack.*

Yes.

What did you mean when you said I've known you before, under another name?

The feline shook its head, then entered the radiance in one single leap. As it disappeared along with the glow, O'Keeffe heard an echo of words spoken only to him. *Remember long, long ago, Seamus... And thank you for sheltering Freya as you promised.*

By the time realization dawned on Seamus, it was already too late – the tiger was no longer present. But the elder Sage didn't linger on it. He was thankful for the introduction, and settled in the belief that the entity meant no harm to either of them.

His twinkling eyes met Freya's gratefully. "Thank you," was all he said.

The Sage was taken aback by her mentor's expression. The meeting had meant more to him than she could grasp, and it was a cruel reminder of all she didn't know about him. For the time being, she didn't think to push it further, choosing instead to focus on the fact he was no longer mad at her.

Freya then turned to Emmanuel. "We'll need your help on this. Sam will be rescued – tonight."

Freya was expecting O'Keeffe to protest, but instead he took a seat down and nodded. "I agree. There is no need to delay this any longer. Besides, Cortés already has another plan ready, you heard Tyr."

Freya leaned forward. "We're listening."

"It isn't for nothing that Cortés rallied over a thousand ghosts. I researched him, and the characteristic that usually echoes everywhere is his thirst for power. I suspected this conquistador was plotting something big with the phantoms he has rallied, but I was not able to deduce what exactly. In the past, he has often struck after rich empires and civilizations, such as the Aztecs. But no matter how much time I spent on it, I could not see what could be of great interest to him now. With Tyr's warning that he is planning on attacking France, it makes sense, if only because of what is hidden there – more clues to the map to the relics."

Freya started, then shared a long look with Brennan. An uncomfortable silence reigned over the table for a few moments, until Seamus broke it.

"What is it?"

"Nothing," Freya muttered, then cleared her throat uncomfortably. "I was just thinking how Cortés is planning to hide so many ghosts, and keep them under his command for such a long time."

"I'm not sure about that last part," Emmanuel intervened, "but for the first, humans will see only what they want to. From what Gustav let escape, Cortés has certain powers, he will surely be able to keep his army invisible."

"Yeah, but he wouldn't," Freya whispered.

"And just how would you know that?" Brennan asked icily.

Freya glanced at him in surprise. "What—" She started, only to realize the Wiseman was addressing Emmanuel.

She rolled her eyes before the ghost could answer. "Let's make one thing clear, Bren. I trust Emmanuel, all right?" Brennan met her glare with one of his own, and a staring match ensued. After a few seconds, he broke eye contact with a snort, and Freya shook her head. "*Now* can we get back to the matter at hand?"

Reluctantly, both Brennan and Emmanuel nodded, though whenever their gazes met, tension reigned again.

This did not pass unnoticed by Freya, but it was a hostility she could do nothing about.

"You are hiding something."

The statement from Seamus was enough to freeze both Brennan and Freya. The Wiseman then glared at the ghost, who huffed and stepped away. "Fine, you...*hombre obstinado*..."

"*What* was that?" Brennan got out of his seat, about to follow the phantom and get answers as to why he was being insulted and called a stubborn male. Freya's fierce grip on his wrist had him settle back into his chair, grumbling under his breath.

"This morning, we didn't quite sleep right away," the Sage admitted. "I had a nightmare, and Brennan came by..."

Another shared look, and the Wiseman took over. "We did what you wanted us to – shared stuff about our pasts, trusted each other. Something happened, and the medallion and the book sort of picked up on it..."

"There was a moment when they merged," Freya revealed in a whisper, "and this map appeared. Seamus, I've never seen anything like it! It split into two, then became these tiny dragons..."

She trailed off, and Brennan squeezed her hand at the memory. Then he met Seamus' stunned gaze. "They entered us, one each. I think the map, well, it's in us now."

O'Keeffe glanced between the two as though seeing them for the first time. Then he cleared his throat, and said, "Just to be clear here, we are referring to the map revealing the relics' location?"

"The same one," Brennan confirmed, while Freya nodded.

Seamus ran a hand over his face, thinking he really had failed in his duty. Nothing could cause her more danger than what had just happened – and yet, nothing could be safer, at the same time.

"Very well," he finally said. "This cannot be undone, quite obviously, but you both need to be incredibly careful going forward. This makes you great tools for Raksh, you must have realized it." When he received confirmation from the pair, he continued, "So Cortés and the demon are unaware their plan is useless. This puts us at an advantage. The only problem is that sword."

At Freya's signal, Emmanuel headed back to their table, just in time to hear the last part.

"Cortés found it in the Aztec treasure," Seamus was saying.

"And we know Raksh was involved in him getting it back," Brennan leaned forward eagerly. "This makes sense, doesn't it? A sword that can enslave hordes of ghosts to Cortés. A demon that wants to use that to take over France. A country that hides clues to the map to the relics... It all comes around full circle."

Emmanuel snorted. "You think so?"

The two glared at each other until Freya placed her hand on Brennan's arm. "That's enough. Both of you," she added as she turned her piercing gaze to Emmanuel.

The spirit held Freya's gaze for a short moment, then dropped his own in a sign of submission. She turned to Brennan and, after a beat, he nodded. "So, the sword."

Seamus frowned. "Its powers are strong. *Very* strong. No one has been able to figure out exactly how powerful Cortés' sword is, so be wary of it. Neither of you can be too arrogant in your own power, or else it will destroy you."

Brennan smirked, jerking his head towards his partner. "Freya's got that part covered."

The Sage mock-glared at him, but Brennan could tell she was only joking.

O'Keeffe glanced from the Wiseman to Freya, and suppressed a smile. *It seems my old Wiseman friend has been right, once more. They can be more powerful than they can imagine if they work together. And with this new milestone, something has changed. I can see it in their eyes – they trust each other more. Maybe, just maybe, all is not lost.*

O'Keeffe cleared his throat to get the attention of the three teenagers. When he had it undivided, he announced, "Very well. We need a plan to save Sam, and it has to be a good one, because neither Cortés nor Gustav are fooling around."

"Wait, before we get into that... Let me just see if I got this straight," Brennan intervened. "So Cortés wants France. Gustav wants Freya. And now, according to Tyr, the demon wants her angry to lose control. That about sum it all up?"

Seamus nodded wearily. "I would say so, yes. Which means your job while you fight will be to also keep her calm."

A snicker had them turn to Emmanuel, who wisely pointed out, "You really think he's the best man for the job?"

Brennan scowled, but Freya's light touch on his arm was enough to stop him from lashing out.

"Enough!" Seamus added, surveying the table. "We have to play on our best strengths. We need a battle place, a plan and bait."

Freya smiled, a twinkle O'Keeffe knew only too well in her eyes. "There's no need to trouble yourselves with the bait. I've already got it."

"And what is it?" O'Keeffe asked.

Brennan turned a warning look towards Freya. "Yes, do tell." Unfortunately, he had a feeling he knew what it was.

Ignoring the Wiseman's silent plea, Freya shrugged and said, "Me."

"No way!" Emmanuel burst. "You cannot be allowed to offer yourself. I know my ancestor, and he has an ugly vengeance in mind, Freya."

"I can't believe I'm saying this," Brennan muttered, "but I agree with him. You're not taking that great a risk."

Freya glared at him. "Just watch me."

"Silence!" O'Keeffe thundered. His voice quieted the roar that was about to erupt around the table. "Why you?"

"That's easy," Freya smiled. "Gustav is beyond pissed at me, and he'll do anything to capture me or have another chance to teach me a lesson. And as for Cortés, let's just say he didn't enjoy that I escaped through his fingers too much."

O'Keeffe was pensive for a few moments, then he gave a curt nod. "You are not going there alone, Freya."

The Sage smiled widely as she processed the words – Seamus had just given his blessing. "Of course not. Brennan is coming with me."

The Wiseman glanced from Freya to O'Keeffe, his jaw nearly dropping to the ground. "You're going to support her in this?"

"*Estás loco!?*" Emmanuel exclaimed at the same time.

The old Sage ignored the crazy comment from the ghost, and leveled an icy glare on both of young men. It was enough to make them cower in a sulking silence. "For once that you two agree on something," he pointed out. "Yes, I am letting Freya do this, because it is the quickest way we can get Sam out of the Cathedral. *Quick* being the operative word here."

At their blank stares, Seamus added, "Thanks to your little revelation, it is evident we need the security of my castle as soon as possible. Thus, we have to make haste."

Freya bit on her bottom lip, trying her best to be apologetic in her expression. Brennan sighed, his defensive posture deflating. "You make a good point, professor. But we still need a battle place."

"Not to mention a plan," Emmanuel added.

"For the battle place," O'Keeffe started, "I would suggest we use the city's Historical Museum."

Emmanuel gasped, which attracted Freya's attention. "Is that good or bad?"

The ghost tilted its head to the side, pondering the matter. After a few moments, he admitted, "Good, actually. The Museum has no barriers like the Cathedral, is big enough to hold a fight, but small enough to not accept more than a hundred ghosts at the maximum. Plus, considering these soldiers all have weapons, it's the perfect place to get supplies."

Freya nodded and turned to Brennan. "Sound okay to you?"

After a slight hesitation, the Wiseman said, "Fine by me."

"What about the plan?" Emmanuel asked.

Freya, Cortés has his ghosts at the border! Tyr's voice warned in the Sage's head.

What? Already? Freya's eyes widened and her face took on a look of sickness.

After visiting your realm, I went to have a closer look... They are lining the border, child, but no sign of the leader. The tiger seemed worried, and it was potent enough to impact their link and have Freya sense it.

Brennan immediately caught the change in Freya's demeanor, and his stomach churned in response – the breakfast was unsettled.

"Freya?" he asked out loud. "Are you all right?"

"Freya!" O'Keeffe yelled.

The Sage got up from the table and took a deep breath to master her powers. Already, her forces were mixing with the elements and Freya was afraid she would lose control.

"We need to move, *now*! Tyr just confirmed Cortés' army is at the border with France." Freya's gaze was piercing as she clenched her fists and threw O'Keeffe a determined look. "He isn't getting away with this. That, I swear."

"I'm with you," Brennan added, standing by her side. "We'll give him a battle he won't soon forget."

Freya nodded, and Emmanuel got up too. "I'm in. I'll do my best to help you."

Seamus's gaze settled on each one of them, and he smiled. They were not perfect, but they'd be a team worth reckoning. One that would defeat Cortés – or die trying to do so.

Chapter 27

F reya inspected the Cathedral from top to bottom, searching for any signs of ghosts before facing her companions. Brennan and Emmanuel were standing apart in a stubborn silence, and she barely held back a roll of her eyes.

"Either they're not there, or they really know how to hide," she declared. Brennan only nodded, whereas Emmanuel glanced away.

Freya decided to give it another try. "All right, so first we have to get Sam out of there. Emmanuel, you'll then dematerialize with him back at the hotel, where Seamus can help you. With you guys out of harm's way, me and Brennan can finish the fight."

Emmanuel inclined his head in assent, but still didn't voice whatever was bothering him.

Freya tapped her foot impatiently, and when that didn't seem to work either, she snapped. "What's going on with you two? Do you really expect to go on like this?"

Brennan shrugged. "Well, we wouldn't have to if *someone* would stop sulking."

"He doesn't trust me," Emmanuel replied. "I refuse to work with someone who doesn't trust me."

"Ugh, boys!" Freya screamed to the skies, then stomped over until she was in both of their faces. "Listen here, both of you. Sam is in there," she pointed to the Cathedral, "held captive by Gustav and Cortés, both remarkable foes. They're expecting us, knowing we would be back and plotting to catch us as you would flies on a spider web."

It was like she was addressing walls. Neither Brennan nor Emmanuel reacted to her words.

Freya set her jaw firm, decided to win this fight. But she couldn't without Emmanuel and Brennan's help, and she was very aware of it. Underneath their facades, she could guess at a deeper resentment – the reason for it eluded her.

Fine then. I guess a little acting's in order... Good thing I'm not bad at it!

"What is your problem?" she burst out, putting just enough tremors in her voice. "We can't go on like this, so you'd better get your act together, both of you! I plan on getting Sam out of there in the next hours, and you two will work together, whether you like it or not!"

Is this how Tyr felt when preaching to me to work with Brennan? Jeez, they're twice as stubborn as I was!

For a grand finale to her act, she added on a disappointed tone, "I thought I could count on both of you. You said we'd get Sam back *together*. I guess that was all talk, huh?" Freya threw both Emmanuel and Brennan a hard stare. "No matter. I can do this by myself."

With a huff, she turned her back to both teens and started walking away. *Three...Two...One...*

"Freya, wait!" Brennan called out. His words were like music to her ears.

And that is how it's done! Freya mused, satisfied that her little act had worked.

The Sage spun around and folded her arms on her chest. "What?"

"You're right," Brennan admitted grudgingly. "We haven't been acting exactly in a mature way and, uh, we're sorry."

He and Emmanuel shared a look that wasn't friendly, though it could have passed for one.

Freya glanced between them, not fully convinced. "So, you're ready to work together?"

"Yes," Brennan mumbled.

Emmanuel nodded his answer.

"Good!" Freya had to fight to keep off her smug expression. "I knew you'd see it my way."

Just don't count on me trusting him with my life, Brennan grumbled telepathically.

Why do you have to be so difficult sometimes? Freya complained. *One day you act your age, the next you're worse than a baby! Not exactly what I need, Brennan.*

I'm sorry, but I can't help my instincts. Some people just can't be trusted, the Wiseman stated.

Freya threw him a dark look. *And let me guess, Emmanuel is one of them?*

Yes.

Jeez, Brennan, if I didn't know better, I'd say you're jealous of him. Whatever. Just work together without fighting, that's all I'm asking from both of you.

She took Brennan's silence as an agreement. Little did the Sage know, she'd struck a chord with her comment about jealousy. The Wiseman decided to ignore the emotions brimming at the surface, and instead focus on the mission. Freya's next instructions brought him out of his thoughts.

"Showtime, guys. Up and at 'em!"

The next minute, they were climbing the stairs at a quick jog. Both Brennan and Freya could feel the anticipation of the fight, humming in the atmosphere surrounding them.

Brennan flashed a smile at her. "Piece of cake."

He thought she'd still be mad, but Freya rolled her eyes and returned the grin. "Sure thing, partner!"

Much too soon, they reached the big doors, and she stepped at the head of their little group, grinning mischievously. "Which one do you prefer, boys? Big, awesome entrance with a bang or a smaller, less flashy one?"

"I'll go with the first," Brennan chuckled.

Emmanuel smiled. "Same here."

At least they're agreeing on something, Freya thought.

"All right," she said and faced her palms to the doors. She called her spiritual energy forth, and mingled it with the surrounding elements. Air answered quick, forming a ball of power in her palms.

"Get ready," Freya warned, then allowed the blast to escape her. It slammed forward and struck the large doors with a huge bang. They submitted easily and creaked open to the darkness within.

Freya entered, followed shortly by Brennan and Emmanuel, and let her eyes adjust to the slight change in the light. *All right. Now all I have to do is find Sam.*

Be careful, Tyr warned. *Gustav and Cortés are cunning, they surely have something planned for you.*

Oh, I figured as much, Freya said. *But I don't mind. If anything, it'll make this all the more challenging.*

The whole point of this little mission is to distract them. Do not stay more in that Cathedral than necessary, Tyr advised.

I wasn't planning to, Freya said. *I promise to contact you as soon as I'm out of here. Shouldn't be longer than a few... minutes, say?*

She was answered by a chuckle. *Don't get ahead of yourself, child,* Tyr chastised gently.

You really don't need to worry.

"We can't split up under any pretense," Freya said to Emmanuel, "or else they'll get us one by one. So even if we get surrounded, stay between me and Brennan, we'll shield you."

The ghost nodded. "Gustav won't be able to resist the bait. When he's not granted something immediately, he gets angry and starts making mistakes."

"Perfect," Brennan drawled. "In that case, we can count on having a raging beast with us within minutes."

Freya only absently paid attention, her senses already scanning the space around them. She couldn't see – nor feel – any ghosts. "I hate to say this, but I have a bad feeling about this."

"What do you mean?" Emmanuel asked, his gaze darting around furtively.

"I can't even get a whiff of the energies of the go—" Freya stopped halfway through her sentence, having caught something. "Never mind. Our friends are here."

"Freya, how many phantoms are there in total, in Spain?" Brennan wondered, an edge to his tone.

"A few thousands," she replied. "Why?"

"I was just thinking... Gustav better not have borrowed a few of those from Cortés..."

Freya threw him a look, then expanded her senses again. "I think we should be fine."

To Tyr, Freya said, *Please keep an eye on the ones at the border. Let us know if there's any movement.*

Very well. Remain cautious and alert, and remember – if you and Brennan work together, there's a lot you two can accomplish.

I know.

And do not *engage in battle with the ghosts until you are out of there.*

The second after, the connection was ended, and Freya shook her head at the constant reminders. She was well aware of the danger awaiting and what they needed to do.

"Let's go," she whispered to the boys, and moved farther inside.

As they advanced cautiously through the church, Brennan pressed, "Well?"

Freya heaved a sigh. "Tyr will keep an eye on them and let us know if they try anything."

Brennan said nothing for a few moments, then, "You're aware that we can't exactly fight them all if they *do* try something, yes?"

"Yes, Brennan," Freya said. "But they won't."

"How can you be so sure?"

"Because for one, any big army needs a leader. And in this case, the leader will be way too busy with us to go and lead his subjects into battle."

"Makes sense," Brennan commented. "But what if he put Gustav in charge?"

"He wouldn't," the Sage retorted confidently. "Because I promised Gustav we'd finish our previous fight."

"Oh, right. And since he hates you, he'll be here to finish that." Brennan snickered at the ghost's predictability. "Well, that settles that."

"Indeed, it does," Freya agreed, grinning his way.

There was still no sign that the specters would try and attack. The further they stepped in, Freya caught drifts of their presence in the shadows, but nothing further. Finally, too perplexed by it, she muttered, "Why aren't they attacking?"

Brennan glanced over his shoulder, then slowed his steps. "Say what?"

"I mean they're all around us, though I can't see them. And yet, they won't make a move."

"Do you think they're waiting for a signal from Cortés?" Brennan asked.

"That, or..." Freya frowned. "They're delaying until we get deep enough!" The realization came with a sinking feeling and she held her hands out. "Stop walking. We need to have a clear sight of the doors."

She looked behind herself, then ahead tauntingly. "Too scared to fight, Gustav? Or is your so-called master holding you back? What a pity!"

Emmanuel winced at the direct challenge, but it only enhanced his admiration for Freya's boldness. He only hoped it would work.

"Uh, Freya?" Brennan frowned.

"What?" she asked, looking around herself for any sign of Gustav's presence.

"Not what," Emmanuel corrected. "Who!"

Freya arched an eyebrow as she turned to the guys. "What are you two going on about?"

Brennan and Emmanuel both pointed to something behind her. Warily, Freya turned around... And burst out laughing immediately as she scanned what she was seeing.

Emmanuel stared at the Sage. "Freya are you... feeling all right?"

The Sage clutched her sides in laughter, unable to stop.

Freya! What the hell is so hilarious? Brennan probed telepathically. Despite his stern tone, she only shook her head, cheeks red from trying to control herself. *Have you completely lost it!?* Brennan continued. *Or are you blind?*

Freya finally got a grip, and straightened up. Pressing her lips together to avoid another fit of giggles, she took a closer look at what had both Emmanuel and Brennan so edgy.

About ten meters away from them was Gustav, surrounded by a few hundred ghosts, and Sam held captive between two of them by Cortés and his sword. What triggered her hilarity was only too visible, but not to Brennan, apparently.

The Sage wondered for a split of a second if it was because he was unable to use his powers in the Cathedral. Then she shrugged the matter off and focused on their foes – and the fact Gustav thought them so gullible.

Swallowing a snicker, she mumbled, "Of course I can see this, Brennan."

"And just what is – or was – so funny?" Emmanuel asked, perplexed.

"You'll find out soon enough, my friends." She then yelled to the phantoms, "Nice to see you're here, Gustav and *Cortés*." The last name was said on a slightly chuckling tone.

Gustav glared at the Sage. "You won't find this so funny once your friend disappears. Or have you forgotten that he is in our power?"

Freya dropped her gaze to her nails with a very bored expression on her face. "No, I haven't."

"Your attitude is fooling no one, Freya," Gustav declared. "Deep inside, you are scared out of your wits for the fate of your friend. You would be ready to do anything to save him, but you're putting up a safe front so that I won't see that. Well, you will soon be begging me for Sam's release."

Gustav's evil smirk sent shivers down Brennan's spine, but as he glanced at Freya, he only saw a smug expression, like before.

What is she playing at? Brennan wondered. He knew Freya could act when needed, but this was taking it just a notch too far. Maybe she really was afraid for Sam, and maybe this was all just a diversion... But then, why was that gleam present in her eyes?

Freya didn't seem unsettled – at all. If anything, she still appeared amused by what she was seeing. Brennan would have loved to share her optimism, but Sam's capture by Cortés stopped him from doing that. Perhaps Gustav was right for once, and the Sage really was just afraid.

Brennan shook his head, not quite trusting it, and yet...Freya was acting odd.

"You don't believe me, do you?" Gustav was saying. "Well then, how about I let you see exactly what my master can do?"

Brennan clued in, and narrowed his stare onto the ghost. *Hold on a sec... Gustav's giving orders? Since when?* He spared another glance for his partner's calm face. *I'm starting to think there's more to this than meets the eye...*

Before he could further investigate, Gustav turned to Cortés and the captured Sam, whose eyes widened. "Freya!" he yelled.

The Sage didn't even flinch.

"Sam!" Emmanuel went to run to the ghost, but Freya grabbed his arm. She pulled Emmanuel back, until he was behind her.

"What are you doing?" Brennan hissed.

Leave it to me, Freya answered telepathically.

Then, she turned back to Gustav and with that same smirk plastered on her face, started clapping. Freya could see Gustav's pissed off face, and that only made her grin widen.

"What is the meaning of this?" the leader questioned.

"Very impressive, Gustav. You know, I'd be shaking with fear if it weren't for one small, teensy-itsy detail."

"And what would that be?" Gustav glared.

"I'm asking myself the same question," Brennan whispered loud enough for the Sage to hear.

"Well, you see, Gustav," Freya started, ignoring her partner, "it all would have been mighty good and scary if Cortés *was* here. Tell me, was this your idea or his?"

"What are you...? He *is* here," Emmanuel stated.

Freya shook her head, pointing to Cortés. "Nope. *That* is an illusion, created by the real Cortés."

It took some time for the information to sink in, but when it did, both Emmanuel and Brennan cracked up.

Freya threw them an amused look over her shoulder, then focused back Gustav. "Sorry to have ruined your plans, but I'm afraid such old tricks don't work on me."

"You're telling me," Brennan choked out, "that he was trying to get us to surrender with an illusion?"

Emmanuel chuckled. "I guess you're more afraid of facing us than you're letting on."

"I am not afraid!" Gustav bellowed.

Hang on, Brennan sobered up as a thought struck him. *If Cortés isn't here, what exactly is he doing?*

We'll find out soon. I have a plan.

It had better work, Freya, or else the French will have a huge problem on their hands.

The Sage could only nod as her cold gaze locked on Gustav, and behind him, on Sam and the illusion. Freya could only hope that Cortés was not at that precise moment leading his thousand or so ghosts to pass the border between Spain and France, because in that case, they were doomed.

Or... not quite, Freya thought pensively. As a plan slowly formed in her mind, she faced her palms to Cortés' illusion. "Be gone!" she shouted. The power that had gathered in her hands escaped and hit the illusion in the chest. It shattered into shiny pieces at once, then dissipated into thin air.

"*No*!" Gustav yelled, staring around in shock. He pointed his hand at Freya. "You will pay for that!"

"I think not," Brennan growled as he stepped in front of Freya.

What are you doing? she questioned him telepathically.

Diversion, Brennan answered smugly. *Also saving your life, but yeah. Go get Sam, what are you waiting for?*

Freya was about to protest against needing saving, but she swallowed the retort and turned to Emmanuel. "Get ready to leave at my signal."

The ghost nodded, then took a step back to give Freya space to move.

At the same time, Brennan turned his back to Gustav and stretched his arms out, crossing them in a horizontal X-shape. Freya took support on his shoulders – squeezed them gently in sign of gratitude and encouragement – then propelled herself upwards and, flipping in the air, extended her leg.

Her balance perfectly held, Freya's leg connected with Gustav's jaw strongly. Unfortunately, she hadn't counted on the phantom grabbing her leg and throwing her over his head.

"Ow," Freya groaned as she hit the floor hard with her back. Rolling over, she immediately raised her hands and released a blast of air towards the ghost, sending him flying far away.

"Freya! Are you all right?" Sam's voice came from close by.

Freya jumped back on her feet, ignoring the pain. Sam rushed over, trying to check her state of health.

"Time for greetings later," she muttered, grabbing his hand. "Sorry it took so long, but let's get you out of here, Sam."

He smiled and squeezed back. "I won't say no to that!"

"Good."

Brennan, anytime now, Freya announced.

Give me a second or two, will you? the Wiseman said.

A quick peek his way confirmed the worst – while she'd neared Gustav, the rest of the soldiers had closed in. The two boys were now surrounded by phantoms, and they were getting their swords out.

"Damn it!" Freya swore under her breath.

With Brennan stuck, he couldn't help out in Sam and Emmanuel's escape. And a more pressing issue was the number of ghosts now starting to circle her – and *they* were no illusion.

"Uh, Freya?" Sam asked hesitantly. "Is this part of the plan?"

Though he was immensely grateful that Freya had come after him and was currently risking her life to save him, Sam could see that there were some things that Freya hadn't planned for. And he *really* wanted to escape this time.

The Sage scanned her surroundings as though she was counting stock in a retail store. "Keep it calm, Sam, I'm on it."

Just how is she going to get rid of nearly fifty ghosts? Sam wondered, but didn't voice his thoughts out loud. Over the years, he'd learned not to underestimate the Sage.

A growl to her right redirected Freya's attention to Gustav. He moved through some ghosts until he was only a few feet away from her. His expression was one of pure glee, already tasting his victory.

Freya had the sudden urge to wipe the smirk off his face, but mastered that impulse – for the time being. *Need to get Sam out first.*

Gustav's eyes glinted of malice, aware now was the time to put into motion what the demon wanted. *Use her parents,* was what Raksh had advised.

"Too scared to fight me alone, little girl? I would think so, after our last encounter."

A wave of fury washed over Freya, and already her fingers itched to strangle him. Gustav stared back for a moment, then smirked.

Freya made to move closer, but Sam stepped between them. "You can't!" He tried to push against Freya's shoulders to move her backwards, to no avail. She was frozen, glaring at the still-talking Gustav.

"Of course you cannot finish your battles on your own. Same like your parents."

Freya froze, her every muscle paralyzed. "What?"

Shit. Brennan heard the ghost's words and in that moment realized he needed to get his partner out. *Freya, time to go!* Unfortunately, she didn't react to his words.

"That night we fought, things would have ended differently," Gustav continued taunting. "And I plan to get my hands on you and finish everything I wanted to do then."

Freya growled, and Sam backed away. When she raised her head, her eyes were icy silver, and her hair was flying wildly.

"Your parents would be disappointed in the weak girl I see before me!" Gustav delivered the final blow.

With a shout of anger, Freya pushed Sam out of her way and launched herself at Gustav. The ghost deflected her blow easily, and kept pushing.

"I know how they died. How you couldn't help them, just watched in the back like a baby."

Freya tried to hit him again, but wavered.

"You could have saved them!" Gustav cackled at the look on her face.

There was a split moment, when Freya tried to hold on to her sanity – and then she lost control. Outside, the wind blew open the doors, bringing with it hail and rain inside the Cathedral.

Gustav glanced around, fearful at the avalanche of elements. There was nothing natural about the overflow of energy he sensed, and it caused him to back away. The Sage before him seemed to have paled, fists clenched and knuckles white, jaw clenched and eyes burning with hate.

Brennan had been watching from afar, fighting ghosts and protecting Emmanuel. When the elements burst in, his attention was dragged to Freya and he was torn. He wanted nothing more than to go to her, but his duty towards the ghost prevented him from moving.

In a last effort, Brennan threw his thoughts to Tyr. *She's doing it again! Freya's losing it.*

The answer was immediate. *You cannot let her! Brennan, tap within your own well of spiritual energy, like you did last time. You cannot let Freya do this.*

The Wiseman glanced to Emmanuel, then the Sage. He punched the last of the ghosts trying to get to him, and knew it bought him a few seconds before they charged again. *It'll have to do.*

He reached deep inside, searching for that same well that had helped him. He caught hold of Freya's anger, bubbling like a stream around her, and latched on. *Enough, Frey,* Brennan whispered mentally.

His voice was a cooling wave, and Freya breathed deeply. Her even stare met Gustav's, who continued backed away. There was mocking still in his smug expression, as though he'd expected her not be able to follow through. When she lifted her palm his way, the Sage was fully aware of her actions.

Brennan sensed her intention a second too late. *Freya, no!*

A burst of energy escaped her and hit Gustav full blast. As he disintegrated into nothing, Freya hissed, "You're through messing with my mind."

&&&

Raksh pulled away from the Cathedral, mouth downturned in anger. "That Sssage is much too capable!"

He'd seen Gustav fumble, and saw the blow before it even came. Without a henchman now, the demon would be left to his own devices.

"No matter," he muttered. "I will handle this myssself."

&&&

Freya stared until there was nothing left of the ghost, then turned to Brennan and winked. "One down!"

"Behind you!" Brennan yelled loudly.

Freya turned to see another ghost heading towards her. He was about Emmanuel's size, but bulkier.

"Raoul!" Sam breathed in shock. To Freya, he muttered, "He's the one I originally saw speaking with the priest."

"I see..."

Tricky, Freya thought, evaluating the distance between herself and Brennan. *But not enough.*

Though she believed in the possibility to get Sam, Emmanuel, Brennan and herself out of the church safe and sound, Freya was also aware of the glitch in her plan. A huge one, too.

I don't have time for this. Getting Sam out of here is way more important than what will follow ... And I'm ready to take the risk.

Just what are you talking about? Brennan questioned.

Get ready for Sam, was all Freya said.

Freya! Brennan yelled warningly, pushed by an instinct warning she was about to do something foolish. But no matter how hard he tried to reconnect with her, Freya was blocking him now – and he couldn't get past the barrier, strong bond or not.

Brennan turned to Emmanuel. "Keep an eye on where Freya and Sam are, will you?" He was starting to have a weird feeling of déjà-vu. And he didn't like it one bit.

He recalled Freya's tendency to sacrifice anything to help the people she loved, and uneasiness crept on him. *Oh, crap!* Brennan swore as realization dawned on him. She was doing it again –helping them all escape and not caring about whether or not she actually made it.

Emmanuel nodded at Brennan's request and immediately directed his gaze there. It took him a moment to locate his friends, but when he did, a gasp escaped him.

That attracted Brennan's attention. "What? What is it?" he asked, worried Freya might have done something foolish.

"Just don't move, Brennan," was all Emmanuel said.

It was enough to get the Wiseman to stop his fighting and look in Freya's direction...in time to see energy heading his way.

Oh, shit! was the first thing he could think of. The second one was, *Is she trying to get rid of me for good?*

But the blast was not meant for Brennan, as it passed by his left side to hit the twenty-something ghosts that were there. As a result, they got knocked out. The second strike that followed got rid of the ghosts on Brennan's right side, effectively wiping them off.

Brennan and Emmanuel stared at each other, before turning to Freya.

The Sage had already turned to Sam and ordered, "Cross your arms." She then blasted about fifteen ghosts that still stood in between her and Brennan.

Next, she grabbed Sam's outstretched arms and threw him up in the air with all her might. The moment she let go of him and he floated like a cannon ball, she coerced air to push him forth faster. At the same time, she ordered Brennan mentally, *Take Sam and get the hell out of here!*

The following instant, Raoul's arms wrapped around her like caging irons, having moved from behind.

Chapter 28

B rennan caught Sam by the arm and stopped his fall, then let go of the ghost. He pushed the younger boy towards Emmanuel. "Both of you, get out of here and dematerialize!"

Sam glanced at Freya. "But what about—"

"I'll take care of her, I promise," Brennan said reassuringly. "There's no way they're getting their hands on her."

Sam frowned, still undecided.

"Come, Sam," Emmanuel intervened. "We should go. We'll only get them in trouble if we stay here. You know as well as I do that we're not able to fight our kind."

Sam nodded, though reluctantly. "All right." He turned to the Wiseman, an unspoken plea in his blue eyes. "Bring her back to the hotel safe, Bren."

"I will," he said gravely, then watched as the two floated off. As soon as they were out the huge doors, Brennan turned to Freya.

His heart pounded as he took in the scene. Not only was she held immobile to the ground by a ghost, but Raoul also had in his arms what seemed like a sword... A pretty sharp one, too.

"No!" Brennan wanted to shout, but the cry didn't leave his lips, blocked in his throat.

Without even thinking about what he was doing, Brennan started running towards Freya, his heart in his stomach. As Raoul raised the sword, the Wiseman's anger and fear rose along with a resolute determination to not let anything happen to her.

The emotion was so strong it freed the power he held within, and let it reach Brennan's hands. The teenager's eyes locked with Freya's, and he gave an almost imperceptible nod. The second after, a strong blast of pure white light had escaped his palms and hit Raoul in the back, knocking him in the air.

Brennan reached Freya at the same moment and he punched the specter that was holding her to the ground, releasing the Sage. The ghosts around them backed off, shocked and afraid of their enemies' abilities.

Brennan offered Freya his hand, and the Sage gratefully took it, then hurled herself in his arms.

"Thank you," Freya whispered in his chest, then pulled away.

She hadn't expected to survive past the next minute. Yet on some deeper part of herself, Freya had known she could count on Brennan. And now, he'd been able to free his own powers as well.

"Is this a fairy-tale situation or what?" she whispered in his ear. But for once, it didn't bother her that her partner had heroic tendencies. After all, he'd just saved her life.

"You didn't think I would leave you here alone to have all the fun, did you?" Brennan said mockingly, but Freya could feel the rush of relief spreading through his whole body. That, and something else. A feeling that was trying to make its way out, both in herself and the Wiseman.

"No," Freya smiled softly to his question.

"This... isn't... over!" Raoul yelled a few meters away.

Freya turned to him, smirking. "Oh, no, it's far from over, Raoul." She walked over to him, knowing Brennan had her back. "But I want a full fight, not some distraction with a simple puppet."

Freya leveled an ardent gaze on the ghost. "Tell Cortés I will be at the City's Historical Museum in five minutes. Don't be late or else I might just think you're afraid."

With that said, Freya spun around and walked back to Brennan. To make sure the ghosts would not follow them – yet – Freya blasted ten on her side, as Brennan blasted ten others. The two then walked out of the Cathedral freely.

As soon as they were in the late afternoon sun, Freya and Brennan broke into a run, going straight to the museum. Luckily, they knew it had closed just an hour before –for siesta time – and thus would be empty by the time they got there.

Freya breathed the fresh air and was even more grateful to Brennan for having saved her from what had seemed like a certain death. She turned to him, biting her lip. "Brennan, about what happened in there... I..." In front of his expecting gaze, the Sage found herself at a loss for words. Finally, she smiled, "Thank you."

Brennan returned the grin. "My pleasure. But let's not tell anyone about it... It'll just get O'Keeffe more anxious about you and cause unnecessary complications."

Freya's mouth was slightly open, and she looked at Brennan in confusion. How he could read her mind that well, she'd never know. "I was thinking the exact same thing."

"What can I say?" Brennan smirked. "Great minds think alike."

Freya nodded in response. Remembering her promise to the tiger, she contacted Tyr. *We're out and heading to the Museum as planned. Emmanuel and Sam are back to the hotel, safe and sound. How are things on your side?*

They were not looking too bright until a moment ago, Tyr answered. *Cortés appeared shortly after you entered the church and has been planning to cross the border for the past hours, but never did. I figured he was expecting some sort of confirmation from Gustav...*

Oh, yeah, Gustav tried to trick us with some illusion of Cortés, Brennan intervened. *Luckily, Freya saw it for what it was.*

So did Cortés get his confirmation? Freya asked.

Not from what I can tell, the feline rumbled, slightly amused. *A ghost just materialized down here. He is passing on a message about a challenge at the City Historical Museum and how there is no time. Cortés is not too pleased.*

Freya and Brennan shared a knowing look.

"I'd expect him to be pissed off," Brennan chuckled.

"He just took the bait," Freya declared smugly.

What are you two referring to? Tyr asked demandingly, though Freya could detect the smile in its voice.

Oh, just a small trap we've got planned, the Sage said.

Exactly. Just a teensy bit of trouble coming ahead for Cortés and Raoul, Brennan declared.

Raoul? The new ghost? What happened to Gustav? Tyr questioned.

Freya smirked wider. *Gone for good.*

Well done! the tiger complimented them. *I am proud of your teamwork. But, Freya, remember this – you do not need to send all the phantoms back to their graves like with the Vikings. It would be a foolish thing to do. If you cut the serpent's head, its tail will stop moving.*

Freya nodded and stopped running as she and Brennan had reached the Museum. Unfortunately, Tyr's words had brought back to Freya's mind the image of the desert and the hypnotizing eyes of the hawk.

"Are you all right?" Brennan asked, having sensed the Sage's confusion.

"Yeah, I'm...okay," Freya said, burying at the deepest of her mind the image of that bird. Tyr's warning was ever-present in her. "Let's get ready, shall we? I have a feeling we won't have to wait too long."

Brennan nodded, then the two entered the building through the back entrance, which Freya had opened without making too much of a ruckus. Moments later, they were standing in the middle of the weapons' room.

Freya scoped the surroundings, unwilling to be taken by surprised. Once she was satisfied they were alone, she turned to Brennan. "How were you able to use your powers in the Cathedral? I thought it wasn't possible for you."

"To be honest, so did I," Brennan shrugged. "But the truth is, when I saw Raoul ready to lower that sword, I... I just couldn't let him do that. Something snapped in me, an emotion so strong it could get rid of anything. Then I just let it fill me and activate everything and..."

"And it struck," Freya finished.

Brennan nodded, and their gazes locked for a split of a second. Something passed between them again, an unreadable emotion that left their pulses racing, and the bond that much stronger.

Seeing his gaze darken with something she couldn't read, Freya blushed and looked away. Brennan caught on to her embarrassment, and rubbed the back of his neck in frustration.

What in all hells is happening to us?

Before either of them could follow the train of thought, a cold voice said mockingly, "That's it? I was expecting more of a challenge."

Freya spun in the direction of the voice and was met by Cortés' frosty gaze a few meters away. Behind him was Raoul and what seemed like fifty ghosts.

She raised an eyebrow. "That's *it*?" she mocked Cortés. "Are you two expecting to get rid of us with a few puny soldiers?"

Nice one. Keep them talking and then attack. Oldest trick in the book, but it could work.

Could? Freya mentally snorted. *It* will *work, Brennan, just watch.*

"To be perfectly honest," Cortés said, "I did not think there was need of more. After all, you are only two. You'll be outnumbered."

"Listen to him, little girl," Raoul said with that evil glower of his. "Surrender and we'll give both of you a short death."

Freya was boiling inside with anger. Raoul had evidently not learned from Gustav's errors, and was already tasting his victory. Too bad they weren't planning to hand it down so easily.

Brennan, are you ready to go to the end with me?

You bet!

Freya extended her palm behind her back, and Brennan's hand placed itself in it. He squeezed it gently and said, *Let's send these guys back to where they belong.*

Right with you, Freya agreed.

Her gaze met Cortés', and she spoke icily. "It seems your puppet has once again underestimated me. You'd have thought after Gustav's untimely demise, he would have understood what a terrible mistake it was. Do you really just expect me to surrender without a fight?"

Before the conquistador could answer, Brennan added, "Instead, we'll do you guys a favor. Drop the weapons now and we promise to send you to the great beyond real fast."

Cortés' loud laugh got on Brennan's nerves, and he was about to listen to his impulsive self and blast the leader when Freya squeezed his hand hard. *Don't. Whatever we throw at him at this point won't touch him.*

What do you mean?

I mean that Cortés has a barrier around himself. It's disturbing the composition of the air, that's how I knew it's there. We'd be slightly disadvantaged.

Well, how do we get it off? Brennan asked, slightly impatient for some action.

Freya thought for a beat, then said, *The sword. It all comes down to it. We have to hit it and the shield will be destroyed as collateral.*

All right. How do we do that?

We can't immediately, if that's what you're asking, Brennan. We have to wait longer.

Why?

If we hit Cortés now, he'll be expecting it and you can be sure he'll find some way to repel it. And then the blow will have been wasted and so will have your energy.

All right, I get it, Brennan said. *But we need to move fast, you know how useless I can get if a fight lasts long.*

There was a pause, and Freya threw him a look he couldn't decipher. *You're never useless, Bren.*

He snorted to cover his own emotion at the words, then cleared his throat. *So, Cortés' sword, how do you plan on doing that?*

Simple. I'll fight Cortés until I know I've pissed him long enough that he's no longer paying attention to the invisible shield, then I'll signal you.

And then we'll hit him together, Brennan finished. *Sounds like a plan to me.*

Good. Because for the time being, I don't have another one, Freya admitted.

Brennan directed his gaze to Cortés and Raoul, then to the ghosts behind them. *Fifty ghosts!* he mentally scoffed. *And just as I was hoping for a full hundred welcoming.*

Don't be so disappointed, Freya mockingly cheered him up. *We still have these to beat off. Not too bad if you ask me.*

Hmm, I guess, Brennan mumbled, almost sulking.

You're impossible! Freya threw him an amused look. *Just pick your fight and get to it, Wiseman!*

Brennan smirked at her. *If it's all right with you, I'm going to take the big guys on. The fifty big guys, to be more precise. Much more challenging. I'll let you deal with Cortés and Raoul.*

Freya's expression said it all. *Nice, Brennan. A very diplomatic way of backing off.*

I am not! Brennan protested. *Really, if you need help with them, just call me.*

Yeah, right, like I will, Freya mentally snorted. *Just get ready to jump into action.*

As she said that, Freya released a blast of energy towards Raoul, sending him flying in – and through – the wall. Cortés stared at the spot he disappeared through for a few seconds, then he turned to the Sage.

"You shouldn't have done that," he said.

"Oh, yeah? And why's that?" Freya asked.

"Because now I have a reason to attack you," Cortés hissed as he drew his sword out and held it in front of him.

Freya smirked mischievously, not the least bit afraid. "What makes you think I wasn't baiting you into doing exactly that?" A flicker of something moved in the conquistador's eyes, but it was enough for Freya – he was getting annoyed at her already.

In the meantime, Brennan had moved by Freya's side. "Well, Cortés, you might want to be careful there. It wouldn't look too good if you were beaten by a mortal girl in front of your men, would it?"

"I do not plan to let that happen," Cortés said icily. He turned to look behind him, presumably to give an order to one of the ghosts.

Brennan didn't give him the chance to do so. He extended his hand and blasted a light of energy at the ceiling. A block of cement fell right by Cortés' leg.

The specter turned to Brennan a hateful look, but the Wiseman shrugged it off. "My bad. Next time, I won't miss."

"Do try," Cortés said, an evil smirk on his face.

"I don't think so," Brennan grinned. "I'm more interested in those guys," he pointed to the soldiers behind the conquistador, "than you. I'm sure Freya can handle *you* all by her lonesome."

Letting the subtle insult register, Brennan winked at Freya, then ran in the middle of the ghosts, where he started battling them. Freya was left facing Cortés, nearly bouncing on the soles of her feet with trepidation.

As Cortés went to strike with the sword, Freya avoided the blow and instead the blade got stuck behind her, in a wooden wall.

Freya kicked Cortés in the stomach, and grinned as she heard his groan of pain. *This means that he can't block physical blows, only spiritual ones. Sweet!*

Freya!

I'm in the middle of something here, Tyr, Freya retorted.

Is that Cortés' energy I sense you are fighting?

Yup, Freya answered as she ducked the sword once more and punched the ghost in the jaw, making him spin around.

When their gazes collided, Freya's was fire opposing ice.

Be careful, and stay away of that sword, Tyr warned.

Why? Freya questioned, her curiosity piqued.

I had a chance to scan it when I was keeping an eye on him in France. If the blade makes contact with a Sage's – or Wiseman's – skin, it will drain the person's vitality with every second that passes! The explanation made her gulp, and she fought the uneasiness settling in her stomach.

Let me guess... And it doesn't stop until they're dead? Freya finished.

Yes! Tyr answered, and Freya detected the urgency in its tone. *Please stay clear of it.*

Now you tell me, Freya muttered as she eyed the sword curiously, but with absolutely no fear.

Oh, and while I am here, Tyr added, *it might interest you to know that Raoul is on the other side of the wall behind you, planning to pierce you with his own blade in a few seconds.*

Freya jumped out of the way just in time as Raoul's sword had nearly cut her. She then turned around and caught the blade with both hands, pulling the ghost with it through the wall.

"Stay where I can see you!" Freya scowled, a burning fire in her eyes.

You ok? Brennan asked, sensing her emotions.

Nope, Freya answered.

Do you need any help?

Unless you've got a sword, no. You? How are you coping with the ghosts?

Piece of cake, I told you so before. I'd be surprised if I get out of this with a tiny scratch, if that!

Freya frowned slightly. *Brennan? Just be careful. Oh, and stay clear of Cortés' weapon. Apparently, if it cuts you or me, it'll suck our energy.*

The Sage bit her lip to stop from screaming in pain as Raoul hit her in the back with a pretty heavy vase. The wave of pain went up her spine, nearly making her lose her balance. But Freya held well, and spun on her heel, kicking Raoul in the stomach, then once more in the head.

She then turned to Cortés, who was advancing towards her menacingly. Freya narrowed her eyes. "Now you're starting to piss me off. And trust me, you don't want to do that."

"The angrier you get," Cortés stated coldly, "the more you will make mistakes. All the better that shall be for me."

Freya's face relaxed, and she let a grin creep on her face slowly. "Actually, it'll be way worse for you. You see, Cortés, the angrier I get, my powers tend to break free, and I have absolutely no control over them. The last ghost that pissed me off was forcefully returned to the world of the dead. And so were his henchman and ghosts."

"Is that supposed to frighten me?" Cortés asked coolly.

"No," Freya smirked. "It's supposed to warn you."

At that moment, a ghost materialized in front of Freya. Eyes wide, she realized it was none other than Emmanuel.

"What the hell are you doing here?" she hissed.

Raoul, about to attack her again, froze. The former friends stared at each other, Emmanuel with a sad look on his face.

"You chose the wrong side, my friend," he whispered.

"No. You did!" Raoul hissed, and launched towards the other ghost.

Freya pushed Emmanuel away, yelling, "Go away. Now!"

At the anger in her eyes, he didn't dispute and disappeared. Freya faced Raoul, who tackled straight into her. They rolled on the ground, but she managed to break away before he got hold of her. Kneeling, she lifted both palms up and a burst of energy hit the ghost full center, and he dematerialized forever.

Umm, Brennan... Freya massaged her shoulder, trying to ignore the pain shooting through her. Noises behind made her turn to face Cortés.

Yeah?

Can you find me a blasted sword?

"You lost me my two best men," he stated, jaw clenching in anger. His palms curled into fists, and she had no doubt he was imagining wringing her neck in that exact moment. "Say your prayers while you still have breath left in you, little girl!"

Turn around, now!

Freya did as asked, and Brennan threw her way a sword he'd found in a display. Freya lifted her palm, controlling it until it smoothly slid in her palm, the pommel fitting perfectly.

She turned around just as Cortés struck, the blade lifted high in the air to block it. As Cortés parried again, the Sage mentally thanked O'Keeffe for having introduced her to sword fighting. If he hadn't insisted on those practices long ago when she was only ten, it would have turned out to be quite a problem by now.

But as it was, Freya raised her weapon just in time to block Cortés' blow. Still, the force of it made the Sage back up slightly.

Freya pushed the conquistador away and kicked him in the gut. Cortés' next blow nearly got her in the stomach, but the Sage jumped in the air and avoided it. She landed behind the ghost and they circled each other for a few seconds, before Cortés launched at her. Freya blocked the blow he intended at her leg, but his next blow got her in the shoulder.

&&&

Brennan was fighting three opponents at a time, with others around him that wanted a piece of him, when he felt the weakness hit Freya. His eyes widened and he turned to the door that led to the chamber where Freya was fighting the conquistador.

Freya?

A ghost punched him, distracting him, and he dropped to the ground. A surge of concern for the Sage hit him, and Brennan didn't bother to control it. He let it run free, and it hit the ghosts around him full force. They were blasted all over the place, and ended up groaning on the floor and walls.

Brennan threw them one last look, then rushed out of the room to where his partner was, well decided to help her escape.

&&&

Freya let out a small gasp of pain as the blade retreated from her shoulder, and the blood started spilling. She went to hit Cortés again, but he easily deflected her blow and kicked her in the stomach. The strike sent Freya into the wall, and she slid to the ground with a groan.

Freya! Brennan yelled mentally.

She opened her eyes, but her gaze was blurry and unfocused. Freya shook her head and supported herself with her hands. She could see Cortés nearing her, his sword in hand. She searched for the blade she'd had, and found it was only a short distance away from her – but still too far in her current state.

"Now what do you say, Sage? I've got you down and your forces are draining. How do you think you can get rid of me?"

Freya raised her head, a fierce look in her eyes. It angered Cortés more than anything. "Why won't you give up? What makes you stand up in spite of all?"

Freya felt Brennan's energy in the room, and she smirked. "As long as I'm alive, and there's a reason for me to live, there's no way I'm letting you win this, Cortés."

With the last of her forces, she threw herself across the floor and reached for the sword. Cortés went to strike, leaving himself open in a rookie mistake. Freya shoved the blade through his gut, impaling the leader in the stomach. Though no blood spilled from the wound, Freya knew it hurt.

When he staggered back, eyes wide, Freya knew they had him. The barrier was weaker around him, making him easy prey.

"Now!" she yelled and extended her palm. Brennan did the same behind the conquistador.

Both teens let their powers invade them, to the point where they couldn't contain them anymore. The energies struck Cortés at the same time, combining their strength and inflicting pain like no other on the ghost. His sword, proud jewel and antique weapon, shattered in millions of pieces, never to be used by a mortal or immortal again. With the blade vanished, the weakness escaping the Sage stopped.

Freya narrowed her eyes towards the leader, then lifted her other palm. She focused her spiritual energy as she had before, with the intent to erase him from existence. A burst of pure white energy escaped her hands and hit Cortés straight in the chest.

Freya staggered, as two separate flows of energy escape her. For once, she knew what Brennan must feel when he lost vital energy due to his powers.

This isn't normal, she gritted her teeth against it, trying to focus. Then it hit her – the ghosts were linked. She was doing exactly what Tyr had warned her against, and it would kill her if she kept at it.

Brennan, I need you! Find the link!

The Wiseman didn't need a lengthy explanation. Reading his partner like a book, he focused his senses on Cortés' glowing form, and found the link the demon had created with the other ghosts. With his free hand, he touched the medallion around his neck.

The warmth he was used to permeated his hand, and he let go. A ray of light escaped him, joining Freya's. The blasts mingled until they formed a faint orange glow, which surrounded Cortés. The link snapped between the remaining ghosts, and they were blasted into various walls, falling down with grunts and groans.

No longer protected by their souls mingled together, the full wrath of the Sage and Wiseman's combined blasts hit the conquistador. A scream of pain was all that was left, then Cortés' glowing form shattered.

As he disappeared, Brennan ran to Freya. He helped her up, beaming victoriously. "We did it! We combined our powers again, and *won*!"

Freya's grin mirrored Brennan's. "Cortés is done for! We did it, Bren!"

For once not overthinking it, she hugged him, putting her gratitude for everything he'd done in that simple embrace. Brennan's arms tightened around her, pulling her closer and inhaling her scent, grateful they were both alive.

"I knew we could."

Lost in their moment, the presence of the awakened soldiers didn't immediately register. When their displeased whispers got to their ears, the two partners pulled back and faced them, though Brennan still maintained an arm around Freya's shoulders.

"Your leader is dead. Forever this time," Brennan announced to the confused ghosts.

"Get back to your own cliques if you don't want to join him where he is now," Freya warned them.

The phantoms shared glances and mutters, but Freya and Brennan felt the undercurrents of their energy. They would disperse as they had before, in all of Spain. Once the specters dematerialized, they shared a look.

"I think it's about time we went back to the hotel," Freya pointed out, feeling her knees almost give way.

"I agree entirely." Brennan grabbed his partner's hands in his own, and maintaining eye contact, they both thought of home.

Their energies once more mingled together, giving each other the strength to go on. Though their bodies were weak, the youngsters had enough fuel left for one last thing.

In the blink of an eye, a vortex appeared above their heads, maintained by their joint energies mingling. Freya and Brennan were sucked through the hole and reappeared shortly in O'Keeffe's room.

Seamus, Sam and Emmanuel rushed to them as they materialized, but neither the Sage nor the Wiseman could keep standing up. They dropped to the floor as dolls would, fast asleep.

Chapter 29

"Tyr!" Osiris thundered, and the tiger lifted its head off the ground.

Since returning from helping Freya and Brennan, it had been tired. Exhaustively so, from the trips between the realms.

Can this wait?

"No!" the god's face was furious, fists clenched, zaps of power exiting them. "You broke every rule we laid in place, all to ensure Freya's safety?"

Yes. And it is something you should understand. You would have done the same for Horus.

"I am not the one on trial here!"

I did not realize I was on trial.

Isis appeared, apparently having tried to stop her husband. "Osiris, please—"

"No! I listened to you when you told me this was a good plan, that Tyr could remain objective and watch from afar. But this is too much. You are done, tiger, you are—"

A sudden growl filled the room, and the gods froze in shock.

Tyr was staring at the fireplace, panting heavily. *Release me, Osiris! Release me* now!

The god deigned to look within, and stumbled back in shock. Having seen the same image, Isis lifted her palm and intoned a spell.

"Go," she murmured softly. "May our grace protect you."

The feline threw her a grateful look, then jumped into the portal without further thought. Once it had vanished, the gods moved closer to the fire. With his hand, Osiris enlarged the image, until the truth was staring them in the face – the demon was still on the prowl.

&&&

Raksh was angry, yes, but it didn't stop him from thinking clearly as he hopped the balcony, then with a whiff of darkness entered the room.

Barely glancing towards the two dormant forms, he moved towards the hiding spot. The closet door squeaked lightly open, and a red glow emerged from underneath a pile of clothes.

The demon scowled. "You can reject me all you wisssh, damned book, but you will ssstill unleasssh your secretsss."

Without further ado, he bent over and extracted the manuscript from the clothes. As he touched the cover, it burned hotly against his skin, sizzling in the night air. Raksh grunted at the pitiful defensive mechanism, then turned away.

His beady eyes fell upon the Wiseman on the couch, unaware of the danger he courted. Unwilling to get close to him, the demon simply lifted his palm towards the medallion. It lifted in the air, hovering for a moment, then floated over his head and into the wraith's expecting hand.

Ignoring the similar burn, Raksh threw one more look around. He was about to blast the room – and its inhabitants – open, when he sensed the change in the air, and knew he was being watched.

"Another time, then. Your deathsss will have to wait."

He turned and jumped out of the room, running among the empty streets, even as Tyr appeared on the balcony through the portal. The tiger rushed into the room, but didn't see anything other than Freya and Brennan's unmoving forms. The two were still recovering from their fight, their senses dead to the world.

Tyr sniffed around, but could no longer sense the manuscript and the medallion. Snarling, it turned away and started hunting the demon. It was only moments later, in a darkened park, that the trail ran cold.

Tyr stopped in its tracks, glancing around in confusion. *Where did he go?*

The crack above was the first warning. Before the tiger could move, something landed on its back, and pain lacerated its muscles.

Growling and roaring in pain, Tyr arched its back and kicked with its back paws. When it did not work, the feline jumped in the air and rotated, landing on its back. The movement had the advantage of shaking the demon off, and the tiger was finally able to face him.

Raksh was crouched in an animalistic position, pointy teeth showing, claws extended – and dripping blood. Tyr glanced over a shoulder, noticing the deep gashes on its back.

"Wounded, pet?" Raksh taunted.

No worse than you! Those are pure objects you hide, they will burn through your intestines if need be.

Tyr lunged at the demon. The fight was long, each inflicting pain on the other. It was a miracle the noise didn't attract humans in the area, nor police.

Despite its best efforts, Tyr was soon panting, red gashes on its back, bleeding strongly. Smirking at the being's weakness, Raksh straightened up and materialized the chains of fire in his hand.

No...

Tyr tried to feint to the right, but the chains wrapped around its body unyieldingly. Tyr roared in agony, attempting to escape their grasp, but it was to no avail. They tightened until its body went limp, and dropped to the ground.

Raksh stepped closer to the feline, nudging it with a booted toe. When no movement answered, he snickered in satisfaction. "Now if you will excussse me, I have a massster to go sssee."

The demon left, leaving the expiring tiger behind.

&&&

Freya's eyes snapped open, but she immediately closed them again and groaned. "Someone stop the room from spinning." The sensation was making her sick, and yet the hole she could feel in her stomach indicated she hadn't eaten anything for at least a day or two.

"Someone stop Freya from talking," came a voice near the Sage.

"Crap, who the hell's that?" With great effort and ignoring the pain in her head, she opened her eyes once more and glanced to her left.

Brennan smirked at her from the couch. "Morning, sleeping beauty."

The Sage took in his appearance. His left arm was bandaged, he had multiple cuts and bruises on his face, and a pretty nasty cut on his right cheek. But he was alive.

"What was that you were saying," Freya started, overcome by an urge to laugh, "that there was no way you were going to get even a simple cut?"

Brennan scowled at her, "Very funny, Freya." His relief was palpable that she'd woken up, despite all he tried to do to hide it.

When he'd opened his eyes and she hadn't, he'd immediately started to worry and asked Seamus and Sam what was happening with Freya. O'Keeffe had calmly explained that, due to the large amount of energy they'd used, each of their bodies would take different lengths of time to recuperate and wake up.

When Seamus and Sam had offered to grab some breakfast for him, Brennan hadn't moved. He'd been watching Freya ever since he woke up, events of the battle with Cortés coming back to him. It made sense she would take longer to recover, considering his sword had touched her.

Now that she was up, he could finally relax and smile. "Well, let's hope we'll be able to walk soon. The sun's up, the birds are singing, everything's sunny around here."

"Why are you so cheery?" Freya groaned, taking in her own bruises. She could feel the cut on her lip and forehead, and her shoulder was bandaged. The wound from Cortés' blade still hurt, but luckily it wasn't sucking her energy anymore.

"Don't ask me, but maybe the fact that I woke up an hour ago after three days of sleep..." Brennan said casually, observing Freya's reaction. "Yeah, that may have something to do with it."

"Wait, *what*?" Freya yelled, then immediately regretted it. The sound of her own voice was ringing in her ears, and she felt like dying.

"You're hurting yourself by yelling," Brennan observed calmly.

"I know that," Freya retorted, clearly pissed off.

Dropping the smile, Brennan inched closer to Freya's bed. Alerted by the serious look in his eyes, she frowned. "What is it?"

"I need to tell you this quick, but don't fill Seamus in until we're back in Scotland. The medallion and the book are gone."

Freya's eyes widened, and a shiver of fear ran up her spine. "No!"

Brennan's dismayed expression confirmed it. "I think it was Raksh, while we were unconscious. No one else would have known..."

Freya bit her lip, then asked, "Have you tried contacting Tyr?"

Another sober look, then he nodded. "No answer. I tried many times."

Tyr? Despite Brennan's words, she had to try. *Tyr, please...*

When nothing responded, the Sage bit her lip. The tiger was gone, and so were the objects of power they were destined to protect. *What can this mean?*

She was about to say more but at that moment, O'Keeffe and Sam entered the room, carrying two trays of a full breakfast. Freya's stomach growled at the sight, but she hugged Sam heartily as he ran to her.

We'll figure it out in Scotland, she promised Brennan with a loaded look, then turned to Sam. It felt good to have the boy around again.

"I'm so glad we were able to get you out of there," Freya said, eyeing the ghost. "I'm just sorry it took us that long."

But Sam only shook his head. "It's all right. You had plenty on your hands, and honestly, I'm glad of one thing – at least your wounds aren't because of me."

"No, that would have to be because of Freya pissing Cortés off," Brennan said jokingly. He held his hands up in mock-surrender when the Sage glared at him.

"Brennan, you and I need to have a little chat," Sam announced gravely. "About the way you treated Emmanuel, namely."

Brennan groaned. "Don't start. I had every right not to trust him – at least I think so – and yes, I may have been harsh at points, but—"

"Hang on, where *is* Emmanuel?" Freya cut Brennan off.

"Hopefully, far away from here," Brennan said under his breath, then coughed to disguise his words when Sam threw him a look.

"Actually, he's in your room, Freya," the spirit revealed. "He wants to say good-bye before he goes back to the city."

O'Keeffe, who'd been uncharacteristically quiet up until that moment – except for the hug he'd given Freya – then said, "I have spoken with Emmanuel, and he has agreed to keep an eye on the phantoms here and alert us if, by any chance, they start rallying again."

Freya nodded, then gave a sheepish grin. "I'm not going to hear another lecture on how dangerous the mission was, etc., am I?"

"No. Not yet, at least," O'Keeffe smiled at her. "If you two feel ready, we can take the plane tomorrow and go back to Scotland."

Freya turned to Brennan, noticing his half-smile. "So, you're joining the team?"

He shrugged, attempting to appear indifferent – and failing. His golden-brown eyes shone with something she hadn't seen there before. "How could I resist?"

Freya felt her cheeks warm up, and looked away. It would be good to have Brennan around – especially as they could use the time off-mission to figure out how to get rid of the demon. Her vow of getting revenge for her parents' murder came back to mind, ringing with purpose.

But before all of that, I have to at least thank Em for his help.

The Sage set her breakfast tray away and immediately got up and headed for the bathroom, stumbling a bit. "Sam, pass me a t-shirt and a pair of jeans, will you?"

The ghost did so, and Freya got changed in the bathroom. She washed her teeth, brushed her hair and, letting it loose on her back, was ready. Though her bandaged shoulder had posed a problem, there was nothing the Sage could do about it.

"Your turn," she said to Brennan as she got out.

Grumbling, the Wiseman went in and got out five minutes after, perfectly refreshed, looking very sour as he followed Freya. Neither of them saw the mischievous gleam in Sam's eyes...

&&&

The two partners left the room and went to Freya's room. As they opened it, they saw Emmanuel half-way through a painting. He stopped when he heard the door, and turned around to them.

Brennan rolled his eyes and went and leaned right next to the painting, eyes narrowed in dislike. In just a few moments, he'd be rid of the ghost for good. For some reason, the animosity between them was still very present, despite Emmanuel having proven where his loyalties lay.

The spirit took one look at Brennan, then hid the smile that was creeping onto his face. It was time to put Sam's plan into action, and see just how right they both were about the two teenagers.

Freya sat on the bed, facing the painting. "So, you're leaving?" she asked Emmanuel. "Seamus said you'd keep an eye on the ghosts for us."

"Yes," he nodded, gaze raking over the Sage one last time. To his side, Brennan growled low, only audible to Emmanuel. He pursed his lips to avoid the grin threatening to escape, then addressed Freya. "It's the least I could do to prevent anything like this from happening again. I wanted to thank both of you for helping me, and ask a favor if I may, Freya."

"Go ahead."

The ghost seemed to hesitate for a moment, and his eyes lifted slightly to Brennan, then he made up his mind. "*Un beso*."

Freya smiled, but Brennan's expression was nowhere close as fury filled his eyes. His fist clenched reflexively, itching to punch the ghost in the face before she got anywhere near him.

Under his incredulous gaze, Freya approached the painting. Brennan grabbed a hold of her arm, whispering furiously, "You aren't seriously going to do this, are you?"

She stared at him, surprised and yet mad. "Why do you care?" Freya snatched her arm away from Brennan's grip and reached Emmanuel, who was looking at her with adoration in his eyes.

"*Gracias, querida*... For everything," he said.

Freya's grin softened, a bit regretful knowing she wouldn't see Emmanuel for probably a long time. Nonetheless, she was thankful to have met him and count him as a friend.

"*De nada,* Emmanuel. Take care," she wished the ghost, before leaning over and placing a friendly peck on his lips – his one request. Before he disappeared, Freya heard Emmanuel whisper words she never would have suspected otherwise.

"*Él te ama...*"
He loves you.

She turned towards Brennan and realized their faces were only inches apart. He was mad. Oh, boy, was he mad! His anger vibrated in the air around them, and Freya sensed it as if it was her own.

Like a veil being lifted, the reason behind it finally dawned on her. And in that moment, everything else made sense, for the first time in a long time. Brennan's unreasonable mistrust of Emmanuel, his animosity towards the ghost, his hostile approach...

Brennan opened his mouth to probably shout at her, but Freya didn't give him a chance. "Oh, shut up, Brennan!"

Then she closed the gap that was separating them and kissed him – a *real* kiss. After a fraction of surprise, the Wiseman's lips pressed against hers eagerly, and one hand went around her neck, the other wrapping around her waist.

The fierce jealousy left him, and all that was left was a sense of belonging. His muscles relaxed under Freya's touch, though his embrace only tightened.

We make a pretty good team, once we're over the whole jealousy thing...

The echo of her words reached his dazed brain, and Brennan pulled away, scowling. "I was *not* jealous!"

"Who said you were?" Freya smirked, then pulled Brennan in for another kiss. She couldn't recall a single moment in her life she'd ever felt this complete. Nothing could compare to it.

They were forced apart when they heard a cough, then a very amused voice said, "Am I interrupting anything?"

"Sam!"

Their joint shouts had the ghost laughing long after he'd left the room, leaving them to some privacy.

&&&

Three days later, back at the grand château in Scotland, Freya was practicing at her meadow once more, trying to sort through her confused thoughts.

Since returning to the castle, everything had been grand – everything, that was, except for her cat. Artemis was acting up, lazing around and unwilling to move much. To make matters worse, Freya hadn't been contacted by Tyr in ages.

They'd come clean with Seamus about the loss of the medallion and book. As predicted, he wasn't pleased, instead believing an imminent attack would fall upon them. He'd strengthened the defenses of the castle with their help, and now, all they could do was wait.

Or so her mentor thought.

At night, Freya snuck to Brennan's room and they spent hours plotting revenge, and reading up on the gods of Egypt. Knowledge was their most powerful weapon and before they set out to carry out their plan, it was important to gather every tidbit of information.

After their chat the previous night, however, the Sage had been unable to rest easily.

Freya was perturbed, yes, and knew Brennan sensed it, which was why she'd sought some time alone. Since their return, their relationship hadn't changed as much as she'd feared. Rather, it seemed only to grow. On top of having her partner, she now had a friend and a boyfriend. It was odd, but left her with a feeling of completeness.

If only Tyr would answer my calls...

Frowning, the Sage was about to go back to her training when a cocky voice said, "Honestly, Freya, did you think those new defenses could keep me away from here?"

The Sage turned to the golden-eyed teenager, pouting. "Damn it, Brennan, I thought I said I wanted to be alone."

"Which is exactly why I came," the Wiseman grinned. "I knew you'd be out here for hours on end, and really, I'm getting bored not doing anything."

Freya smirked, "Bored, are you?"

Recognizing the gleam in her eyes, Brennan mock-groaned. "Please tell me you're kidding. Freya, *come on*! I did it once, do I really have to re-experience that?"

"It's practice for both of us," the Sage chuckled at Brennan's dismayed expression.

"Practice? I think it's your way to punish me," he muttered under his breath.

Freya laughed, the worries easing off her shoulders. Sure, they were hunted by a demon. And soon they'd have to take off on a quest, probably hurting Seamus' feelings in the process. Not to mention she desperately missed Tyr's presence and advice... But despite it all, she was enjoying teasing her boyfriend as if such a thing was perfectly normal, in their lives that were all but normal.

"Come on, lazy," Freya smiled. "Let's see what you have. Unless, of course, you're scared I'll kick your butt."

"Please, Freya," Brennan scoffed. "Let's settle it right here and now."

She watched as Brennan stretched a bit, cracked his knuckles, and then flashed her a charming grin. "Whenever you're ready, love."

"You're going down, Brennan," Freya laughed.

And soon enough, they were once more testing each other's skills, challenging, until the day went away and night took over. When the fight finally came to an end – this time, undisrupted – they were both panting heavily, but their eyes gleamed of joy.

"I told you I'd win!" Freya laughed.

"That…" Brennan panted. "Is entirely ridiculous… I couldn't have…"

But he soon realized he was talking to himself, as Freya had sprinted off into the woods, back to the castle for dinner.

Shaking his head, Brennan yelled, "Freya! Hey, come on, wait up a second!" Half-laughing, he chased after her. "I want a rematch!"

And the rest, as they say, is history.

Epilogue

In the palace of the gods, Isis and Osiris had finished gathering the tools needed. They turned to the immobile tiger laid out on the carpet, no longer breathing.

"Are you sure about this?" Osiris asked his wife for the thousandth time.

"Yes. We need help, and so will the two youngsters."

Osiris nodded, then they both knelt next to the animal. The god picked up a sacrificial knife, and cut into the tiger's chest. Blood poured out, flowing over his clothes and Isis'. Yet the god of the Underworld was unmoved.

They'd done their best to keep the link between Tyr and Freya from toppling over and causing her massive losses. Their last chance had been to seclude Tyr, until such time as they could heal the being.

Only, this was not healing. It was a rebirth.

Hands deep in the feline's cavity, Osiris grasped onto the heart and gently cut around it, until he had it in his hand. Isis lifted her palms and encased it, then murmured, "Let the one that was two be split again. Let the two that had been one be reborn. Let life infuse what was once dead..."

She stared at her husband expectantly, and Osiris gave a brief nod. His palms glowed with the magic he pulled from the earth.

"As Lord of the Underworld, I can take life, and give it back. I so choose this, bless my wife's words. Let the one that was two, the two that were one, be reborn tonight."

Under their determined gazes, the heart radiated softly. Osiris placed it back inside Tyr's body, then they stepped back. With a wave of her hand, Isis mended the carcass of the blood and gore, until the fur was immaculate once more.

And then they waited.

For a moment, nothing happened. Then a thud echoed loudly in the room, followed by another, then another... Until it seemed as though two hearts were beating instead of one. When the rhythm picked up, Tyr's form shimmered, and two shapes seemed to overlap.

The tiger groaned, turning its head this way and that. The two shapes became solid, until not one, but two tigers lay on the ground. They groaned in tandem, then slowly stood. They glanced towards each other, one with eyes as grey as ash, the other green as the deepest forest.

Then they turned towards the gods in confusion. Isis smiled, and waved her hand again. This time, their bodies shimmered until the two animals became human.

One was a woman, with long dark hair reaching past her waist, grey eyes and beautiful features, fair and feminine. The man was her opposite – taller, broad of shoulders, with green eyes and a few days' worth of stubble.

"Welcome," Osiris greeted, opening his palms.

"Welcome, Evelyn and Mark," Isis repeated.

&&&

Entering the Underworld was an easy feat, if one knew where to find a backdoor. Remaining hidden in said Underworld was harder, but Raksh managed just fine. He moved undetected all the way to Set's cage, where the guardians stood.

Unleashing his true form, a snarling beast, and aided by his master's power, he quickly disposed of the jackal guards, despite their best efforts.

Then he turned to Set. The bars around him were indestructible, but there was enough space to get the book and medallion through.

Eagerly, Set grasped the two and knelt on the ground with them. He placed the necklace onto the manuscript, knowing exactly what to expect. The disappointment was worse when he realized they were empty.

Like a caged lion, he roared and moved to the bars, eyes burning into his servant's. "Fool! The map is not here!"

"That cannot be, massster." Raksh looked at the inert objects, reflecting on all the trouble he'd gone through to get them. He gulped – his master was not pleased. "What...What ssshall I do now?"

"Bring them to me. *They* have it."

When Raksh turned to do so immediately, Set whispered, "No. Not now. My brother will be on alert. Wait...and lead them to you."

"Yesss, massster."

End of Book II

Did you love *The Dragon Manuscript*? Then you should read *Relics of the Underworld* by Alexa Whitewolf!

Freya and Brennan barely have time to settle in their new romance when tragedy strikes. Sick of waiting for the axe to drop, Freya convinces her partner it's time to fight back.Armed with only the knowledge gained from their respective objects of the power, the two start on a perilous journey to find and destroy the Relics of the Underworld.Unfortunately, they are not the only ones in search of the mythical treasures. The demon Raksh, more determined than ever to free Set, comes up with his most evil plan yet.From Scotland to Slovakia and Egypt, this last installment is packed with action and surprises at every turn., while the gods observe their champions and each challenge they face. As Freya and Brennan get closer to their goal, neither is aware of the ultimate sacrifice awaiting them - nor the ancient god pulling their strings.

Read more at https://www.alexawhitewolf.com.

Preview of Book III:
Relics of the Underworld

F reya jumped awake in her bed, panting. *That damn hawk...*

It had been a dream, only a nightmare, but her heart thudded wildly, and she felt the pain of its claws on her back.

Absentmindedly, she reached behind to touch the skin - and her eyes widened in shock.

Brennan!

She jumped out of and ran to the bathroom, turning her back to the larger than life mirror and biting her lip to stop from screaming.

The door to her bedroom opened and footsteps headed her way. "What is it?" Brennan's voice, still groggy from sleep, reached her before he entered the bathroom.

He took in what she was wearing – a top and shorts – and grinned. "Is this all for me?"

When Freya did not respond, he met her teary gaze. Stricken, his eyes flicked to the mirror.

Three large scratches could be seen peeking from the top of her tank top, and blood permeated the rest of the material across his girlfriend's back.

The grin slipped off his face, and he moved closer. "What the *hell*?"

"I don't know, Bren," Freya whispered. "I had that nightmare again, with the hawk, and in it the stupid bird hurt me. I woke up and the pain was real!"

"This is impossible," the Wiseman murmured, passing his hand over the wounds to see if he could pick up anything.

Images of a bird of prey, coal dark eyes and feelings of ruthlessness passed through him.

He gasped, and his stunned golden eyes met Freya's. "We need Seamus. He'll know what to do."

Continue reading! [1]

More at alexawhitewolf.com/books

About the Author

Alexa Whitewolf is a dog-loving, caffeine-addicted, all-around traveling enthusiast. Author of three series of fantasy, paranormal and young adult, she spends her nights dreaming up new stories and her days fighting reality. She lives in Ottawa, Canada, with her husband and two mischievous furballs- Zeus and Achilles. Check out her website at www.alexawhitewolf.com !

Read more at https://www.alexawhitewolf.com.

ALSO BY THE AUTHOR

The Avalon Chronicles series
Avalon Dreams
Avalon Wishes
Avalon Nightmares
Atrox - A Novella

The Sage's Legacy – YA series
The Dragon Medallion
The Dragon Manuscript
Relics of the Underworld

Moonlight Rogues series
First to Fall
Second to Surrender
Third to Tumble
Last to Love
Moonlight Rogues: Origins

Standalone novels
Blood Ties, Love Binds
Unconditional Love
Blazing in a Storm of Ashes (Coming Soon)
More novels coming soon!

Sign up for my readers' group **at
www.alexawhitewolf.com/contact** and receive
a copy of *Unconditional Love* for **FREE,** as
well as first dibs on cover reveals, discounts,
giveaways, prizes **and more**!